Gilt

Gilt

Jamie Brenner

THORNDIKE PRESS
A part of Gale, a Cengage Company

This is a work of fiction. Names, characters, places, and incidents either are the product of the author's imagination or are used fictitiously, and any resemblance to actual persons, living or dead, businesses, companies, events, or locales is entirely coincidental.

Thorndike Press® Large Print Basic.
The text of this Large Print edition is unabridged.
Other aspects of the book may vary from the original edition.
Set in 16 pt. Plantin.

**LIBRARY OF CONGRESS CIP DATA ON FILE.
CATALOGUING IN PUBLICATION FOR THIS BOOK
IS AVAILABLE FROM THE LIBRARY OF CONGRESS.**

ISBN-13: 978-1-4328-9715-4 (hardcover alk. paper)

Published in 2022 by arrangement with G. P. Putnam's Sons, an imprint of Penguin Publishing Group, a division of Penguin Random House LLC.

Printed in Mexico
Print Number : 1 Print Year : 2022

GILT

▪ ▪ ▪ ▪

Part One

▪ ▪ ▪ ▪

One empire falls, another empire rises, all because of the inherent human weakness for pretty things.

— AJA RADEN,
STONED: JEWELRY, OBSESSION, AND HOW DESIRE SHAPES THE WORLD

1

New York City, 2004

She reached for her mother's hand, excited and just a little bit afraid. The sun was beginning to set on Fifth Avenue, and cars were at a standstill. Reporters crowded the sidewalk and onlookers pressed against metal security barriers.

"Over here, over here," photographers called out, and her parents stopped for a moment, her mother leaning down to whisper to her, *Smile for the camera.*

"Paulina, show us the ring," someone called, and her mother flashed her left hand. A woman stepped forward holding a copy of a magazine and asked for an autograph.

It seemed to take forever to reach the jewelry store on the corner of Fifty-Third Street, a seven-story limestone and granite building her grandfather called a "monument to love." The entranceway was engraved with her family name. Tonight, display windows were filled with black-and-white photographs of legendary couples: Elizabeth Taylor and Richard Burton, Marilyn Monroe and Joe DiMaggio, Grace Kelly and Prince Rainier. And in front of each photo, a Pavlin & Co diamond engagement ring, just waiting to be bought by a customer with a love story of their own.

It was the tenth anniversary of Pavlin & Co's most famous diamond of all, a thirty-carat pink stone called the Electric Rose. Her grandfather Alan gifted the treasure to the first of his three daughters to get engaged: her mother.

That afternoon, her mother had let her try it on. It was so beautiful she couldn't take her eyes off it, the color of a pale rose petal but also clear like a drop of water. Gemma had to clamp her small fingers tightly together to keep the ring from tilting over.

"One day it will be yours," her mother said.

The thing was, while everyone in the family loved talking about the ring, no one seemed to ever want to talk about her parents' actual engagement. Or wedding. Or anything about her parents at all. Gemma was too afraid to press with questions. Sometimes she worried things were too perfect. That it could somehow all disappear.

Gemma and her mother spent all day getting ready for the party. A stylist visited their apartment, piling her mother's blond hair into an updo and blow-drying Gemma's until it hung down her back like a golden sheet. Both of their gowns were white and embroidered with butterflies, each delicate wing hand-sewn by another visitor to the apartment earlier that week, a man with a white ponytail and dark glasses and an accent, who her mother called "Mr. Lagerfeld."

"We're twins tonight," her mother said with a wink. "No one will be able to tell us apart."

When the car arrived to whisk them down Fifth Avenue, her father looked at them both and said, "You two are more beautiful than any diamond in the world."

Gemma's parents guided her inside Pavlin & Co, the vast sales floor transformed into a wonderland of sparkling diamonds everywhere you looked: in glass display cases, on the hands of the glamorous guests, and in the framed photos on the walls.

The photos were advertisements from the long history of Pavlin & Co, starting back in 1947 with a black-and-white picture —

now recognized all over the world — of a man on one knee in the snow, slipping a diamond solitaire ring on the finger of a willowy brunette in a ball gown. Above them, in elegant script, the sentence *A Diamond Says Love.* With those four simple words, her great-grandfather had created the idea of the diamond engagement ring.

Her mother told her the story over and over again, the way other little girls were told fairy tales.

"There was a time when people didn't buy diamond engagement rings," her mother said, "not until our family made them important."

Gemma's eyes skipped forward eagerly, alighting on her favorite series of ads, the ones featuring her mother. She'd modeled for the 1994 ads wearing furs and her own pink diamond. Whenever Gemma looked at the photographs of her mother with her chin resting in her palm, the spectacular gem flashing on her finger, her big blue-green eyes staring directly into the camera, they didn't make her long to get engaged so much as they made her long to be Paulina. She was sure lots of women in the 1990s felt the same way. Buying a Pavlin diamond wasn't just buying a piece of jewelry — it was buying the promise of love.

They passed the orchestra playing near the gilded elevators, and her grandmother rushed toward them. Constance, with her eternally blond bouffant hair and head-to-toe designer outfits, seemed like a queen to her.

"You're late," Constance said. "Come along, everyone's waiting for you."

The rest of the family was assembled on the podium: Alan, looking distinguished in his tuxedo, and her mother's two older sisters, Aunt Elodie and Aunt Celeste. Like her grandmother, her aunts seemed regal and somewhat unknowable. Aunt Elodie was Alan's right hand at Pavlin & Co, while Aunt Celeste lived far away at a beach. Gemma wished she was closer with her mother's sisters. Maybe that would help fix the nagging sense that something was wrong. She was especially uncomfortable around Elodie. There was just something about the way her aunt looked at her.

Uniformed guards encircled the podium as her grandfather stepped toward the microphone. On either side of him, glass cases displayed glittering diamond rings in every shape and color, yellow and white and even a rare blue stone set in platinum. Of course, none of them compared to the ring on her mother's finger.

"Gemma," Aunt Elodie said in a loud whisper, placing a hand on her shoulder. "Don't you find it interesting that with all this security, a thief can still hide in plain sight?"

What?

"Oh, give it a rest, Elodie," her mother said.

"You'd like that, wouldn't you?"

Confused, Gemma looked between her mother and her aunt. Her stomach tensed, and that feeling came over her again — the sense of something terribly wrong.

"Gemma, go over there and stand with Grandma," her mother said.

"Why?" She didn't want to leave her side.

"Please just do it," her mother said, a rare flash of annoyance in her voice.

Biting her lip, she dutifully walked to the other end of the podium. *What just happened?*

She blinked back tears, then told herself she had no reason to be upset. Looking out at the crowd, she knew she was lucky to be exactly where she was in that moment. Everyone wanted to be a Pavlin, to have beautiful things and be surrounded by love. So what if her aunt Elodie and her mother didn't get along? It wasn't the end of the world.

But something deep down told her that it could be.

2

New York City, Fifteen Years Later

Gemma was the only student at graduation without some kind of family. She'd considered not even attending, but she'd been looking forward to the awards ceremony for a long time. And so, wearing her blue cap and gown, she took her aisle seat in the third row.

The auditorium was warm, teetering on the brink of overheating. Air-conditioning vents wheezed loudly, as if they hadn't been intended for a room filled to capacity.

She looked across the aisle at her classmate Mae Yang.

Did you bring it? she mouthed.

Mae interned at *New York* magazine, and Gemma needed to borrow a press pass — the only way she was going to sneak into the Pavlin & Co centennial celebration tomorrow night. A party she hadn't been invited to.

The dean took to the stage. "Welcome, graduates, friends, and family . . ."

She slumped back in her seat, urging herself to stay in the moment — no matter how imperfect. Directly behind her, her best friend — and former boyfriend — Sanjay squeezed her shoulder. He leaned forward.

"Thanks again for the extra tickets," he said.

"No problem," she said. It was the least she could do for him. She'd give anything to have his trust again.

Gemma opened her compact to use her pressed powder. Her long hair, the color of white corn, was pulled back in a low ponytail. She always looked pale and tired during finals week, and this time was no exception. Except this time, her eyes — a startling deep teal color — were bright with something new. The spark was like a pang of hunger just as dinner was being pulled from the oven — so close to satisfaction, but not quite there. It was standing on a diving board, looking down from a great height. It was the final toll bridge on the long drive to a beach. Anticipation, she was learning, was most painful when you were close to the finish line.

The dean announced the beginning of the awards ceremony. Since the first day of her freshman year Gemma had dreamed of earning first prize in jewelry design; the NYSD Senior Award winners were profiled in *The New York Times,* and it was a distinction that awarded visibility to young artists and artisans at a time when they needed it the most, launching them into the real world.

For Gemma, it would have the added value of helping her reclaim what had been taken from her.

Her project was a jewelry collection she called Old New York. Gemma got the idea from visiting Sanjay at his job working the front desk of a historic hotel called the Casterbridge. The place captured her imagination the moment she walked into the lobby; it was like she'd stepped into a different century. The lobby walls were red damask and the room packed with heavy mahogany furniture. An entire wall was floor-to-ceiling bookshelves, all leather-bound volumes with wildly romantic titles: *My Last Duchess, Wide Sargasso Sea, The Wings of the Dove.* The guest rooms were named after classic English novelists like Browning, Rhys, Waugh, and Austen, spelled out on the doors in brass letters.

When Sanjay told her the hotel was being renovated and selling off all the old fixtures, she knew she needed the brass door letters to turn into charms.

Gemma saw the world through the lens of objects turned to jewelry. She spent every weekend scouring markets downtown or stoop sales in Brooklyn and Queens for knickknacks that could be turned into necklace charms. A lot of them reflected a little piece of Manhattan history, and all were affordable. She wanted people to feel they could build a jewelry collection without spending a fortune. Ideally, on pieces that represented something special to them.

Today, under her gown, Gemma wore a charm necklace that included a gold-plated Casterbridge "G," a faceted aquamarine (her birthstone), and a gold and enamel daffodil — her favorite flower.

"Gemma? You have to go up onstage," Sanjay whispered, nudging her from behind.

Applause surrounded her, and the dean stood onstage waiting expectantly. Had he just called her name?

She walked as quickly as possible but still felt like she was moving underwater. By the time the dean handed her a glass plaque for the top honor in jewelry design, she was so winded she could barely muster a smile.

"Congratulations," he said, shaking her hand.

She knew she was expected to make a speech, but she hadn't prepared anything out of superstition that she'd jinx herself. She looked out at the audience, and Sanjay gave her a thumbs-up. Gemma took a deep breath.

"I wouldn't be here if it weren't for my mother, Paulina. She's my inspiration. Mom, this is for you." The mothers in the audience glanced around, smiling, wanting to acknowledge the woman who must be so proud in that moment. But that woman had been gone for over a decade.

She slid back into her seat and then fanned herself with her program, vibrating with adrenaline.

Sanjay leaned forward and put a hand on her shoulder.

"Congrats. See you at the party tomorrow?" he said. She nodded, but the answer was no. There was only one party she wanted to attend.

Whether her family liked it or not.

3

Elodie Pavlin sat in her sun-filled office on the top floor of Pavlin & Co's flagship building. Behind her vintage brass and leather desk, the window offered a view of the busy streets of midtown in late spring, the worker bees on their lunch breaks, the tourists filing in and out of Gucci, Prada, and Versace, the police taking a break from their post outside St. Patrick's Cathedral. But Elodie didn't waste time with the view. She hadn't gotten to the helm of the company by daydreaming. At fifty-three years old, she was a woman with tunnel vision, and her focus at the moment was the party she was hosting tomorrow night.

Her eyes glanced toward *The New York Times* unfurled across her desk. It was a three-week-old copy she kept in her top desk drawer, open to the style section. The headline read, "One Hundred Years of All That Glitters."

This summer marks the centennial anniversary of Pavlin & Co, eponymous jewelry company founded in 1919 by Isaac Pavlin, whose son, Elliot, made *engagement* synonymous with *diamonds.* To mark the occasion, the family's private jewelry collection will be on display at the flagship store through the month of June.

"My father, Alan, spent his life celebrating the idea that a diamond says love," said Elodie Pavlin, now CEO. "He marked many occasions with a piece of jewelry gifted to my mother. Now I want to share these treasures with our devoted customers to show our love for them."

The exhibit opens the night of May 25 with a private party. It opens to the public the first week of June.

The black pug by her feet, Pearl, let out a sneeze that sounded like it came from a much larger creature. Pearl, her only trustworthy companion.

"You hate this air-conditioning, don't you?" she said, reaching down with an affectionate pat.

Elodie closed the paper, inhaling with satisfaction. Tomorrow's party was going to truly showcase her talents as CEO. She only wished her father had lived to see this day.

Growing up, Elodie loved nothing more than following her father around the Fifth Avenue store and feeling the buzz of the customers, the click of metal and glass as cases were opened and locked, the crinkle of stiff paper bags in Pavlin & Co's trademark green — the color of emeralds.

"Emeralds don't sparkle, they shine," her father always said. The shopping bags themselves even had a gleam to them. Emerald green had always been the brand's signature color.

The store was her second home and had been for as long as she could remember. Starting her freshman year of high school, Elodie spent every summer at the office. She didn't have the glamour job of catering to celebrities trying on jewels for the Academy Awards or showing multimillion-dollar engagement rings to high rollers. Instead, she had a desk at a cubicle and took orders, learned how to weigh loose diamonds, picked rings up from the setter, and arranged for deliveries. She was happy to pay her dues, to learn the business from the ground up. Someday, she would be the one hosting luminaries at the fifth-floor salon. She would be the one greeting the press at the annual holiday launch party.

That day had, at last, arrived. Since her

mother's passing, Elodie had presided over two successful holiday season launches, and now was preparing for the company's centennial year — an anniversary she needed to leverage as spectacularly as possible. It was increasingly difficult to keep jewelry in the minds — and budgets — of customers.

People simply didn't buy jewelry like they used to. The entire business model was based on tradition — a tradition engineered in part due to the marketing genius of her grandfather. What would an anniversary be without a pair of solitaire diamond earrings or a string of pearls? An engagement without a big diamond ring?

But these millennials! They preferred the latest technology gadgets for their birthdays. A trip to Phuket for their one-year anniversary. An engagement ring and wedding ring might be the only pieces of jewelry someone ever buys for their spouse, and even those sentimental items were becoming less and less essential. It was hard for her to believe, but it was true. This is what it had come to. And for all the big splashy pieces that generated press, for all the borrowed glitz and glamour during the television and film awards seasons, it was the buying habits of the average person that sustained a business over the decades. And the average person needed to be coaxed, prodded, and lured in like a fish on the line. That's what made evenings like the one she had planned so important. Desire had to be invented.

Her assistant buzzed in with a call. "Sloan Pierce from Whitmore's for you," she said.

Sloan was the daughter of one of Pavlin & Co's longtime customers, the socialite Harriet Pierce, and worked at the venerable auction house Whitmore's.

"Hello, Sloan. I hope you're not calling to say you can't make it tomorrow night." With this, Elodie pulled Pearl onto her lap and got a sloppy kiss.

"I wouldn't miss it for the world. But I'm expecting it will be such a smash event I might not get a chance to speak with you, and there's something I want to discuss," the woman said, her voice breezy. Confident. "Are you free for drinks at the Carlyle on Friday?"

Elodie assumed some charity event needed a chairwoman. The polite thing to do was say yes, of course. And while it was tempting to think she didn't have time for such things, the truth was her life outside the office was quiet.

She looked around her green-accented space, as finely appointed and as still as a photograph in an interior design magazine. Everything in its place. Her life was ordered and in control. She'd never had a husband or children, and this left all her energy for Pavlin & Co.

"I think that could work," Elodie said. Elodie always had weekend cocktails at the Carlyle. Clearly, this had become common knowledge, and Elodie was flattered. Finally, the type of attention — the type of power — she had long been due. It was a new era for Pavlin & Co — her era.

Hers alone.

4

Gemma's fourth-floor walk-up, in a charmingly dilapidated brownstone on West Twenty-Fourth Street, was more of a work studio than apartment. The six-hundred-square-foot space was just a few blocks from school and for Gemma functioned as design studio and sales floor.

As soon as the graduation ceremony ended, she couldn't resist announcing a flash sale on her social media. It was her own way of celebrating. Gemma checked the time; customers would be arriving any minute.

Whenever Gemma accumulated a few dozen pieces, she held a sale. All it took was the right photo and just a few seconds to get the word out on Instagram, where she had close to a hundred thousand followers. Today, she piled three chunky rings on her right forefinger and snapped a shot and posted with the caption: *How sweet is this?*

New Rock Candy rings available now . . .

Her Rock Candy rings sold out as fast as she could make them, gold-plated, sterling silver, and fourteen-karat-gold rings set with large semiprecious gemstones: bright citrines, sumptuous lavender amethysts, rich amber quartz. She also offered a costume-jewelry version in gold-plated brass with cushion-cut, colored glass "stones."

To Gemma, costume jewelry was just as precious as real jewelry. Sure, if you took an expensive diamond and set it in expensive platinum it would be appealing. But it took imagination and craft to transform non-precious metal and rhinestones, beads, or glass into something equally compelling. When she looked back at work by Elsa Schiaparelli from the 1950s, playing with color and shape to make crystal bracelets as extraordinary as anything diamond, she understood the true power of creation.

Gemma pushed her furniture and tools to one side of the room. Aside from the fold-away daybed, her apartment was dominated by jewelry-making equipment she'd bought with the dwindling remains of a small inheritance from her paternal grandmother, her nana — the woman who raised her after her parents' deaths when she was eight years old. Nana had only seen the apartment once. That was enough.

"How, Gemma Louise, can you live this way?"

Anne Maybrook was a simple woman from Pennsylvania farm country who didn't understand why Gemma couldn't be happy attending a more local school like Penn State. Or, if Gemma really wanted to be fancy about it and got a scholarship, she could apply to her late father's alma mater, Cornell. "But," Nana warned, "it was that kind of uppity crowd that got him into trouble in the first place. Filled his head with ideas about moving to the city — ideas that didn't turn out so great in the end, did they?"

Gemma told her that New York School of Design was the best place for the career — the future — that she wanted.

"That's what I'm afraid of," Nana said.

Gemma had been so certain that she'd have the chance to show her grandmother that she had nothing to worry about, that she'd become a successful jewelry designer and make her proud. But Nana passed away in her sleep a few years ago, not living to see her graduate NYSD, never mind become a success.

In her studio, Gemma had a workbench, torches, metal shears, pickle pots, jewelry wire, and every imaginable sort of hammer and pliers. It also served as a showroom/ pop-up store since she couldn't afford a storefront. But she had to be careful not to use her apartment for selling jewelry too often since it violated the terms of her lease.

Sure, she could probably sell all her merchandise online. But in-person contact with customers was valuable. By talking to them about her pieces she made personal connections that created brand loyalty. And seeing their reactions gave her feedback that she used to improve every new collection. As much as she recognized social media as a valuable tool, she knew she couldn't rely solely on it. If the best jewelry really was personal, she had to *be* personal.

After setting out the rings in clear plastic trays, she placed pieces from her Old New York collection on tables the way they had been displayed at the showcase. In addition to her Casterbridge letters, she had charms made from vintage subway tokens she'd found at a flea market on Elizabeth Street.

A buzz from the street-level intercom came ten minutes before the official eight P.M. start time, and she decided to let them wait. She needed to keep things somewhat organized.

Someone knocked on her door. She

jumped up from her workbench and looked out the peephole.

Oh, no.

"Open this door right now!" It was her upstairs neighbor, an older woman named Evelyn Woods, who wore floral housedresses from the 1950s and whose sparse, bleached blond hair had lately taken on an unintended lavender hue. "I know you're in there and I'll call the landlord."

It wasn't an empty threat. Evelyn had already called the management company on her several times. Gemma had the strongly worded letters from her landlord to prove it.

Gemma opened the door. "Hi, Mrs. Woods. There's no one in here . . . see?"

"No one's in here because they're all outside blocking the entrance! I just came back from Gristedes and there's a line down the block. You're a security hazard to this building. Letting all sorts of riffraff in here day and night . . ."

Gemma wanted to tell her that the "riffraff" were people simply buying jewelry — it wasn't as if she was hosting a rave.

"It's my college graduation, Mrs. Woods. I'm just getting together with a few friends."

The woman narrowed her eyes. "If you let all those people into this building, you're going to have a big problem. Am I making myself clear?"

"Very clear," Gemma said, just wanting her to leave so she could start letting people in. It was eight and the clock was ticking.

She watched Mrs. Woods shuffle off and pressed the button to buzz open the building. After tonight, she'd have to wait awhile before holding another sale. In the meantime, she'd focus her attention on her next big hurdle for getting her business off the ground: finding an investor. Thankfully, she already had a meeting set with a finance guy next week, an Israeli named Jacob Jabarin. And the only reason she was able to get in the door was one of her customers was Jacob Jabarin's niece.

Pretty much all of Gemma's customers were artists or young, in-the-know New Yorkers. Her work had been written about in cult magazines like *Speciwomen* or on trend-casting sites like Refinery29. Then six months ago, Hunter Schaefer from the show *Euphoria* was photographed wearing an onyx Rock Candy ring, and that pushed her brand into another stratosphere. Gemma could only hope that progress would be enough to attract money people.

The sound of customers heading up the stairs was louder than she'd like considering the run-in with Mrs. Woods, but there was nothing she could do about it now.

The first person through the door was Mae.

"I'm here to collect," she said with a grin. Gemma had offered to let Mae pick out a piece of jewelry in exchange for the press pass.

Mae gravitated to the trays of Rock Candy rings, sifting through cushion-cut citrine, amethyst, and white topaz rings. There was one pink topaz and one violet-colored stone called iolite.

"Love this," Mae said, picking up the citrine. "It looks like a canary diamond. I've been obsessed with these photos on your Instagram."

In keeping with her belief that the best jewelry was meaningful, the Rock Candy collection was deeply personal. It grew out of her memory of — and longing for — her mother's spectacular thirty-carat pink diamond engagement ring. As a young girl, she found that the gem seemed to overtake her entire hand. It was vividly pink but at the same time as clear as water. Her mother had promised Gemma it was her inheritance. Gemma hadn't seen it since shortly after her mother's death.

She was certain it would be on display at

the Pavlin & Co party. How could it not? It was the most famous piece Pavlin & Co ever created.

And like everything else that had been taken from her, she was coming for it.

5

Gemma flashed her borrowed press pass at the gatekeeper, glanced at her family name carved above the entrance, then followed the tide of reporters as she crossed the threshold of Pavlin & Co for the first time in a decade and a half.

Nothing had changed. Not the deep green awnings over the windows, not the entrance itself inlaid with stainless steel columns, and not the sprawling main floor filled with glass display cases under twenty-four-foot ceilings. The double-height windows offered a view of one of the most famous retail blocks in the world.

A man dressed in a double-breasted suit directed the crowd to the far wall, where a continuous, long glass case was flanked by guards and lit from above with bright light.

"Please feel free to peruse the Pavlin Private Collection, on exhibit in its entirety for the first time . . ."

Gemma's heart began to beat fast. She was so close. She couldn't believe she'd finally get to see her mother's engagement ring again. The last time she'd touched it had been in the chaotic days following her parents' deaths. Her maternal grandmother, Constance, an imposing woman with a tiny thin frame and blond hair that never moved in even the stiffest wind, had been the one to break the news of the accident to Gemma. Surreal days blended into one another, as Gemma wandered her grandparents' palatial apartment on Park Avenue, irrationally waiting for her mother to come get her. Out of habit, craving the ritual of watching her mother do her hair and makeup for a night out, she ventured into Constance's bedroom. Shockingly, she saw her mother's pink diamond engagement ring resting on a crystal dish on the dresser. This, more than anything else, made the news of her parents' deaths seem real. At the sight of that ring separated from her mother, she burst into tears. Trembling, she slipped it onto her finger. Then, hearing her grandmother's footsteps, she just as quickly slipped it off.

"It will be yours someday," her grandmother said. "It's what your mother wanted. So, something to look forward to when you're grown up."

Well, now she was grown up. But she'd had almost no contact with the Pavlins for the past fifteen years. They never reached out to her, and Nana discouraged her from contacting them — or asking too many questions.

"You're better off without those people," she'd said.

Gemma was confused. Wasn't she herself one of "those people"?

She fell into the makeshift line of reporters, noting that even the jaded Manhattan press was quietly reverent in the face of such treasures, some — but not all — of which she recognized. The Daisy necklace, a graduated series of circular-cut diamond daisies, each set with a circular-cut yellow diamond bombé pistil, spaced by chrysoprase leaves with circular-cut diamond trim; the Lemon Drop, a detachable pear-shaped fancy yellow diamond, 9.66 carats, attached to a colored diamond neck chain, mounted in gold-plated platinum; the Constance, an art nouveau enamel and multi-gem heron designed with a cushion-cut aquamarine and cabochon opal body, extending blue and green plique-á-jour enamel wings, enhanced by cabochon rubies and calibrécut emeralds, accented by gold wirework detail.

All breathtaking, but somewhat dated. Gemma, a student of the history of jewelry as well as its creation, had noted that Pavlin & Co had long since stopped innovating. They were coasting on their name, on people's perception of luxury and quality. But Gemma knew times were changing, and the Pavlins' laziness would make her job of outshining them that much easier.

Still, there was one piece Gemma's modern creations could never compete with: the Electric Rose. But as she moved from case to case, a feeling of unease came over her as she approached the end of the exhibit.

Her mother's engagement ring was not there.

Elodie, dressed in a custom emerald green St. John dress, greeted the press and felt like a bride on her wedding day. Or, at least, what she imagined a bride to feel like. Despite being the heiress to a fortune built on diamond engagement rings, neither Elodie nor her older sister, Celeste, had ever married. The irony had not escaped the notice of gossip columnists over the decades.

The media assembled before her now

were of a different generation; aside from a few familiar faces from *The Wall Street Journal* and *The New York Times,* she doubted any of them remembered when more ink was spilled on the glamorous Pavlin sisters than on Pavlin & Co itself.

"I'm delighted to welcome you here tonight on such an auspicious occasion, and I know my parents would be touched to see such an enthusiastic celebration of our one hundred years on Fifth Avenue. Since opening these doors a century ago, Pavlin & Co has become one of the most sought-after retail destinations in the world . . ."

Elodie moved through her speech, adrenalized by the camera flashes and the anticipation of fielding questions about each of the eighty heirloom pieces on display. The press had been given a walkthrough in advance of the party guests' arrival, and their appreciative sighs and murmurs had fueled her like a drug.

Elodie's publicist gave her the signal that it was time for the Q and A.

"I'll take a few questions," Elodie said. The first hand that shot up belonged to a young woman in a black dress. Elodie pointed to her and nodded, an alarm bell sounding deep inside as she noted there was something eerily familiar about the beautiful blonde.

"Why isn't the most famous piece in the Pavlin collection included in the exhibit?" the woman said. "Where's the Electric Rose?"

Elodie felt the blood drain from her face, her heart pounding as recognition materialized: That woman was her niece, Gemma. Every nerve in her body wanted to summon security, to have the interloper thrown out. Instead, she smiled calmly.

"The Electric Rose has not been shown in public since the death of its owner," Elodie said. "Nor will it be."

A reporter raised her hand. She was in her early fifties, with straight red hair the color of a new penny. Elodie recognized her, too: Regan O'Rourke from *The New York Times,* formerly a gossip columnist who'd written some absurd items about Elodie and her sisters. And some not so absurd.

"Is that because of the curse?" Regan asked.

Oh, not that nonsense again. It had been years since she'd thought about the old rumor that the Electric Rose diamond was cursed and doomed her family to be unlucky in love. Leave it to Regan to bring it up. She was probably the one who'd started it.

"No, we don't make decisions based on tabloids from the 1990s," Elodie said with a forced laugh. She glanced once again at her niece, a mirror image of her mother.

She stopped taking questions.

Gemma followed the tide of journalists from the press area back onto the main floor.

She walked directly behind the red-headed reporter who asked about the curse. Growing up, Gemma had tried to make sense of her parents' deaths, searching online and finding a revolting trove of gossip items about her family. Yes, some said the Electric Rose, just like the Hope Diamond, was "cursed." Some claimed that her mother's oldest sister, Celeste, ran away to New England and joined a cult. She read that her mother stole her father from Elodie, and that her grandfather had an affair and originally unearthed the Electric Rose to win his wife back. Gemma knew every gossip item was garbage, but out of all of them, the curse story was the one that persisted. But even as a teenager Gemma knew it was childish — lazy — to try to explain away real-world tragedy with magical thinking.

The front doors were now open to the wider party, well-heeled guests pouring in, vibrating with the specific energy of people who felt included, chosen, special. The last time Gemma had been inside the store, she had felt that way: Included. Chosen. Special.

Being around diamonds and emeralds could do that to a person. Her mother always told her that the value of precious gems went beyond their beauty — that each stone had unique properties that enhanced the spiritual life of the owner. "They're little bits of magic." Emerald stimulated the heart chakra, healing emotions as well as the physical heart. Rubies improved energy and concentration.

"What about pink diamonds?" Gemma once asked, because of course that was her favorite stone of all.

"Pink diamonds heighten our intuition." And she wagged her ring finger with the breathtaking gem.

Has not been shown in public since the death of its owner.

She felt a hand on her shoulder.

"I need to speak with you," Elodie said.

Escorted by security guards, Gemma had no choice but to follow Elodie out a side entrance onto East Fifty-Third Street.

"You're trespassing," Elodie said, her ash blond hair pushed back in a headband that matched her dress. Her only jewelry was a gold chain-link necklace and a gold Pavlin & Co watch. Her figure was matronly; her voice had the huskiness of a former smoker, and a slight twang that suggested nonexistent Southern roots. She had deep creases around her mouth, but was blessed with the same beautiful blue-green eyes as all the Pavlin women.

"Do you know who I am?" Gemma said.

"I do. That's how I know you weren't invited."

"Where's the Electric Rose?"

"That's none of your business. It's a family piece."

"And I'm family. My mother left it to me."

"It wasn't hers to leave. It belongs to Pavlin & Co. At best, it was loaned to her. I hate to disappoint you, but you'll have to go gold-digging elsewhere."

Gemma felt a fury she'd never experienced before. She would never understand why the Pavlins cast her out as they did, but at least in this moment she knew what to do about it.

"I'm not going anywhere. That ring belongs to me. And the future of jewelry belongs to people like me. The glory days of Pavlin & Co are over."

She turned and walked away, leaving behind the celebrated building that haunted her dreams. Knowing that in order to fulfill her destiny, she had to destroy her legacy.

6

There had been a time when Elodie walked into the Café Carlyle and felt utterly at home amidst the elite crowd of New Yorkers and moneyed tourists. The Carlyle, on the corner of Madison and East Seventy-Sixth Street, shined like a beacon of the best New York City had to offer. It represented an old world that Elodie increasingly felt slipping away.

The staff still greeted her by name. But since her mother had passed away, there was a hollow feeling to the space. The first night she'd come for dinner after losing Constance, it was all she could do to keep down her martini — Belvedere Vodka, straight up with a twist. Two years later, seated in that dark and clubby room, she felt surrounded by ghosts. The ghosts of her parents, the ghosts of the legendary artists who had performed at the piano bar, and maybe the ghost of her former self, the one who believed she'd be truly happy once she was finally given her rightful place at the helm of the company.

Now she had the position she'd always wanted. But in some ways, it felt like it had come too late. The world was changing. Just the other day she'd overheard a young man saying he'd ordered an engagement ring *online.* Where was the joy in that? Did tradition have no place in society anymore? There had been a time when the appointments for ring consultations were booked six months in advance. Customers took the elevator up to the fourth floor, sat in a velvet cushioned wing-backed chair, and were offered champagne while her father himself counseled them on the "four C's" and discussed the merits of platinum versus yellow gold settings. Now what? People preferred to just click a button?

Truth be told, as much as the current state of the industry dismayed her, she'd been in a foul mood ever since the unfortunate appearance of her niece earlier in the week.

She checked her watch, hoping Sloan would be on time. Lately, her dog, Pearl, seemed depressed when Elodie stayed out late at night. She didn't want to have to put her on Prozac like her neighbor had with her terrier.

A woman with sleek good looks entered the room, her dark hair loose to her shoulders with razor-sharp bangs that could only have been cut by Shereen at Oscar Blandi. She was dressed in a dove gray pantsuit and a Pavlin & Co platinum chain-link necklace from the spring 2016 collection. Sloan Pierce.

They exchanged an air-kiss before Sloan took the seat across from her.

"The party the other night was just exquisite," she said. "Congratulations."

The waiter reappeared and Sloan ordered sparkling water.

"Sloan, dear, I insist you at least consider the wine list. It's a travesty not to." Elodie knew there were certain people who didn't drink, and she found them dull. Sloan ordered a glass of the Burgundy. It was a point in her favor — that would have been Elodie's selection as well if she had been having wine.

"How are your parents?" Elodie inquired politely.

"Wonderful, thank you. Mummy is already planning the gala for next season." Harriet Pierce was on the board of the New York City Ballet and never let anyone forget.

"She always does a fine job," said Elodie.

The waiter placed a glass of wine in front

of Sloan and she raised it.

"To new endeavors," Sloan said with the buoyancy of the young, for whom the future was just one big adventure.

Elodie took a large gulp of her martini and smiled tightly.

After some small talk, Sloan folded her hands in front of her and said, "You must be wondering why I called."

"I assume you need someone to chair an event. I'm happy to lend a hand. Charity is very important to me." It was true now more than ever; her mother had raised her to always find a way to give back. Constance had been on the board of Mount Sinai, the Met, and Children's Aid. Elodie had not been the chair of a fundraiser since her death, and it was time. It would make her feel closer to her.

"Oh, well, there certainly could be a charitable angle," Sloan said carefully. "That's entirely up to you."

"How so?"

"Elodie, I've always been a huge admirer of Pavlin & Co. Your family commissioned some of the most iconic pieces of American jewelry of the last century. I'm certain you'll continue that tradition well into the next few decades. And as a scholar of fine jewelry, as a passionate enthusiast for your stellar brand, I'm proposing an auction of the Pavlin Private Collection."

Elodie's jaw dropped. Neither her grandparents nor her parents had ever sold anything from the private collection. These were pieces that had been created as gifts for members of the family, or pieces that had been designed for the floor but ultimately considered too special to part with. It even included pieces that had been purchased at one time but then quietly sold back to the family — sometimes a generation or more later.

"The Pavlin family has never put any of our pieces up for auction."

Sloan nodded. "Historically, I know that to be the case. But I thought this centennial anniversary might be a time to revisit that."

"How so?"

"This is the moment when a brand moves from classic to legendary. The party was a wonderful start. But why stop there? With an auction, you could cap this year off with something that would go down in history."

Interesting. Try as she might, it was getting more and more difficult to get press, to distinguish Pavlin & Co from the competition, of which there was more and more with each passing day. Not to mention the internet.

"I know it's a big decision," Sloan said. "My boss was part of the team that put together the auction for Elizabeth Taylor's jewelry. Ms. Taylor oversaw every detail. Not only every piece that was chosen for the auction, but how it was positioned in the catalogue, how it was advertised, how the event was planned down to the type of canape served. The auction, as you well know, was one of the great jewelry events of all time."

"May I ask how old you are, Sloan?"

"I just turned thirty."

"Quite young to be undertaking such a project," Elodie said.

"I'll admit, this would be a career-making event for me." She met Elodie's gaze, unwavering.

Ambitious. Elodie could relate.

"Well, it's an intriguing proposition," she said. "I'll think about it."

"Great. Also, I do have a question about one particular piece."

"Oh?"

"At the party the other night, someone asked about the Electric Rose. You mentioned that it hasn't been shown publicly since your sister's death. I hope you will at least consider including it in the auction. It would make for spectacular publicity."

Elodie sat back in her seat, narrowing her eyes. "That's not going to happen. And if that ring is your entire motivation behind this conversation, then we have nothing left to discuss."

"No, no," Sloan said quickly. "Absolutely not. There's certainly no shortage of remarkable pieces to build a promotional campaign around. Really, I think it would be the auction of the decade. And again, we'd welcome your input. You *are* Pavlin & Co."

Yes, she was. And really, what better way to make use of the collection? She would never have someone to hand the pieces down to. And selling it off would at least prevent her niece from claiming it.

"I'll think about it."

7

Gemma stood outside the Union Square Barnes & Noble and checked her phone. Sanjay was ten minutes late, but he was doing her a favor, so she knew she couldn't complain. She had a bunch of new pieces she needed photographed for Instagram and he agreed to help.

It was the day of the farmer's market, so she at least had great people-watching to pass the time. You never knew when you'd spot a celebrity on the hunt for prime butternut squash.

Her phone rang.

"May I speak to Gemma Maybrook?" a female voice said.

"This is Gemma." She stepped closer to the bookstore awning and covered one ear with her hand.

"I'm calling from Jacob Jabarin's office. Mr. Jabarin unfortunately needs to postpone your meeting."

"Postpone? Why?"

"I'm not at liberty to disclose all the details, but he said you have a product more than a business, so it's premature to discuss any potential investment."

A product rather than a business? But that was why she needed seed money — to grow *into* a business. She needed to invest in materials and at least the occasional pop-up before a physical store. She needed a marketing campaign to get her message out. Sure, she had a respectable following on Instagram and she was making some money. But she'd gotten as far as she could on her own. She had to take things to the next level and knew a real investor would get her there. She'd seen too many other promising NYSD graduates fail to segue from wunderkind to serious competitor in the marketplace. She didn't want to fall into that trap. She had the New York City and LA crowd wearing her designs. What she needed was the homemaker in South Carolina buying her daughter a charm necklace for Sweet Sixteen, or a workingwoman in upstate New York buying herself a Rock Candy ring for her own birthday.

"Feel free to check back in a few months. Perhaps the end of the summer?"

Gemma forced herself to reply with detached politeness, not betraying the frustration she felt. What was going to change by the end of the summer? As the call ended, she spotted Sanjay emerging from the subway station. At least she still had him on her team. Barely.

A gifted photographer, Sanjay had been assigned to her group for a project in a business elective freshman year. They had to create a marketing campaign for a product, and the group decided to use her jewelry and his photography. She got an A on the project, but more important, found a new friend in Sanjay. They shared the same obsessive drive, the same sense of having something to prove. She had jewelry-making in her blood but had been cast out of the family; Sanjay was from a strict Indian household that believed any career for a man other than medical or scientific was a waste of time. For both of them, NYSD was more than just a school: It was their launching pad for proving their families wrong.

At the end of junior year, when she created her first real line of jewelry with the Rock Candy rings, she enlisted him to help her take photographs for Instagram. At first, he said he just didn't have time: He had a full course load and worked every weekend at the Casterbridge.

She considered other photographers within the school directory, but Sanjay's work stood out. The way his shots conveyed texture and light was unique. She couldn't take no for an answer; instead, she told him she'd rent a room at the hotel one night, bring all her things, and if he could just run up to the room after work and shoot, she'd "pay" him with some of the pieces that he could give to his sisters. They negotiated: He said his sisters didn't wear jewelry, but he'd do it if he could keep some of the photos for his portfolio or even to sell in the future.

"Deal," she said.

The Casterbridge was a redbrick and stone Georgian Revival building overlooking Central Park. A room was a big expense, but she knew she would make it back if she sold just a quarter of the rings Sanjay photographed. She brought along a bottle of prosecco to celebrate when the shoot was finished.

He finished his shift at midnight and worked methodically but quickly; he tried different backgrounds, some white light box, some colorful textile, some taken of the rings on her fingers. The ones she liked best were the close-ups of a ring with the bright white background. They allowed the gems to pop, vivid and enticing as actual candy.

As she watched him work, trusting his art direction instead of her own urge to call the shots, she realized for the first time how attractive he was. With his intelligent dark eyes, thick black hair, and dimpled smile, she could only assume her admiration for his talent led her to prematurely put him in the friend zone. And Sanjay must have felt something different that night, too, because somehow, between breaking down the lights and camera setup and opening the bottle of prosecco, they kissed. It was a great kiss, one that made her knees weak.

A kiss worthy of launching a real love affair. And it did — until she screwed it up.

It had only been a few weeks since he'd forgiven her and they'd tentatively found their way back to friendship. With school ending, they both wanted to set things right, and Gemma was grateful to have her friend back. Still, she longed for him in a way that would make it impossible to be satisfied with just friendship. And there was absolutely nothing she could do about it.

"Wanna grab something to eat?" she said.

"I don't have a lot of time," he said. "Let's just get to work."

"Oh? Big plans tonight?" she teased to

cover up her disappointment. She thought with a pang of the days when they met up at her apartment, had heart-stopping sex, ordered in food, and then finally got around to photographing her work around midnight. Then more sex. Then waking up in each other's arms . . .

Stop it.

They walked west, passing the shuttered restaurant Coffee Shop. Sanjay stopped at a hot dog vendor to buy a bottle of water. At five in the evening, it was still close to eighty degrees out — the warmest day of spring so far.

"Why didn't you come by my graduation party?" he said.

She hadn't told him about the Pavlin & Co event.

Growing up, Gemma never discussed her relationship with the Pavlins, not even with her closest friends. It was a habit she'd gotten into because of Nana's attitude toward her maternal family. It was an unspoken rule that they didn't ever acknowledge that side of Gemma's life. As she grew up, hungry to know more about the mother she'd lost, she learned to swallow her curiosity. It became almost a superstition not to mention the Pavlins — like avoiding stepping on the cracks in the sidewalk. In contrast, her grandparents' house was a shrine to her father. His photos were on every flat surface in the place, along with his high school soccer trophies, plaques for his honor roll in college, and the awards he won in advertising. Because she was raised in that environment, it was like she was one hundred percent Maybrook.

Sanjay was one of the few friends of hers in whom she'd confided about her actual family background, and only then because she'd had one too many glasses of wine at her birthday dinner. She instantly regretted it. She hated to think of Sanjay googling her famous mother, seeing the photos of her in the Pavlin & Co ads that were plastered all over the city — all over the country — thirty years ago. She was afraid he'd look at her differently. But to his credit, he never even brought it up again except when he read her sales pitch for the investors. He'd suggested she include it in her bio, and she hadn't listened to him. Considering the call from Jacob Jabarin's office just now, maybe she should have.

"I'm sorry. I had a . . . thing I had to take care of."

"You should have been there to celebrate with everyone. Graduation is a big deal, you know." He shook his head. "Sometimes I feel like you go out of your way to avoid being happy."

Gemma couldn't help but think this was a dig at how she messed up their relationship.

They walked in silence until they reached her building.

"I think you were right about leaning into my family connection more in my business plan," she said, stopping on the front stoop to fish her keys from her bag. "But it would have to be done in the right way."

Pavlin & Co might have outdated designs, they might not have innovated in decades, but it was, at least, a company. A world-renowned company. Legendary. Her connection to it might give her legitimacy in the eyes of investors. But it had to be something more than just a line in her bio.

She'd once read that a single tabloid photo of her mother wearing the Electric Rose generated more sales at Pavlin & Co than a six-figure advertising campaign. What if she were able to use the ring to generate that kind of buzz for her own brand? She'd find an angle, something like "tradition reimagined." The only way she could compete with a monolith like Pavlin & Co was to show it was a dinosaur — that the customers and creators of jewelry were different in the new millennium. She could design a new setting for the Electric Rose, transforming it from an engagement ring into a pendant that symbolized independence. Women didn't need to wait around for someone to buy them a diamond ring. They bought their own jewelry. They knew how to celebrate *themselves.*

They climbed the stairs to her apartment, each floor more stifling than the one below it. When they reached her front door she found a piece of paper taped to it.

"What's this?" she said, leaning closer to read it. The words "commercial enterprise" and "lease violation" swam before her eyes.

Sanjay pulled it off the door and looked at it closely. "This," he said, "is an eviction notice."

Elodie sat elbow to elbow at a long table inside the Hall of Ocean Life at the Museum of Natural History on the Upper West Side. She wished she hadn't committed to the fundraiser, but she was a sucker for anything animal-related. And the museum still had its butterfly room, so technically it qualified. With a rush of nostalgia, she remembered how her younger sister, Paulina, had loved butterflies. She shook the thought away.

Inside her handbag, her phone vibrated.

She gave her screen a quick glance and sent her lawyer's call to voicemail.

"The problem is these young people don't understand that not all money is created equal," said the woman next to her.

One of the eternal downsides of being a single woman on the fundraising circuit was that she was always trapped in conversation with people she had no interest in talking to. She couldn't even look across the table at a spouse or partner for a sympathetic nod whilst trapped in a boring conversation.

Today, she had Esther Dernhauser on her right talking her ear off about co-op board problems. On her left, she had Joe Lavendero, an eighty-year-old billionaire who was considered quite the catch. Had she been seated next to him in some sort of misguided matchmaking attempt?

That was the other problem with being single in New York society. Everyone wanted the feather in their cap of being the one to pair you off. A hundred years after Edith Wharton, and matchmaking was still the preferred sport of the rich.

Elodie had been in love precisely once, back in the early nineties.

Four years out of Columbia, Elodie was hitting her stride as her father's heir apparent. As far as her sisters went, it wasn't even a contest: Celeste was away at grad school, and Paulina was flitting around the world being photographed by tabloids and sleeping her way through Europe's most eligible gene pool. Elodie was delighted. After being in the shadow of both of them for her entire life, she finally had her father's attention — and the company — all to herself.

Every year the agency built a campaign around Pavlin & Co's holiday collections. Alan paid a small fortune for the annual blitz of magazine ads and television spots. As he always said, desire had to be invented.

"Miss Pavlin, we have a new account executive working with us on this project," said the agency CEO, Jim Rizzi, when the conference room was fully seated. "This is Liam Maybrook."

Elodie took in his wavy dark hair, cornflower blue eyes, and sharp cheekbones. He was tall and lean and when he reached over to shake her hand, Elodie felt as if the chair dropped out beneath her.

"We just lured him away from TBWA/Chiat/Day and we're delighted to say he's hit the ground running on this," Jim added.

Liam Maybrook gave her a brief nod before launching into his presentation, using a projector to run through a slide show.

He was dressed in a jacket and tie, and he

moved with a stiff formality. But there was something devil-may-care in those deep blue eyes. He spoke with an absolute command of the room, and she found herself almost holding her breath.

At the end of the presentation, it was as if she snapped out of a dream. She was there to either sign off on the pitch or ask for a different direction. She found herself unable to do either.

"You've given me a lot to think about," she said. Jim Rizzi, sensing that she was being euphemistic for "I hated it," jumped in with, "Look at the time! It's almost five. Who can make decisions on an empty stomach? Let's discuss this over dry martinis and rare steaks."

The Palm was just a few blocks away on Forty-Fourth and Second Avenue. The maître d' seated their large party immediately.

"I eat here four or five nights a week," Jim told her, either bragging or to explain how they bypassed all the patrons waiting at the bar.

The table for six was round, and the group politely waited for her to take a seat before filling in the chairs around her. Fate smiled at her, because Liam Maybrook ended up directly to her right.

She spent the first round of martinis and the appetizer course talking to the man on the opposite side. It took her that long to get her bearings. Only then, fortified by the vodka, could she turn to Liam and attempt small talk. She noticed he stopped drinking after the first round.

"Do you prefer wine?" she said, wondering if they should order a bottle. She wouldn't have minded switching over herself. Between the hard liquor and her attraction to this stranger, she could barely keep her head straight.

"I like martinis just fine," he said. "But I stop at one when I'm on the clock."

"Oh?" she said. "I didn't realize you were still on the clock."

He turned his empty cocktail glass, glancing sideways at her with a small smile that made her melt.

"I'm always on the clock. But someday I hope to spend a lot of time traveling. There's so much to see in the world. I think a lot of people in New York City forget that."

Elodie picked up her water glass and held it out toward him.

"I'll drink to that. But are you *really* always working, Liam?" she said with out-of-character flirtatiousness. The man did something to her.

He nodded, a twinkle in his blue eyes. "If I wasn't — and if my work didn't involve your ad campaign — I would ask you out to a proper dinner."

She felt her heart stop.

"In that case," she said, "maybe I should quit."

Now, three decades later, she could still see him like it was yesterday. More, she could still feel the rush of longing.

Elodie tried to root herself in the present, looking around the packed luncheon hall, barely aware of the Emmy Award–winning actress taking the stage to juice up the crowd so they opened their wallets.

"Elodie Pavlin! What a surprise to see you out and about," said Isabel Haupt, wife of hedge fund honcho Ian Haupt and one of the wealthiest women in Manhattan. "I guess you haven't been feeling very charitable lately." No matter what planning committee they were on together, Isabel was always the contrarian when it came to Elodie's suggestions and opinions. And since planning committees were never about who had the best ideas but rather who would be bringing in the biggest donors, Isabel's opinion won out every time.

"Some of us have full-time jobs, Isabel," Elodie said.

"Still," Isabel said, looking grave and putting a bony hand on her forearm, "one must always make time to give back."

"As a matter of fact, I'm working on something for charity right now." She made a mental note to talk to Sloan Pierce about partnering with a charity.

Just a day earlier she'd decided to move forward with the auction. She'd get a year's worth of publicity out of it, she'd unburden herself of caretaking all the pieces, raise some money, and, best of all, that niece of hers would have less reason to keep sniffing around.

Her phone buzzed again, and again she checked. Her lawyer. At least this time the call would extract her from the conversation with Isabel. She excused herself and stepped away from the table.

"Elodie speaking."

"I've been trying to reach you all morning. We need to discuss the auction paperwork you sent me," said her lawyer.

"Right now? I'm at a luncheon."

"There's a problem. The Pavlin Private Collection is part of a trust. You can't sell any of the items without sign-off from the co-owners of the trust."

Had he been day-drinking? "There aren't any co-owners of the trust."

"I'm afraid there is. Your sister Celeste."

"*Celeste?* Celeste hasn't had anything to do with the company . . . ever!" It was an outrage. A grotesque mistake that she would immediately remedy.

"And your niece, Gemma Maybrook."

8

Gemma had thirty days to vacate her apartment. She didn't have any idea where she was going to find something as affordable. Her studio was a unicorn that she'd gotten through the NYSD student center. Now that she'd graduated, she was on her own.

She hadn't realized, until faced with eviction, how buffered she'd been within the NYSD community. Her professors had been surrogate parents, her friends surrogate siblings. Now, with everyone either back to hometowns or hunkered down looking for jobs or already paired up with roommates, she was faced with a real problem to solve, without a safety net.

"I would offer to let you crash with me but that probably wouldn't be the best idea. Considering," Sanjay had said when they discovered the notice.

Sanjay shared a Brooklyn town house with his two older sisters, Daksha, a cellist, and

Prishna, a med student. During the months of their relationship they rarely spent time there because the two women were always practicing or studying. And after the New Year's Eve disaster, his sisters definitely weren't her biggest fans.

Sanjay had taken her to a New Year's Eve party at his friend Monica Del Mar's apartment in SoHo. Also in the photography program, Monica was a tall brunette with attention-grabbing piercings. She bragged, a lot. Gemma had always found her irritating but it didn't matter — she'd be with Sanjay, and wherever they went it felt like they were in their own little universe. They'd been together for over a half a year, and for the first time, Gemma was in a relationship with someone who was her best friend. They had passion without drama — something she previously believed to be impossible.

Monica Del Mar lived in a loft on Greene Street. Her parents got the apartment through an artist's grant back in the 1970s, a time when artists could actually afford to live in SoHo. The space was cavernous, with big pillars the only dividing marks in the open living space.

The party had a DJ table and serve-yourself bar filled with bottles and bottles of vodka and tequila and trays of Jell-O shots. The latter, ultimately, did her in. Gemma did a few, felt nothing, and then within ten minutes was wasted. That's when she saw Noam.

Sophomore year, Noam Levy had been the only classmate who shared her nearly obsessive interest in metalwork. Gemma had originally enrolled in NYSD planning to focus on gemology. It was, after all, her namesake. But she soon found herself just as enthralled with metals. There was something endlessly fascinating about the way metal and its alloys behaved, and how she could manipulate that behavior to create something new. And really, what was a stone without the setting? For Gemma, the ring itself — be it gold or platinum, silver or bronze, pure or plated — was as interesting as the gem it framed. The first time she made a necklace chain from scratch, a basic loop-in-loop, she felt like she'd invented the wheel.

Gemma and Noam could talk for hours about the science behind metalwork, how heat from the torch forced the crystals of metal to move apart. He was a master at forging; in his hands, a hammer was as precise an instrument as a scalpel. His hands were equally skilled on her body. They had sex more than once in a studio after hours, their bodies connecting wordlessly and perfectly, like a well-orchestrated solder.

But a few months into their relationship, Noam changed. He stayed up all night creating intricate metal sculptures that he was convinced would be displayed at the Whitney Biennial. He didn't go to class and they stopped having sex. After not hearing from him for a few days, she went to his apartment and learned from his roommate that Noam's mother checked him in to a psychiatric hospital. He was bipolar and had stopped taking his meds.

The sighting at the party was the first time she'd seen him since he took a leave of absence from school. Through the haze of alcohol, she couldn't process it. Instead of seeing her ex-boyfriend, someone from the past, she was jolted right back to the headspace she'd been in when she last saw him. Since they hadn't had a fight or a proper breakup, there was no closure. Even though she was happy with Sanjay, in the back of her mind Noam was still an open wound. And when he leaned forward and kissed her, she let him. It felt natural. It felt like . . . a punctuation mark. And if their hostess, Monica Del Mar, hadn't seen them from across the room, that's all it would have been. But then Monica told Sanjay.

Now, sitting alone in her apartment four months later, she was still paying the price.

Her phone rang, a number she didn't recognize.

"Hello," she said, standing up from her workbench for the first time in hours. Her back ached, and her thumb was turning black and blue from where she accidentally hit it with a hammer. Still, she'd gotten in a full day of metalwork; she had to replenish her stash of necklace chains for her Old New York collection. They were distinct, thicker than a typical necklace chain. Some were oval-link chains, some more industrial-looking edge link. All were finished with her signature lobster-claw clasp with *GEMMA* engraved in script.

"Hello, may I speak to Gemma Maybrook?" a female voice asked.

"This is Gemma."

"Gemma, my name is Sloan Pierce. I work at Whitmore's Auction House in the jewelry department. I believe you were at the Pavlin & Co party last week?"

"Um, yes. I was."

"I noticed you because of your question about the Electric Rose. It seems we share an interest in it. Do you have time to chat over a cup of coffee?"

Gemma's first instinct was to say no; the call violated her sense of privacy, her strong desire to stay under the radar when it came to her connection to the Pavlins. But maybe this woman was willing to tell her what Elodie Pavlin had not been: where to find her mother's ring.

"Sure," Gemma said. "Let's talk."

Elodie hated meeting with the accountants. Numbers didn't lie; no matter how brightly the showroom glittered, the health of the company was determined by the spreadsheets and executives on the top floor. And today, the news was not good.

"That's two bad quarters in a row," her accountant said.

"I'm not an accountant, but I'm quite capable of counting to two," Elodie said dryly. "There's no need to panic. We've already seen a bounce from all the party publicity."

But the problem, she knew, was that they couldn't throw a party every day. It wasn't just about two bad quarters; Pavlin & Co was losing its allure. Maybe it was time to reinvent the brand, the way her grandfather had in the 1940s, or the way her father had commanded the market in the mid-nineties. But Elodie wasn't creative; she knew her best bet was to lean into their deep history. It was the one thing the flavor-of-the-month jewelers couldn't compete with. She also knew the best way to do this was to move forward with the auction of the Pavlin Private Collection.

"You need to do more," her accountant said.

Yes, she did. That's why she was headed to Provincetown.

9

Provincetown, Cape Cod

It was the unofficial start of her twenty-fifth summer in Provincetown, and Celeste Pavlin was supposed to be working. She had, in fact, told Jack — her partner in business and in life — that she was running out to look at an estate sale to find things for their antiques shop. Instead, she was sitting in the wild garden behind a historic Victorian on Provincetown's famed Commercial Street.

Late May was go-time in town, when everyone was in a mad scramble to get their businesses ready for the rush of tourists. Celeste, who had been running her store for two decades, was no exception. There wasn't any time to waste. But, of course, Celeste would never consider getting her cards read a waste of time. Jack, however, would feel differently.

"Do you have a question for me today?"

asked the woman seated across from her. Maud Bigelow was sixty, with salt-and-pepper hair, very thick and straight, chopped in a ragged line just below her ears. Her skin was leathery after decades of beach living, but her eyes were the bright ice blue of a Siberian husky with a deep, soulful intelligence. She was medium height and wiry, and her nails always looked like she'd just been gardening.

Maud was a Provincetown fixture since she "washed ashore" in her late twenties, and had been reading Celeste's cards for years.

Celeste appreciated having a like-minded person in Provincetown. Whenever she told her friend Lidia that Mercury was in retrograde, all she got in response was an eye roll. When she told Jack that it wouldn't be the worst thing in the world to time their special sales event with the full moon, she got silence. But Maud understood.

That was one of the things she loved about her adopted town; the year-round population was only a few thousand people, but among them, you could always find the support you needed, no matter how quirky or demanding your needs.

Celeste met Maud a decade and a half ago in a moment of sudden, crushing grief. By

2004, she'd created a happy life for herself up on the Cape. She had Jack; she had his family, who lovingly embraced her; and she had their store, Queen Anne's Revenge. Jack gave it the name after Blackbeard's pirate ship. At first, he'd hesitated to join her antiques store venture. But once he saw how important it was to her, he was all in. Now, all these years later, she knew she wouldn't have been able to manage without him.

So yes, Provincetown gave her many gifts, the most important being distance from her own family's drama — a distance that came at the price of her father cutting her off financially. But Provincetown gave Celeste something money couldn't buy: peace.

That came to a swift end with a phone call in the middle of the night from her mother.

"There's been an accident . . ." Constance was hysterical; it took Celeste a few minutes to make out the news. Her sister Paulina had died.

She never went back to sleep that night. Instead, she walked on the beach and then, after the sun came up, she wandered the side streets. That was when she noticed a tiny storefront tucked down an alleyway near Freeman Street. The sign read, *Life is full of questions.*

That wasn't the beginning of Celeste's interest in astrology. No, it had started with the horoscopes in the back of her mother's *Vogue* magazine. But what was once a casual curiosity changed that morning when she felt everything she believed about the world had been pulled out from under her. Her baby sister — dead. Celeste rang the bell above Maud's door, and kept ringing it in the years that followed.

Maud's storefront was long gone now. Over the years, she'd become one of the town's most productive businesswomen, with a successful restaurant and several rental properties. Now she only read cards and astrology charts by appointment at her home, and always made time for Celeste.

"I want to know what this summer might bring," Celeste said, settling back in the lawn chair with a deep inhale. "I love this time of year. So many possibilities!"

Maud instructed her to cut the deck three times, and Celeste felt the usual frisson of anticipation. In a world full of uncertainty, there was something comforting about being able to commune with the universe.

When the deck had been adequately shuffled, Maud directed her to ponder her question. Celeste then halved the deck, and pulled the first card and set it facedown in front of Maud. She pulled another card, and then one more.

"Are you ready?" Maud said. Celeste nodded, and the cards were turned faceup in the order they had been pulled. The first card pulled represented the past, the second represented the present, and the third represented the future. Since life was a shimmering thread between the three, all were needed to tell the story of any given moment. She looked down at her cards: The Fool. The Wheel of Fortune. The Lovers.

"With the Fool, we are connected back to our childhoods — a former state of wonder. The Wheel of Fortune suggests change. And the Lovers suggests a new phase or compromise is coming in your relationship. Reading these, I would say prepare yourself for the past to revisit you in some way, and this will bring a transformation either to your life in general or your romantic life." She looked up. "Either way, change is coming."

Celeste shuddered. If there were two things she didn't welcome, they were her past and change. She turned to such mystical comforts as tarot to keep things steady and rooted in the present.

Maybe she should have gone to the estate sale after all.

10

Gemma chose the meeting place: City Bakery on Eighteenth Street. The bi-level, open-space restaurant with a double-sided buffet in the center and a gourmet salad bar in the back was familiar territory for her. Besides, it would be nice to have someone else pick up the check for the pricey pretzel croissants.

She waited for Sloan Pierce at a table on the mezzanine, which afforded her a clear view of the entrance. Gemma had already looked up Sloan online and was able to recognize the pretty brunette the moment she walked in the door. She left her knapsack on the chair to reserve the table, and headed down the narrow stairs to meet her.

"Wow. You look just like your mother," the woman said. Gemma blanched; few people knew about her parentage, never mind enough to comment on a family resemblance. "I'm sorry," Sloan said, noting

Gemma's reaction. "I'm just a fan of your family's work and legacy. I wrote my graduate thesis on how your great-grandfather essentially invented the modern-day engagement ring."

"I'm going to get a hot chocolate," Gemma said, suddenly losing her appetite for the croissant.

"Oh, yes — please get whatever you'd like." The woman whipped out a gold corporate American Express card and they fell into line. It was crowded and noisy, and mercifully Sloan didn't try to talk again until they were seated at the table, Sloan with her latte and Gemma with her hot chocolate and croissant, which she wrapped in a napkin and put in her bag for later.

"Thanks for taking the time to meet with me," Sloan said. She was dressed in a blazer and cream-colored pants. Her jewelry was all yellow gold and understated, including a Cartier bracelet and a Pavlin & Co tank watch. She didn't wear earrings, though Gemma noted her ears were pierced. Her left ring finger was bare. "So do you write for a magazine or a newspaper?"

"What?" Gemma said, confused. Then she realized: Sloan had seen her at the party, where she posed as a member of the press. "Oh — neither. I'm a jewelry designer."

Sloan nodded. "I thought maybe you did both. I've seen your Instagram and you're quite talented. Congratulations on the NYSD award. You're in good company; the head designer for Tiffany won that award when she was a student there."

Gemma gave her first genuine smile of the meeting. "Thank you."

"The reason I wanted to talk to you, as I mentioned on the phone, is my interest in the Electric Rose. I'd been hoping to see it at the centennial exhibit, but as you noted that evening, it wasn't included. Do you have any idea if anyone else in the family wore the ring after your mother?"

It was strange, surreal actually, to hear someone talk so casually about her mother. It took all her effort to stay businesslike.

"I don't know anything about the ring. I was hoping you did."

Sloan nodded. "I'm working on it. Do you think there's any chance someone in your family would have sold it?"

Gemma felt her face drain of color. The thought had never crossed her mind. "Wouldn't you have heard about the sale of such a significant diamond? I mean, being in the business?"

Sloan sighed. "Typically, I would say yes. But there are private sales, and important pieces do go underground for any variety of reasons."

While Gemma had no reason to think highly of the Pavlins, she still couldn't believe they would part with the Electric Rose. It was synonymous with the company, just like the famous diamond worn by Audrey Hepburn was a hallmark of Pavlin's biggest competitor, Tiffany.

"Why are you so interested in the diamond, anyway?" Gemma said.

"Your aunt didn't tell you?" The way she asked told her that Sloan knew full well that Elodie hadn't told her anything, and the fact that she would pretend otherwise put Gemma on guard.

"Tell me what?"

"We're planning an auction to celebrate the centennial with the historic pieces that have come to represent the brand. Elodie made it clear the Electric Rose wouldn't be included, so I'm just wondering where it might be. The question is going to come up once we publicize the auction, and I'd rather not have any surprises. So I guess you could just call this my due diligence."

Gemma was relieved to hear that her aunt wasn't trying to sell the Electric Rose out from under her. But the fact that this well-connected woman couldn't find any clues about its whereabouts was discouraging. Was it possible her grandparents simply locked it away somewhere after her mother's death? It seemed the most likely explanation. She said as much to Sloan, who looked dubious.

"It's possible," she said. Then she pulled her handbag onto her lap and fished out a business card, sliding it across the table, avoiding a puddle of spilled hot chocolate. "If you think of anything, feel free to be in touch. I'll keep my eyes out, too."

Gemma took the card, knowing that when she got her hands on her mother's ring, the last thing she would ever do was call Sloan Pierce. The problem was she had no idea how to go about finding it on her own.

11

For Celeste, antiquing was never about the object itself. It was the thrill of the hunt.

It had taken a few seasons for her to get to know the sweet spot of her Provincetown clientele. They had impeccable taste and plenty of disposable income, but they didn't come to her for million-dollar paintings or rare Chinese porcelain. They wanted things that spoke to them: a great piece of pressed glass, a wooden medicine cabinet from the early 1900s, a Baccarat paperweight. At this point, she could spot something at an estate sale and purchase it with a specific client in mind. She'd text that client from the road and they'd be at the store first thing in the morning. Sometimes that client was herself. Just last week she'd found a Federal-style mahogany sideboard for their bedroom. Of course, this sort of impulse buying was an occupational hazard — one that drove Jack crazy. Just that morning, as she headed out for the sale, he'd said, "Remember, you're looking for the store *only.*"

They both knew it was likely she wouldn't find anything even just for the store. Queen Anne's Revenge had become so well-known on the Cape that they fielded dozens of calls a week to come visit estate sales. More often than not, Celeste had the unenviable task of disappointing them — either declining to attend or showing up only to leave empty-handed.

Today, the seller was the daughter of a recently deceased author of several acclaimed bird-watching guides. The family was fifth-generation Cape Cod, a promising pedigree for estate-hunting. Sure enough, just a half hour into her perusal of the tagged items throughout the Craftsman house, she found some unusual Bakelite buttons, a goose-necked copper kettle from the 1800s, and a gold-topped wooden walking stick. The walking stick was just the type of thing her customer Clifford Henry, the town Realtor, had been asking for. This particular piece was beautiful but needed a little restoration. She'd ask Jack for help with that.

On her way out to her car, she thanked the seller and noticed the woman was teary-eyed as she looked at the walking stick.

Celeste didn't understand the intense sentimentality people felt toward objects. She didn't understand their attachment to their families in general. How could she?

She'd carefully arranged her entire life to make sure she had nothing to do with her own.

The drive to Provincetown seemed to take forever.

Elodie sat nestled in the back seat of the Lincoln Town Car, Pearl on her lap. Once they reached the Cape, she thought, *Finally.* But then, another hour to the godforsaken town her sister called home.

Elodie's driver pulled up in front of the building with Celeste's address. It was a Queen Anne house with a storefront on the lower level.

"You can just let me off here and find a place to park," she said to her driver. "I'll text you when I'm ready to leave."

She adjusted Pearl's leash and lifted her out of the car. The only wrinkle in her trip was her inability to find a hotel room on such short notice. The entire town was booked; apparently, according to the third hotel receptionist she spoke to, she was arriving in the middle of something called CabaretFest, and her options were limited.

Some of these places didn't even have turndown service! And while most places were pet-friendly, the few left available did not.

She decided she wouldn't even stay the night. She would get Celeste's sign-off on the auction contract and turn right back around for Manhattan. Then she'd worry about that niece of hers.

Inside, the store looked like a bohemian marketplace, with textiles and clocks and objets d'art. It took her a few seconds to spot Celeste's longtime partner, Jack, behind a checkout counter to her right. He looked as scruffy and rakishly handsome as she remembered, with olive skin, silver hair in need of a trim, and white stubble along his square jaw. His small but expressive dark eyes widened when he saw her. She couldn't blame him for being surprised; in the quarter of a century that her sister had lived on Cape Cod, she'd never once visited.

Pearl tugged on her leash and Elodie relinquished hold of it so she could meander over to a water bowl set near the counter.

"Elodie?" he said.

"Hello, Jack. You're looking well. Is my sister around?"

"I'll be darned. She didn't even mention you were coming."

"I wanted to surprise her," said Elodie, mustering a smile that suggested whimsy and affection, not impatience and business necessity.

"She's at an estate sale. You're welcome to wait —"

Her sister breezed in the door, carrying an armload of items and talking a mile a minute.

"You wouldn't believe the crowd," she said, focused so completely on Jack she didn't notice that someone else was there. "I thought today was the preview but I almost got my hand bitten off by some of these people who clearly have no sense of etiquette. And we're not putting this tea tray onto the floor. I'm going to call —"

"Elise and Fern. Great thinking," Jack said. He cleared his throat. "And . . . you have a visitor."

Celeste turned, taking a few beats to register that it was her sister standing in front of her.

"Good lord — what are you doing here?" Celeste said.

"Hello to you, too," Elodie said, shrugging off her cardigan.

Celeste's hair was loose and a bit stringy and she was dressed in some sort of embroidered caftan.

"Elodie, seriously. What's going on?"

Pearl strained at her leash. She needed to be walked. Elodie mustered a smile for her sister.

"Can we, perhaps, talk outside?"

12

Elodie followed her sister up the street, which was packed with pedestrians. Bikes whizzed past in every direction and cars moved at a crawl. Celeste told her she picked the first busy week of the season.

"Apparently," Elodie said. "I couldn't find a decent hotel."

"Where are you staying?"

"I decided just to make it a day trip."

Celeste raised an eyebrow. "That's a hell of a long day trip. So what brings you here? CabaretFest?"

Elodie offered a tight smile.

"No. I needed to talk to you."

"Uh-oh. Sounds serious." A pedicab drove past, the two people in the back blasting dance music from their phones. "Should I be sitting down for this?"

They crossed the street and followed an alleyway to the water. It turned breezier, the air thick with brine. They passed a few wooden buildings — a house and a garage, some kayaks on a rack, and a wooden shack — like a small tollbooth or mini office — under a boat rentals sign. Beyond that, the area splintered off into separate docks. They sat on a bench.

"How lovely," Elodie said.

Celeste turned to her.

"Yes. It is. And I'm happy for you to finally see it after all these years. But I'm guessing you're not here for the view. What's going on?"

Best to just come out with it. "I need your signature on a document."

"Mine? Why?" Celeste seemed genuinely confused.

"Just some minor bureaucracy before I proceed with an auction." She opened her bag and pulled out the contract. "Whitmore's likes to make sure all their T's are crossed, that sort of thing."

Celeste looked skeptical. Elodie anticipated this. "If you want a share of the proceeds, I'm willing to negotiate." Pearl barked, and Elodie knelt down to calm her.

"No — it's not that. I'm just surprised that you need my signature. I have nothing to do with Pavlin & Co." She stood up and walked toward the water. Elodie followed her, thinking, *No more surprised than I am, believe me!*

"Again, just a formality."

Celeste stopped walking when they reached a dock. She turned to her and said, "I need to think about it."

"Think about it? What on earth for? You just said yourself that you have nothing to do with the company."

"Mercury's in retrograde."

"I'm sorry, *what*?" So clearly Celeste had never outgrown all that astrology nonsense. When they were young, it was all, "I'm an Aries and you're a Gemini, so even though we don't have a lot in common, we won't be in conflict or competition." *Wrong. Wrong, wrong, wrong.*

"It's bad luck to sign contracts when Mercury is in retrograde."

Elodie exhaled loudly. "When is it *out* of retrograde?"

"In twenty-three days."

Elodie crossed her arms. A strong breeze off the water lifted her hair and she patted it back into place.

"I just told you I'm not staying overnight."

"And that's entirely your choice. Now I have to get back to work."

With that, Celeste walked away.

Unbelievable! Did she really think that would be the end of it? That Elodie would just retreat back to the city, tail between her legs?

"You don't even have *your* tail between your legs, Pearl," she said.

That's two bad quarters in a row . . . You need to do more.

She wasn't waiting twenty-three days to lock in the auction, that was for damn sure.

As usual in their family, things were going to get ugly. She texted her driver that her plans had changed: She was staying. Of course her sister had to choose to live in a beach town that could not be more out of the way.

With a sigh, Elodie stood up from the bench and walked away from the marina back toward the street. On her left, a house caught her eye: A sign hanging off the deck announced, *Room for rent, water view. See Lidia for details.*

The house was a bit ramshackle, all weathered clapboard with a cluttered garage or workshop of some sort on the ground level. Stairs led to a deck and a second-floor entrance, and a Portuguese flag waved from the roof.

It wasn't exactly the Carlyle, but surely it would be tolerable for just one night. All she needed to do was to make her point by not driving off the second Celeste gave her a little resistance.

Elodie looked around and turned back to a small booth offering boat rentals and tours of the bay. A man stood inside selling tickets. He was broad-shouldered, with deep-set dark eyes and white hair. His baseball cap read *Long Point.*

"Excuse me. Do you know where I can find . . . Lidia?"

He pointed to the house.

"I meant, is there a number I can call?" Elodie said.

"It's up to you," he said, smiling in amusement. "But I don't know why you'd call on the phone if you can just stand at the foot of the stairs and holler up to her."

Uncivilized, she thought, marching toward the house. The town, her sister, that man. She'd long ago accepted the fact that money couldn't shield her from all of life's indignities. But it should at least buffer her from this type of nonsense.

Although it violated all sense of propriety, Elodie tied Pearl's leash to the wooden banister and climbed the steps to the second-floor entrance of the house. She knocked twice and got no response. She peered through the screen door and saw a kitchen.

"Hello?" she called out. No response.

Elodie walked back down to the boat rental booth.

"Excuse me," she said to the man.

"I'm Tito," he said.

"Tito," she said, "it appears no one is available." She reached into her bag for her business card, then realized she hadn't brought any. "Do you have a piece of paper I could write my number on?"

He handed her a brochure for Barros Boatyard. The name was familiar. She thought for a minute and realized it was Jack's last name.

"Do you have a brother?" she asked.

"Sure do. Manny. Do you know him?" He looked skeptical.

"No," she said. And then, thinking of last names, she realized she should use her mother's maiden name for this inquiry. People saw the name Pavlin and always charged more because they knew she had deep pockets. She pulled a pen from her bag and jotted down the name "Elodie Lowe."

"Please give this to whomever is in charge and let them know I'd like the room for the night. And I'd like to check in as soon as possible."

"I certainly will . . . Elodie," he said, reading the card. Something about the way he said it seemed rude. Presumptuous. Perhaps the town was just very informal, but either way it ruffled her feathers. She needed a strong martini.

"Thank you," she said. "Now, if you could please direct me to the nearest place I can find a cocktail."

13

Celeste slipped into bed next to Jack, using a finger to hold her spot in the paperback she was reading. Jack had his reading glasses on, thumbing through a wooden-boat-restoration magazine.

"I just can't believe Elodie showed up here like that," Celeste said. Jack put down the magazine and looked at her.

"Try to look at it this way: It took two and a half decades, but at least she's finally paid you a visit."

"I knew you'd say something like that." Jack had never understood her fraught relationship with her family. How could he? He saw his first cousins daily. He'd visited his mother at the senior home in Falmouth every Sunday until her death at age ninety-five. His entire family genuinely enjoyed spending time together, and Jack wouldn't have had it any other way. It was just one of the many things she loved about him.

The Barroses had been on the shores of Provincetown for generations, ever since Jack's great-great-great (however many greats) grandparents landed there from Lisbon. When Celeste first arrived in town, she was told the Barroses were the best people to rent a room from. At the time, Jack's aunt and uncle owned a three-story house at the boatyard, right at the edge of Cape Cod Bay. She and her friend Nathan, who'd just graduated from Philadelphia's University of the Arts, rented two rooms on the third floor of the house — a place now inhabited by Jack's cousin Manny and his wife, Lidia.

It had been Nathan's idea to leave Philly for P'town. While she was busy licking her wounds after a bad breakup and feeling alienated from her family, he won a writing fellowship at the Fine Arts Work Center and suggested a change of scenery would be good for both of them. It was only later that she learned Nathan hadn't moved to Provincetown for the writing fellowship; he'd learned weeks earlier that he was HIV positive and had gone there to spend his final days. Six months into their new life there, he was gone. Celeste had no real reason to stay in town. She was barely making ends meet with a part-time sales job at an antiques shop. And yet, she found herself in no rush to leave.

It wasn't just the astonishing sunsets, or the majestic wildlife, or the arts scene. It was the people. She was eternally moved by the way virtual strangers had rallied around Nathan. They delivered meals. They organized his drug cocktails. They showed up in the backyard to sing and recite poetry while he sat bundled in blankets on a lawn chair. *This,* she thought, *is family.* Not the bunch of petty infighters she'd left behind in the city. No, she decided. Provincetown was meant to be her home.

The following summer, her landlord's nephew passed through town in between runs as a merchant marine. Jack Barros was striking, with dark hair, a tan, and mischievous dark eyes. Celeste, wary from her last romantic disappointment, didn't want to give in to her attraction. But her landlord's sons — Manny and Tito — started teasing her that they hadn't seen so much of Jack since their grandmother used to serve them fried dough in the afternoons.

By the time she finally agreed to go out to dinner with him at Ciro & Sal's, she knew deep down she was already smitten. They'd been together ever since. The only tricky part had been convincing Jack to accept the fact that she never wanted to get married. "Marriage just isn't for me. I don't want any part of engagements, engagement *rings,* labels . . . none of it," she'd said. That was true. But there was another reason, one she wouldn't admit: She was afraid of the Pavlin curse.

Thankfully, over the years, marriage hadn't been much of an issue. Their life was peaceful. It had a rhythm, a wonderful predictability. Making it all the more vexing that her sister had just shown up like that.

"My sister's not here to *visit.* She wants something." She'd mentioned the auction over dinner, fried oysters from his cousin's oyster farm and a few cold beers, but he didn't share her concern.

"Why not just sign the papers then and be done with it?" he'd said.

She couldn't tell him about Mercury in retrograde. She and Jack were like-minded in so many ways: their love of P'town, antiques, the sea, cold beer on a warm night. But Jack's patience for what he called her "hocus-pocus" was limited. And so she told him the second truest thing: "I feel like our parents are still manipulating us — even from the grave."

Elodie's temporary landlady, Lidia, seemed

to be a competent, pleasant woman. She had silver-brown hair to her shoulders, deep-set brown eyes, olive skin with the hint of sunspots on her cheeks, and just enough New England saltiness to appear trustworthy. Yes, if she had to prolong her stay to put pressure on her sister, this place would do just fine.

The third-floor bedroom had plain wood-paneled walls, a queen-sized bed with an iron frame and headboard. The cotton sheets were crisp but mismatched. There were two white wicker chairs and a distressed wood bedside table also painted white.

Pearl seemed to feel right at home. She climbed the newly purchased doggie steps, which Elodie had found that afternoon in town, to reach the bed and promptly fell asleep. Elodie set her water bowl and food dish in the corner near the bathroom.

She opened her laptop, scrolled through some work emails, and resisted the urge to call her sister and yell at her.

Her phone rang. She sat up in bed, almost hitting her head on the dormer ceiling.

"Hello?"

"Elodie, Sloan Pierce. Sorry to call so late — I'm still at the office and just realized the hour. Here's the deal: The team here is very excited at the prospect of the auction, but they do think we're short on time if we're going to get it launched during this centennial year. Publicity wants to start on the press release as soon as possible. Where are we with the paperwork?"

Elodie glanced out the window at the moonlit Cape Cod Bay. New York suddenly seemed very distant, and she felt a flash of anger at her father. Why had he tied her hands like this? What reason could he possibly have had to require she get her sister's and her niece's signatures before making a business decision? Or maybe it hadn't been her father's decision after all. Maybe the three-signature stipulation was something her mother put in place after his death. But why?

"I'm waiting for my attorney to get back to me," she lied. "We should be wrapping it up shortly." Tomorrow was a new day, and she'd figure out a way to apply pressure on Celeste. But that was only her first problem.

What was she going to do about Gemma? With no time to waste, how was she supposed to convince her sister to sign on the dotted line and then get Gemma to cooperate from three hundred and sixty miles away?

The answer was, she wasn't.

She needed to find a way to bring the girl to her.

14

The storage unit in Weehawken, New Jersey, was five by ten feet. Gemma booked it online, and it was clear as soon as she looked inside that it wasn't large enough to fit her workbench, tools, and supplies.

"You can't take this stuff with you to your next apartment?" Sanjay said, surveying the situation alongside of her. She'd enlisted him at the last minute for help driving the U-Haul.

"Considering my budget, I'll be lucky to find a room to rent that fits my bed." The way things were looking, she might have to start *living* in the storage space.

"Okay, let's do this," he said.

They staged all the boxes outside the storage unit, arranging them by size before positioning them carefully inside. Sanjay made sure all the labels were facing out so she could find things when she needed them. Gemma was creative and hardworking, but spatial organization had never been a strength of hers, so she let Sanjay take the lead. While he took care of some of the heavier metalworking equipment, she bent down and checked the boxes labeled *Photos* and *Press,* sealing them with an extra layer of packing tape. They contained the things she was most reluctant to leave behind: photo albums, newspaper clippings, and magazines featuring her mother.

The mementos started arriving by mail four years ago. The first package was an old-fashioned leather photo album, the type where photos were arranged four at a time on a page and held in place by sticky plastic sheets. The spine was embossed with *1980–1981* in gold lettering. Every picture was of the Pavlin sisters, or the sisters with their parents. The package didn't include a personal note of any kind, but the return address was Park Avenue — the sender: her maternal grandmother, Constance. Over the next year, seven more packages arrived, some photo albums, some meticulous scrap-books. Every time she found one waiting inside the vestibule of her apartment building, she was tempted to try to contact Constance. But loyalty to Anne Maybrook, knowing her wishes where this was concerned, kept her from reaching out. Two years after the first package arrived, she saw the *New York Times* headline announcing Constance Pavlin's death. The realization that she was too late, that she'd hesitated too long, took her breath away.

Her phone rang with an unfamiliar number. She had the impulse to send it to voicemail, but considering she was simultaneously looking for an apartment, a lead for financing her business, and a part-time job, she was in no position to ignore her phone.

"Hello?" she said, glancing at Sanjay. He seemed to be fitting the last of the larger boxes into the space and gave her a thumbs-up.

"Gemma," the voice said on the other end. "It's Elodie Pavlin. We need to talk."

She stood up, walking a few paces away. Her heart began to race.

"I'm listening," Gemma said coolly, still feeling the sting of their confrontation at the party. She hated to admit it, but deep down, she'd had a fantasy that the estrangement had ultimately been in her imagination; her mother's sisters had actually tried to be in touch with her but simply couldn't find her (a scenario that she knew was more plausible before the internet had been invented). Still, in her weaker moments, she imagined she'd cross the threshold of Pavlin

& Co, and her aunt would spot her, and like in a film they'd run toward each other in slow motion and Elodie would say, "I've been waiting for this day. We all have."

"I spoke to my sister — your aunt Celeste — and it seems she might have an idea where the pink diamond can be located."

Gemma didn't know much about her mother's oldest sister. The photo albums included snapshots of all three girls. She could always identify her mother, the youngest. But her two aunts looked alike: long-limbed preteens with shoulder-length bobs, dressed in the preppy fashion of Manhattan's upper class circa the 1970s: pleated skirts, pearls, and penny loafers. The one difference she was certain of was that the oldest had never worked for Pavlin & Co. Out of all the Pavlin relations that haunted her dreams and fantasies, Gemma had always given Celeste the least amount of thought.

Why would Celeste know the whereabouts of the Electric Rose, and not Elodie?

"Does she have it?" Gemma said quickly. She felt like someone on the phone with a kidnapper waiting to hear the ransom, like the caller might end the call at any moment and leave her hanging.

"I think you should go and talk to her

yourself. In person," Elodie said.

Gemma didn't know why Elodie suddenly had a change of heart, but she couldn't worry about that now. After the discouraging conversation with Sloan Pierce, she was willing to follow any lead.

"Okay," Gemma said. "Where can I find her?"

"Provincetown," said Elodie. "Provincetown, Cape Cod."

15

Celeste clicked open the email account for Queen Anne's Revenge, continuously amazed at how many antiques hunters reached out to her.

It was late afternoon and the back office was sticky with heat. The old ceiling fan whirred with valiant effort. When they'd first moved into the house, there hadn't been air-conditioning or even so much as a table fan. The four-bedroom Queen Anne cottage, built in the early 1900s by Jack's great-grandfather Silverio, had been in a state of disrepair when Jack inherited it in 1998. When he brought her to look at it three years into their relationship and with the invitation to move in together and make it their home, she immediately envisioned using the first floor as an antiques shop. Jack, to his eternal credit, supported her dream. No, more than supported — he helped make it happen. Was still making it happen.

"Celeste, are you in here?"

The office door opened to reveal their one employee, Alvita Thompson, who went by the nickname Alvie. Alvie arrived in town three summers ago from Boston's Hyde Park. Like so many young people, she was searching for a place to live a life without judgment. Her parents, Haitian immigrants who made their career and their community in the local church, struggled to accept that she was gay.

"Hey, Alvie. Do you know where those brass candlesticks went? I'm going through this inventory and it says they haven't sold but . . ."

Alvie pulled out a metal folding chair tucked behind a pile of boxes and sat across from her. She was a pretty young woman, with an oval face defined by a cleft chin and long eyelashes. She'd bleached the ends of her dark curls blond and wore her hair in two low bunches. Her sunny demeanor added to her attractiveness, but today the look on her face was serious.

"Is everything okay?" Celeste said.

"I have to give notice."

"Wait — you're quitting?" It was the first week of June. This was their busiest time of year, and the three months that made their entire balance sheet work had just begun.

Even if she was able to find someone else to hire — an impossible task since the stores and restaurants had already soaked up all the job-seekers like a sponge — they wouldn't be Alvie. She'd spent so much time with Celeste and Jack, even living in one of their guest rooms for most of last summer, that she knew and loved the shop in a deep way that was irreplaceable.

"Maud needs me at the restaurant."

Celeste sighed. She should have seen this day coming. Alvie and Maud met at Jack's cousin's Fourth of July party last summer. Alvie was instantly smitten with the much older woman and agonized for days after that Maud didn't take her seriously.

"Don't get involved," Jack warned. But Celeste, after checking that Maud's and Alvie's charts were aligned, couldn't resist talking Alvie up to Maud and nudging them together, even saying to Maud, "You know, there was an even bigger age gap between you and Sylvie."

Maud moved to P'town in the late 1970s along with her girlfriend, Sylvia Shuttle of Sandwich, Massachusetts. They both started as dishwashers at the Flagship, a restaurant made famous by their former co-worker Anthony Bourdain's bestseller *Kitchen Confidential,* where the restaurant was dubbed "the Dreadnaught." In fact, it was Maud's short-lived breakup with Sylvia — and Sylvia's subsequent quitting of her job — that brought Anthony Bourdain in as a replacement and launched one of the most storied culinary careers in recent memory.

Celeste wouldn't be so bold as to claim credit for Maud and Alvie's romance (by Labor Day weekend, they were inseparable), but facts were facts. Making this current situation all the more irksome. Maud could have at least given her some warning.

"I really wish you'd given me more notice," Celeste said.

Alvie nodded in remorse. "I wasn't planning on this. But Maud asked me to move in with her — she wants us to really share our lives together. And that includes the restaurant and the work. I mean, you and Jack are a huge inspiration for me in that way. I promise I'll stay until you find a replacement."

Celeste smiled at her, feeling bad for only thinking of herself. "I'm glad you two are happy. It's okay, we'll figure it out."

Alvie thanked her for understanding and scampered back out to the sales floor. Celeste sighed, reaching for her phone to send off a text to Jack when her computer pinged with an incoming email. Another customer inquiry could wait. But a quick glance told her this one wasn't from a customer. It was from her niece, Gemma Maybrook.

Alvie and the store were immediately forgotten.

16

Elodie awoke to Pearl's wet kiss, sun streaming through the flimsy curtains. Disoriented, she wondered if her dog walker was on the way and then realized with a start that she was still on Cape Cod, not Park Avenue. *She* was the dog walker.

She sat up quickly, checking the time. It was seven in the morning.

"Up we go," she said, pulling a button-down shirt over her pajamas and slipping into a pair of Tory Burch ballerina flats. She pushed back her hair with a headband and picked up Pearl. The solidness of her little dog body never failed to make Elodie smile. So much spirit packed into that compact corporeal form.

She carried Pearl down the hall, down the stairs, and outside to the deck, where she knelt to fasten the leash. Behind her, the screen door opened and she turned to find the man who'd been working in the boat rental booth the day before.

"What are *you* doing here?" she said.

He broke into a wide grin. "I live here," he said. "At least, for the summer I do. Tito Barros. Pleasure to meet you. I assume the room worked out?"

"Uh, yes. It did. Thank you."

Pearl barked and only then did Elodie notice a dog by the man's feet. Another black pug.

"And who's this?" Tito said, reaching out to rub Pearl's head.

"This is Pearl. And yours?"

"Bart," he said. "I'm taking him to the beach. You're welcome to join us."

"I'm just walking her," Elodie said.

"All the dog parents around here go to the beach at the West End Parking Lot just down the way. Come along."

Well, why not? It was a beautiful day out, and the beach would probably be a great place to find someone she could hire to do this work for her.

Elodie followed Tito down Commercial, cyclists whirring by in both directions. Couples strolled past holding takeout coffee and eating pastries out of paper bags.

They passed a gated Coast Guard station before the street curved even farther left toward the water. On this end of Commercial, the shops gave way to classic Cape Cod houses lining both sides of the street. The lawns were lush with green grass and colorful hydrangea bushes. A few front yards had a more untamed aesthetic with thickets of wildflowers.

"So what brings you to P'town?" Tito said.

"Business." She'd been distracted up until that moment from thinking about the argument with Celeste.

"What business is that?"

"Jewelry."

"Interesting," Tito said, though his tone of voice suggested just the opposite.

Again she wondered: What could she do to coerce her sister into signing the paperwork? Elodie had long ago learned from her father that everyone had a price. And she was willing to do whatever it took to figure out Celeste's. In the meantime, she wanted more luxurious accommodations.

"So you work at the boatyard?" she said. He nodded.

"It's the family business," he said. "Started by my grandfather. It's changed a lot over the years. Used to be repairing and building fishing boats but eventually evolved to a mooring field. And we have the boat rentals — you can rent kayaks, pontoon boats, et cetera. Last year we started seal tours."

"Interesting," she said — about as enthusiastically as he'd responded to her work.

"It's seasonal. And it's flexible enough for me to continue to do volunteer animal rescue on the side."

"Animal rescue?"

"You'd be surprised how much trouble dolphins can get themselves into."

They passed a small café called Relish, and Pearl relieved herself.

"How far is this beach?" Elodie said.

"Almost there."

On the corner to their right, Elodie noticed an extraordinary white clapboard, octagon-shaped house with a widow's walk.

"That's a fantastic house," she said.

"It was built by a whaler in 1850," Tito said. "It's had as many lives as a cat: Inn. Restaurant. Retirement home. Today it's a privately owned house."

Now, *that* was the type of place she could settle in to for a few weeks.

"Do you know anyone else who has a place like that to rent out?"

"For next summer?" Tito said.

"No — for the next few weeks."

He looked at her like she was from another planet. "This season is booked. I rented out my house back in February. That's why I'm staying at my cousin's. And the only reason

Lidia had a room for you is because her daughter decided not to come home from school for the summer."

They reached a parking lot, and beyond it, a sprawling view of the bay and a narrow stretch of beach.

"Lidia's your cousin?"

"No. Lidia's husband, Manny," he said.

They cut through the parking lot to a bench at the edge of the beach. Cement stairs led down to the sand.

"I'll have to wait here. I can't ruin these shoes," she said. She sat on the bench and Tito offered to bring Pearl down to the beach and let the dogs off their leashes.

"Is that allowed?" she asked.

"Sure. But no dogs on Race Point Beach. And I'd think twice about Herring Cove because of the coyotes."

Coyotes?

Tito was already heading down the steps with both dogs. She sat back, watching Pearl hesitate before gingerly trotting around after Bart. She could tell she was both confused by the wide-open space and thrilled by it. The best she got in New York was a crowded pen at the Central Park dog run.

When she was satisfied that Pearl was okay, Elodie turned her attention to a pair of men launching a kayak into the water. A small bird landed on the bench beside her, tilting its brown head quizzically before taking flight once again.

Elodie inhaled, realizing that, as frustrated as she was, there were far worse places to be stuck for a short while. She had no doubt she'd prevail with Celeste. It was just a matter of how long it would take.

Gemma, however, was another story. She'd been noncommittal — disinterested, even — on the phone. If she didn't take the bait and run out to Provincetown, it would be time for a plan B. But Elodie didn't think it would come to that.

People always took the bait.

17

Constance, 1993

The times were changing, and not for the better; Constance Pavlin would never step out of the house looking like the models in the pages of that month's *Vogue.* More than being in poor taste, all that anti-glamour, minimalist, grungy heroin-chic was bad for business.

"This will pass," she assured her husband. After thirty years of marriage, she'd ridden the highs and lows of Pavlin & Co long enough to know that trends — no matter how good or how onerous — were temporary. Her husband seemed to have lost sight of that.

Alan had been in a bad mood all day. Still, they'd gone to the party. She wore Azzedine Alaïa — the one designer who she felt hadn't yet lost his mind, unlike the house of Perry Ellis, who'd hired that young Marc Jacobs kid. The Alaïa was a form-fitting red sleeve of a dress. She'd barely eaten all week in anticipation of wearing it, but even her success in pouring herself into the unforgiving frock hadn't put a smile on Alan's face.

At fifty-five, Alan Pavlin had aged into a distinguished head-turner of a man. The boyish, uncertain person she'd married all those years ago had finally come into his own. It wasn't just that he was more confident; the good looks of his youth had been honed by the passing years into something sharp and deeply attractive. And she wasn't the only woman who'd noticed; all night long, that opportunist Betsy Laurent-Leeds had been making eyes at him. Alan, to his credit, paid little attention. But he did drink too heavily, which was very much out of character. His father, Elliot, had been a big drinker. It wasn't uncommon for Scotch to appear at the lunch table. And Alan made a point of doing everything differently than Elliot.

Alan's father, second-generation president and CEO of Pavlin & Co, the family's eponymous jewelry company founded in 1919, had always treated Alan more as a child than a business partner. Two years after his father's death, Alan was still trying to prove himself. But Elliot cast a long shadow over Pavlin & Co. After all, how did one compete with the man who single-handedly created the entire market for diamond engagement rings?

Elliot, in his day, faced the same sort of downturn Alan was grappling with now. In the 1940s, diamond sales plummeted. Post–World War II, expensive jewelry suddenly seemed frivolous. Faced with a crisis, he conducted a marketing survey, and what he found surprised him: Middle-class women preferred that their husbands spend their money on something practical, like a washing machine. Diamonds, it appeared, were only for the very wealthy.

Elliot immediately recognized the challenge in front of him: how to make diamonds a necessity instead of a luxury. To do this, he knew he would have to appeal to customers' emotions. And what was the strongest emotion? Love. What occasions marked true love? Marriage and engagement. A rite of passage millions and millions of women experienced each year. And yes, rings were involved. But at the time, it might be a family heirloom opal or a small moonstone.

Until Elliot reminded everyone, with a dramatic and visually captivating ad campaign, that the "great" love story between Archduke Maximilian and Mary of Burgundy in 1477 began with the first-ever faceted diamond engagement ring. And the classic "A Diamond Says Love" campaign was born, changing the industry — and the very concept of engagement — forever.

Elliot had endless strategies to get the rings in front of the public, including gifting diamond rings to actresses and society women on occasions like the Academy Awards or the Kentucky Derby, then hiring photographers to get clear photographs of the baubles on display. "People don't know what they want until you tell them what to want," he'd said.

Now, in the last decade of the century, it again seemed difficult to convince people that what they wanted was fine jewelry.

It was a relief to be back home after the party. Their sprawling Park Avenue apartment felt empty now that two of their three daughters were out of the nest, but at moments like this she was grateful for some privacy.

"You looked very dashing in your tux tonight," she said, asking him for help unzipping the back of her dress. The touch of his fingertips against her bare back gave her a shiver. She pulled the clips out of her hair, still long and lustrous and just now showing the first few threads of silver. She shook it loose and turned to him, wanting to remind him that Betsy Laurent-Leeds wasn't the only woman who noticed him. But he had already retreated to the other side of the room, shedding his shirt and jacket while sitting on the edge of the bed and staring out the window.

"Alan," she said. "It's Friday night. You can't carry the stress of work through the entire weekend. One bad year isn't the end of the world."

He looked at her with irritation. "I wish it were just one bad year."

She sighed. Their middle daughter, Elodie, was involved in the business as well and had recently expressed her own concern.

Alan pulled back the covers. Since sex was clearly out of the question, Constance slipped into a fluffy robe and sat on her side of the bed, reaching for the hand cream on her nightstand.

"I know you'll think of something," she said. "You always do." The latter comment was a small wifely lie. The truth was, while Alan was a hard worker, even a non-business-minded person like herself could see that Pavlin & Co hadn't innovated since the "A Diamond Says Love" campaign half a century ago.

Alan climbed out of bed and left the

room. When he returned he was holding a Pavlin & Co ring box. He handed it to her. "Open it," he said, his eyes shining.

Confused, she gave him a small smile. While a gift was always appreciated, it seemed like an odd moment for one.

She lifted the lid and gasped. It was a pink diamond, *the* pink diamond.

Alan, in a quest for a precious stone to compete with some of the flashy gems that rival jewelers were marketing, had commissioned a dig in a remote Western Australia mine. After several years, they'd unearthed a Fancy Vivid pink diamond that was 59.6 carats in the rough. The discovery made the international news: Only one percent of all pink diamonds were larger than 10 carats, and only four percent classified as Fancy Vivid.

Alan's gemologist studied the stone for a full year before cutting it, and then took another ten months to transform it into a 30-carat, cushion-cut gem of extraordinary beauty.

This was the first time Constance had seen it in person. Hands shaking, she shed her wedding band and slipped the ring onto her finger. She couldn't take her eyes off it. After three decades with Alan, she was spoiled. Jaded, even. She had jewels to rival the royals, and yet this ring took her breath away. She didn't know if it was the size, the clarity, or the delicate pink color, but the gift left her almost speechless.

"I never want to take it off," she breathed.

"Well, you're going to have to," he said. "I'm giving it to one of the girls."

She looked up at him. "Which one?"

"The first to get engaged. I'm planning a big launch event introducing the diamond. We need to remind the world that luxury makes people happy, and that romance is alive and well in the nineties."

Constance raised her eyebrows. "Okay. But none of the girls are even close to getting engaged."

"Well, with this incentive, that should be changing soon," he said.

"Alan, don't be ridiculous." She couldn't imagine a worse idea. Their daughters were already so competitive with one another. "They squabble over everything. This will just make that more of a problem. There must be some other publicity idea . . ."

"I've already summoned them back. It's done."

"They're coming home?" Paulina had been in Europe for months, and Celeste rarely visited from grad school in Pennsylvania. Even Elodie, working long hours at the corporate office, might as well be in another country considering how rarely Constance saw her.

She didn't like this idea. Not one bit. But it was Alan's time, and he wanted to seize it. She thought of the way Betsy Laurent-Leeds had gone after him earlier that night, and the way he hadn't noticed. He was a devoted husband. And she, in turn, had to be a supportive wife.

No matter how big a mistake he was making.

18

Finding contact information for her aunt Celeste — or her store, rather — had been easy. The hard part had been deciding what to say in her email. Gemma decided the less, the better. And so she wrote that she was visiting Provincetown and would like to see her if possible. Her aunt's reply had been immediate and welcoming, if brief: *What a lovely surprise. Of course. Looking forward to seeing you.*

As for her other aunt, she hadn't told Elodie she'd taken her up on the idea of talking to Celeste.

Gemma leaned over the ferry railing for a better look at Provincetown during the approach. She spotted boathouses and clusters of small buildings, some topped with steeples. The only tall structure was a single monument towering above everything else.

Other passengers on the deck began trickling down to the lower cabin. She followed, her hand almost slipping on the wet rail. She carried a duffel bag stuffed with clothes over one shoulder.

From the metal gangway, she saw a crowd of people gathered on the pier, waving at the new arrivals. She fell into the line of people disembarking. The sky was a vivid periwinkle blue, the sun was bright but not hot, and a gentle breeze blew off the bay. She checked the address of her aunt's store and mapped the directions on her phone.

Walking the length of the pier toward the main street, she passed people selling tickets for whale-watching tours, artists painting at easels, and information booths. Once she reached Commercial Street, she was surrounded by colorfully painted two- and three-story buildings packed closely together. A pedicab whirred past, shuttling two buff, shirtless men.

Music emanated from every direction: Eighties pop. Show tunes. A young woman seated in a chair on one street corner playing the cello. The air smelled like salt and honeysuckle. Gemma stopped dragging her suitcase, light-headed with sensory overload. Or maybe she just needed coffee.

A patio with tables filled with people sipping cold beverages alerted her to a possible caffeine source. The sign out front read, *Joe Coffee.* Inside, she found an oasis of croissants, cookies, and muffins. A young man behind the counter with a platinum buzz cut and wearing black liquid eyeliner took her order. His T-shirt read, *Bradford Goes Both Ways.*

She tipped him with the last of her singles, making a mental note to look for an ATM later. With coffee in hand, she had a singular focus: her aunt Celeste.

"Excuse me," she said to the barista. "I'm looking for the store Queen Anne's Revenge?"

"Oh, I love that place," the barista said. "Yep, just two blocks down on this side of the street."

Gemma followed Commercial, the suitcase feeling heavier by the block. By now, the stores were interspersed between pretty clapboard houses. And then, a black-and-white sign hanging from a wooden post with a pirate-skull-and-crossbones flag announced: *Queen Anne's Revenge.*

Wide-open French doors welcomed her inside. The store was bright and airy, with a vaulted ceiling and shelves crammed with all sorts of things: lamps, old clocks, china, porcelain teapots, a bronze lobster, a large punch bowl painted with peacocks.

An older man stood behind the counter.

He had wild gray hair and deep-set dark eyes, a heavy five o'clock shadow, and a red bandana around his neck.

"Excuse me," she said. "I'm looking for Celeste."

He looked up at her, narrowing his brown eyes.

"You must be Gemma," he said.

"Um, yes. How did you know that?" She adjusted the bag on her shoulder.

"You look just like your mother."

The comment took her breath away. This man had known her mother?

"I'm Jack Barros. Nice to meet you. Let me get Celeste."

When the man returned, he was trailed by a woman wearing a sarong in a batik print and who had long dirty-blond hair threaded with gray and a sun-weathered, makeup-free face. Was this her aunt? It was hard to believe this was the preppy little blond girl from the photo albums. The only clue that she was the eldest Pavlin sister was her blazing blue-green eyes.

"Aunt Celeste?" Gemma said, suddenly feeling like a little girl herself.

"Yes, yes — welcome! How was your trip in? Did you take the ferry?"

Gemma nodded.

Jack cleared his throat. "I'll mind the shop

if you two ladies want to take a walk."

Celeste smiled at her. "Shall we? You can leave your bags here."

19

Celeste found herself looking at the mirror image of her lost sister: the curtain of blond hair, the Cupid's bow lips, the dramatic cheekbones.

She felt a wave of guilt and loss, the pain of a phantom limb she'd long since amputated. And then, a flash of irritation at the stranger standing before her who made her feel these things. She shook it away, disgusted at her selfishness.

"Thanks for seeing me on such short notice," Gemma said.

"No problem at all," Celeste said quickly. "I'm glad you looked me up."

They waited for cyclists to pass by and then scooted across Commercial. Music blared from somewhere, the Madonna song "Holiday." The source of the music approached: an open-topped Jeep filled with three men who rented the same house on Commercial every summer.

"Hi, boys!" Celeste said with a wave.

"Hi, Mama!" one called out to her.

She led Gemma to a nearby bench in front of the Thai restaurant, Joon.

Oh, it was such a beautiful late spring day, one of the last before the town became truly overrun with tourists. All winter, when stores were shuttered and just a few perennial restaurants like Napi's were open, when the sky could seem endlessly gray and high tide could bring flooding, they waited for days like this. The sun dancing on the bay. Storefronts with their doors propped open, people strolling Commercial eating ice cream, cyclists riding up and down in both directions, a new crop of puppies being walked, and Monday night live music on the front porch of the Beach Rose Inn.

Celeste wanted to look forward — to this summer. Not back at the past. But the past was now staring her in the face.

"So . . . what brings you to town?" Maybe she needed money. Of course, Celeste would help in any way she could. Looking at her sister's daughter, she felt overwhelmed with guilt for not reaching out herself all these years. It's not that she hadn't thought about it — she had. Many times. And Jack had encouraged her. But something held her back, and it wasn't just her father's warning that the Maybrooks could make trouble for their family if any of them contacted Gemma. Once her niece became a legal adult, she knew that wasn't really a threat. The truth was, if she reached out to Gemma, it would mean dealing with all the messiness and heartache she'd tried to forget about.

"I need to speak with you," Gemma said.

"Are you in trouble?" She would help the girl. Of course she would.

"What? No," she said, crossing her arms. "I just graduated from college. I'm a jewelry designer."

A jewelry designer. Interesting that Gemma, raised away from the Pavlins, had grown up to be the first designer in their family since Celeste's great-grandfather Isaac. Her father and grandfather had been businesspeople who hired design talent. Personally, Celeste couldn't draw so much as a stick figure, and neither of her sisters had been particularly artistic.

"Congratulations," Celeste said. An uncomfortable silence settled between them. There was so much to say that it made saying anything difficult. She felt she should apologize for not being in touch. Was that what her niece had come for? An explanation?

"I actually wanted to talk to you about the Pavlin Private Collection," Gemma said. "A specific piece. My mother's engagement ring."

Celeste blanched. She thought she'd heard the last of that thing ages ago. And good riddance.

"Why?"

"Well, it's my understanding that my mother left it to me," Gemma said, looking uncomfortable. "It's what I was told when I was young. I'm not — it's not about the money. It's just hugely sentimental to me."

She seemed so earnest; Celeste wished that she could help her. But she hadn't seen the ring since the last day she saw Paulina alive. And couldn't imagine why her niece thought otherwise.

"Gemma, I think you need to talk to my sister Elodie. I have nothing to do with the company or any of the jewels."

Gemma looked bewildered. "But Elodie told me that I should talk to *you.*"

Now Celeste was confused. "You've been in touch with Elodie?"

Gemma nodded, and out came a halting story about a party at Pavlin & Co, the ring not being on display, and Elodie accusing her of being a gold digger. "But then she called and told me you might know where to find it. That I should come out here."

Elodie. What on earth was she up to, sending Gemma to the Cape on a wild-goose chase?

Her phone rang.

"Sorry to bother you," Jack said. "But a customer's here to pick up an amberina pitcher and I have no idea where you put it."

"I'll be back in a minute." She put down the phone and said, "I'm sorry. I have to go back to the store." As much as she wanted the conversation to be over, she knew it was far from finished. "Gemma, I'm sorry you came all this way for something I can't help you with. But for what it's worth, I'm happy to see you. Please . . . stay at our house tonight."

20

Gemma walked up Commercial Street feeling like a fool. She'd run all the way out to Provincetown based on a single phone call from Elodie. That's what happened when you felt desperate: You *acted* desperate. She'd let everything from the past few days rattle her. And now she'd wasted precious time and money.

At least her aunt Celeste offered to let her stay at her house. She canceled her hotel reservation — a place in town that didn't allow pets and therefore had openings — and lost her deposit but got the rest refunded thankfully. First thing tomorrow, she'd head back to the city. In the grand scheme of things, very little harm done. And yet . . . why had Elodie lied to her?

She'd felt like such a brat asking her aunt Celeste about the ring. As if she just wanted a big fat diamond. Gemma wasn't a diamond type of person. Even if she got engaged someday — hard to imagine with her current track record — she hoped her husband-to-be proposed with a ring that meant something, not just a generic gem. No, this wasn't about a diamond. This was about her mother.

Gemma walked the length of Commercial, passing cute shop after cute shop, each window tempting her more than the next: sumptuous throws, robes, and textiles at Loveland, surprisingly hip clothing at a store called MAP, the Provincetown Bookshop, marked with a wooden sign painted with an owl.

The past four years in Manhattan had made long strolls a habit. A tide of pedestrians swept her up toward the East End, past Cabot's Candy and a second bookstore, East End Books, with a view of the bay. Here, clothing shops and cafés gave way to art galleries.

She decided to climb the brick stairs to the Harrison Gallery. Sometimes, looking at paintings or sculpture helped give her ideas for her own work. No matter what was going on in her life, work — creating — was always the answer.

The gallery was long and narrow, the white walls filled with large oil paintings illuminated with spot lighting. It was cool inside, the first breeze of air-conditioning since she'd gotten to town. She paused in front of a painting of a poppy field, the orange-red so vibrant she wanted to reach out and touch it. It was how she felt when she saw a beautiful stone.

"It's special, isn't it?" a man said, walking up to her. "She's a local artist. I'd be happy to answer any questions."

He looked to be in his mid-twenties. He had sandy blond hair and a strong jaw and navy blue eyes, and looked like he should be riding a horse on the cover of a romance novel instead of standing there in the gallery.

"Thanks," she said, turning back to the painting. She waited for him to move on but he kept standing beside her. She didn't care how good-looking he was, or how much he knew about the art. She was in no mood for small talk. "Um, there's no chance I'm buying anything in here. Just so you know — I don't want you to waste your time talking to me."

"Always happy to talk," he said.

"Okay, then . . . I don't want to waste *my* time."

He laughed and pulled a business card out of his pocket. "In case you have some time to waste one day."

When she was back outside, she glanced at it briefly before tossing it in the trash.

Celeste typically looked forward to their weekly dinners at the Barroses' house. She adored Jack's cousin Manny and his wife, Lidia. Lidia was a fantastic cook, and there were few spots more scenic than the century-old house on the bay. They ate on the deck, the table just a few feet away from the front door. The setting sun painted the sky in pastel colors that, over decades, had inspired countless works of art. But tonight, she couldn't enjoy it. She was uncomfortable thinking about Gemma being all alone back at the house. It felt rude to go out to Lidia and Manny's and leave her there, but when Jack suggested Celeste bring her, she refused.

"Why not?" Jack said.

"It's a boundaries thing," Celeste said. "I have no problem offering her one of our guest rooms, but dinner at Lidia and Manny's . . . that's too close for comfort."

"I'm sure they'd love to meet your niece."

"Not tonight, Jack," she said, and the tension in her voice told him not to push.

The attitude at the Barroses' was always the more, the merrier. Dinner groups had been known to swell to as large as a dozen, depending on how many members of the extended Barros family were in town. Typically, they were seven: the two couples; plus Jack's cousin Tito; and Lidia and Manny's son, Marco, and his wife, Olivia. Tonight, Celeste was relieved to find it was just the four of them.

"So, we ended up with a full house after all," Lidia was saying. "Tito's in Marco's room, and we've got our first tenant of the season in Jaci's room."

Every summer brought the Provincetown housing shuffle; locals rented spare bedrooms for extra income or moved out of their homes entirely to rent them for the season. For a lot of people, three months of summer could make their entire year. Lidia and Manny had successfully rented out their daughter Jaci's room for the summer. She was staying at school, and they were able to get a last-minute tenant from New York.

"It's been lonely with Jaci away, but at least we're making it productive," Lidia said with a sigh.

"I didn't know Tito was renting out his place this summer," Celeste said, refilling her glass of merlot.

Manny nodded. "Clifford Henry told him what he could get for it, and that was that. He didn't even ask us about moving in —

he told us."

"I hope you gave him a good rate," Jack joked.

"Don't think Manny didn't try to charge him," Lidia said.

"We have a guest under our roof tonight, too," Jack said, giving her a wink.

"Oh?" Lidia said, standing up to clear the dishes.

Celeste hadn't even mentioned to Lidia that her sister showed up in town, never mind her niece. It had been years since she'd talked about her own family.

There had been a summer night, not long after Lidia and Manny got married, when a party at the house had lasted until the earliest hours of the morning. The dozen or so revelers still hanging around all gathered on the beach to watch the sunrise, and Celeste and Lidia had ended up talking for hours over way too many bottles of wine. Celeste told her about the younger sister she'd lost, and that she was barely on speaking terms with the one who remained.

"You should invite her to visit you," Lidia said. Everyone in Provincetown believed that a visit to the place could cure anything.

"I never want my family visiting me here," she'd said. *"Never."*

Now Lidia and Manny looked at her expectantly.

"Yes. My youngest sister's daughter. It's just for one night," she said.

"I didn't know you had a niece," Manny said. Was that a touch of judgment she detected in his voice?

"She grew up with the other side of her family," Celeste said.

The front door swung open, and someone walked out of the house. The woman gave a quick glance at their group. Then she stopped moving, turning around slowly.

Celeste jumped up from her seat, nearly knocking over her glass of wine.

"Elodie?" she said. "What are you doing here?"

How could this be?

Lidia put down the plates she'd been gathering. "You two know each other?"

"How do *you two* know each other?" Celeste said, sounding angrier than she intended.

"She's our tenant," Lidia said, clearly understanding something was very wrong but unable to imagine what it could possibly be.

Celeste walked over to face her sister.

"Are you stalking me? Trying to pressure me to sign those papers by moving in with Jack's family? This is so typical of you . . ."

Jack got up and walked over. "Ladies, come to the table."

"This is as much a surprise to me as it is to you," Elodie said, looking indignant. Her small dog strained on her leash. "I told you I didn't have a place to stay and you just left me standing on the dock —"

"What is going on here?" Manny said.

"What's going on here," Celeste said, "is that your new tenant is my sister."

21

The ceiling slanted so low that Gemma almost banged her head when she woke up. The room had a small nightstand with a tiny lamp, and across from the bed was a fan plugged into the floor. The walls were clapboard wood, with lots of knots and marks in the boards, and the skylight let her stare up at the stars, which she had plenty of time to do last night since she had a hard time falling asleep.

Why had Elodie manipulated her? Wasted her time? She would text her. No, she'd call her. But first: coffee.

Gemma pulled on a pair of denim shorts and a black tank and pulled a comb through her long hair. She peeked into her suitcase, comforted by the sight of her charm necklaces. She fastened one around her neck, then covered her sleep-puffy eyes with her sunglasses and made her way down the narrow staircase to the first-floor kitchen. The shop was dark and quiet.

Yesterday, after Gemma had tentatively accepted her offer of hospitality, Celeste gave her a quick tour of the house. Aside from the shop on the ground floor, there was a kitchen in the back and a screened-in porch overlooking a small yard. A narrow staircase led to the second floor, and then there was the third floor, where she had her room.

"Who are you?" a voice said from out of nowhere. Gemma shrieked, then the voice shrieked.

A tall and striking young woman appeared from behind a hanging tapestry. She was dressed in an orange halter top, orange and white striped cinch-waist pants, and had oversized gold hoops in her ears. Her dark skin was accentuated by the platinum blond tips of her pigtails.

"We're not open yet," the woman said, hands on her hips.

"I'm staying upstairs . . . I'm Celeste's niece. Gemma."

Her eyes narrowed. "Well, *Gemma,* I've worked here for two years and never heard of a niece." She crossed her arms and stared at Gemma in appraisal. "The only reason I'm not calling Celeste right now to report an intruder is . . . I have to know where you got that necklace."

Gemma smiled. "I made it. Now, can you tell me the nearest place to get coffee?"

Commercial Street curved around and she followed the water on her left, visible between neat clapboard homes. To her right, more houses were hidden behind green hedges. Bikers whizzed past her, and a large dog-walking contingency streamed in the same direction. Lots of French bulldogs and pugs.

Celeste's employee/watchdog Alvie told her to find a place called Relish — and to get her a latte while she was at it.

Coffee in hand, walking back to the store, she noticed a spectacular house across the street from Relish. It was white clapboard in an octagon shape, with a widow's walk that had to offer a panoramic view of the town. It was lovely and dramatic. She had always appreciated grand homes and apartment buildings, wondering about the lives unfolding within the walls, always imagining that it was impossible to be truly sad in a place of great beauty. A man wearing a Harvard sweatshirt sat on the front porch looking at his phone. He looked up as if sensing her gaze and smiled when he saw her.

It was the guy from the art gallery. Lord, he was attractive.

She quickly looked away.

Elodie knew the expression "Keep your friends close and your enemies closer." But staying at Jack's relative's house was simply too much, even for her. And so, first thing in the morning, she made a trip to a Realtor.

Clifford Henry & Associates was just two blocks up the street. The office was a storefront on the ground floor of a yellow house on Commercial. She walked in and was surprised to find a man sitting at a neatly ordered desk just a few feet from the door.

"Hello, welcome," he said, looking up from the magazine he was leafing through. It appeared to be called *ptownie*. The man had bright blue eyes, a pleasant face, and brown hair with chunky highlights that he styled slicked back. He wore a pink button-down with a plaid bow tie. She guessed he was in his forties.

"Is there someone I can speak to about a house rental?" she said.

"You're looking at him: Clifford Henry, at your service."

"Wonderful. I just recently arrived in town and I'm looking for a waterfront house. I'm flexible on the number of beds and baths. Although yesterday I saw a home with the loveliest widow's walk. That would be a plus."

The man frowned. "I don't do Truro or Eastham or Wellfleet. Just Provincetown."

"Yes, that's where I'm looking."

The man laughed. "Listen, gorgeous, I know I have a reputation as a miracle worker, but I don't have a time machine. Hello — it's *June*!"

All Elodie heard was the word "gorgeous." No one had ever called her gorgeous in her life. She'd read once that the light in Provincetown was special. Maybe that was true.

"I'm willing to go beyond the asking price. I'll make it worth their while," she said.

"I'm renting for *next* summer. Why don't we plan ahead for you, hmm?"

"Mr. Henry, I have no intention of being here next summer. I simply have some business to attend to and need a rental for a few weeks."

"Where are you staying now?"

"I have a room at the boatyard."

He nodded. "Manny and Lidia's place. Sweetheart, I suggest you stay there." He handed her a business card. "If you change your mind about next summer, you know where to find me."

This was ridiculous. Elodie walked back outside in a huff.

Her phone rang. It was Sloan Pierce.

"Sloan, I was just thinking about you," she said, stomach tightening.

"I don't mean to push but . . ."

Elodie felt a flash of anger. How could her parents have put her in this position?

"Working on it. Just a few bureaucratic loose ends. Just keep the ball rolling on your end and I'll do the same."

"Elodie, I am extremely excited to get to work on this. We all are. But we do need the legal formalities out of the way. Do you want to come to the office sometime next week to finalize the contract?"

"Actually, I'm on Cape Cod at the moment." Across the street, a woman with a curtain of blond hair blowing in the breeze caught her attention. "Provincetown. Quite a distance."

Was that *Gemma*? So she'd come to town after all.

"Sloan, I have to call you back."

On her walk back to Celeste's, Gemma stopped in front of a store called Ball Beachwear, the windows dressed with bathing suits for men and women and two dresses in a 1950s silhouette, a white one with a cherry pattern and the other blue polka dot. She wondered what it would be like to simply be in town on vacation, hitting the beach and having drinks with friends.

She checked her phone to find the departure time for the afternoon ferry.

"Gemma?"

She looked up to find her aunt Elodie crossing the street, dodging a bike soaring against traffic.

What was she doing here? Had she mentioned in her phone call that she was in town? No, she hadn't. Gemma would have remembered. It would have made her think twice about heading out here herself.

"So you made the trip after all," Elodie said, her pale cheeks shiny with perspiration. Her faded silver-blond hair was pulled up in a clip, large solitaire diamonds in her ears. "Why didn't you contact me?"

"So you could waste more of my time? No thanks," Gemma said. "Why did you lie to me? Celeste doesn't know anything about the Electric Rose."

"You should have told me you were coming," Elodie said.

"You should have told me you were *here*!" *Unbelievable.* "Are you playing games with me? Is this some sort of payback for showing up at your party?"

"No," Elodie said. "But we do need to talk. All three of us."

"I'm leaving," Gemma said, flashing her the ferry schedule on her phone. She turned and walked back toward Celeste's house, Elodie close behind on her heels.

"Oh no, you're not," Elodie said. "This conversation is a long time coming. And I'm not waiting another minute."

22

Celeste, 1993

Bryn Mawr College was only two hours from Manhattan, but felt like a world away. That, along with its excellent graduate program in art history, was its selling point for Celeste.

The Philadelphia suburbs were the perfect place for her to lose herself in her studies. There were only two main newspapers, *The Philadelphia Inquirer* and the *Daily News,* and neither devoted much ink to gossip pages. For the first time in her life, she wasn't one of the Pavlin sisters; she was just Celeste. She even went by her mother's maiden name, Lowe, to stay under the radar completely. But she didn't have to worry; the Main Line functioned like its own universe, with its local celebrities and socialites and big-money power players. And in her academic niche, her neighborhood populated primarily by health food stores, yoga studios, and coffee shops, no one cared about even local notables.

She lived in an apartment building just off Lancaster Avenue, shedding her Manhattan socialite skin like a chrysalis. She wore Birkenstocks and flannel shirts and hadn't picked up a mascara wand in ages. She spent most of her time on campus or down the road at Ludington Library. Sometimes she ventured out with friends to hear indie bands play in Center City or passed entire afternoons at the Philadelphia Museum of Art. And best of all, she hadn't gone to a Pavlin & Co event for at least a year. She told her parents she was studying or working and couldn't get away. Her mother always quipped, "When you're ready to be a member of this family again, you let me know."

Celeste didn't take the jab too seriously; her parents were guilty of a gross double standard. Her younger sister Paulina dropped out of school to run around Los Angeles and Europe, but because she was dating men with titles and was written about in *Town & Country* and *Vogue,* she was deemed "good for the Pavlin name." Celeste's descent into academic bohemia . . . not so much. As for Elodie, who had worked in the family business since her undergraduate years at Columbia, she now seemed to be pursuing a master's degree in kissing their father's ass.

After a while, both her parents stopped asking — aside from Thanksgiving and winter break — when she was coming to visit.

So Celeste was surprised one afternoon to return to her apartment to find an urgent answering machine message from her father summoning her to New York. She called him at the office, expecting that her usual excuses would work. But Alan was having none of it.

"This is non-negotiable. All three of you girls will be at this event."

"Paulina's coming in for it?" she said.

"She is indeed," her father said.

And then the conversation took an even stranger turn: "And please bring your young man friend. We'd like to meet him."

This left her speechless. She didn't know how her father even knew of her boyfriend; Elodie must have mentioned it. She knew she shouldn't have told her! But she was lulled into a false sense of safety when Elodie had uncharacteristically confided in her. Her wallflower sister had fallen in love with some guy who worked at the ad agency the company used. In their last few phone conversations, she'd been like a different person, bubbly and chatty. Celeste was happy for her, and when Elodie asked about her own dating life, she told her the truth: She'd met someone.

His name was Brodie Muir, a recent Villanova law school graduate toiling at a small Center City firm. Tall with dark hair, he'd been the only other person at a midnight showing of the movie *In the Name of the Father.* They both left the theater sobbing and ran into each other in the lobby. When they began chatting about the film, it was the first time she missed New York City. If they'd been in Manhattan, they could have gone to an all-night diner and talked about the movie. But since there was absolutely nothing open in the suburbs at that hour, they reached an awkward moment when the usher kicked them out of the theater and they walked to their respective cars in the parking lot.

Brodie had grown up in a blue-collar Delaware town he visited often, always without her. He came from a close-knit family of six boys. His mother taught middle school math and his father worked for the postal service. They were old-fashioned; if his mother called him on a morning when Celeste had stayed overnight, Brodie never let on that she was in his bed.

"I don't want her to get the wrong impression of you," he said.

And she didn't want Brodie to get the wrong impression of her, either. Celeste never said much about her own family, except that her father was in the jewelry business and she had two sisters.

Eight months into their relationship, she still hadn't met the Muirs. She wasn't offended when Brodie said he was waiting until things were "serious." She wasn't in a rush to introduce him to her family and the circus that would inevitably follow, so living in their own little bubble suited her just fine. Besides, he worked long hours at the firm and she was committed to her studies. Neither of them wanted to put pressure on the relationship.

So when her father insisted she bring a date, she was at a loss. She tried to explain that they weren't even serious, but her father wouldn't take no for an answer. "If you want to continue making the most of *my* tuition dollars, I suggest you make an appearance with your beau. Really, Celeste — do we ask so much of you?"

The truth was, she did think she might be falling in love with Brodie. The day would come, sooner or later, when she had to admit that she wasn't just a simple grad student. That there was a limestone building engraved with her family's name on one of the most illustrious corners of Manhattan. That she'd been photographed in her mother's arms by Scavullo for *Vogue* when she was born. That, unlike the Muirs, she would never have to work a day in her life.

Maybe it was better to get it over with. If he loved her, it wouldn't matter. And it might be nice to bring someone home who she could roll her eyes with. She might actually have fun for a change.

Maybe the summons was a blessing in disguise.

23

The way Gemma saw it, things were pretty simple: Either Elodie told her where her mother's ring was or admitted she was hiding it from her. A famous thirty-carat diamond ring didn't just disappear.

But Elodie insisted she wouldn't talk without Celeste and followed her into the antiques store.

"Celeste has nothing to do with this," Gemma said. "You're playing games with me."

"I'm playing games? What do you call pretending to be a journalist to crash my party?"

"I should have been *invited* to that party," Gemma said. "I only had to crash it because for some reason you people decided to pretend I don't exist!"

"I see you share your mother's sense of entitlement," Elodie said.

Gemma wanted to punch her, and Alvie

clearly sensed this because she stepped in between them. "Why don't you two take this outside?"

"*What* is going on here?" Celeste appeared, rushing toward them.

It had been many, many years since Celeste had played the part of peacemaking big sister. How many times had she been caught between Elodie and Paulina, who bickered over everything? Who got to ride shotgun during the drive to the Hamptons? Who got the bigger room on family vacations? Who had this, who had that. It never ended, the battle over things large and small. Until the ultimate battle that tore the family apart.

She had no interest in seeing history repeat itself.

"You two: Follow me." She sounded more weary than commanding, but still, Elodie and Gemma listened to her. As in many stressful situations, one thing was needed: food.

Liz's Café was just around the corner on Bradford. The restaurant was a relative newcomer at only two years old, but the owner, Liz Lovati, was a town fixture. She'd owned and operated the mainstay corner market Angel Foods for the past two decades.

The café, with its maritime décor and Italian comfort-food menu, stood where the former Tips for Tops'n restaurant had been for forty years. Tips had been well-known for its breakfast specials, and a section of Liz's menu paid it a tribute. Celeste loved that every place in town had a story behind it. It made it particularly ironic then that she chose to celebrate these places steeped in history while being confronted with the avoidance of her own.

When Elodie and Gemma realized Celeste intended for them to have a meal together, and the length of time that implied, they balked. "We have to eat, don't we?" she said. No one could argue with that, at least. They were seated at the front, next to a window. Her sister and niece were too agitated to even glance at the menu.

"We'll have three orders of the pancakes, two sides of bacon, three coffees . . . and that should do it," Celeste said to their server.

"I prefer not to eat anything but fruit before noon," Elodie said. Celeste turned to her.

"And I prefer not to have a major emotional event before noon. But I guess we're all out of our comfort zone. Look, I have a peaceful, wonderful life out here. You can't just show up and create drama. Do you understand?"

"I'm happy to leave — as soon as you sign the auction paperwork."

"I told you I can't sign paperwork until Mercury is out of retrograde," Celeste said.

"Hold up," Gemma said, looking back and forth between her two aunts. "What paperwork?"

"Contracts for an auction of the Pavlin Private Collection," Elodie said, looking directly into her eyes. "And I need your signature, too."

24

Gemma couldn't believe what she was hearing: Elodie couldn't sell pieces from the family's private collection without *her* signature? She'd been cut off from the Pavlins — and the company — since she was a child. It didn't make any sense. But it did give her leverage.

"Well, I'm not signing anything . . . unless you hand over my mother's ring."

Elodie pursed her lips. After a pause, she said, "That's a big ask. But I *am* willing to negotiate — with both of you. That's why I wanted the three of us to talk in person."

The waiter appeared with coffees, detected the tension at the table, and discreetly slipped away after setting down the mugs.

"I understand that I'm asking both of you to sign paperwork allowing me to sell off valuable jewelry, and you're wondering, what's in it for you? Well, I'm happy to share some of the proceeds from the auction."

"I'm not interested in Pavlin blood money," Celeste said. Gemma looked at her in surprise while Elodie just sighed.

"Please don't be so dramatic," Elodie said. "If you don't want any money, that's fine. But then don't stand in the way. You can't have it both ways."

To be honest, Gemma wouldn't mind some money. She had no idea what an auction would bring in, but she was pretty sure even a fraction of the proceeds would allow her to grow her own company. This could be her answer to the investor issue. She could incorporate, develop a better website, buy more material for making inventory — possibly outsource production to scale up. Who knows — she could even lease a storefront. When money wasn't an issue, anything was possible.

But it was a catch-22. Her ultimate goal was bigger than just money. She wanted to change the jewelry industry; she *believed* in changing the industry. She wanted to put the old guard — specifically, Pavlin & Co — out to pasture. She wanted to push them to the side — as they had pushed her aside. The auction wouldn't just raise a lot of money, it would no doubt generate a lot of publicity. And she had no interest in helping Pavlin & Co with publicity.

But then, the money guy Jacob Jabarin had invited her to return at the end of the summer. She had to do something to raise her profile. Yes, she wanted the famous diamond for personal reasons. But she *needed* it for professional ones. If she could relaunch it in the context of contemporary jewelry, with her own "jewelry should be personal" ethos, it would amplify her brand in a way investors would take seriously.

"Again, the only thing I want is my mother's ring."

Elodie's face turned red. "It was never her ring. It belongs to Pavlin & Co."

"Alan Pavlin gave it to my mother as an engagement gift," Gemma said.

"That was a loan — for publicity," said Elodie. "Tell her, Celeste."

Celeste put up her hands. "I don't want any part of this."

The server appeared with plates of fluffy pancakes and perfectly crisped bacon. Gemma's stomach rumbled, but she made no move to eat. Again, she was brought back to the last time she saw her mother's ring, resting on a tray on her grandmother's nightstand. *It will be yours someday. It's what your mother wanted.*

"It's the ring or no signature," Gemma said.

"So you'd rather walk away with nothing?" Elodie said. "I don't believe you."

"I've done fine with nothing the past fifteen years," Gemma said.

Elodie stood abruptly, nearly knocking over her chair. It bumped back against the restaurant's front window frame.

"Celeste, you know where to find me when the moon is out of Venus or whatever you're waiting for. And, Gemma, I expect to hear from you, too, when you realize this is a once-in-a-lifetime opportunity that you're squandering."

She pulled her orange Hermès handbag into the crook of her arm and stormed out. Gemma exhaled. She hadn't realized she'd been holding her breath. She glanced at Celeste, who picked up her knife and fork and cut a bite off her pancakes.

"Please," she said, "eat."

Gemma bit into her bacon and sipped her coffee. It was strong. They ate in silence, her mind racing. Was she being foolish? Should she take the money and run? She wished she had a mother to talk to. *Anyone* to talk to.

"Gemma, this might not be what you want to hear, but I wish you'd forget about the Electric Rose."

She looked at her aunt, feeling stricken.

Was she taking Elodie's side on this?

"Why?"

"It's bad luck. It's cursed. I don't know where it is, and I don't want to know. Please, for your own sake, forget about it."

"Aunt Celeste, you don't really believe that, do you?"

Celeste nodded vigorously. "I do. The first time I saw an article that suggested the curse, I knew in my bones it was true. And if you'd seen how drastically things fell apart once that diamond came into the family, you'd believe it, too."

Gemma didn't know about that. She'd stumbled upon a few mentions of the curse online but didn't give it any more credence than she did stories of haunted houses.

"And I overheard some of your argument in the store," Celeste said slowly. "The part about our family pretending that you don't exist. I feel terrible. I'm sorry. I should have reached out."

Yes, she should have. And maybe she should feel more bitterness toward her aunt. But the thing was, Celeste welcomed her the minute she appeared in town. She welcomed her the way, deep down, she'd wished Elodie had the night of the Pavlin & Co party. "I guess you had your own reasons for keeping your distance, not just from me but from the whole family. I'm not taking it personally."

"Please don't," Celeste said. "And I know it's probably too little too late, but would you consider staying here a bit longer? We have the extra room. And I know you mentioned not having an apartment in the city right now."

Gemma felt like she could cry at the kindness. It was sweet and well-intentioned. But she had to get back to her own life. She had to get back to work.

"I appreciate that, Aunt Celeste. But I can't stay."

Celeste nodded in understanding. "Okay," she said. "Well, at the very least, would you be interested in coming with me to an estate sale this afternoon? It might be fun. And I don't want your last memory of your visit here to be this unfortunate breakfast."

An estate sale could be fun. She might find an interesting piece or two. Then at least the whole trip wouldn't have been a waste of time.

One more day wouldn't hurt.

Elodie fumed the entire walk back to the Barros house.

Unbelievable. She'd made that grifter a generous offer, and she'd refused. Now what? And as if that weren't bad enough, the house now smelled dank and briny, as if somehow during her walk the bay had seeped into every floorboard.

Lidia sat at the kitchen table chopping up what appeared to be dried plants. It was immediately clear this was the source of the very strong odor.

"What *is* that smell?" Elodie said, bending to undo Pearl's leash.

"Oh, hi, Elodie. Dried seaweed. I'm immune to the scent at this point. But don't run off — I wanted to talk to you."

Reluctantly, she took a seat. She didn't particularly want to talk, and she certainly didn't want to be exposed to the seaweed for a minute longer than she had to be. Pearl sneezed.

"Dare I ask why you're chopping up seaweed? Is this a local custom I should know about?"

"Marco and Olivia farm it, then we mix it with fresh tea leaves for a special blend sold at Tea by the Sea. If you haven't visited there yet, I highly recommend it. It's right across the street from East End Books."

"I prefer my tea without seaweed, thank you," Elodie said.

Lidia laughed. "Most of their tea doesn't have seaweed in it. We came up with this blend last summer. It was my son's idea; seaweed is full of antioxidants, and farming it is great for the aquatic environment."

Elodie nodded, impatient for Lidia to get to the point. If Lidia wasn't going to get right to it, then she might as well. "For the record, I had no idea you knew my sister. I wasn't trying to be deceptive with my last name. It's standard practice to protect my privacy."

Lidia moved the seaweed aside, put down the knife, and clasped her hands together.

"I understand. And you don't owe me an explanation. I'm a professional, and we have a business arrangement for the room. But on a personal level, I need things to be harmonious around here. I don't want you to be uncomfortable, and I don't want Celeste to be uncomfortable. So . . . maybe you can make amends?"

"Me? Why should *I* make amends? I don't know what my sister told you but —"

"Celeste never told me a thing. I have no idea what the problem is between you two, but around here, family is family. If you only knew all the issues we've had with Manny's sister Bianca. Look up 'troublemaker' in the dictionary, it's got her name there. But when she's here, we keep the peace. For our own sanity. Maybe take a similar approach with Celeste? And I'll tell her the same thing." She smiled and went back to chopping the seaweed.

"Well, Lidia, I can certainly try," she said. "By the way, is the ocean beach walkable from here? I could use some fresh air."

"Technically, yes. But it's far on foot. You're better off biking," Lidia said.

Elodie hadn't been on a bike since she was twelve. She'd call a cab.

25

Paulina and Celeste, 1993

Paulina Pavlin stretched under the covers of her luxurious king-sized bed at the Four Seasons Hotel in Florence. The suite had frescoed ceilings and overlooked the Giardino della Gherardesca. It had been her home for the past two months.

She'd only intended to stay in Florence for a week before meeting up with friends skiing in Zurich, but she quickly realized the only thing more delicious than Italian food was Italian men.

Beside her, her *uomo del giorno* snored softly. She'd met him two days earlier when she stopped by a café after visiting the Uffizi. Three hours of looking at Renaissance art got her in the mood for romance; Alessandro served her a shot of espresso and when she left a few lire for the bill, she included a scrap of paper with her hotel phone number. He called her as soon as his shift was over and arrived at the hotel on a red Vespa. He hadn't left since. For now, she was more than content to have him in her bed. But she knew it was just a matter of time before the restlessness set in; it always did.

Paulina was in love with the idea of love. Unfortunately, she had yet to fall in love with an actual person. No matter how handsome the stranger, how great the sex, how fabulous the setting, she lost interest after a week or two. He'd start talking about the screenplay he hadn't finished, or his ex, or his mother issues, and the bubble would burst and she'd be over it.

Maybe this was normal for age twenty-three, but Paulina wasn't a normal twenty-three-year-old. She was a Pavlin, heiress to a jewelry fortune, with the tabloid following to match. And they were relentless. A few months ago, the *New York Post* ran a piece about her with the headline "The Count, the Duke, and the Wardrobe" — a play, no doubt, on the book *The Lion, the Witch, and the Wardrobe* — documenting her consecutive flings with a French count, a British duke, and one of the Missoni fashion heirs. To top it off, it included a paparazzi shot of her topless on the latter's yacht.

Ever since, she found it easier to have affairs with more low-profile men, and so . . . the barista in her bed. Who knew how long this particular fling would last, but she hoped at least until the weekend; she was meeting friends on the coast for a day of yachting, and she knew her barista would look beyond hot in a bathing suit.

Paulina slid gingerly from under the covers, not wanting to wake him. But she couldn't wait another minute for coffee. The strong Italian coffee had exacerbated her caffeine addiction. She slipped on her jeans and well-worn ankle boots for the trip down to the espresso cart on the street.

"Ms. Pavlin, *un minuto,*" the front desk clerk called out.

"I'll be back soon, Umberto," she said. "I need *caffeina.*"

Italian had proven so much easier to pick up than French. Maybe it was because the people were kinder about it, quick to let her mistakes slide and eager to offer help.

"I have a telephone message for you — from two days ago."

She'd turned her room phone off and asked not to be disturbed. Her heart skipped a beat in alarm.

"Oh?" She hurried closer to the desk. Umberto handed her a slip of paper with three words on it: *Call your father.*

Of course, she imagined the worst: that something had happened to her mother or one of her sisters. She hadn't heard from Celeste, toiling away in grad school, in a while. And she never heard from Elodie, who worked long hours in the family business and was about as much fun as a root canal.

Paulina did a quick time difference calculation and realized it was only five A.M. in New York. But her father was an early riser. She hurried to the phone banks on the far side of the lobby. Her hand shook as she punched in all the numbers for the collect trans-Atlantic call.

"It's about time!" her father said without so much as a hello. She supposed she deserved it.

"I'm so sorry," she said. "I literally just got the message from the front desk." Well, it wasn't a lie. "Is everything okay? Is it Mom?"

"Everything — everyone is fine. But I do need you to come back to the city."

"When?" She knew she would have to go home eventually, but she was in no rush. She felt better out from under the shadow of her older sisters, brainy Celeste and ambitious Elodie. She didn't want to have to answer her parents' nagging questions about what she planned to "do" with her life. As far as she could tell, she was *doing* what she planned to do. It seemed self-evident to her.

"I want you on a plane tomorrow. We have a big family event coming up."

"Dad! I need more notice than that."

"You'd have had more notice if you returned my first message forty-eight hours ago. Oh — one more thing. Bring a boyfriend. Your sisters are bringing dates."

"I'm not seeing anyone right now, Dad."

"Well, that's a first," he said. "Either way, let me know what time your flight lands so I can send the driver."

She hung up the phone with a sigh. *So much for seeing the barista in his bathing suit.*

No matter how much time Celeste spent away from her parents' Park Avenue apartment, it always felt like she'd just left. It never changed.

The first thing her boyfriend, Brodie, said when they walked into her parents' duplex was, "I didn't believe people really lived like this."

Seeing the place fresh through Brodie's eyes, it all looked like a cartoonish version of the opulence she remembered. The ceilings looked higher, the sunlight pouring into the living room brighter, her mother's stark minimalist décor (the brainchild of her interior designer, a woman so pricey Alan called her CV, for cash vacuum) more dramatic. Every inch of the place screamed "expensive." Celeste was embarrassed; she wished she hadn't let her father pressure her into bringing Brodie. Especially since Paulina, apparently, had managed to fly solo for the weekend.

A housekeeper informed her dinner was scheduled for six o'clock in the dining room. While Brodie was getting changed, Celeste slipped down the hall to Elodie's room. Even though Elodie had been working for the company since graduating college, she still hadn't moved out of her childhood bedroom. While Celeste hadn't been able to leave fast enough, Elodie was clearly in no rush to cut the cord.

"I wish we were going out to a restaurant," she said, sitting on the edge of Elodie's bed. Elodie sat at a mahogany vanity, trying to pin her hair back. "It just feels so . . . intense with all of us here."

Elodie, who had always been game to join in for a session of complaining about the quirks and vagaries of their parents, was in no mood to play along.

"I think it's nice," she said. "It's more

intimate this way."

More intimate? When Celeste moved to Philly, Elodie declared that New York City wasn't big enough for her and Paulina without Celeste around as a buffer. Clearly, something had changed. She took a closer look at her sister. Elodie had replaced her old tortoiseshell glasses with a sleeker pair of black lacquered frames. Her hair, naturally a mousier color than Celeste's and Paulina's golden blond, seemed to shimmer with new highlights and it was longer than Celeste had seen it since they were teenagers.

"Look at you. What happened to my sister Elodie? I demand you return her immediately," Celeste teased.

Elodie turned away from the mirror to face her. Her blue-green eyes seemed lit from within.

"I think I'm in love," she said.

At dinner, she could see why. The twenty-seat table — white Carrara marble imported from Italy — was set for seven. Celeste was next to Brodie and across from Liam Maybrook, Elodie's guy. He was handsome, seemed intelligent, and when he looked adoringly at Elodie, it warmed Celeste's heart. He was mid-story about something at an advertising agency when she took her seat. She had learned from Elodie that they met at a brand strategy creative meeting.

Beside her, Brodie sat stiffly without saying a word. She reached for his hand under the table.

"Sorry I'm late," Paulina said, strolling in wearing a spaghetti-strap black dress with a plaid shirt tied around her waist and black combat boots. Her pale hair hung down to her waist. She looked like the poster girl for grunge chic.

Elodie's boyfriend stared at their youngest sister. Who could blame him? Still, it made Celeste shift uncomfortably in her seat when Paulina stared right back. No one else seemed to notice.

"Celeste, when are you moving back to civilization?" her father asked while the sommelier filled everyone's wineglasses. "I've got a desk with your name on it."

"Philadelphia isn't exactly a desert island, Dad," she said. "And I'm getting my master's degree so I can teach."

"How about you, Brodie?" Alan said. "You have your head stuck in the books, too?"

"No, Mr. Pavlin," Brodie said. For the first time, Celeste could detect the slight muddiness of his Delaware accent. And she hated herself for noticing. "I'm a first-year associate at a law firm."

"A lawyer!" Alan said, smacking his palm onto the table. "We can always use more of those around here." He turned to Paulina, seated to his left. "Why don't you try dating someone with a job for a change?"

"Because it's so much more fun dating someone with a *title,*" she said.

Even the new-and-improved Elodie rolled her eyes at that.

"Alan," Constance said, her lips pursed in displeasure at the direction the conversation had taken. Paulina was Constance's favorite, always had been, and Celeste had finally reached an age where she accepted this without judgment or too much emotion. "Why don't you give the kids a little preview of what you have planned for tomorrow night."

Her mother looked elegant as usual in a navy Chanel suit, her blond hair parted at the side and tucked behind one ear with a diamond clip. Her blue eyes were perfectly made-up with smoky shadow and liquid eyeliner. Her nails were polished a deep crimson, her lips nude gloss. She smelled like her Opium perfume.

"Excellent idea, my love." Her father, for all his faults (controlling, workaholic, judgmental), had one unimpeachable quality: He adored his wife. "Everyone, tomorrow night will be a historic moment for Pavlin & Co. As you know, I'm introducing the Electric Rose to the press and the public. But I also want to bring Pavlin & Co back to its roots; as my father put it, 'A diamond says love.' That's why I wanted everyone together tomorrow night. Because there's no greater love than my love for my family." He raised his glass. "To my girls, my greatest treasure."

Everyone raised their glasses, and Celeste felt a lump in her throat. It was the warmest expression of feelings she'd heard from her father in years.

Maybe some things could change.

26

As soon as Celeste pulled the truck into the nearby town of Wellfleet, Gemma knew she'd made the right choice in accompanying her to the estate sale. The narrow streets and small shops selling ice cream and crafts gave her a feeling of tranquility. A wooden sign in the center of town pointed arrows in different directions, directing people to Provincetown or Wellfleet Harbor. A teenage girl sat at a table selling shells painted with the words "Wellfleet Summer." A line had formed in front of her.

"People are really into shells around here," Gemma said.

"They're not buying shells," said Celeste. "They're buying memories."

Gemma nodded. She knew exactly what Celeste meant. It was the whole idea behind her brand: Build a necklace from charms that reflect your memories, your experiences.

She glanced at Celeste from her passenger seat, wondering if her aunt resembled what her mother would have looked like if she'd reached her fifties. Paulina was frozen in Gemma's memory as an eternally young woman. Would her hair still be blond? Aunt Celeste's was still faintly gold, an ash-blond with streaks of silver. She didn't wear makeup, and her crow's feet and laugh lines were deep — the byproduct of sun-drenched summers. And she dressed like a hippie, always in flowing caftans and sandals. But her eyes; it was like looking directly into her mother's.

They arrived at their destination, a classic three-quarter Cape framed by a white picket fence. Near the trim board of the front of the house, a metal plaque declared the home part of the National Register of Historic Places circa 1800.

"Sometimes these old houses themselves are more interesting than anything that's for sale. They have all these quirky features, like beehive ovens beside brick fireplaces," Celeste said.

She'd explained to her that each sale was slightly different. Some were as loosely organized as a yard sale, with people browsing inside and out freely and sometimes aimlessly. Others featured attendants offering a guided tour like a museum visit. Most fell somewhere in between, with a sales crew around to monitor the room and answer questions.

"I'm mainly looking for porcelain and cut glass," Celeste said on their way inside. "They sell like hotcakes in the summer because people are staying at friends' homes and they need host gifts."

She led Gemma through a room filled with Federal-style furniture and asked an attendant where to find housewares. They were directed upstairs, where Celeste gravitated to an alcove stuffed with vases and chandeliers.

Gemma drifted into the next room, where tables were covered end-to-end with trays of costume jewelry. She picked up a sterling silver and rhinestone owl, and a small brass stamped cat with green stones set as the eyes. She found an elaborate collar that looked like French poured glass, with cut and carved glass beads shaped like leaves with oval beads at the end. It resembled the work done by Gripoix for Chanel, but she knew it probably wasn't.

Gemma snapped a photo, adjusted the contrast, and posted it to Instagram with the caption *Treasure hunting.*

She walked back across the hall to find

Celeste.

"This stuff is cool," she said, showing her the rhinestone owl. "And this pin . . . amazing." It was a painted enamel flower with pavé set rhinestones.

"I don't sell jewelry at the shop," Celeste said quickly.

"Yeah, I've noticed. But why not?"

"That was my family's business — not mine."

Okay.

Gemma returned to the jewelry tables and couldn't resist other trinkets: an emerald-cut piece of white glass set in silver, a blue cabochon glass bead that looked like turquoise but wasn't, a two-inch gold egg decorated with swirls of color, a beaded necklace that looked like jade but was probably just glass. All of them would make great charms. She'd just need to create some bezels and hooks.

And then she saw a piece that froze her hand midair: a metal butterfly brooch. It was an earthy coral color, probably copper.

A copper butterfly, she said to herself, incredulous at the find. Her mother's favorite creature was the copper butterfly, a species so common in the Northeast that the Pavlin Hamptons house had been overrun with them during her mother's childhood summers. Her mother loved all animals and animal imagery. She used to have little figurines on her bedroom dresser, some crystal, some silver, some carved wood. A butterfly represented transformation.

She felt like it was a sign. Maybe she'd been too quick to turn down her aunt's offer to stay a little longer. What if she spent a week or two scouring local antiques shops and estate sales while she figured out her next move?

Besides, she still hadn't given up on finding a clue about her mother's engagement ring. As long as Elodie was still in town, she shouldn't be in such a rush to leave.

Maybe Elodie should see that she wouldn't be that easy to get rid of. Not this time.

27

Lidia insisted on giving her a ride to the beach. She drove a battered pickup truck, and Elodie settled in the passenger seat with Pearl on her lap. Heading down Commercial, she felt every bump in the road. She realized she hadn't seen a single traffic light in town.

"So you met my brother-in-law, Tito?" Lidia said.

"Yes. We walked our dogs together."

"We encouraged him to get a pet because we thought he seemed lonely," Lidia said. "He never married, you know."

Elodie glanced over. "Yes, well, not everyone gets married."

They passed marshes and a long stone jetty. In the far distance, a small island with a lighthouse.

"You can walk the jetty all the way to Long Point," Lidia said.

She looked out at the jetty. It seemed an

unwise endeavor to traverse the uneven rocks out into the water as far as the eye could see. But people were apparently busy doing just that.

"How many miles is that?"

"Six," said Lidia. "It goes surprisingly quickly. But when my kids were growing up I always warned them not to go out there after dark, and certainly not to go out after they'd been drinking. Just the thought of it kept me awake at night. I'm sure you can imagine."

Actually, she couldn't. Why did people always assume that just because she was a woman of a certain age she was also a mother? The only thing more irritating were the people who called her *Mrs.* Pavlin.

Lidia continued along Province Lands Road. A breeze blew off the salt water and Elodie inhaled. To their right, houses sat high on the grassy hilltops. The road became flanked by sand dunes. They passed a sign that read *Entering Cape Cod National Seashore* and reached a stretch where the side of the street was filled with dozens of parked bicycles.

"What's that all about?" Elodie said.

"Oh, that's just Boy Beach."

What on earth was "boy beach"? She'd never heard of such a thing. Was she going to "girl beach"? Was there a "middle-aged woman beach"?

They turned in to a large parking lot and the ocean stretched out like a deep blue, undulating blanket. The sand was obscured behind tall seagrass and beach roses. Lidia pulled into a spot but didn't turn off the engine.

"There's the entry point to the beach — you'll see a blue tarp path. Back there are the snacks and bathrooms. Have fun. Let me know if you need a ride back."

"That's very kind of you but I'll get a cab later."

"Give me a call if you change your mind. Oh — and you're welcome to join us for dinner tonight. I'm just doing oysters and rice — very simple."

Elodie thanked her, but she was distracted. Stepping out of the truck, watching Lidia drive away, something deep inside her felt off. Maybe it was the talk of marriage, of loneliness. She ignored it, getting Pearl hooked onto her leash and heading to the clearing where people entered the beach with their fold-up chairs and coolers.

No, it wasn't the conversation with Lidia that left her unsettled. It was her niece's fixation on the Electric Rose. She wished her father had never discovered that diamond! She knew, or should have known, from the very beginning that the diamond was cursed. Not in the sensationalist way the stupid tabloids implied, but it was truly a trigger for misfortune. No one could deny that.

The first warning bell should have been that after years of her father bringing her into every meeting, consulting her about everything from brand strategy to design, he was suddenly tight-lipped about the launch of the Electric Rose. All she knew was that he was hosting a black-tie party at the store, with hundreds of press and VIPs invited. She and her mother went to Vera Wang for custom evening gowns, and her mother said with a wink, "Maybe we'll be coming back here soon for a white dress." Elodie, who prided herself on being grounded and work-focused, almost swooned.

Her father encouraged her to bring Liam as her date to the party. She hesitated; six months into their relationship, it was their first public outing and she was nervous that he'd find it overwhelming. Growing up in the Manhattan spotlight, like other children of the rich and famous, she was used to cameras and the occasional odd item in the gossip columns. But Liam was from a small town in Pennsylvania. His parents had never even been to New York City. He once told her he hadn't eaten in a real restaurant until college.

"I want you to be there, but I'm warning you it'll be a circus," she said.

The night of the party at Pavlin & Co, they arrived together in a Lincoln Town Car, and when he came around and opened the door for her, she felt beautiful for the first time in her life.

The crush of press outside the store on Fifth Avenue was overwhelming. Security had to help them through the front door, and they traversed a red carpet as if they were going to the Academy Awards.

Paulina arrived in a car with Celeste and Brodie, and photographers called for Paulina by name, jockeying for a photo they could use in gossip columns. She was dressed in hot-pink silk, a vintage Halston gown that tied around her neck and billowed out below her waist. But even her attention-grabbing sister couldn't outshine the true star of the evening: the Electric Rose. Elodie had devoured that morning's *New York Times* article about the remarkable size and clarity of the stone her father was introducing into the public view. It was a heady thing to be custodian of such a treasure. She couldn't help but feel a touch of reverence for the moment at hand.

The publicity team arranged for the three sisters and their dates to stand side by side next to the podium where her father was speaking. A few feet away, roped off and flanked by armed guards, the pink diamond was displayed on a base of black velvet. The overhead light gave it an otherworldly glow.

"Now, while some notable diamonds have been worn only by movie stars, that will not be the case for the Electric Rose," Alan said. "This stone will only be worn by one of my daughters standing before you here tonight. Because Pavlin is about family."

The room burst into applause. Celeste exchanged a surprised glance with Elodie. *What was this all about?*

"The Electric Rose will be gifted to the first of my daughters to get engaged," Alan said, beaming.

Someone gasped. It might have been her. Or one of her sisters. She turned to look at Liam. He smiled at her and squeezed her hand, and there was no diamond in the world that was as valuable as the way he made her feel. And yet, she wanted that diamond. It was symbolic; the greatest treasure of Pavlin & Co should go to the daughter who was *part* of Pavlin & Co. And as her father always reminded them: A diamond says love.

She didn't want Liam to feel pressured to propose, but a part of her was already fantasizing about it, how it was all coming together for her. The man, the ring, the company. She was the future of Pavlin & Co. The long competition she'd felt with her sisters was over, and she'd won.

Now, all these years later, on a strange beach in a distant town, she was still grieving for what should have been hers.

Celeste insisted on cooking Gemma a farewell dinner. Jack picked up steak at Mac's market and she bought asparagus at Angel Foods and a bottle of sauvignon blanc from Perry's. At the last minute, she made a quick trip to Connie's Bakery for pie.

She set the beat-up picnic table in the back with citronella candles from Good Scents, and the blue and white striped runner in Turkish cotton she'd splurged on at Loveland. Shopping in Provincetown always felt delicious and special and a little bit like she was discovering things no one else had, even though everyone shopped at the same places. But the shop owners were such devoted curators that their passion spilled over into the experience for the buyer. It was a high bar that Celeste strived for with Queen Anne's Revenge.

"This is delicious. Thanks, Aunt Celeste," Gemma said.

She was a sweet girl, really. It had been a great idea to bring her along to the estate sale. Gemma enjoyed it, and Celeste had the satisfaction of getting to act like an aunt for the first time in far too long. Still, she was ready for things to get back to normal. She was glad she'd made the offer for Gemma to stay but, at the same time, was a little relieved she insisted on leaving tomorrow morning. The ugliness of the conversation at Liz's Café was bad energy that she didn't want to be around. The sooner Gemma and Elodie went back to their own lives, the sooner she could return to her own.

All around them, nocturnal insects clicked and hummed in the bushes. Something scurried nearby, and she wondered if it was one of the baby rabbits she'd seen nibbling in the grass earlier.

"So what did you two ladies get up to today?" Jack said. His tan had deepened after a day on the boat. He'd gone out to the oyster beds with Manny's son, Marco. Lately, he seemed more interested in spending time on the water than at the store, and Marco's nascent oyster farm seemed to tap into Jack's nostalgia for his seafaring days. It was fine — the store was really her baby and she didn't mind doing most of the work. But until they replaced Alvie, he might need to be more hands-on. It was a conversation for later.

"We went to an estate sale in Wellfleet," Celeste said.

"You didn't buy more, did you?"

"I did. Why?" She knew why: Sometimes she spent too much and they didn't sell-through by the end of the season.

"Celeste, we have a ton of inventory. Please: No more buying until after the Fourth of July. Then we can at least see where we're at."

He was right. Always so maddeningly practical. She knew opposites attracted, and opposites balanced each other. But sometimes it was irritating.

"They had beautiful things," Gemma said, clearly trying to be on Team Celeste. "I couldn't resist buying a few pieces myself." She went on and on about the remarkable costume jewelry selection, 1940s pieces by designer Miriam Haskell and a 1950s brooch designed by Elsa Schiaparelli.

"Well, I hope you snatched them up," Jack

said. "Not all sales are treasure troves. We've gone to more than our share of duds, right, hon?"

Celeste nodded. "That's true."

"Sadly, no," Gemma said. "They were too expensive. But I did find some collectible pieces that I can use in my own jewelry designs and I bought those."

"Oh, I wish you'd told me," Celeste said. "I would have . . . Were they really that expensive?" Maybe she could go back for something and send it to her. She thought of the extravagant pieces Gemma's mother used to wear — five-carat diamond earrings for a day at the beach — and yet this young woman wouldn't buy fake jewelry at a house sale.

"It's fine," Gemma said with a wave. "I don't wear that stuff. But I studied a lot of jewelry design history and some of the artisans working with non-precious stones were the most inventive. I admire their work."

Jack's eyes narrowed, looking at Gemma with interest. "You know a lot about antiques?"

"Just antique jewelry," she said.

"We do need a new part-timer . . ." he said.

Celeste glared at him. How could he make

such a suggestion without discussing it with her first? She'd told him she felt uncomfortable with her family around. She had no interest in turning a casual visit into an employment situation.

"Gemma's leaving tomorrow," Celeste said quickly.

Gemma sipped her wine, placing the glass down carefully on the wooden table and not the runner. "Actually, Aunt Celeste, I was rethinking your offer. About staying longer. I really don't have anything to rush back to. I can manage my Instagram from anywhere, and if you need help in your store, I'm happy to pitch in."

So this was happening. Paulina's daughter was moving into her house and working at her store.

"Glad this worked out," Jack said, pushing his seat back and collecting a few plates. "You two can chat about the details. I'll go fetch the pie."

28

"Customers want to feel like they're buying something with history," Alvie said. "Do you know the difference between an antique and a collectible?"

"Yes. Age."

Gemma had a lot to learn about the shop, and Alvie was an eager guide. She walked Gemma through every table, piece after piece, sharing encyclopedic knowledge about each one.

"Exactly. For something to qualify as antique, it has to be a hundred years old at least. Anything 'younger' is considered a collectible. We sell both."

"Did you study antiques in school? How did you get into this?" Gemma said.

"I learned everything from your aunt. Absolutely *everything,*" Alvie gushed. "I can't pretend that I can teach you all you need to know in one day. You have to just be here and absorb."

When customers wandered in, Alvie greeted them with enthusiasm and made sweeping declarations like, "Vintage copper is back!" In between, she grilled Gemma about her connection to Celeste.

"My mother was her sister. But after my parents died I was raised by my father's family, away from the Pavlins."

"That's so Dickensian. So romantic."

Gemma rolled her eyes. "It's really not."

"Do you have a boyfriend? Girlfriend?"

"No." Not her favorite subject, but at that point she was relieved to just be off the topic of family. "I have terrible luck in that department."

Alvie tilted her head in sympathy. "Let's grab drinks tonight."

Before she could answer, her phone rang. Sanjay.

"I'm sorry — I have to . . . do you mind if . . ."

Alvie waved her on. "Be my guest. But let me warn you: Keep that thing out of Jack's sight. He considers cell phones a personal affront."

"No calls in front of Jack — got it." She slipped around the counter and crouched out of sight. "Hello?" she said quietly.

"Gemma?"

"Yes. It's me. Hi."

"You sound weird," Sanjay said.

She straightened up a little. "Sorry. I'm at work, so I'm trying to talk quietly."

"Work? Where?"

"In Provincetown. At my aunt's store."

"You're still out there?" he said.

"Yes. Um, my aunt needed some help in the shop." If she was honest with herself, Celeste had looked completely surprised by Jack's offer last night — and not entirely happy. But she quickly recovered and agreed it was a good idea, and that Alvie could train her before her last day.

"What about your jewelry?" he said.

"What about it?"

"I thought this summer was all about finding an investor."

"It is. That's definitely a priority. But I told you I want to find my mother's ring and maybe that can help."

His silence made his disapproval loud and clear despite the three hundred miles between them.

"Is that why you called? To check up on me?" she said.

"No. I'm calling because you left the storage locker key in my car. I didn't know if you realized it was missing or if you'd need it soon. But I guess it's not a pressing issue."

She'd been so distracted in her last week in the city, it was a miracle she hadn't left more things behind in random places.

"Thanks. Can you just hold on to it for me?"

"Yeah, yeah. Sure. But, Gem, I'm worried you're letting this family stuff distract you. You won the NYSD award. You're at the start of such great things. Just come back here and get to work."

She felt a flash of annoyance. "Why are you lecturing me? You're working a hotel desk more than you're doing photography. We all have to make compromises."

"Yeah, but you're more talented than I am. That's why I take all those pictures for you. Your work makes my work better."

She smiled, even though he couldn't see her through the phone. It was classic Sanjay: admonishing her and then complimenting her all at the same time. "Then I guess you're going to have to come out and visit me," she said flirtatiously.

"Gemma," he said, decidedly not flirtatiously, "as your friend, I really think you should get back to New York."

Celeste reached for Jack's hand and he helped her onto the skiff. She hadn't expected today to be the inaugural sail for the season, but the conditions were perfect and his sailboat was tuned up and ready to go. When his father died Jack inherited his vintage 1964 Bristol 40.

Marco had given them a lift out to the moorings.

"All right, you two — have fun. Say hello to *Pacheco* for me," Marco had said. Jack's father had named the boat *Pacheco,* after Duarte Pacheco Pereira, a fifteenth-century sea captain and explorer from Lisbon. The Barroses were fascinated by the seafaring legends in their culture. Apparently, Duarte Pacheco Pereira had been the first to calculate the degree of the meridian arc with remarkable accuracy for his time.

Celeste settled onto a bench and Jack motored out past the breakwater.

"I don't know if the wind is going to cooperate today," he said from behind the wheel.

"That's fine," she said. There was a transcendent calm when the motor was off and they were reliant just on water and wind, but today she wasn't in the mood to drift along. She wanted speed, forward motion. Something to distract her from her troubled thoughts.

She still hadn't confronted him about his overstepping last night with Gemma. After all the wine, she was too tired to get into it before going to bed.

"Penny for your thoughts," Jack said. The sails were up and he'd cut the engine. She heard the water gently lapping against the boat.

"Don't you think maybe you should have talked to me before offering Gemma a job?" she said.

"It seems like a win-win," he said. "You have some family around; we fill the spot Alvie left open."

"But, Jack, you know I don't necessarily *want* my family around."

"She's a good kid. And you know it or else you wouldn't have taken her antiquing yesterday."

"That's beside the point," she said, softening just a little. She knew he meant well. "You should have asked me first."

"I'm sorry. You're right. But Provincetown always makes room for its wash'ashores," Jack said. As someone born and raised in P'town, he could say this with authority. Anyone else was a "wash'ashore" for life — no matter how long they lived there, no matter how rich, no matter how famous. And some of the most famous artists of the twentieth century had called Provincetown home. "Celeste, look at this gorgeous day.

The open sea . . . what more could we ask for?"

She smiled at him. It was true.

Jack asked her to fetch his sunglass case from underneath the bench. "Can you take the glasses out for me?" he asked from behind the wheel.

She set the case on her lap and opened it. Inside, instead of sunglasses, she found a ring. A delicate 1920s ring with a transitional cut small diamond. It had a deco platinum setting with small diamonds surrounding the main stone in its square bezel. It was absolutely stunning.

Celeste's stomach dropped.

"What is this?" she said, looking up at him but not removing the ring.

"That, my love, is my sixtieth birthday present," he said.

"You bought yourself a ring?" She wanted to keep things light. She wanted to not go down this road.

"No. The ring is for you. I'm asking you to do me the great honor of becoming my wife."

Celeste snapped the sunglass case shut.

"Jack."

"I know, I know. You don't believe in marriage. But, Celeste, I hope by now you do believe in *us*. We're great partners."

"Of course we are. So why change anything?"

"Because I'm turning sixty years old in August and I want you to be my wife. Forever isn't such a long time anymore, Celeste. After all these years, I want to make it official."

Celeste knew this should be a romantic moment. She loved Jack and didn't want to spend her life with anyone else. But that didn't mean she wanted to get married. But he did. So now what?

It would be insensitive in that moment to remind him of how badly her first marriage proposal had turned out. Of course, that had nothing to do with Jack. Unless, of course, the rumors of the Pavlin curse were true.

She wished she'd never given in to her father's insistence that she go back to New York City that fateful weekend. She should have seen the red flag when he insisted she bring her boyfriend. And she didn't just bring him to New York. She pulled him into the white-hot center of Manhattan media and society only to find out the whole evening was just a publicity stunt.

After the Electric Rose party, they took the first Amtrak back to Philadelphia in the morning, and she promised Brodie — and herself — that they wouldn't be going back again. Not for a long time at least.

Two nights later they went to a concert at Penn's Landing. It was an all-female group from Seattle that was one of Celeste's favorites. Brodie surprised her with the tickets.

"Sitting here, it's like New York City doesn't even exist," she said to him that night, relieved to be back in her own milieu, her feet solidly on the ground. "I'm sorry the other night was such a circus. But I'm glad you were with me."

"I'm glad I was with you, too," he said, his arm around her shoulders. She smiled at him and then glanced at the women onstage rocking out against the backdrop of Center City.

She felt Brodie's eyes on her, so she turned back to him. He slid a few inches away, so they were facing each other instead of side by side.

"Celeste, the past year has been amazing. But going to New York with you . . . it makes me realize how close we've really gotten. And how much more is ahead for us."

"Brodie. That's so sweet." She felt her chest swell with happiness. Maybe bringing him home hadn't been a disaster after all. Maybe she'd been silly to even have worried about it.

"I'm not trying to be sweet. I'm trying to say . . . that I want to spend the rest of my life with you." At first, the words didn't register. But understanding slowly dawned with the intensity of fireworks.

"Wait, are you —"

"I love you, Celeste. Will you marry me?"

"Yes," she breathed, leaning forward to kiss him. After a moment he pulled back.

"I almost forgot," he said, handing her a small box. She opened it to find a silver claddagh ring.

"It's beautiful," she said as he slipped it onto her left ring finger.

"It's just a placeholder," he said.

"For what? It's perfect." She knew he didn't have a lot of money and certainly didn't expect — or want — a diamond.

"Well, until you get the pink diamond from your father," he said.

Her mood instantly plummeted.

"You didn't feel pressure to propose to me because of my family, did you?"

"No — no. Of course not."

She wasn't so sure.

"For the record, I don't want that insane diamond. I don't want anything from my parents. I'm here to live my own life."

"Well, let's live it together," he said. She

told herself to stop being cynical, to just accept the happy moment.

The following days were a blur of sharing the good news, drinks to celebrate with friends, and the delicious feeling her life was about to begin for real. The only people she didn't tell were her parents and sisters. She wanted to savor the happiness inside their little bubble for as long as possible.

"We should go to New York this weekend and tell your parents in person," Brodie said.

"A phone call will be fine," she said.

"I'm sure they're going to want to see us. And besides, your father will want to give you the ring."

She pulled back. "I already told you I don't want that ring. Maybe *you're* the one who wants the diamond."

"Celeste, you come from a family with money. Why are you pretending you're just another broke grad student?"

"Well, when you thought I was 'just another broke grad student,' we never even talked about a commitment. Now that you've seen my family, suddenly you want to get married?"

"That's unfair," he said.

Her heart was pounding.

"Well, that's how it feels. And yes, my father pays my tuition, but aside from that,

I have no intention of taking money from them — or help in any way. Do you understand that?"

She went home to her own apartment that night, wanting time to cool off. And never heard from Brodie Muir again.

If that had been the end of it — the drama with the Electric Rose — she maybe could have chalked it up to one random bad experience. But then, Paulina's engagement. Paulina's death. And the tabloids starting up with the Pavlin curse. Like several other accounts of extraordinary diamonds bringing misfortune — the Hope Diamond, the Black Orlov — the Electric Rose became tarnished with tragedy.

She couldn't talk to Jack about this; he didn't understand her interest in tarot cards and belief in the zodiac. The last thing he would give credence to was her feeling, her deep-seated certainty, that she and her sisters were under a dark cloud of bad luck, and that getting engaged would be tempting fate.

The sun beat down on her face, and she used it as an excuse to close her eyes. *Don't blow it,* she told herself. *The past is the past.*

"So, my dear . . . whadya say?" he said.

She opened her eyes, ignoring the glare, focusing on the face that she loved so much.

"Yes," she said. "Yes, Jack, I'll marry you."

29

"And I thought New York had the best people-watching," Gemma said.

Spindler's restaurant was located on the East End and had a front deck, rear garden seating, and an upper level with water views where Alvie chose to sit. Gemma looked down at the colorful tide of people roaming Commercial Street. Cars were at a crawl; on the nearest corner, a man in a top hat belted out Frank Sinatra with a karaoke machine. Families with small children carried bags from Cabot's Candy, and drag queens handed out flyers for that evening's shows.

"My girlfriend says New York hasn't been interesting since the eighties," Alvie said from across the table.

Their drinks had barely arrived and she'd already mentioned Maud, her much older girlfriend, repeatedly.

"So you don't have any hesitation about

quitting the store to work with your girlfriend? I mean, not everyone can work together," Gemma said with a twist in her gut. After hearing from him earlier, she realized how much she missed Sanjay. Worse, she couldn't even tell him how she felt. That definitely would fall outside of the careful friend zone they'd established.

"Celeste and Jack don't seem to have a problem," Alvie said.

That was true. And there were probably countless other examples. Not everyone messed things up as spectacularly as Gemma had. There were moments when she was tempted to wonder if the Pavlin "curse" was actually a thing. She raised her margarita glass and a dusting of salt fell to the table.

"I guess some people are relationship people and some aren't," she said. "I'm done at the ripe old age of twenty-two."

Alvie put down her glass. "You are too gorgeous to be cynical. I bet you have guys throwing themselves at you."

She took a slug of her drink. It was sweet and tangy and she licked the salt from her lips. "I have more important things to think about."

"Like what?"

"Like my business. My jewelry work."

"Did you make that ring?" She looked down at the silver and peridot piece from Rock Candy on Gemma's middle finger. Gemma nodded.

"So . . . what do you want to do? In life, I mean."

Alvie shrugged. "I want to marry Maud. I know — it's so 1950s. If two women were allowed to get married in the 1950s. But you know what I mean."

Gemma nodded. When she had been a little girl, looking up to her parents who were so in love, she dreamed of being married someday. Not anymore.

"We're programmed to believe in the fairy tale," Gemma said.

"You don't believe in true love?" said Alvie.

Gemma considered the question. She had a fleeting image of her beautiful parents. And the look on Sanjay's face when he confronted her about Noam. She shook the thoughts away and glanced across the street at East End Books.

"I believe in love," she said, turning back to Alvie's hopeful face. "But I don't believe in happy endings."

Her phone rang with an unfamiliar 212 number. Someone from Manhattan. She was tempted to send it to voicemail, but then had the long-shot hope it was one of her leads on a potential investor.

"Sorry, I have to take this," she said. "Hello?"

"May I speak to Gemma Maybrook?"

"This is Gemma."

"Gemma, this is Regan O'Rourke from *The New York Times.* We would like to do a feature on you as this year's New York School of Design award winner. Are you amenable to an interview?"

The New York Times! She'd forgotten all about the profile piece that was part of winning the NYSD award. A feature in the Style section could give her the bump she needed to justify going back to Jabarin at the end of the summer.

"Yes, absolutely."

"Great. And you're in Manhattan?"

"I'm in Provincetown right now. But . . . I can come back."

"Actually, Provincetown would make a great setting for the piece. Very photogenic. How's a week from tomorrow for the interview?"

A week from tomorrow? Out here?

"Yes, that works," Gemma said.

The woman gave her contact information and said she looked forward to meeting her. "Oh — one more thing. We'll want to photograph your work space and the collection, so please have that available to us."

She didn't have *any* of that available. Her studio was packed up in her storage space. She didn't want to admit to *The New York Times* that she got kicked out of her apartment and couldn't afford a new one. Not exactly the image of success.

She'd figure it out. She always figured things out.

Alvie looked at her expectantly.

"Sorry about that," she said. She took another big gulp of her margarita, the citrus and salt a little rough going down this time.

"You know what, Gemma? This is going to be your summer of love. I'll be your support system — like AA. Or Weight Watchers."

Alvie raised her glass again. She raised hers, too.

"I'm all for support. But I can guarantee that what I need has nothing to do with love."

30

Elodie, 1993

Two days after the extravagant launch of the Electric Rose, the family decamped for East Hampton. Elodie invited Liam along for the weekend.

Celeste had already rushed back to Philadelphia, and Elodie assumed that Paulina would jet back to Italy or France or wherever their parents had summoned her from. But Paulina decided to stay.

"I've missed you guys!" she said in that deep-throated purr of hers.

Their first morning at the house, Elodie and her father and Liam gathered around the poolside table, the ocean rumbling at high tide just a few yards away. It was late October but unseasonably warm. Liam sat across from her, so handsome it took her breath away. It was an effort not to break into a smile every time he spoke, but she maintained a professional neutrality while her father brought up plans for spring advertising.

At first, she'd protested the shoptalk, reminding her father that Liam had joined them for the trip as her boyfriend, not as the Pavlin & Co advertising account executive. But Liam was more than happy to toss around some ideas.

Paulina climbed out of the heated pool wearing a skimpy black bikini and a solitaire diamond on a platinum chain dangling between her breasts. Uninvited, she joined them at the table, water beading across her glistening skin. Her eyes were so blue-green they matched the sea, her face as obscenely perfect as the film star Bo Derek.

Elodie felt like she was holding her breath, resisting the urge to glance at Liam to see if he was looking at her sister.

"I'm heading to the beach," Paulina said, leaning over and kissing their father on the cheek. She reached for a piece of watermelon. She wore a canary diamond the size of her knuckle on her middle finger.

"You look like a walking jewelry advertisement, my dear," their father said.

"I'll take that as a compliment," Paulina said.

"Actually, that's not a bad idea," Liam said.

Elodie shifted uncomfortably in her seat. "What do you mean?"

He smiled at her, then turned to Alan. "The other night at the launch, you emphasized the family nature of the business — that Pavlin & Co had real people behind the brand name. I think it was brilliant to give the Electric Rose emotional weight by evoking engagement. You could lean into this strategy even further by putting your family into your ad campaign. If you think Paulina is a walking ad for your brand, make it official. Make her the face of Pavlin & Co."

Elodie drew in her breath, silently willing her father to call this idea what it was: absurd. And couldn't Liam see how appalled she was at his suggestion? But no, how would he? She'd never admitted to him how competitive she felt with her younger sister. It would seem weak. Nothing good could come from such a conversation. And nothing good could come from letting her true feelings show now. All she could do was wait for the moment to pass, a temporary squall in the midst of an otherwise flawless day.

"Brilliant," Alan said, bringing the palm of his hand down flat on the table with such force it rattled the bottles of Perrier. "Let's do it."

"Wait — what?" Elodie said.

"Hello, don't I have a say in this?" Paulina feigned irritation but her eyes were bright with excitement.

Liam turned to Elodie.

"What do you think?" he said, reaching for her hand.

"I think . . . I think it's interesting in theory but maybe a little too on the nose. Too much of a good thing. Separation of church and state and all that . . ."

"Nonsense. I like it," said Alan. "How soon could we shoot?"

Liam launched into a potential timeline, talking about storyboards and media buys. Elodie faded out. It was as if a green mist of envy separated her from the rest of the table.

Fine — let Paulina be the face of Pavlin & Co. Elodie would still be the brains of the operation. And she would be at her father's side long after Paulina tired of playing cover girl and flew off to the next place that offered her amusement.

Besides, work wasn't the only thing she had going for her anymore. She had something far more important in her life.

She had Liam.

31

Jack wanted to have the family over to celebrate their engagement. And he meant the *whole* family.

"I'm not inviting Elodie," Celeste said, twisting the ring on her finger. It had only been a few days since he proposed, and she couldn't quite get used to having it there. She never wore jewelry, and somehow wearing a diamond for the first time in her life made her feel like she was in costume.

"Why not?" Jack said. "She's your sister, she's in town, we're having a family celebration. If Bianca were in town, I'd invite her."

Bianca was Jack's cantankerous — okay, hostile — cousin who moved to Florida. She knew he honestly *would* include her, and it was hard to make the case that Elodie was anywhere near as bad as Bianca.

"It's not just about my own comfort level. Elodie and Gemma don't get along, and Gemma's our houseguest. So, for tonight, no."

She won that battle. But the war was ahead of her. Now that the initial thrill of the proposal — romantic, unexpected, and typical Jack in its sweetness — was wearing off, fear was setting in.

When she moved to Provincetown in the mid-nineties, she'd done so with the intention of living her life differently from her parents in every way. Where she worked, where she lived, and *how* she lived. After the Electric Rose fiasco, she never wanted to hear the word "engagement" again. And after Paulina's death, she found it difficult to believe in happy endings. If she hadn't already been with Jack, she might never have found her way to a loving relationship.

It was around this time that she turned to astrology in a serious way. She felt so unmoored, so adrift and cynical, she could only look to the stars to make sense of it all. It was comforting to find a system that told her that while life could be random and cruel, she could at least have a greater understanding of herself and the people around her and make decisions with some guidance. As long as she understood the moon and the stars, she wasn't alone. She wasn't lost.

"Who's the extra place setting for?" Jack

said, mopping up water that she'd spilled setting out mason jars stuffed with wildflowers.

"Maud's able to join us after all." Maud usually didn't have time for socializing at dinnertime once the season kicked into full gear, but she told Celeste she wouldn't miss the celebration for anything.

"The more, the merrier," Jack said, kissing her on the cheek. "A preview for our wedding."

"Did I hear the word 'wedding'?" Lidia said, traipsing through the grass holding a bottle of champagne. Celeste swallowed hard. Lidia rushed over and hugged her. "This is so exciting! Oh, and Manny should be here any minute. He had a late seal tour."

"Can you believe it?" Jack said, beaming. "She's finally letting me make an honest woman out of her."

"So have you set a date?" Lidia said.

"I'm thinking my birthday," Jack said.

Celeste looked at him. "On your actual birthday? But that's . . . the first week in August."

He smiled at her, either not noticing or choosing to ignore the alarm in her voice. "Perfect, right?"

Gemma called Sanjay to tell him about the

New York Times interview, and that she might need a tiny little favor: help getting her equipment and jewelry out to the Cape in time for the interview. "I'll totally mention your photography," she promised. "It will be good for both of us." She said if he could bring her stuff to Provincetown, she'd find him a place to crash for a day or two.

After the phone call from the reporter, the interview was all she could think about. Alvie said they had five bedrooms at Maud's and that Sanjay could absolutely stay for a night.

"I'm not sure that's going to work, Gemma," he'd said. "I have to look at my schedule."

"Okay — no worries," she said, thinking the exact opposite. "Just let me know."

Before dinner, she took a walk to the edge of the bay and snapped a photo of her outstretched hand with two of her Rock Candy rings stacked on her forefinger. The water complemented the large, emerald-cut blue glass stones set in silver. She saved it to post to Instagram later.

Now, surrounded by Jack's family at the dinner table, she tried to be in the moment.

Everyone seemed to be talking all at once — at one another, over one another. The only person not talking a mile a minute was the woman sitting next to her, Alvie's girlfriend, Maud.

Maud was tall — close to six feet. Her silver hair was cut into a shag; she had deep-set blue eyes and smoker's creases around her mouth. Her voice was husky, and her laugh was big. Gemma immediately understood her appeal to Alvie, no matter the age difference.

Celeste's picnic table had a white and blue striped runner down the center and flickered with candles. At first, it seemed too large with only Gemma, Alvie, and Maud seated, but then the Barros clan arrived.

Lidia, wife of Jack's cousin Manny, was attractive in a careless way, with thick silver-threaded hair and a cleft in her chin. She gave Gemma a hug in greeting, then introduced her husband. He was pleasant looking, with a broad nose and kind dark eyes.

"And this is my brother, Tito," Manny said.

Tito was broad-shouldered, with the same dark eyes as the rest of them but with a thick head of white hair. Next to Tito was a young, gorgeous man with bedroom eyes and thick dark hair curling around his ears. She learned this was Lidia and Manny's son, Marco. The pretty blonde next to him was introduced as his wife, Olivia.

Corks popped, wineglasses were filled, and Celeste and Jack served plates of takeout from Liz's Café.

"So you're here for the summer?" Olivia asked.

"I'm not sure for how long," Gemma said. "I'll be heading back to the city at some point."

"Yeah, that's what I said when I first got here. Now my husband and I work together on the oyster farm."

"Amazing," Gemma said.

"It's a lot of hard work. But it's his passion, so now it's mine, too. You can't separate the Barros men from the water."

Everyone at the table was talking about summer work, going on about how "the season" was the time when everyone had to hunker down and wring as much revenue as possible out of everything. Gemma, meanwhile, just kept eating like it was her last meal. In addition to the Italian food from Liz's Café, Lidia had brought over codfish cakes, baked oysters, and grilled shrimp with garlic and cilantro.

"Is it too early to put in menu requests for Fourth of July?" said Jack's cousin Tito. "I think we were light on the dessert last year."

"You've got to be kidding me," said Lidia.

"We won't miss it this year," Celeste said. "Promise!"

Watching the banter, Gemma felt an unfamiliar sensation, something like belonging or contentment. It was the feeling that there was nowhere else to be, no one better to be with. It felt like family.

After dinner, Celeste stood to clear the dishes. Marco stood to help but she insisted she had it covered.

"Oh, let him help," Olivia said. "Maybe he'll enjoy it so much he'll try it out at home."

"Very funny," Marco said.

Tito launched into a story about tourists he took out for a seal-watching tour who wanted their money back when the seals didn't swim close enough to the boat.

"It's going to be a long summer," Tito said.

"I thought you'd be excited for summer, Uncle Tito," said Marco. "You could take Iris McGinty out for a sail, a little dinner on the beach . . ."

"We broke up," Tito said.

"What? Since when?" everyone at the table seemed to ask at once. Gemma basked in the warm glow of all the affection volleying back and forth. She felt herself smiling.

"Months ago. She said her children don't

approve. She's so recently widowed."

"Sean died eight years ago," said Jack.

Gemma's phone beeped with a text. It was Sanjay.

Okay I'll do it.

She breathed a sigh of relief. She knew she owed him one, for this, and for so much else.

Your the best, she typed back, purposefully writing "your" instead of "you're" because he told her once he broke up with someone because she didn't know the difference and they'd laughed about it so hard it became a private joke between them. She waited for his response, watched three dots form, and then disappear.

Okay, well, at least he was coming. That was the important thing. And as for where all of her stuff would go, she had an idea for that, too: Across from her bedroom on the third floor, there was an empty room with a skylight. It would be a perfect studio — or at least a staged studio for the purpose of taking photographs. She'd just have to ask her aunt if she could use it.

Lidia offered to help her with the dishes. Celeste would typically tell her to sit and relax, but it was the only way she could get her alone to talk. Halfway through dinner, the engagement ring burning on her finger, she realized the one person who could possibly help her with the dilemma was someone who had also joined the Barros family from the outside: Lidia.

In the kitchen, the light fading outside as the nocturnal insects began to peep — not nearly as loud as they would be by late summer but enough to make the outdoors feel alive — Lidia rinsed the dishes while Celeste dried. The music and laughter from the yard drifted in the open window.

"Lidia, can I talk to you about something?" Celeste said.

"Of course. Anything." She smiled at her and adjusted her yellow rubber glove.

Celeste took a deep breath. "It's just . . . I'm not sure about this engagement."

Lidia immediately turned off the faucet and looked at her, concerned.

"Don't get me wrong — I love Jack. I want to be with him always," she said, suddenly feeling foolish. "We're so happy together. I don't want to change anything by getting married."

"Okay. But now, don't you think things will change if you *don't* get married?" Lidia said.

"Well, yes. I feel damned if I do, damned if I don't. If I go through with it, I'll resent

Jack. If I don't, he'll resent me. I don't know what to do."

Lidia gestured for her to sit down with her at the kitchen table.

"What's the real problem here, Celeste?"

She hesitated, knowing that what she was going to say would sound questionable at best. But she needed to get it off her chest, and if she couldn't talk to Lidia, she couldn't talk to anyone. "Bad luck comes to the women who get engaged in my family."

Lidia frowned. "What do you mean, 'bad luck'?"

"I mean . . . tragedy."

"Oh, come on. You really believe that? I know you're into astrology but —"

The kitchen screen door opened again, and Gemma walked in carrying plates.

"Oh, Gemma, you don't have to do that. We've got it," Celeste said.

"I don't mind," Gemma said. She set the plates on the counter and lingered.

Lidia, understanding they couldn't continue the conversation in front of her, said, "Dear, go on outside and enjoy yourself. We've got the cleanup under control."

"Actually, I wanted to ask you something, Aunt Celeste," Gemma said. "Can I use the spare room across the hall from my bedroom just for a little? I need my jewelry-making equipment."

She looked nervous, as though she were requesting something huge. Celeste told her yes, of course she could use it for as long as she needed. Really, she was thankful for the interruption.

It was clear from even their brief chat that Lidia wouldn't see her perspective on the engagement issue. Now she wished she hadn't brought it up.

She needed to consult with Maud.

32

A week without progress. How much more time could she waste in the middle of nowhere, waiting for Celeste to sign the papers? The answer: not much. Elodie had to push things along. But how?

The early morning sun cast a pink glow on the bay. All was quiet except for a chorus of birds, including an owl hooting somewhere nearby. On the dock, two men wearing high rubber boots climbed into a small boat.

Still wearing her pajamas and robe, she carried Pearl down the deck stairs to the street level. Pearl had made such a fuss upstairs that Elodie worried she didn't have time to dress or she'd risk an accident in the room.

Elodie had never understood people's complaints about how much work it was to have a dog. She now realized that was because she hadn't done most of that work.

At Commercial, she bent down and fastened Pearl's leash. Then she tugged her along toward the beach but hadn't gotten half a block before Pearl stopped to do her business. While she waited for her, she spotted Tito heading up the street with Bart in tow.

"You're out early," she said.

"I could say the same to you," he said. "I'd have waited if I knew you'd be on the crack-of-dawn shift."

Elodie smiled. "This is unusual. I'm going to try to get her back on a later schedule. In the city I have a dog walker, so it's enough of an adjustment without starting at this ungodly hour."

"A dog walker?" he said. "You mean, when you're away on a vacation?"

"No," she said. "Every day."

He laughed. "You're pulling my leg."

"No," she said slowly, suddenly self-conscious. "Why would you think that?"

"You pay someone, every day, to walk your own dog?"

"Well . . . yes."

He laughed harder.

"I don't see what's so funny." She crossed her arms.

"It just seems like a waste," he said.

"I can afford it."

"No. I mean, it's a waste to have a dog but not really care for it. These morning walks with Bart are my favorite time of the day. I wouldn't miss them for the world."

"Well, I find it to be a chore," she said. "And that has nothing to do with my love for Pearl. It's just grunt work."

"So you're one of those people who paid someone to diaper your kids," he said.

"I don't have children," she said.

"No? Me neither," he said. "I was too busy working."

"Me too," she said, and smiled. "But I thought women were the only ones who had to choose between parenthood and career. At least, that was the prevailing wisdom when I was growing up."

The truth was, work had nothing to do with her childless lifestyle. She had no desire to be a single mother and had simply never found a romantic partner, at least not one that stuck. There had been a few dalliances with men who ran in her circles, people she could call when she needed someone on her arm for this benefit or that, and people who called on her for the same. But it had rarely gone beyond that, and if it did, she always pulled herself back from the edge of developing any real feelings.

"The sea is a demanding mistress," Tito said.

Her phone rang. Sloan Pierce. Again. She sent it to voicemail.

"Well, who needs kids and marriage? We have our four-legged children."

"True. But I gotta admit I think about it sometimes. You don't?"

"No," she said quickly. "Never. I'm devoted to my work. Relationships have always seemed a messy distraction to me."

Tito seemed to consider that. Pearl sniffed around Bart and began straining on the leash. "I should get going. She needs exercise."

Tito gave her a small salute and began walking toward the house. But then he turned and called out to her. "I have a thought, just an idea to make walking her less of a . . . chore. What if we meet up in the morning and keep each other company?"

Well, why not? She missed seeing her usual people in the city. The doormen. Her dry cleaner. The woman at Eli's who made her cappuccino. It might be nice to have a Provincetown routine.

"I like that idea," she said. "Just not the crack-of-dawn shift."

■ ■ ■ ■

"If you have any questions, just ask. And don't feel intimidated: Most customers walking into the store during the summer know less about all this stuff than you do," Jack said.

He was so kind, and a seemingly endless font of information. Gemma followed him around the store, listening more than talking and feeling, happily, like she was back in school.

She picked up a colorful glass bowl. It was floral on the outside and deep pink on the inside and the waffled edges were gilt.

"That's called a bride's basket," Jack said. "It's colored Victorian glass. That edge there? It's quatrefoil."

"How old is it?" she asked.

"That piece is circa 1885."

She checked the price tag: seventy-two dollars.

"Is this missing a zero?" she asked. He told her no, that was the price. When she said surely they could get more for it, he explained, "The market for Victorian glass is soft right now. It's selling for half the price it was just eight years ago."

"Why?" By her logic, eight extra years

added that much more to its pedigree as an antique.

"That's the way things are in this business. There's no absolute value. It's mostly perception, and supply and demand."

Interesting. Very different from dealing in gold and other precious metals.

"So did you get into the antiques business first or did Celeste?"

He smiled. "This was all Celeste's idea. I'm just along for the ride. But I did get on board quickly to impress her. I guess I did my homework."

His unabashed affection for her aunt was really very sweet.

"Speaking of Celeste, have you seen her this morning?" he said. Gemma shook her head.

A customer walked in, and Jack moved behind the counter to give her the space to spread her wings. Gemma approached the man perusing a display of candlesticks and cut-glass vases.

"Let me know if I can be any help," Gemma said.

He turned to her and she recognized him as the guy from the art gallery. He was even more handsome than she remembered, with long eyelashes and flecks of gold in his blue eyes.

"I need a gift for my mother," he said.

"Great. Um, birthday?"

"No. It's an apology gift."

"Oh. Okay. Well, those two candlesticks you're looking at are both brass. But the one with the wider base is more valuable. It's from Spain, late 1500s."

"Do you know the provenance of every piece in this store?" he said, looking at her closely. He seemed amused. Or impressed. She couldn't decipher his expression except to say it was one of interest.

"Not yet," she said. "I just started working here. It's my aunt's store."

He smiled and held out his hand. "Connor Harrison," he said. "I believe we met at my gallery the other day."

"Gemma Maybrook," she said. He held her hand just a beat longer than it took to shake.

"I'll take the Spanish candlesticks," he said. "And . . . your number?" He grinned in a way that was almost irresistible.

Almost.

"I think we should keep our relationship professional," she said. "But if you irritate any more of your relatives, you know where to find me."

Maud could only fit her in first thing in the

morning, before she started her day at the restaurant, where Alvie was already doing prep.

"So what seems to be the emergency?" she asked as Celeste settled into her lawn chair, swatting away a bee.

"Your last reading was spot on," she said. "My sister showed up for the first time since I've lived here. And then my niece, whom I haven't seen in fifteen years. And then, Jack's proposal."

"All good things," Maud said.

"Well, on the surface. But you know how I feel about marriage."

"Because of the curse," Maud said, her eyes soft with empathy.

"I can't tell him that. But . . . yes."

Maud was the only person aside from Lidia she'd confided in about the whispers of a curse in her family. They'd parsed the idea endlessly, the way a person might examine their early childhood with a psychiatrist. They compared the history of the Electric Rose to other cursed diamonds, the most famous being the rare, blue, forty-five-carat Hope Diamond.

Four centuries ago, the Hope was stolen from a Sita idol in India, and the thief was soon after killed by dogs. Every subsequent owner suffered financial ruin or premature death. Then there was the Black Orlov, originally 195 carats, which was set as one of the eyes in a statue of the Hindu god Brahma. It was also stolen from India; a diamond dealer brought it to the U.S. in 1932, before jumping out of the window of a Manhattan skyscraper. The Russian princesses who later acquired the diamond also leapt to their deaths.

"A curse starts with a transgression," Maud told her years ago. "The notoriously cursed diamonds were all stolen. Your family was the first and only owner of the Electric Rose."

She had a point. And yet, the minute her father brought the diamond into the family, bad luck started. Elodie lost her first love when Paulina was summoned home for publicity, her parents became embattled for the remainder of their marriage, and ultimately Paulina and her husband were killed in a freak accident, leaving their daughter orphaned. Even *The New York Times* mentioned the curse in Paulina's obituary. She believed her relationship with Jack had remained unscathed only because they never tempted fate by getting engaged.

"Celeste, I've known you and Jack a long time. Speaking as your friend here, I don't want you to let this get in the way of your happiness."

She looked at her incredulously. "What's that supposed to mean? You suddenly don't believe in these things now that you're happy with Alvie?" She hated herself for lashing out, but Maud's new skepticism felt like a betrayal when she needed an ally the most.

Maud didn't flinch.

"I believe it takes a lot of factors for bad luck to dominate a situation. You have to look at the entire picture. I would never want to see a client act or not act based on one reading, or one element in the overall universe."

Celeste pulled a rubber band from her wrist and gathered her hair into a knot. "Well, let's see what the cards have to say."

With the deck in her hands, she felt steadier than she had since the moment she set eyes on the engagement ring. The familiar motion of shuffling was like a big exhale.

Maud turned her first card over. The Tower.

"How's that for the entire picture?" she said, heart pounding. The Tower indicated danger. Crisis. Destruction.

"You still have to pull two more cards," Maud said. "We don't know what it means yet."

Celeste stood up, her legs shaky. "I'm afraid I know everything I need to know."

33

The orders came in overnight, a flurry of requests after she posted photos of her Rock Candy rings against the backdrop of the water. She was counting the minutes until Sanjay arrived tomorrow with her equipment. Now she didn't need them just for the photo shoot: She'd have to create new pieces to replenish her inventory.

At eight in the morning she walked up Commercial to the post office, a redbrick building in the center of town, to buy packing material and get her pieces out to customers.

She knew she couldn't keep going like this forever: a one-woman operation schlepping jewelry in her backpack to the post office every day, secretly checking her Instagram all day long while trying to work a paying job. She was starting to wonder if she was delusional about having a real business. That guy Jacob Jabarin had been right. Of course he was right; that's why he was a billionaire investor and she was at the mercy of her ex-boyfriend and a U-Haul.

But Provincetown made it hard to sink into a truly bad mood. Early risers were rewarded with spectacular light and a calm before the tourist storm on the main drag.

After the post office, she took a walk to quiet her anxiety and ended up across the street from the Harrison Gallery. Two men carried a large painting wrapped in brown paper up the stairs. One of them was Connor.

Her first impulse was to duck behind a street sign covered in winding vines. But she was too late; with a double take, Connor set down his end of the painting.

"We've got to stop meeting like this," he said, walking toward her.

"Don't let me interrupt."

"I was just finishing up and about to get some coffee," he said, calling out to the other guy to take five. "Care to join me?"

"I'm fully caffeinated, thanks," she said.

"If I can't interest you in coffee, maybe a little sun and sand? It's a great beach day."

A beach day? She barely knew the guy.

"Thanks, but I don't even own a bathing suit," she said.

"I promise you won't get wet," he said.

She startled for a moment at the possible double entendre, but the expression on his face was neutral. Innocent.

She shook her head. "I should get going."

"Consider it an act of charity. I need to come up with some gift ideas. I've alienated at *least* two or three members of my family this week."

She laughed and was surprised at how good it felt. Really, what was the harm? It was a trip to the beach, not a marriage proposal. And she needed to get her mind off work.

They rode to the beach in Connor's Range Rover. The short drive had the perfection of a Coca-Cola ad: the weather, the sun-dappled bay on the left, the salt marshes populated by cranes and herons. Gemma couldn't help but think, *This is not my life.*

But it used to be.

As a child, she'd traveled endlessly with her parents: Phuket, the Amalfi Coast, Andalusia, Corfu, the Côte d'Azur. And then, her world became confined to rural Pennsylvania.

A year ago, one of her friends invited her along on a trip to the Hamptons, and Gemma felt completely out of her element. But Provincetown was like a welcoming pair of outstretched arms.

The Herring Cove parking lot was nearly full. Even before she set foot on the sand she could see the untamed, expansive beauty of the place. They walked down a blue tarp framed by shrubbery and wildflowers. A posted notice warned people to be mindful of their dogs at night because of the coyotes. Other signs offered trivia about local birds.

The beaches, Connor explained, were a part of protected federal wetlands.

"Some of the greatest natural wildlife in the country can be found right here," he said.

Connor knew a lot about Cape Cod. He'd grown up in Boston and spent summers in nearby Chatham with his family. She tried to stay focused on his chatter, to be in the present. But her mind kept slipping into the past. Perhaps it was being back by the water. Or all the thinking about the Electric Rose. Either way, in that moment, she was mentally eight years old again, waking up in a strange hotel room, surprised to find her grandmother had suddenly arrived. The sinking feeling in her stomach.

"Tell me more about the gallery and how that all came together," she said, trying to bring herself back to the beach.

"The art world is intense. And risky," he said.

She nodded. "What world isn't?"

"Antique shops?"

She smiled. "It's my aunt's store. I'm sure she has her own stress."

For two hours, they watched the waves roll in and out. They talked about music, movies, the restaurants in Provincetown. It was unspoken, but they both clearly avoided any serious topics. As usual, she didn't talk about herself. And like most people, Connor didn't notice. She'd read once that the surest way for another person to find you interesting was if they do all the talking.

"Well . . . thanks," she said when Connor dropped her off on Commercial Street. He'd offered to drive her home, but she said she wanted to walk a bit, so he parked the car in a lot on the East End.

"How about dinner tomorrow night?" he said.

She hesitated. "Look, today was fun. But I'm not planning on being here much longer."

"Big plans back in the city."

"Yep. World domination."

"I'd expect no less," he said. "How about this: I just might pop into the store now and then to see if you're still around. I wouldn't call it stalking exactly, but if you're still around . . . then dinner?"

He looked so sincere, so deeply hopeful, she could only nod. Maybe, just maybe, this change of scenery would change her luck.

34

Paulina, January 1994

The photography studio bordered Alphabet City, which had a fabulous edgy energy that was unmatched anywhere in the world. Paulina had loved this area of New York, but still, it wasn't enough to keep her rooted in her hometown. She couldn't stay in any one place for too long; she'd had to really fight her parents to drop out of college, just barely convincing them that she'd learn more traveling the world.

After today's Pavlin & Co "Electric Rose" shoot, she'd be jumping back on a plane, looking for the next adventure. The tickets were in her bag, and a friend was on standby to meet her in Africa for a trip to a wildlife sanctuary. But for today: work.

The music was already blasting when she walked into the studio — Tupac's "Keep Ya Head Up" — and the space was buzzing with the energy of the stylists and makeup artists and the photography crew. Paulina enjoyed modeling — she'd done a bunch of it in high school, a lot in Europe. She loved the constant go-go-go, which was how she caught the travel bug. But since she didn't need the money, after a while she shook herself free of the punishing schedule and unrelenting pressure and just kept the travel part.

She arrived to set dressed in tight jeans, a simple white buttondown shirt with the sleeves rolled up, and Converse sneakers. She wore ropes of gold chains around her neck, including one dangling with animal-shaped charms. Her Prada bag was a gift from Miuccia herself after a night of partying together in Milan.

A Black guy dressed in leather pants and a Soundgarden T-shirt ushered her into the makeup chair. It was a typical fashion scene except for the armed guards; they had the Electric Rose on the set.

She spotted her sister's boyfriend hovering near wardrobe. Paulina was happy for Elodie. Liam Maybrook was incredibly attractive and seemed liked a genuinely nice guy. Elodie was moody and never had a positive thing to say to her, but Paulina hoped now that she was getting laid regularly she'd be more cheerful.

"Hey — didn't know you were going to be here," she called out to him. "Is Elodie coming, too?"

He shook his head. "Just me. You excited?"

She gave Liam a thumbs-up and sat for the makeup artist. His name was Sebastian, and he did not look happy.

"I told them minimalism was the way to go with the makeup but they're insisting on going heavy glam," Sebastian said. This didn't surprise Paulina; her parents weren't exactly cutting edge. Her mother still thought it was the 1980s.

"Let's go rogue," Paulina said. Sebastian shook his head of blond dreadlocks. He couldn't. He was paid to follow the art direction, not to improvise. "Liam, come here for a sec."

He strolled over, checking his watch. "We're getting a little behind schedule. Everything okay?" he asked.

"Well, this will save us some time: I don't want makeup. Just some mascara and lip gloss."

Liam looked confused. "That's going to read washed-out on camera," he said.

"Washed-out is in. Look, why not let the diamond be the only shiny, glittering thing in the photos? It will be so much cooler that way." She glanced at the racks of clothing.

"And I'm not wearing fur, so you might as well just get rid of those."

"She *does* look pretty fab just the way she is," Sebastian said.

Liam crossed his arms. "The art direction was carefully thought out and your father signed off on it."

Paulina jumped out of her seat and walked over to the clothes. Ralph Lauren, Escada, Armani. *Boring.*

"Are you trying to make me look like a Beverly Hills housewife?" she said.

"Who do you think is shopping at Pavlin & Co?" Liam said.

He had a point.

"Please, go get the makeup done. I'll be right back."

When she was in the makeup chair, her face covered in foundation and midway through the application of fake eyelashes, Liam stood in front of her with a velvet jewelry case. Behind him, two burly security guards stood close watch.

"I thought this would help you get into the right frame of mind," he said, opening the case to show her the Electric Rose. Paulina, exposed to precious gems her entire life, afforded almost every luxury imaginable, still felt awestruck at the sight of it. She held out her left hand and he slipped it on her ring finger.

"Fine, fine, this is worth wearing fake eyelashes for," she said, laughing. She held her hand up against her shoulder, wagging her ring finger. "Amazing."

"It suits you," he said. "Now let's do this."

After ten hours in heavy makeup and furs under bright lights, Paulina needed to let off steam. Live music and tequila shots would do the trick.

"Let's go to Brownies," she said to the crew when they wrapped, suggesting the hole-in-the-wall bar on Avenue A that always had the best bands.

She didn't expect Liam to come along; even though he was only a few years older than she was, he was a suit — he looked it, he acted it, he lived it. When she told him this, he laughed.

"Even suits need to have fun once in a while," he said with a wink.

The band that night was an all-female group from Portland called Dorothy Is Dead. The commercial crew filled two tables up front. Paulina was back in her street clothes but still had a face full of makeup and felt out of place. She told this to Liam after their first round of shots.

"I should have stuck to my principles on

the makeup," she said, annoyed with the smear of lipstick on her shot glass.

"It's a job, Paulina. We all make compromises. Just be thankful you don't have to go to an office every day."

"You don't like advertising?"

"I mean, I like it. But it's not what I would choose to do if I could do anything I wanted." Their gazes met as a lock of dark hair, damp with perspiration, fell against his cheek. She had the urge to brush it away. She wanted an excuse to touch him, and it horrified her.

"Um, so what would you do?" she said, trying to even her breathing.

"Travel the world."

She bit her lip. "Now I feel bad."

"Why should *you* feel bad?"

"Because I get to travel all the time."

He nodded. "I know. I think that's great. You have an adventurous spirit."

"I guess we both do." She looked into his intense navy-blue eyes. He truly was gorgeous. She forced herself to look away, down at his hands with long tapered fingers like a piano player's. It took all of her will not to lean forward and kiss him.

She reached into her bag for a cigarette.

"So where's your next adventure?" he said.

"Africa. I'm leaving for a safari tomorrow

to meet up with some friends." She lit up, took a deep drag, and told him the details of her two-week itinerary. "I want to see lions roaming free. I want to experience something totally outside of regular life." Yes, in twenty-four hours she would be far away. And she'd never think about her sister's boyfriend again.

He nodded. "I get that. I've always wanted to see elephants in the wild, in all their majesty. It must be awe-inspiring."

"Well, someday you and Elodie can go." Although her sister's idea of travel was a jaunt to London for a jewelry conference.

"I'm going to end things with your sister," Liam said abruptly.

"What?" She turned to him, squinting to see through the dim lighting and haze of smoke.

"Yeah. To be honest, I've been avoiding it because I don't want it to get awkward with work."

"But why? You guys seem . . . happy."

"I thought we were. Happy enough. But then, the night your father made the announcement with the Electric Rose? I knew in that second it was over." His voice grew more animated, his words tumbling out faster and faster. "Elodie looked so excited, and I just knew I didn't want to be that person — the one to propose. Not to her, at least."

"Okay, you're freaking me out. Don't break up with her. It's all good." Paulina didn't want to hear that her sister was about to get her heart broken. She wanted to forget this conversation ever happened. More, she wanted to forget her own unwelcome urges.

"It's *not* all good," he said. "I don't love her. Doesn't she deserve that?"

Paulina stood up. "I'm going to the bar to get another round. What do you want?"

Liam stood, too. "I'll get the drinks."

"And for the record," she said, unsteady on her feet but not sitting down. "You can learn to love someone. So just . . . learn to love her."

He looked at her, his face serious.

"I can never love her," he said. And then, his voice lower and calmer, "I want to spend more time with you."

"With me? *Why?*"

"I don't know," he said. "Ever since that dinner at your parents' — the night before the Electric Rose launch — I've been thinking about you. I've tried not to, but it's like . . . your face and your voice . . . like one of those songs you get in your head playing over and over. And with Elodie, it was never like that. We made sense together on paper. And I do like her. But I can't pretend I'm not feeling what I'm feeling right now. Even though this is not good on paper. Not good any way you look at it."

Paulina sat back in her seat, biting her lip. No, this wasn't good. Not at all.

"I'm leaving tomorrow for my trip. That should give you some time to forget about me. And I'm going to pretend this conversation never happened," she said, standing up to leave.

Her flight couldn't come fast enough.

35

"It's just temporary," Gemma said, uncomfortable with how quickly Celeste's spare room filled up. Sanjay and Jack carried her folding workbench, side drawers, and chair up three flights of stairs. And her Flexshaft motor for her various drills and cutters. *And* those various drills and cutters.

"Seems like the perfect fit to me," Celeste said. "Like the room was meant for this."

Sanjay took a swig from his water bottle. The room didn't have a ceiling fan and the breeze through the open window did little to combat the heat. She watched him while trying not to look like she was watching him. His thick dark hair was slightly longer, and the summer clothes — crew-neck T-shirt, cargo shorts — reminded her of his off-the-charts body.

"What a good friend you are to make this trip for Gemma," said Celeste.

"Well, it's not entirely selfless," Sanjay

said. "I've heard all about the legendary Provincetown light. I'm not sure if Gemma mentioned, but I'm a photographer, so I brought my camera and plan to make the most of it."

Celeste nodded with enthusiasm. "Painters and photographers come here from all over the world. Starting with, oh, Charles Hawthorne back in the 1890s. There was Jackson Pollock, Lee Krasner, Franz Kline, Max Ernst, Helen Frankenthaler. I don't know as much about photographers but I'm sure you're in good company."

Sanjay grinned. "I'm looking forward to the sunset tonight."

Gemma wanted to see it with him, but she wasn't holding her breath for an invitation.

"Where are you staying?" Celeste said.

"Alvie hooked him up with a room at Maud's," Gemma said.

"Oh, don't be silly! I have an extra bedroom down the hall. I know I really should rent out the rooms but I've never gotten used to the idea of having strangers in my house all summer. That's how you know I'm not a native Cape Codder."

Gemma didn't dare look at Sanjay, silently bargaining with the gods of fate to let him accept the offer.

"Thanks, that's very generous of you," Sanjay said. "But I don't want to cancel on the other house at the last minute." His voice and expression were so even-keeled, she could almost believe him. There was nearly no tension, no hint of subtext: *I can't stand sleeping under the same roof as my ex.*

Stop thinking like that, she told herself. He was there. That was all that mattered.

Celeste left for the shop, and Sanjay checked his phone. Gemma fidgeted with her bench pin, an attachment that functioned like a third hand when she was drilling or filing. Reunited with her equipment, she was itching to get back to work. But even more than that, she found she wanted to spend time with Sanjay. The way her heart fluttered when he pulled up to the curb in the U-Haul was like if a dozen birds took flight in her chest.

"Thanks again, Sanjay. You're a lifesaver."

He looked up. "No problem. Like I said, I'm going to make the most of the trip."

An awkward silence settled between them.

"So . . . the interview's tomorrow?" he said.

She nodded.

"Okay, I need to drop off the truck and then I'm going to head over to the house." He pulled his duffel bag over one shoulder.

"Can I at least buy you dinner? As a thank-you, I mean."

Their eyes met, and she knew — *she knew* — from the expression in his that he wanted to say yes.

"It's fine. You already said thanks." He gave her a complicated look, one that was part pity, part regret. He brushed past her, out of the room. She followed him into the hallway. Before he reached the stairs he turned. "Good luck tomorrow. Enjoy your moment. You deserve it."

And then he was gone.

Elodie, not a patient woman to begin with, was losing the last of her forbearance.

Every day, she made a solid effort to irritate her sister. She loitered around that antiques shop of hers, she reminded her that she wasn't going anywhere until the papers were signed — she'd moved into Jack's family's house, for heaven's sake! And nothing. Celeste had clearly become too comfortable with Elodie's presence in town.

It was time to make her uncomfortable.

The empty storefront on Commercial was sandwiched between a T-shirt shop and a bakery. The past few days she'd tried calling the number posted in the window for leasing, but no one ever answered. Things were clearly not very buttoned up in this town, and so she would have to try a different tack. Today, she was going to make an attempt in person.

She found the front door propped open.

"Hello?" she said, stepping over copies of the *Cape Cod Times* and *ptownie* magazine left in the doorway. She almost collided with a ladder.

"Whoa — careful down there!"

Elodie looked up and found Tito perched near the ceiling, working on dangling wires.

"Tito?"

"Elodie? What are you doing here?"

Trying to save my company. And yes, it was starting to feel like that *was* just how important it was to get the auction underway. While she was busy putting the pressure on Celeste, her CFO was putting the pressure on her. "This is no time to be taking an extended vacation," he said during their morning phone meeting. "This is the worst June we've had in a long time."

What he didn't say was that it was also the most competition they'd ever had. Jewelry companies — especially online companies that could sell close to cost because they didn't have the expense of a physical space — were starting to cannibalize the market. It was getting more and more difficult to make the case that buying your engagement ring at Pavlin & Co was special. She needed something to resuscitate their glamorous image, their place above the rest. She needed this auction.

"I'm here to look at this space. I've called the leasing number posted in the window but I never get anyone on the phone."

Tito climbed down the steps and removed his thick gloves.

"The owner went fishing."

"Very funny," she said.

"No, literally. The family is on a fishing trip all week. I'm just helping out here with some odds and ends until they get back."

"Oh. Well, that explains things, I suppose."

"You want to lease this space?" His dark eyes focused on her with a sharp intensity she hadn't noticed before. He was actually quite attractive, in a ruggedly handsome sort of way. Not her type, of course. But then, she didn't have a type. She was finished with all that nonsense.

"I'm thinking about it, yes."

He seemed amused. "For what?"

"Well, as you know, I'm in the jewelry business. I was thinking of opening a little summer outpost here, a sort of . . . Pavlin & Co by the sea." The idea came to her shortly after her CFO's latest alarming email. Did she have any actual interest in opening a shop in that town? Of course not. But she was certain that as soon as her sister got wind of the news, she'd change her mind about continuing to delay the auction contract.

"Well, that's a fine idea," he said. "Tourists seem to love buying jewelry while they're here. Not sure why. It seems people splurge for things on vacation they wouldn't spend a dime on at home." He smiled at her. "Can I give you a tour?"

She didn't need a tour. She could see the entire space from her vantage point in the doorway. But for some reason, she didn't mind the excuse to spend a few more minutes with her housemate.

She smiled back. "That would be delightful."

Race Point Beach at sunset was one of Provincetown's great gifts. One of life's great gifts, really. Celeste followed the narrow path shrouded in tall seagrass, Jack a few paces ahead carrying their folding chairs. When they cleared the dunes, the wide expanse of deep blue sea seemed to stretch into infinity.

The afternoon revelers had decamped to the bars and restaurants, leaving a mellow crowd of mostly couples patiently waiting for the famed sunset.

They settled into the chairs and Jack passed her the mini thermos filled with chilled rosé they picked up from Perry's on the way. She took a sip and dug her toes into the sand.

"So you've officially given up the entire third floor to Gemma," Jack said, smiling at her.

"Not the entire third floor. There's still the other spare bedroom."

"I'm just teasing you."

"You're the one who wanted me to be more in touch with my family. So . . . be careful what you wish for," she said.

"There's only one thing I've been wishing for, and you've given it to me," he said, reaching for her left hand, the diamond winking in the sun. Celeste smiled, her stomach tightening. "We need to start making some plans, though. Have you given any thought to who should officiate? And where you want to have the ceremony?"

"I haven't," she said, feeling like the world's most delinquent bride-to-be.

"Maybe Clifford Henry could officiate? He did a great job at Tom and Aaron's wedding last summer."

She nodded. "I'll talk to him."

"And we need to figure out the guest list. You really should invite your sister, you know."

"Oh, Jack. Don't start with that. I doubt she'll even be out here in August. I'm going to sign the paperwork she wants. Hopefully, that will set a good example for Gemma and she'll do the same. I just want Elodie to tell her where the ring is . . . for closure. And then we can all move on." Herself especially. The past few days she'd allowed herself the small hope that maybe the ring was somehow gone, and that's why Elodie was being evasive. If it was out of the family, she was in the clear. She would be free of the curse.

"Celeste, that competition was a lifetime ago. I think everyone has moved on. You're holding on to the past."

It was low tide and the receding water left a band of stones and shells. An older man with linen pants rolled up to his knees picked through them, collecting some into a reusable shopping bag.

She turned to Jack. "The past just showed up on our doorstep. I'm doing the best I can."

It was hard for her not to think of the time when Paulina had been the one to show up on her doorstep.

Celeste had just moved to Provincetown a

few weeks earlier, and she and Nathan were just settling into their rooms at the Barroses'. They had a routine meeting every morning for coffee in the kitchen, served by Mrs. Barros, along with homemade Portuguese rolls. Then they went off to work, Celeste at an antiques shop, Nathan at his writing space. At the end of the day, they met up again for drinks before heading home together.

One night, they reached the house sometime close to nine and spotted a couple on the second-story deck. It was just about dark out, only a faint stripe of fading pink in the sky, endless stars, and a bright three-quarter moon. Celeste remembered the way light seemed to play tricks with them at that hour; the couple on the porch seemed to radiate their own glow. They didn't see Celeste and Nathan approach, they were so wrapped around each other, kissing in a way that felt obscene to have stumbled upon.

That's when Celeste recognized the unmistakable long blond hair.

"Paulina?"

Her sister scrambled to her feet, the man standing up beside her. They held hands. The man looked familiar, but it took her a few seconds to place him: Elodie's boyfriend.

"Hey. Sorry to just show up like this. I left you a message on your machine."

Sensing the tension, Nathan continued inside, leaving the three of them alone.

Standing in the moonlight, urging Paulina to keep her voice down so they didn't disturb the Barroses, Celeste listened calmly while the story came pouring out: They were in love, neither of them planned this, they tried to stop it but they were soul mates.

They both kept saying the same thing: "It just happened."

Now they needed to tell Elodie. And they wanted her help.

"I'm not okay with this," Celeste said, looking up at the stars and wondering what to do. As the eldest, she'd always felt removed from the scrum of competition between her younger sisters. Although, if she was being honest, it was really a one-way competition: Elodie had always been jealous of Paulina and never the reverse. It was their mother's fault; Constance fawned over the baby, never failing to mention her beauty while always chiding Elodie for being bookish and dowdy.

Her first instinct was to tell Paulina to back off — to throw this particular fish back into the sea when there were so many others readily available to her. But confronted with the pair, their hands entwined, the palpable energy sparking between them, she knew it was a lost cause.

"I don't want to hurt Elodie," Paulina said. "That's why we waited so long. We both hoped this would pass, that we'd get it out of our system."

"I knew it wouldn't pass," Liam said, gazing at her adoringly.

Celeste shifted uncomfortably. "Look, things happen. Fine. But why are you dragging me into this?"

She already knew the answer. Elodie adored Celeste. She looked up to her more than she respected her own mother. Celeste was the one who turned her on to Virginia Woolf and Charlotte Perkins Gilman. Who introduced her to great works of art and the importance of history. Celeste and Elodie were the only two in the family who had true intellectual curiosity, and that had always been Elodie's escape from the demands of life in the Pavlin orbit.

"I thought if *you* told her, if you somehow suggested that we can all get through this . . ." Paulina said.

"I'm sorry," Celeste said. "I can't condone this. And I don't want to be a part of it. I love you, but you're on your own with this one, kiddo."

She let Paulina and Liam crash in her room for the night under the condition that they go back to New York the following day and talk to Elodie. "No matter how difficult the truth is, a lie is always worse."

The decision the following morning to visit the beach had been a last-minute one. After a sleepless night of thinking about this disastrous turn of events, obsessing about it from every angle, Celeste felt more compassion for Paulina. Her youngest sister wasn't malicious, but she was spoiled and naïve. There was no scenario in which this was going to go well.

She didn't want Paulina to leave on a bad note and suggested a quick walk on Race Point Beach as long as they discussed anything *but* Elodie. The walk had been innocent. But it came back to bite all three of them. Badly.

Celeste, consumed with the memory, zoned out and missed the sunset. The beach erupted in applause as it always did for nature's light show. Jack leaned over and kissed her.

"Another day in paradise," he said.

Yes. It was their paradise. And she intended to keep it that way.

36

Gemma recognized the *New York Times* reporter, but couldn't place where she'd seen her before. Regan O'Rourke was in her fifties, with sleek orange-red hair, pale brows, and no makeup except for lipstick in an ill-advised shade of coral. She wore a navy linen dress that buttoned up the front and small gold hoop earrings. She arrived at Celeste's house at precisely the agreed-upon time.

"The camera crew will come on a separate day," Regan told her in advance. It took some of the pressure off, but Gemma still dressed carefully in a simple white T-shirt and jeans, her hair pulled back in a ponytail. She wanted to let her jewelry take center stage, and wore two necklaces, one short chain and one long, both gold-plated, with charms, including a vintage "Y" cutout subway token, a Casterbridge letter "G," a gold-plated key to Gramercy Park, and a purple Met admissions button she set in a bezel. She wore citrine and aquamarine rings from Rock Candy stacked on her right forefinger.

They sat across from each other at the picnic table in Celeste's backyard. Kate Bush music emanated from a neighbor's house. The sun was bright overhead, so Gemma put up the table umbrella. Across the lawn, a baby bunny lifted its head from the grass.

Regan put her phone on the table. "Do you mind if I record our conversation?"

Gemma realized where she'd seen her before: the Pavlin & Co party last month.

"Sure," she said, shifting uneasily.

"So tell me about your work. What makes you different from other designers? What's your brand?"

Gemma took a breath. "My brand, GEMMA, is about personalization and sustainability. Everything is designed to be personal to the wearer. That's also why I want my work to be affordable. My first collection, Rock Candy, was inspired by birthstones. I created a high-end version and lower price-point versions in colored glass and base metals." She held out her hand with the citrine.

"And your necklace? That's from your

NYSD award-winning collection, Old New York, correct?"

Gemma nodded. "It's all charm jewelry. The first pieces were inspired by the Casterbridge hotel. I collected all the brass letters from the guest rooms and made molds. This 'G' is one of them. Other charms are made from collectibles I found scouring flea markets around the city. All the charms have symbolic meaning for New Yorkers — like the subway tokens that were taken out of circulation sixteen years ago. Or this key to Gramercy Park."

"Great idea. And so the charms can be mixed and matched to different chains?"

"Exactly. I work in silver, brass, and gold-plated steel. My chains are custom-designed so the charms clip easily on and off. I use a large lobster clasp that I find to be the most wearer-friendly."

The reporter asked her about her studio and how much business she did online versus in physical retail sales. Without a good cover story, Gemma admitted she got booted out of her apartment for using it as a pop-up shop, and thankfully, Regan laughed. "Is that why you're on the Cape for the summer?"

"I can really focus on the work here. And I've already been to some local estate sales.

This area is full of interesting collectibles."

"So maybe we'll be seeing an Old Cape Cod collection next?" Regan said.

"I don't know. I might want to do something more general that really opens my pieces up for the individual to create their own meaning. My dream is that someone who buys a GEMMA necklace today will keep adding to it throughout his or her life. It's meant to grow with the wearer. In other generations, jewelry was something people got as gifts. Like, for some women, their first real piece of jewelry might be their engagement ring. But that's old thinking. I believe the future of jewelry is gifts to ourselves. I want us to mark our own milestones, big and small."

It was the first time she'd said the words out loud, but it instantly gave her the idea for a future collection she could call Mile Stones. She'd have to remember to write that down after the interview.

Regan smiled. "It's interesting to hear you speak of the traditional engagement ring as passé considering your family essentially put them on the map."

Gemma swallowed hard and reached for her water bottle. She'd been realistic enough to expect the question and mentally prepared for talking about the Pavlins. At least, she thought she had. Now that it was happening, it took her a moment to find her voice.

"I didn't grow up with that side of my family," she said carefully. "So it's not that remarkable that I have a different idea of jewelry."

"A different idea, maybe. But Pavlin & Co is a century-old company. It's an institution. You have no interest in designing for them?"

With that one question, Gemma felt utterly exposed, as if the woman had seen inside of her soul.

"Yes, Pavlin & Co is an institution," she said carefully.

As a teenager, she dreamed of designing for Pavlin & Co. The thought of working at the company gave her a sense that she could somehow continue her mother's legacy. Both of her parents' legacies, really. Her father had been instrumental in their advertising campaigns, and her mother had been his muse. It was only fitting that her mother's engagement ring was the most important piece in the entire Pavlin & Co collection — one of the most important diamonds in the world. Surely, Gemma was destined to be a part of that ongoing story. Jewelry design was in her blood, and where else would she direct her talent but the company her family had built?

"Don't be foolish," her nana told her. "They don't want anything to do with you. Isn't that obvious? And for the record, you're better off without them. Don't look for trouble."

Gemma didn't believe her. She waited and waited to hear from her mother's family, but the day never came. Not until she was in college, and the first of the photo albums arrived in the mail. By the time her grandmother finally reached out to her, it was too late. Gemma's heart had hardened toward the Pavlin family. The years of silence spoke loud and clear. She was unwanted. She was cast aside. Her only inheritance was grief.

So her dream changed. She wouldn't be a part of Pavlin & Co., but she would be a part of making them obsolete.

"But it's an institution of the *past,*" Gemma said, looking the reporter in the eye. "I'm all about the future. I'm looking forward. And it's a great view."

Alvie insisted on celebrating Gemma's interview and her own last day at Queen Anne's Revenge. They were going to Tea Dance at the Boatslip, a sort of dance-party happy hour. It seemed like a great idea last night when Alvie suggested it, but after talking with the reporter for hours, Gemma wasn't in the mood.

Still, she dutifully met Alvie at Maud's old Victorian with the pink shutters. On the way, she stopped at the post office to mail that day's jewelry orders. Sealing up the Priority Mail boxes, she didn't feel the usual sense of satisfaction.

She thought she handled the reporter's questions just fine. At least, on the outside. But the conversation was eating at her, hours after they shook hands and said goodbye.

Pavlin & Co is a century-old company. It's an institution. You have no interest in designing for them?

She couldn't delude herself that she was anywhere close to disrupting the conventional jewelry business — nowhere near competing with Pavlin & Co. She'd been living in a fantasy world. What had she expected? That she'd graduate from college and some billionaire would throw money at her? That they'd look at her Instagram and anoint her the second coming of Elsa Peretti? Even winning the NYSD award — the small, attainable goal she'd set for herself along the way — wasn't a game-changer. Instead of focusing on what she was doing, the reporter seemed more interested in what she *wasn't* doing. And wouldn't anyone who read the article feel the same?

The redbrick path to the house was lined with flowering bushes. While most of the homes on Commercial had neatly trimmed hydrangea bushes, the front garden of Maud's pink-shuttered Victorian was a maze of tall grass, marigolds, purple zinnias, sunflowers, and ferns. The house itself was marked with a metal plaque — one of dozens around town — designating the building as having once been the home of a notable artist.

Alvie sat on the front porch, nestled in a cushioned wicker chair with an open bottle of wine on a side table.

"Hey," Gemma said, sitting on a swinging bench across from her. "I thought you said we needed to be there by five to get a spot."

"We do," Alvie said. "This is just pregaming. No one shows up at the Boatslip sober."

Gemma accepted the glass Alvie poured for her. It was a pale white, fruity but not sweet. It went down easy and she had to force herself not to drink it too quickly. She hadn't eaten in several hours and in her frame of mind she'd be on the fast track to wasted.

She glanced at the front door, wondering if Sanjay was inside. He'd texted her earlier, asking how the interview went. She'd written back, *Fine.* She'd managed to work in a mention of him when the reporter asked about her success on Instagram. "Photography is instrumental to my business," she'd said, and told the story of how she and Sanjay began working together to launch her brand.

"Maud should be down any minute and then we can head over," Alvie said.

Gemma barely heard her because at that moment Sanjay rounded the sidewalk corner, heading to the house. He had his camera bag over one shoulder and was talking on his phone, not noticing the small group on the porch until he was almost at the steps. He abruptly ended his call.

"Hey, have a drink with us," Alvie called out. Sanjay climbed the stairs and set his camera equipment down on the ground.

"So what happened with the interview?" he said to Gemma.

"Nothing happened," she said. "I texted you that it went fine."

"Exactly. You were interviewed for the most culturally influential newspaper in the country and all you had to say about it was that it went 'fine'?"

"Maud always says that understatement is a sign of confidence," said Alvie.

As if on cue, the front door opened and Maud strolled out with a bottle of vodka in one hand and three shot glasses in the other. She was dressed in the same outfit of rolled-up jeans, black V-neck T-shirt, and white Converse high-tops that she'd worn to the engagement dinner at Celeste's.

"Hello, ladies," she said in her husky drawl. "Oh — and gentleman." She sat on the landing of the front door and set the vodka and shot glasses down beside her.

"We started with wine, babe," Alvie said.

"Wine? I thought you said we were *celebrating* tonight."

Sanjay stood, picking up his bag and pulling it back over his shoulder. "Have fun tonight."

"What do you mean? Come along," Maud said. Sanjay shook his head.

"Thanks but I want to take some photos tonight after dark. The monument, the wharf . . ."

Maud checked her Apple Watch. "It's four hours till sunset. And Tea Dance ends at seven. You haven't experienced P'town until you've danced at the Boatslip. Bring your camera."

Sanjay glanced at Gemma. She shrugged. "Well, I'm all for experience," he said.

37

The club was set right on the water, with a wide deck, hoppin' bar, and a female DJ wearing a fluorescent sports bra and cranking out remixes of Lady Gaga and Kanye West songs circa 2010. Shirtless men abounded — young, old, six-pack abs, and potbellies. No one cared. Gemma felt she could take off her own shirt and no one would raise an eyebrow.

Sanjay had given up on taking photos an hour earlier. But he'd hesitated to leave his camera at their table.

"This is P'town! Lighten up," Maud said, pulling him out of his chair by the hand. Gemma wasn't sure if the comment meant that no one would steal his things, or that dancing was mandatory, but either way, the four of them fell into the groove of the crowd.

Maud ordered food for their table — chicken fingers, a hummus plate, and a spicy noodle salad. She insisted everyone stop and eat something because it was clear they were all crossing the line from pleasantly tipsy to sloppy drunk. But every time Gemma thought about slipping away to grab a bite, the DJ hit them with an even better song. A man wearing a Speedo, a glowstick around his neck, and a sailor hat handed out small water bottles. Gemma wanted to dump it over her head but knew she'd feel better in the morning if she started drinking something other than vodka.

"The club scene is dead in New York," Sanjay said to Maud. "I've been there my whole life and haven't seen anything like this."

"That's because you don't go to gay bars," said Alvie.

"If you think a random Thursday night is fun, come back on the Fourth. Now, that's a party."

The sun began to set, and the music shifted into a mellower, 1970s R&B vibe. Sanjay noticed the quickly changing light, and his eyes became very focused. "I want to get some shots from the beach."

Gemma, breathless and with her tank top clinging to her sweat-soaked skin, said, "I need a break. I'll walk you down to the water."

■ ■ ■ ■

The sky turned violet edged with gold. The breeze off the water gave her a chill in her damp shirt, and her slides filled with sand. She barely noticed.

"I guess what they say about the light here is true," she said.

Sanjay adjusted his camera lens, focusing on the horizon. "One of the few places that lives up to its reputation," he said, lowering the camera after getting his shot.

"I'm glad it was worth your while to make the trip then," she said. He took a few more photos before the sun disappeared. Sanjay recapped his lens and put his camera back in his bag. "All done?"

"Almost. I want to head over to the Pilgrim Monument. I tried to get some good shots of it last night but it was cloudy. Now the sky's clear. If I'm able to get the moon in the frame, it will be amazing."

Gemma looked up at the three-quarter moon and shivered. Sanjay unzipped his bag and pulled out a thin cotton blanket, draping it over her shoulders.

"You carry this with you?"

"In case I ever need to lay on the street for a shot," he said. She pulled it tighter, arranging it around her body like a wrap. The fabric smelled earthy and familiar — it smelled like Sanjay. Her longing for him broke through her alcohol fog, hitting her like a physical blow. She abruptly sat down on the sand, leaning forward to brush the shells out from underneath herself.

"You okay?" he said.

"Yeah. I just need a minute."

Sanjay sat next to her, keeping his camera bag on his lap. "So . . . what really happened today with the interview?"

Had that just been earlier that day? She sighed. Her complicated feelings about the interview were hard to put into words. But if anyone would understand, it was him.

"The reporter started asking me about the Pavlins. She'd done her research. I was prepared for that, but it still felt weird to talk about it."

"Well, you probably should get used to it. Your family background is something you can't avoid if you're going to become really big. And I believe you will, Gemma."

She adjusted to the fresh darkness, the moonlight off the bay giving her enough light to see the expression in his eyes. As she tried to decipher it, he looked away, out at the water. She stared at his profile, taking in the curve of his cheek and the line of his jaw. She could feel the stubble against her neck, against her breasts. Her eyes lowered to look at his hands, remembering what they could do to her.

"Sanjay," she said quietly. He turned toward her, and she leaned forward, kissing him. For a second, he didn't move. The sound of the water seemed to roar in her ears, her heart pounding so hard she felt it might burst. Sanjay touched her face, tentatively at first, then cradling her jaw, kissing her hard. The feel and smell of him was like a homecoming. The kiss deepened, and she felt instantly sober. Her body was on fire, but her mind was clear: It wasn't over between them. Not by a long shot.

She pulled back just long enough to catch her breath. He jumped to his feet.

"I can't do this, Gemma," he said. "I'm seeing someone."

38

Gemma turned on the overhead light and it flickered once before illuminating her workbench. She didn't know how long Celeste would let her keep her things set up, but she intended to make use of it for as long as possible. Work was all she had.

I'm seeing someone.

She set the pieces she'd bought at the estate sale onto the table, contemplating the copper butterfly brooch first. The best strategy for turning it into a pendant would be to drill a small hole near the top, feed a hook-topped wire through it, and then bridge that wire with a simple loop.

Gemma picked through her supply of hooks, clasps, and wire until she found something that would do the trick. Then she picked up the Dremel, attached a fine drill bit, and sat at the spot at the end of the table.

Wielding the tool felt powerful. She might

have lost Sanjay, but at least in this one small way she could control something. She could bend and shape metal. She could drill a hole. She could create. Jewelry was about transformation. Maybe that's why Gemma found it so satisfying. It was easier to change base metals into something beautiful than fix something in real life.

If the average person saw a diamond before it was cut and polished, they'd never dream of spending a dime on it. And metals transformed even more dramatically: Metal didn't just become more beautiful, it became functional. Stainless steel could become a necklace chain, a watch band. Plated, the appearance of the metal itself changed to gold. She always loved the idea that metal could appear like something it wasn't.

When the butterfly was secure in the clamps, she put on a pair of goggles, turned on the Dremel, and got to work. With the startup whir of the rotary tool, with the first give of the metal butterfly as it was pierced with the bit, Gemma experienced a heart-pounding uncertainty whether she would transform the piece or destroy it.

"I thought I'd find you here," Celeste called from the doorway.

Gemma looked up. Her aunt was dressed

in one of her usual cotton tunics, this one peach colored. Her hair was damp and loose, a cup of coffee in her hand. She felt a flood of affection for this woman, a stranger until just a few weeks ago. And now Gemma was working comfortably under her roof, productive. Inspired. Welcome.

She wanted to give something back. And she had an idea.

"Aunt Celeste, thank you again for letting me set up a studio here. And I was thinking . . . unless you have something else in mind . . . I would love to make your wedding bands. Yours and Jack's. You can design them, choose the metal. Whatever you like."

Her offer didn't seem to have the intended effect. Celeste's facial expression tensed.

"I suppose we will need wedding bands, won't we? But you have enough on your plate."

"No, I'd be honored. Really."

"Well, that's very generous of you. We can talk more about it later. But right now you have a visitor downstairs."

"A visitor?" Gemma said.

"A very handsome young man."

Sanjay. Gemma turned off her equipment, mind racing. Of course he couldn't leave town without seeing her one more time. Dating someone or not, they were friends.

Whoever this woman was, the relationship would pass. The fact that he'd shown up made her certain of it.

She took the stairs two at a time, following Celeste down to the store, where she found . . . not Sanjay.

Connor Harrison wore a powder blue T-shirt that brought out his tan and the flecks of gold in his blue eyes. His taut biceps tugged at the sleeves. She couldn't have been less interested.

"Hey," she said, glancing uncomfortably back at Celeste.

"I came to see if you were still in town," he said, smiling.

"I'm working," she said.

"Oh, sorry to interrupt," he said. "Your aunt said you weren't starting until ten."

She cast a look at Celeste, who was suddenly very busy behind the counter.

"My own work. I design jewelry," she said.

"Very cool," he said. "Family tradition, right?"

Startled, she eyed him with suspicion.

"How do you know about my family?"

He tilted his head to the side. "You mentioned it at the beach."

She had? She didn't remember. And if so, it had been a slip. Very unlike her.

"Okay, well . . . I have to get back to it."

"Definitely. Don't want to keep you. Just wanted to invite you over for dinner tonight. I have a great view from the widow's walk."

"Um, I don't know . . ."

"It's just dinner," he said. "You have to eat, right?"

She didn't need a man in order to eat, she thought with irritation. But maybe she needed a man to get over another man. Maybe a no-strings summer fling was just what she needed. If she could shape metal to her will, surely she could control her emotions.

"Sure," she said. "Dinner sounds great."

Elodie never realized how much time she spent at the office until she found a way to manage her workload outside of it. Somehow, between email and video conferencing, she was keeping all the balls in the air. What had she actually been doing in the office for twelve hours a day?

She adjusted the deck chair and clicked on the PDF invoices sent by her assistant for signature. A few days ago, she'd asked Lidia if she had a printer, prompting her landlady to retrieve a model from the attic that was so old it was practically dot matrix. But it got the job done. Lidia kindly set it up in the kitchen for her because the bedrooms didn't have enough outlets to accommodate anything more than a reading lamp.

"Marco has a more state-of-the-art printer at his place," Lidia said. "I'm sure he wouldn't mind if you used his office." Apparently, Lidia and Manny still managed their boating business with handwritten bookkeeping.

Elodie carried her laptop into the house and plugged it into the printer. (It took two adapters from Lands End Marine Supply to make this possible.) As the machine chug-chugged out her paperwork, her phone rang. Sloan Pierce.

Elodie hesitated but knew she couldn't send the calls to voicemail forever.

"Sloan, hello," she said, modulating her voice to sound welcoming — or, at the very least, non-evasive. "I was just about to call you."

"You've been a difficult woman to get ahold of," Sloan said.

A siren blared in the background and Elodie felt a pang of homesickness for the city. She'd been on this spit of land for weeks and was no closer to having the signatures she needed. Again, she wondered: Why had the three-signature stipulation been put in place? And what else could she do to get them?

She knew her sister wanted to avoid drama at all costs. Always had. But her niece? If her only ask was that ring, which was never going to happen, she had to figure out another angle.

"Are you free for a drink tonight? The Carlyle?"

Elodie looked out the kitchen window at the bay. "I'm not in town at the moment."

"Oh? Hamptons?"

"No. Cape Cod."

"I *adore* Cape Cod. Nantucket?"

"Provincetown, actually."

"Of course. Where your sister lives."

Elodie bristled. Did Sloan know about Gemma, too? The thought made her chest tighten.

"I'll be in touch as soon as I'm back from vacation," she said.

"Fabulous. In the meantime, let's get the paperwork wrapped up this week. My PR department is chomping at the bit to announce."

"It's in the works," Elodie said, which was technically true. But by the time she ended the call, she was in a sweat. She pulled out one of the kitchen chairs and sank into it. With both elbows on the table, she put her head in her hands. She looked up at the sound of a dog barking. It wasn't Pearl. She turned just as Tito and Bart walked into the room.

"I was hoping I'd find you around," he said, smiling. "We're headed to the beach. Care to join?"

Elodie glanced at the printer, her invoices piled in the tray. They could wait, but the ticking clock for the contract could not. She wasn't in town for the sun and sand. She needed signatures.

"Not today," she said. The disappointment on his face was surprising, even if he quickly recovered. Well, it wasn't her problem.

She wasn't there to make friends, either.

39

Elodie, July 1994

Elodie planned the romantic weekend down to every last detail: the menu (steaks on the grill), the flowers in their room (bluebells for Liam's favorite color), the CDs in the stereo (Oasis for him, Dave Matthews for her), and the activities: tennis doubles with their friends, pool time, and most important, a midnight stroll on the beach.

They'd been spending nearly every weekend at the Hamptons house, sometimes with her parents, sometimes alone. Either way, it felt like she and Liam were the only two people in the world.

And yet, something between them had changed. There'd been a subtle shift in his attitude toward her, a certain tenderness when he looked at her that made her heart skip a beat. But it didn't quite feel romantic, and they hadn't had sex in months.

Elodie was nothing if not analytical, and it

didn't take her long to do the math: The shift between them started after her father's announcement about the Electric Rose. She was certain of it. And it made sense: They were together, they were in love, and the logical next step was engagement. But how could he propose to her if the traditional symbol of commitment — the diamond engagement ring — had been taken out of his hands? Liam had a lot of pride.

She needed to do something. Sitting around and waiting for things to come to her had never been a luxury she could afford — unlike Paulina. She learned this long ago, striving to get her father's attention as the heir apparent instead of Celeste. Being smart instead of pretty. And it had always paid off. If she had to nudge Liam down the aisle, so be it. And she knew just how to do it.

The only point of contention in their relationship was that she was an early-to-bed, early-to-rise person, and Liam was a night owl. And so, as a gesture to show that their life together would keep up with his preferred rhythm, she planned a midnight stroll on the beach for that night. She arranged to have a bonfire waiting, and the words "Will you marry me" spelled out with stones and shells in the sand.

How was she going to wait thirteen hours? She slipped out of bed, Liam still sleeping though it was close to nine. She'd been awake next to him since the early morning, content just to feel him breathing and to gaze at him — a sight that would never, ever get old. Not even after a whole lifetime together. She was certain of it.

By now, the staff had left coffee and newspapers on the tray outside the bedroom door. She retrieved it and settled back into bed. She liked to pretend she read the *New York Times* business section first, but she was only human and started with the gossipy *New York Post.* She flipped through it, sipping the coffee, which was slightly bitter. She wondered if she should call for a fresh pot when an article caught her eye. The black-and-white photo jumped out at her like it was in Technicolor: Liam, on an unfamiliar beach. Liam, holding her sister Paulina's hand, gazing at her with an expression of adoration she'd never seen on his face before. She could almost think she imagined it, a projection of her deepest fear, her most childish impulses of competition and insecurity. But there, on the other side of Paulina, was Celeste. The three of them, together.

The caption read, "Cape Cad: Boyfriend

of Pavlin & Co heiress Elodie Pavlin caught on romantic stroll with her sister model Paulina Pavlin."

Elodie dropped the coffee mug, sending it crashing to the hardwood floor beside the bed. Liam woke up with a start.

"What's going on?" he said.

She threw the newspaper at him.

"You tell me."

40

"Jack didn't want me buying this and I guaranteed we'd sell it," Celeste said, hands on her hips. "If we don't, I'll never hear the end of it. So if a customer asks for suggestions, this is your go-to."

Gemma helped Celeste move the carved Louis XV mirror onto the sales floor. For the first time all season, the humidity forced Celeste to close the front door and turn on the air conditioner. When she turned around, she did a double take, looking at Gemma's necklace. "That's lovely," she said.

Gemma touched the copper butterfly hanging from her necklace. The *New York Times* photographers had shown up that morning for their scheduled shoot, and she'd made sure to wear her latest piece.

"Thanks," Gemma said. "I found it at the first estate sale you took me to."

"Very creative."

"I was thinking . . . maybe I could sell

them in the store?"

"Sell what in the store?"

"My jewelry. Maybe a small table display near the counter?"

"But it's an antiques store."

"Yes . . . I know. But every charm is repurposed from an antique or a collectible. The only things that are new are the necklace and bracelet chains I've designed for them to clip onto." She held out her wrist.

"I've made a point of not selling jewelry," Celeste said, crossing her arms. "It's nothing personal. Your pieces are beautiful. It's just not the business I want to be in."

The front door opened, letting in a gust of damp air and Elodie.

"Can I interest you in a Louis XV mirror?" Celeste said cheekily.

"No. The only thing I'm interested in is your signatures on this contract." She slammed a document down on the counter.

Celeste shook her head. "Do you have to nag me about this every day?"

"That's the plan. There's one way to put an end to it: just sign."

"I'm going to get my cards read later today. Let me check and see what the climate is for major decisions. I told you I wanted to wait until Mercury —"

"And I'm telling you, this can't wait

another day. Whitmore's wants to announce the auction. And if we can't move forward because you two are holding it up, I'm sure they'd be happy to announce *that* to the press instead. So, if you want that kind of attention, Celeste — by all means keep holding me up. And, Gemma, I'm sure it will be great for your jewelry career to be the one denying the world a chance to bid on some of the world's most important pieces."

Elodie turned on her heels and stormed out, the contract still on the counter.

"Please, don't sign that," Gemma said. "She's up to something."

"Oh, Gemma," Celeste said with a sigh. "You need to let go of that diamond. It's toxic."

Gemma shook her head, emotion welling in her chest. "Not to me it's not."

Celeste's expression softened. She moved closer and put an arm around her niece's shoulders. "I think we need to pay a visit to Maud."

Celeste closed the shop with a handwritten note taped to the door: "We're off scouting more treasures for you. Be back soon!"

"Can you really leave?" Gemma said, following her to the street.

"In the beginning, when it was just Jack and me, we had to close down to go to estate sales or do errands."

Gemma had noticed that it wasn't uncommon in town to, say, stop by a bakery in the middle of the afternoon only to find a handwritten note from the proprietor reading, "Closed for a mental health day."

"And this is important," Celeste said. "You need to learn to let go of things that are clogging your aura."

"Okay. But for the record: I don't believe in this sort of thing."

Maud met them in the garden behind her house.

"Welcome, ladies. Who's going first?"

"She is," Celeste and Gemma said at the same time.

"Don't be shy," Maud said to Gemma. "I promise I don't bite. Have you had your cards read before?"

"No," Gemma said, glancing at Celeste.

"Come," Maud said, leading them to a small table and a set of wooden chaise lounges with purple cushions. "Tarot cards have been used since the Middle Ages as a tool for divination and self-discovery. Now, the clearer your intentions, the more accurate my reading will be. So I ask that you hold a question in your mind."

"I don't really have a question," she said nervously, again glancing at Celeste.

"Not to be too leading here," Celeste said, "but I know Gemma is interested in the comings and goings of a certain object, and perhaps needs to know if she can let this object go."

Maud focused her sharp eyes on Gemma. "Is this accurate?"

"I guess?" In reality, there was nothing this woman could say that would make her feel better about the disappearance of her mother's engagement ring. And yet, she felt anticipation as Maud slid the deck of cards across the table and instructed her to cut it three times. Gemma hadn't held a deck of cards since she was a teenager and played gin with her grandfather.

"Now, think about the object in question."

Gemma envisioned the diamond ring. She focused at first on the gem itself, the remarkable shade of petal pink that appeared lit from within. The name Electric Rose truly captured it. She remembered how it had looked on her mother's slender hand, the stone covering half her knuckle. And finally, she let herself remember trying it on, the way it made her feel pretty, and special, and most of all, close to the mother she adored.

"Now, halve the deck, and draw three cards one at a time, placing each facedown."

Gemma followed the instructions. Her hand felt shaky as she pulled the first card. When the three were set out before her, Maud turned them over one at a time. She contemplated them for a few moments before looking up at Gemma. "Well, I don't see anything here about an object. Your first card here, the Sun, suggests good fortune. Your next card, the World, indicates a major change and the finding of a truth. Your final card is the Lovers. What I see clearly in this is that you have either found your true love or are about to very soon."

"What?" That was the last thing she expected to hear.

"Oh! That young man who visited you in the shop," Celeste said.

No way. She didn't believe in any of this. But she couldn't help but note that while Celeste tried to change the subject, Maud did *not* advise her to forget about the diamond.

And she wouldn't.

41

After a busy weekend at the store, Celeste finally found time on a calm Monday morning to break away for a few hours. She and Jack left mid-morning for an estate sale right in town on Bangs Street. She had no qualms about leaving Gemma in charge. Their customers seemed to love her.

Jack held her hand as they strolled up Commercial. After all their years as a couple, Celeste still felt that antiquing was the most romantic thing she and Jack did together. More than a sunset sail, more than an early morning walk by the salt marshes. Maybe even more than having sex. The store was their baby and collecting pieces to "feed" it was a timeworn, beloved ritual.

"Wait — is that . . ." Celeste spotted Elodie a block away, hands on her hips in her usual imperial stance, looking up at the sign hanging above the empty storefront that had been a stationery shop for decades. She held a paint swatch against the doorway.

Celeste dropped Jack's hand. "Look — Elodie's up to something at the stationery shop."

"So I see," he said.

"What's she doing?" Celeste said, her stomach tensing.

"There's only one way to find out."

When they were within earshot, she called out, "Hey there — what's going on?"

Elodie turned and broke into a suspiciously big smile. "Oh, hello there, you two. You haven't heard? I'm surprised. Good news usually travels so fast around here."

Celeste crossed her arms, sweat trickling down the back of her neck.

"What news?"

"I'm looking into leasing this space. I think what this town needs is a high-end jewelry store, don't you?"

She couldn't be serious. "No. I don't."

"This is the perfect spot for a Pavlin & Co outpost. Or, what do the kids call it these days? A pop-up."

Celeste turned to Jack. "What did she just say?" Of course she'd heard it loud and clear. She was just hoping Jack might tell her otherwise.

"Well, we wish you luck, Elodie," Jack said, taking Celeste by the elbow and steering her back into walk-mode. "We're late for an estate sale."

"Enjoy!" Elodie called out gaily. "Keep an eye out for the invitation to the grand opening."

It was all Celeste could do not to break into a run. As soon as they rounded the corner, she stopped in her tracks.

"I can't believe this!" she said, pressing her hand to her forehead. "I have to talk to Pamela. She can't lease that space to my sister."

"Oh, Celeste. Elodie isn't competition for us. We're in a totally different business."

"That's not the point. This town is my home. Mine. She doesn't belong here."

"The town's not big enough for the both of you?" he teased.

"No. Frankly, it's not. New York City wasn't big enough for the both of us."

"Come on, don't let this spoil the day." He took her by the hand again and led her up the gravel path to their destination. The house was a stunning example of the Middle Georgian architecture that had been popular during the whaling era, with a two-story open porch with a pediment roof and a widow's walk. "I remember the first time I went with you to one of these sales. The only thing that could possibly get me off the water and into an old inland house was my adoration of you."

They stood on the porch, facing each other.

"Oh, Jack," she said, forcing herself to smile. "Well, yes, let's have fun inside. I know a lot of the items will be expensive, but even if we don't manage to sell, it's worth having in the store just for the cachet."

Jack looked skeptical. "I'm not so sure about that. We need to be careful. Sell-through is important this summer."

"What makes you say that?"

"We need to start thinking about retirement."

"Retirement? What's gotten into you? I think this upcoming birthday is messing with your head. We don't need to change everything just because you're turning sixty."

"Easy for you to say as a spry woman in her fifties."

"I'm serious," she said.

"Retirement is a reasonable thing to consider, Celeste. You're just on a hair trigger."

Was she? Well, the run-in with her sister didn't help. She couldn't possibly be serious about bringing Pavlin & Co to Commercial Street. Was this about the auction paperwork? Or was this Elodie making good on her threat from years ago — the promise of payback?

The phone call came on a summer morning decades ago, waking her.

Her sister was yelling, screaming at her. Celeste could only make out every other sentence or so, but they all sounded like "How *could* you?" Then, something about the *New York Post.* About Celeste betraying her ("I'd expect this from Paulina. But you? How could you keep this from me? And *be with them*?"). And then, before hanging up, her final pronouncement: "You'll pay for this." Celeste, completely confused, could only look directly to the source for answers. When the Provincetown library opened, she found the answer in the black-and-white headline of the *Post* gossip pages: "Cape Cad." She'd thought, standing at the periodicals table, still in her pajama pants, confronted with the photo of herself on the beach with Paulina and Liam, that things couldn't get any worse. They did.

Provincetown was her escape from all that. Until now.

"Jack, it's really a lot for me to have my sister and my niece here all summer. It's been great getting to know Gemma but —"

"But what?" He looked at her. "She's doing a good job at the store. And Elodie might not be your favorite person, but I think now that you've spent some time with her, you can see she's harmless."

Celeste swallowed hard.

"Gemma wants to start selling her jewelry in the shop."

"Great. She's talented. The stuff is nice. Figure out a fair cut and let her." He kissed her. "Stop worrying about your sister and your niece. My mother always said, if you look for trouble, you'll find it. So let's look for some bargains around here instead."

With that, he rang the doorbell. The conversation was over.

Connor opened the door before Gemma had a chance to knock. He was dressed in a white linen shirt, navy shorts, and driving shoes without socks. Behind him, sunlight streamed through large windows. It was like he was standing on a movie set constructed to accentuate his New England good looks.

"Come on in," he said.

The front door opened to a foyer leading directly into a spacious living room. The walls were white, the floors red birch. Anywhere she looked there was a window. The space was uncluttered but accented with perfect touches like Turkish throw rugs, nautical pillows, framed photos of sailboats on the wall, and a glass vase of sunflowers on the wood coffee table next to a wide beeswax candle. In one corner, a wicker basket was filled with magazines.

"I brought this for you. A friend told me it's a local favorite." She handed Connor the bottle of Helltown rosé she'd picked up at Perry's on Alvie's recommendation, a tip that came along with a reminder not to have sex, at least not yet.

"What kind of advice is that? Don't act like you don't have sex on a first date."

"I'm gay and you're straight. Different rules," she said.

The truth was, she hadn't slept with anyone since Sanjay and she wasn't sure she was ready to start that night. Even if sex with someone else might be the only way she could move on.

She followed Connor into the kitchen, where he had dinner on the stove. It was another airy room, with windows overlooking the garden, bead-board cabinets, and soapstone countertops with marble, mosaic tile backsplash.

"Shall I open this? I also have a great Cab Franc, or a Riesling. Whatever you want," he said.

"You pick," she said self-consciously.

The kitchen smelled like sautéed onions and peppers. A large wooden salad bowl brimmed with romaine. Connor uncorked the rosé and poured two glasses.

"To the summer ahead," he said, touching his glass to hers. "And to new friends."

"To new friends." She sipped the wine, barely tasting it and resisting the urge to gulp it down. It felt strange to be on a date with someone other than Sanjay. *No, don't think about him now.*

"So, here's the deal: Everything is prepped. All I need to do is boil water when you're hungry. Do you want a tour of the house first?"

"Sure," she said.

He led her through the rest of the first floor, which had two more sitting rooms in addition to the living room she'd seen when she walked in. The rooms all had the same pale, neutral palette — a chic, soothing simplicity. Through the open windows she smelled the briny air coming off the bay and a hint of lavender from the garden.

The red birch stairs leading to the second floor had a blue and white runner down the center and a curved banister.

"Here's the guest room," he said, opening a door to a room three times the size of her space at Aunt Celeste's. "And the bathroom . . ."

Her nerves ticked up again. Of course, this whole tour was leading to one place: the master bedroom. Alvie hadn't needed to warn her; she had no intention of sleeping with Connor on the first date. Maybe not ever.

The minimalist room, all white beadboard walls with a wrought-iron four-poster bed punctuated by an antique trunk at the foot, had clearly been crafted around the spectacular view: French doors led to a balcony and the beach across the street. The light played off the water in a way that seemed to channel it directly into the house.

"Wow," she said. "I don't think I'd be able to get any sleep here because I'd just be staring out the window all night."

"It's even better outside," he said, waving her forward. She followed him onto the balcony, but by the time she was facing the view, he stood so close to her that the water was no longer the thing taking her breath away.

Connor leaned on the balustrade, and the breeze blew a lock of hair into his face. He brushed it back, tilting his head to look at her with a smile. The light caught his golden stubble, his eyes more intense than she'd seen before. And then he leaned forward, brushing her lips ever so lightly with his own. She leaned into the kiss, her intense feelings of attraction taking her by surprise.

"Get a room!" someone called from the street down below, while someone else applauded.

"Maybe it's time to eat?" she said, pulling back. He smiled at her.

"I'm starving."

He was from a "good" Boston family. His father was a hand surgeon at Boston Children's. His mother was a Rhode Island Biddle. Growing up, she'd lived right next door to the Bouviers when Jackie was a debutante. Neither one of them approved of his career in the art trade.

"It's fine to collect art, but dealing it is considered gauche. They wanted me to follow in my father's footsteps but there was no way."

She sipped her wine. "So how'd you do it? Fund the gallery, I mean."

"I found investors."

She perked up. "How?"

"There's a lot of money in Boston," he said. "New York isn't the only playing field."

She looked at him with new interest.

"Could you make some introductions for me?"

"For you? Your family is loaded."

"So's yours."

"Touché," he said. "I guess business mixes better with strangers. Sometimes it's hard for people to see the value that's right there in front of them. But when it comes to you, I don't have that problem."

He leaned forward and kissed her again. She still didn't know if she wanted to have sex with him. But the thought of meeting his money people *definitely* turned her on.

42

Paulina, October 1994

The day Paulina's "A Diamond Says Love" ads were published in magazines all across the country, she woke up in Liam's bed filled with dread.

In the months since the gossip item appeared in the *New York Post,* not a day passed that she didn't grapple with what was happening. Understandably, Elodie wasn't speaking to her. But Celeste, too, was angry.

"You dragged me into this, and now Elodie thinks I was colluding with you to keep it from her," Celeste said.

Her father was irritated that she'd created tabloid drama that threatened to overshadow his marketing of the Electric Rose.

"You go through men like tissues, and your sister was serious about this young man. I hope you're happy with yourself!" he'd scolded. Her mother, at least, had given her the benefit of the doubt. The only thing she'd asked her was, "Do you love him?"

Paulina could tell her honestly, "Yes."

"Good morning," Liam said, walking into the bedroom with a breakfast tray filled with coffee and pastries and a bundle of magazines tucked under one arm. "Coffee, croissants, *Vogue, Harper's Bazaar,* and *Vanity Fair,*" he said. "They were out of *Town & Country.*"

The truth was, she had tried to forget about him. The morning after the photo shoot, she got on a plane and vowed to stay away from New York for as long as possible. But then, three days into her time in Kenya, Liam showed up at her campsite.

"This is madness," she said, trying to be angry but overwhelmed by happiness at the sight of him.

"It *is* madness," he said with a grin. "My first vacation in ten years? I should have done this a long time ago."

"Liam, I'm serious. You can't be here. You have to go."

He looked her in the eyes and said, "Tell me honestly you're not happy to see me and I'll leave."

She couldn't. "But you have to end things with my sister."

Still, she resisted her insane lust for him. For about a week. She ultimately gave in on the darkest, hottest night of the trip. They had outrageous, mind-blowing sex in her mosquito-netted bungalow, an experience she hoped would help get him out of her system. But afterward, breathless and spent in his arms, she had the alarming certainty that the night was just the beginning.

She hoped her feelings would fade. She believed they would; she always lost interest in men after a while, be it two weeks or two months. She warned him of this and begged him not to tell anyone about what was going on.

"What if we lose interest in each other once we're back home, in the real world?" she said. "I don't want my sister to get hurt for no reason."

"These feelings started in the real world," he said. "I'm never going to want her the way I want you, Paulina."

Still, she'd changed her mind about pushing him to end things. "Please, just wait. You might get things out of your system — we both might. Don't do something permanent for what could be a temporary . . . fever between us."

That strategy had been a mistake.

Now Elodie, heartbroken, was becoming

a shut-in. Celeste refused to take her calls and didn't come to the city for their mother's birthday. Paulina felt such guilt and shame that she and Liam avoided being seen in public together. He'd been patient but it was wearing thin.

He waved a magazine at her. "I want to celebrate with you tonight," he said, climbing back into bed. "At a restaurant. In public. Like a normal couple."

"I'm not ready."

"Paulina, it's time. I love you. Elodie will get over it, but not if we continue to slink around like criminals."

He handed her *Vanity Fair,* the page with her photograph dog-eared. She flipped it open and confronted her own image, her eyes exaggerated with shadow and liner, her lips a deep, vampy matte red. Her face rested in her palm, her bejeweled fingernails splayed along her cheek to present the diamond. The deep, dazzling pink of the Electric Rose popped against her ivory skin.

"I hardly recognize myself," she said. But really, she wasn't talking about the photography but rather that she'd never felt so out of control of her own emotions.

Liam moved the tray and the magazines to the floor, kissing her. As always, his touch erased the rest of the world. Paulina gave in to it, melting under him, certain that something that felt so good couldn't be so bad. He pulled back.

"There's one more magazine," he said, reaching for one on the nightstand and passing it to her, his expression mischievous. The magazine was slightly propped open by something in the middle pages.

An enormous, sparkling pink diamond ring was tucked into the crease. The Electric Rose. Paulina gasped.

"Paulina Pavlin," Liam said, "will you marry me?"

It was the second time he'd stood before her holding that ring. The first had been the photo shoot — not even a year ago, but also, a lifetime.

She loved him. She loved him with all of her heart and there was nothing she could do to change that. And now, even with all the problems their love caused, she didn't want to.

"Yes," she said. "Yes, of course I'll marry you."

Liam slipped the astonishing ring on her finger, and she saw that his hands were shaking. She threw her arms around him, kissing him the way she'd wanted to that first night at the bar.

The way she would kiss him now for the rest of their lives.

43

Gemma's first clue that something happened was her pinging phone. She was just too busy to stop and look at it.

The sun was barely up when she set out her equipment: needle-nose pliers, soldering paste, soldering pad, interlocking tweezers, goggles, the torch, and the pickle pot. She'd seen a robin's egg on the ground the other day, and then minutes later spotted a cloisonné egg at a shop called Global Gifts on Commercial. This was the way inspiration worked: She was turning the cloisonné egg into a charm.

She secured the egg in a clamp and looped the wire through the hook with the other end looping through the clasp and then twisted it closed, making the joint meeting as close as possible so she could solder it.

Her phone demanded attention: *ping, ping, ping.*

She fire-coated the top of the egg and the

clasp to protect it from the heat. Next, she used her soldering paste and applied it as accurately as possible just to the joint — she had to keep it isolated from the rest of the piece so the heat didn't melt any other parts. Goggles on, she flipped on the torch and set it to continuous flame. One of the first things she learned in metalworking was that the heat from the flame drew the solder to where she wanted it. She could still hear her professor saying, "Solder flows to the hottest point."

Ping, ping, ping.

She put down the torch. What was going on? She opened her Instagram account and saw it was flooded with orders. More orders than she could possibly fulfill. There was only one possible explanation.

Heart pounding, she clicked over to *The New York Times.* There it was: "Something Old, Something New: Meet Gemma, the Next Big Thing in Jewelry Design."

She scanned the article quickly, looking for any mention of the Pavlins. It came later in the article, only as background. Gemma was relieved to see that the article focused first and foremost on her work. The reporter did a great job articulating her values and vision, and she even included a shout-out to Sanjay and his photography for her online shop and social media. The whole piece was as positive as she could have hoped for, except for the timing. If she'd had an investor in place, the article would have been an accelerant for her scaling up. But without funding, she couldn't buy even a fraction of the supplies needed to meet the sudden demand. All she could do was hope it helped make her case with investors. If she found one to make her case *to.*

Shaking with excitement, she forwarded the article to Sanjay. At the very least, maybe it would bring him some photography work. She hadn't heard from him since he went back to the city the week before. Still, she thought about that kiss on the beach over and over again. Even when she tried to discipline herself not to think about it during the day, she dreamt about him. She'd hoped spending time with Connor Harrison would help her feelings for Sanjay fade, but so far not so much.

Her phone rang, and for a split second she thought it might be Sanjay calling to congratulate her. But the incoming number was unfamiliar.

"Hello?"

"Gemma, Sloan Pierce here. What a fabulous piece in the *Times.*"

"Oh, thanks, Sloan —"

"But I do have to ask: Since things are going so well for you, why do you feel the need to be obstructionist?"

"I'm sorry?"

"Elodie told me you're refusing to sign off on the auction contract."

"I'm not refusing," Gemma said. "I just made it conditional. She can't keep the Electric Rose from me. And since you want to know where the diamond is, too, we have a shared interest in this."

"You need to get out of the way," Sloan said.

The woman had nerve. Even by New York standards, she was getting too pushy for comfort.

"Actually, I don't *need* to do anything."

"You know, it really is a lovely article. But the jewelry business is a very small world. I should know: I've been making a name for myself for nearly a decade. This auction will be a game-changer for me. I'll be able to write my own ticket at Whitmore's or anywhere else. That is, if you don't mess it up. And really, it would be a shame for you to make enemies this early in your career."

Before Gemma could respond, Sloan ended the call.

Elodie pedaled behind Tito on the final

stretch to Herring Cove Beach, then coasted into the parking lot.

Avoiding bike rides hadn't lasted very long. It was a point of pride that Tito didn't drive to Herring Cove unless it was above ninety degrees or if it was late in the day and they risked missing the sunset. Starting a week ago, they daily made the ten-minute bike trip up Province Lands Road, past the salt marshes and Boy Beach. Occasionally, they went all the way to Race Point, but she didn't have the stamina to do that all the time. She was well out of her comfort zone as it was. But Tito had that effect on her. When she was around him, she felt like a teenager again, like she had her entire life ahead of her and anything could happen. She felt a weight lifted. She felt almost . . . happy.

Tito stopped his bike before making the usual left turn toward the beach path. Then she noticed the truck parked off to one side and a small crowd of onlookers gathered behind it. The truck had a large trailer attached to the back and read "Marine Mammal Rescue" on the side.

Elodie pulled up beside Tito and hit the brake.

"What's going on?" she said.

An official-looking woman with wild curly

gray hair and wearing a uniform blue T-shirt with a life jacket around her neck crossed in front of them, speaking into a walkie-talkie.

"Judy," Tito called out. "It's Tito from the marina. You need any help?"

"Oh, hey, Tito. I think we might. We got six adult dolphins who were grounded ashore in Wellfleet. We're just waiting for the rest of the crew to get here for the release. Hop in the truck — there's extra boots and gloves in back."

He turned to Elodie. "Sorry to run off but —"

"Of course! Go — I'll just wait here," she said.

"She's with me," he said to Judy.

Police cars pulled into the parking lot, and two women in sheriff's office uniforms conferred with Judy while Elodie followed Tito to the truck. There was no time to talk. Tito ushered her to the rear of the trailer. It was open in the back with a metal walkway that extended to the pavement. She was shocked to see dolphins lying on the floor, each wrapped in some sort of tarp or blanket. Another woman in a blue T-shirt tended to them. Tito disappeared inside.

More police arrived, conferring with Judy. A van pulled in, and half a dozen women jumped out all dressed in orange all-weather uniforms with long sleeves and long pants, water boots and gloves. A flatbed on wheels appeared, and the women moved it close to the trailer.

The crowd of onlookers had tripled, and there was a sense of urgency in the air. People spoke in hushed tones, a lot of them snapping photos of the dolphins. Elodie wondered how long the dolphins had been out of the water, and how long they could survive like this.

Tito emerged from the trailer dressed in brown waterproof coveralls and boots, with a blue IFAW baseball cap over his thick head of hair. The women in the orange uniforms surrounded him, and they huddled together intently. She thought again in that moment how very attractive he was — a man's man. So unlike the suits she met all the time in the city.

Things moved quickly. The rescuers carried the dolphins out one by one in red tarps and then placed them on the flatbed on wheels. She realized the bed was a mobile stretcher, and Tito pulled it from the front with the six women surrounding the dolphin along both sides and the back. The procession headed swiftly but carefully down the nearest pathway to the beach. The crowd followed, rushing through the nearest alternative path to the shore, giving the procession a respectful wide berth.

The beach was particularly rocky that day and she was thankful that she had sneakers on. The beachgoers in flip-flops did not fare as well, slowed down by the need to step over stones and rocks and shells. Some gravel made its way into her sneakers but she didn't miss a step, so intent was she on not missing a moment of the dolphins' journey.

The police had cleared the perimeter, and some beachgoers were still grumbling about uprooting their umbrellas and chairs and coolers. There was confusion about what was going on, but as soon as the rescue teams were in full view, the sunbathers backed off.

Elodie spaced herself far enough away from the dolphin procession that she felt comfortable she wasn't crowding in. They stopped the first stretcher about twenty yards from the water and moved the first dolphin onto what looked like a blue tarp on the sand. Elodie saw the animal fully revealed. It was very still, and she couldn't tell if its eyes were closed or if that was simply the way it always looked. It was tan on the under half and black on the top, its dorsal fin lying flat. It seemed lifeless, and the high she'd felt watching the team in action gave way to the sobering realization that the outcome might not be good.

A group transported the second dolphin, and then four more teams, each with a dolphin, reached the first. The only thing she could hear was the lapping of the waves. The smattering of onlookers were completely silent, reverent in the face of delicate work. She watched Tito in conference with his team, and after a moment they reconfigured around the tarp and lifted the dolphin, taking slow and steady steps to the water until everyone stood waist-deep. The rest of the groups followed them, and they fanned out, side by side, standing about ten feet apart, each surrounding their dolphin.

Elodie expected the dolphins to perk up and swim right off, but nothing happened. Minutes ticked by, and her curiosity turned to anxiety.

"This is normal," a woman next to her said. "They need to get their muscle memory back. It's almost as if they forget how to swim when they're out of the water for a while."

Sure enough, Tito's team shifted as their dolphin wriggled free of the tarp and swam off. Seconds later, another dolphin followed. After a few more minutes, all of the animals were free. She wanted to clap or cheer and waited for her fellow onlookers to do the same, but the respectful silence continued until the rescue workers turned to walk back to the parking lot. Then the applause began, a smattering that turned into a raucous shouting and whistling.

Tito gave her a wave, and her heart began to race. She wanted to throw her arms around him. She wanted *him.*

Standing with her feet planted firmly in the sand, she knew the dolphins weren't the only ones resuscitated that day.

She couldn't deny it any longer: She was falling for Tito Barros.

■ ■ ■ ■

Part Two

■ ■ ■ ■

Jewelry is a covert language full of secrets.

— GEOFFREY MUNN IN CHERIE BURNS'S *DIVING FOR STARFISH*

44

Elodie, 1994

Thanksgiving Day was bright but shockingly cold. Elodie fortified herself with a glass of scotch before the bracing walk three blocks north on Park Avenue. She'd been tempted not to show up after all. But she couldn't let her father down.

Four months after the paparazzi photos of her sisters and Liam on the beach, she still hadn't seen her sisters. She moved out of her parents' apartment and got her own place a few blocks away on Lexington. Celeste stayed hidden away on Cape Cod, and Paulina continued to flit around like a butterfly, only now with Liam following along like a dutiful dog. And Elodie spent ten hours a day at the Pavlin & Co office, working beside their father. She knew she was becoming a workaholic, but it was her only outlet — not just to forget about Liam, but to secure her place as her father's number two. But on the eve of Thanksgiving, her endless need to please her father backed her into a corner.

"Your mother asked me to make sure you'll be joining us for the holiday," he said. "She wants everyone together. No matter the . . . challenges."

"Who's *everyone*?" she said, her stomach twisting into a knot.

"Your sisters, of course."

"Celeste is coming?"

"We've made it clear we expect her."

"And who else?"

"Paulina. I've insisted. We must find a way past this. I won't have the Pavlin house divided."

So there it was. She would have to face Paulina at last.

She squared her shoulders, looked her father in the eye, and nodded her agreement. She refused to act like the loser. Men would come and go, but Elodie was on her way to becoming one of the most high-profile executives in Manhattan. Paulina was a child. She was the flavor of the month. Really, she'd done Elodie a favor by saving her from the distraction of being in love.

Inside the apartment, her parents' living room was lit with a fire, and one corner was already dominated by a towering Christmas tree even though they were Jewish. Constance and Alan could not resist tinsel and lights — glitter was embraced in any form.

"Mother, the apartment looks beautiful," Elodie said, kissing both parents on the cheek.

"And you look lovely," Constance said. Elodie had dressed carefully for the occasion in a Chanel suit with a spectacular string of black South Sea pearls around her neck. They had just arrived at the showroom a few days earlier and her father said she could borrow them for the night.

Paulina stood in front of the couch. Her long hair was loose, and her flawless face was flushed — either from the fire or from nerves. Either way, Elodie could see how scared she was to finally see her. It was incredibly gratifying. One day, Liam Maybrook would be out of the picture, and Paulina would spend the rest of her life trying to make it up to her older sister. One day, Elodie might even forgive her.

And then a flash of color caught her eye. It was a stone on Paulina's finger, refracting the firelight. Elodie's heart began to race. She stepped closer.

The Electric Rose.

It could only mean one thing.

"I wanted to tell you in person," Paulina said.

Elodie stared at the pink diamond until she was able to summon her voice.

"That ring is a symbol of how you betrayed me. I hope you think of that every time you look at it. I know I certainly will. And I'll never forgive you."

Not as long as she lived.

45

The Fourth of July parade started late morning.

Giant bunches of rainbow balloons traveled down Commercial Street attached to floats shaped like sea creatures, the American flag, and the Pilgrim Monument. Dancing drag queens were decked out in red, white, and blue sequins, and candy-colored vintage cars puttered past the crowd of onlookers.

Gemma and Alvie staked out a viewing spot in front of Maud's Victorian. They were dusted with stray glitter after only a few minutes. Along the parade route, all the shop owners and tourists with children and locals taking a time-out from the beach and pool cheered the participants on.

Gemma felt almost carefree. She'd always liked the Fourth of July. When she was little, she'd watched the extravagant Hamptons fireworks show from the deck at her mother's family's beach house. Later, after she moved in with her father's parents, Nana took her to a little park where the local kids played softball and basketball. Everyone sat on blankets and watched a more modest version of the celebration she remembered from her other life. Once she got to college, the Fourth of July wasn't as big of a deal in the city. Mostly, she and her friends drank too much and hung out in Washington Square Park.

But now, back at the beach, she felt her childlike enthusiasm returning. How could she not? Even on an average day in Provincetown, there was a certain whimsy in the air. On a holiday, you had to work hard not to find something to smile about.

"Isn't that your man?" Alvie said. Gemma followed the direction she was pointing in, expecting, on some gut level, to see Sanjay. But Alvie was talking about Connor Harrison.

"He's not my man," Gemma said.

"I'm sure that can be fixed."

"Very funny. And stop pointing —"

Too late. Connor must have sensed their eyes on him because he turned in their direction as surely as if they'd called out his name. He moved toward them, weaving through the crowd. She hadn't seen him since dinner at his house two weeks ago — not for lack of trying on his part. Gemma just kept telling him she was busy. She'd had a good time; she enjoyed his company. But she needed to keep things casual.

And yet, she kept forgetting how handsome he was. Every time she saw him, he was more tan, more golden.

"Hey, I'm so glad we ran into each other," he said. "Do you want to come over later to watch the fireworks? The view from my roof will be spectacular."

She was about to say no, to tell him that she was going to a party. Jack's cousins Lidia and Manny hosted a clambake every Fourth and that's where she'd be celebrating. But then she spotted another familiar face in the crowd — and this time it *was* Sanjay.

What was he doing there? And why hadn't he called her?

She got her answer as soon as she realized he wasn't alone; he was holding hands with Monica Del Mar. Monica, of the disastrous New Year's Eve party. *She* was the woman he was seeing? The reason why he pulled away from her the night on the beach?

Unbelievable.

So much made sense now. Monica told on her because she was jealous — she wanted Sanjay for herself. Gemma gave her the perfect opening by kissing Noam at the party. And now they were together, two photographers just living it up at one of the most scenic beaches in the country.

Fine. She was officially done flagellating herself. She'd apologized to Sanjay a million times; she'd made it clear she still cared about him. She even mentioned him in her *New York Times* interview. She valued him in every way. But if he couldn't see that, then maybe it was time for her to let go.

"Gemma?"

She looked back at Connor, having almost forgotten he was standing there with her.

"Yes," she said. "I'd love to come over and watch the fireworks."

Elodie poured herself a cup of white wine and looked around for Tito.

The party spilled out from the Barros house all the way to the dock. Paper lanterns topped picnic tables, a DIY bar was set up on a folding table, and off to the side there was a large steaming bed of seaweed surrounded by a buffer of packed sand and covered with lobsters, corn, clams, and oysters. Bruce Springsteen played over the sound system.

People milled around, drinking out of

plastic cups (the stack of cups by the bar had a sign behind it reading *Recyclable!*), eating watermelon and feta salad and other appetizers, and dancing to the music.

She couldn't stop thinking about Tito since the dolphin rescue. It was near constant. She thought about him in a way she hadn't thought about a man in many years. In decades.

She spotted her sister in the crowd. Celeste gave a hearty wave, and Elodie returned the hello with slightly less enthusiasm. It was hard for her to be smiles and rainbows for Celeste when she was half the reason she was still stuck in limbo.

Her phone rang, and she checked it reluctantly, only to immediately wish she hadn't.

"Sloan, hello. You don't take off holidays, I see."

"I'm on a vacation of sorts," Sloan said. "I decided to take a trip to the Cape."

Elodie felt her stomach tense. "Oh? Good for you. Let's talk after the holiday?"

"Actually, I'd love to talk sooner. I'm in Provincetown. How's tomorrow afternoon, say two o'clock? I'm staying at a friend's house. We can chat poolside."

Elodie caught Celeste's eye and waved her over. "Sure," she said.

"Wonderful. I'll text you the address. And

please see if your sister and niece can join us? I figure we can wrap up the paperwork and celebrate with a bottle of champagne."

Little alarm bells went off inside her.

"I can't make any promises . . . but I will certainly stop by to say hello," Elodie said.

Celeste reached her, dressed in one of her usual tunics, this one navy blue with little gold stars. She had a gerbera daisy tucked behind one ear, her sand-colored hair loose and slightly frizzy at the temples.

"Happy Fourth!" she said, smiling like she didn't have a care in the world. It was infuriating.

"Well, it would be happy if I didn't have the rep from Whitmore's calling me," Elodie said.

"On a holiday?"

"Listen: I don't ask you for very much. For anything, to be exact. But this woman is in town and she wants to meet tomorrow. I need you to come, I need you to bring Gemma, and I need you to convince her to sign the contract. Can you do that for me?"

Celeste hesitated. "I'll talk to her. But I can't make any guarantees unless you at least tell her where Paulina's ring is."

"It's not Paulina's ring! That was just a publicity stunt and you know it. Are you really going to rewrite history like this?"

Tito walked over with a smile, handing Elodie a can of wine. Celeste waited for Elodie to inform him that she didn't drink *wine* from a *can,* but instead her sister just smiled at him sweetly and pulled the aluminum tab open. Interesting.

"Listen, Elodie," she said, "do you want to be right or do you want your signed contract?"

"I want the contract."

"I'm not even asking you to give the ring to Gemma. Just let her know that it's safe, let her see it. Tell her you'll leave it to her children someday — *anything.* Just meet her halfway, and I'll do my best with the paperwork."

It was a reasonable request. The problem was, she couldn't tell her the ring was safe. And she couldn't let her see it.

The diamond was long gone.

46

The morning after the Fourth of July party, Gemma woke up to the news that she'd been summoned to a meeting with Sloan Pierce. Right there in Provincetown.

It was her day off from the store and she'd planned to try to catch up on the orders flooding in on the heels of the *New York Times* article. Last night, at Connor's after the fireworks, she hinted around about meeting his investor contacts while he was busy trying to get her into bed. They both ended the night unsatisfied.

And now this.

Celeste drove the five minutes to the meeting place.

The house didn't seem to belong in Provincetown. High atop a hill on Province Land's Road, it was new construction, mostly glass. It looked as if a strong wind had plucked it from East Hampton and dropped it there. Gemma had biked past it on her way to the beach but never imagined she'd see the interior.

"You're sure this is it?" she said to Celeste.

"I'm sure this is it," Celeste said, double-checking her phone before parking in the circular driveway. "And I have to say, I'd been wondering who built this monstrosity."

"The owner is Sloan Pierce's friend?"

Celeste nodded. "I think the woman buys a lot of art at auction. Her name's Sandra Crowe. I asked around at the party last night and Maud said Sandra came to town just a few years ago. She lived on the East End while building this. She also apparently bullied her way into showing her amateur paintings in one of the galleries."

Gemma glanced behind her to take in the sweeping view of the bay, the jetty, and the marshes. They walked toward the front door, white pebbles crunching under their feet. Before they could ring the bell, a young woman emerged dressed in a white linen button-down and matching pants.

"Welcome! I'm Samantha, Ms. Crowe's assistant. Please follow me out back to the pool."

So much for seeing the interior. White hydrangea bushes framed the path to the rear of the house. The grass and hedges were among the most manicured Gemma had seen in town.

The pool was large and oval-shaped, the water a breathtaking aquamarine — the color of the Caribbean Sea. Elodie was already seated in an Adirondack chair alongside Sloan, drinking a tall glass of pink lemonade. As soon as Gemma took her own seat, another assistant pressed a glass of it into her hands.

"So glad you could join us." Sloan Pierce stood from her chair. She wore a khaki-colored, safari-style shirtdress that looked casual but was probably Ralph Lauren Purple Label. Gemma didn't know how she was meant to greet the woman who, the last time they'd spoken, had basically threatened her career.

Celeste bridged the awkwardness by shaking her hand and then sitting in the chair between them. All four seats had been assembled around a glass table with a bottle of Cristal on ice.

"Thanks for taking the time to meet," Sloan said. "I know it's a holiday weekend and you're all very busy. Normally, I wouldn't press. But my team feels strongly about coordinating this with the Pavlin & Co centennial, and the clock is ticking. An event of this magnitude takes a lot of planning."

"Well, now that we're all here, we can sign the paperwork and move forward," Elodie said.

"We never agreed to sign the contract," Gemma said, glancing at Celeste.

"I did," Celeste said.

What? "You did?"

"On the condition that Elodie tell us where to find your mother's ring."

Gemma turned to Elodie, heart pounding. Elodie crossed her arms, her expression steely.

"My parents sold the Electric Rose under the utmost secrecy ten years ago. It was through a private dealer, completely underground," she said.

Gemma felt like she'd been physically struck. It took a few seconds to find her voice. Sold? *Sold?*

"They got rid of it?" Celeste said, sounding incredulous. She moved closer to Gemma, putting her arm around her shoulders. She leaned against her aunt as if she were the only thing keeping her upright.

Her mother's ring was gone.

"Why?"

"It was a business decision."

"She left that to me. The only thing I

would have of hers." Gemma's mind raced. Someone bought her diamond. And it *was* hers. Her grandfather had given it to her mother, and her mother had given it to her. It was a family heirloom, and there was such a thing as succession. Didn't those things matter?

"I know it's not the answer you wanted, but there it is." Elodie turned to Celeste. "So now it's your turn."

"I'm sorry, Gemma," Celeste said before leafing through the document and signing the last page. "I really am."

Gemma felt sick. The ring was long gone. Sold not long after her parents' accident. The news felt like another death. And it brought the feelings of that awful day rushing back to her.

She and her parents had been on one of their many trips. Gemma's early childhood had been a constant rotation of luxury hotel rooms and yachts anchored off the coast of Europe, punctuated by the occasional visit to New York to see her grandparents. It would have been lonely except for all of the time she and her mother spent together while her father was off scuba diving and parasailing and all the other adrenaline-fueled activities her mother wasn't interested in. Instead, the two of them would shop and take long lunches at cafés and sit on the beach. By that time, Paulina was tired of being hounded by photographers and she'd found anonymity in narrow cobblestoned streets and obscure harbors. But on that particular trip, her mother was learning how to sail.

That final morning, her father filled a thermos with white wine and told Gemma to be good for the babysitter, a local village girl. Her mother helped Gemma get the knots out of her hair, tangled from swimming. Paulina was dressed in a black two-piece bathing suit with a sarong tied around her waist. The gauzy fabric had a yellow butterfly pattern, and the color was picked up by the yellow diamond studs in her ears. Her hair, too, was pale yellow, bleached from the sun. She wore it piled on top of her head in a clip, just a few tendrils escaping that brushed Gemma's cheek when her mother kissed her goodbye.

By nightfall, her parents hadn't returned and the village girl put her to bed. When she woke up in the morning, her grandmother was in the living room. Her first thought was, how strange to see Constance outside of Manhattan. Then her instincts kicked in and told her something was very, very wrong. And then Constance stood up, seeming, in that moment, to tower over her. *There's been an accident . . .*

Sloan Pierce looked at her expectantly. Celeste passed her the pen and the document.

Gemma couldn't do it.

47

The lie about selling the diamond came out so easily, it almost felt like the truth. Elodie gulped her lemonade, wishing it had a shot of vodka in it.

While Celeste signed the contract, Gemma's stare was like a dagger. Who was she to judge? She didn't know the first thing about running a business. And no, selling a few things here and there on Instagram didn't count. Elodie had been in the trenches for decades.

Pavlin & Co had overcome obstacles like world wars and cultural shifts that made expensive jewelry obsolete. But by the late 2000s, the industry was facing the biggest threat by far: technology. Lab-grown diamonds were becoming nearly undetectable from their natural, mined counterparts. And they sold for forty percent less. Worse, jewelry buyers who did want the real thing or even just traditional gold jewelry could now shop online and have pieces shipped anywhere. The metropolitan jewelry retail epicenters of the world were losing their hold on the market.

Maybe her father, or grandfather, or great-grandfather could have found some way to pull a rabbit out of a hat and turn things around. But all Elodie could do was think of a way to get a quick infusion of cash to pay the bills. In her business, the business of dreams, cutting back was not an option.

She thought long and hard about what she could do, coming up short at every turn. And then one day, during her obsessive reading of magazines and newspapers, she came across a *WWD* end-of-the-decade fashion retrospective that included a photo of Paulina at some red-carpet event. The caption made a big deal about the famous pink diamond ring on her finger.

The Electric Rose. After Paulina's death, Alan had put it back in the vault. It was never spoken of, all but forgotten about. When her father died, his obituary made a brief mention of the stone. Still, it wasn't on Elodie's radar.

But then, the cash crunch. What was the point of having a treasure like that locked in a vault? It was no use to them hidden away.

"I think we should sell the Electric Rose,"

she said to her mother.

"Oh, yes," Constance said. "I wish your father had done that a long time ago."

"Good," Elodie said. "The business needs the money."

"What? Oh, no no no. If we sell the ring, the money has to go into a trust for Gemma. Paulina intended for her to have it some day."

Elodie couldn't believe what she was hearing. The ring belonged to the company — it was, at best, loaned to Paulina as a publicity stunt.

But there was no use trying to rationalize with her mother. And so she went around her.

The jewelry trade was a business of secrets. It was ingrained in the culture, both on the part of the sellers and the buyers. Still, the sale of a stone as significant as the Electric Rose would be nearly impossible to keep quiet. But there was another way to wring money from it aside from selling it outright.

For one whole year, she devoted most of her time to planning the 2010 holiday collection she called Pink Rapture: understated pink diamond pieces set in gold and platinum, none any more than two or three carats' worth of stones. It was one of their most successful campaigns; the sales were pure profit because Pavlin & Co didn't purchase any of the diamonds.

The collection was cut from a diamond they already owned: the Electric Rose.

Now, years later, she knew how this would look to Celeste: like a crime. She'd chopped up one of the jewelry world's great treasures. And certainly, Gemma would have a fit and cause god knows what kind of trouble if she knew the truth.

It was one thing to sell it, to let someone else other than their spoiled sister enjoy its beauty. But to chop it up like a used car, selling it piece by piece?

She watched her sister pass the contract to Gemma, who then tossed it to the ground.

"You had no right to sell that ring," she said.

Sloan Pierce slowly and with great deliberation stood from her chair and retrieved the papers from the ground.

"Celeste, Elodie — thank you for coming today. But I'm wondering if it might not be best for me and Gemma to have some time to talk in private?"

Gemma, alone with Sloan Pierce, felt that there was nothing left for them to discuss.

She decided she wouldn't say anything and would just let Sloan do the talking. And the first thing out of her mouth surprised her.

"I need your word — your *professional* word — that this is all confidential," Sloan said.

Gemma hesitated. In her silence, Sloan summoned an assistant and asked for an iced tea.

"Okay," Gemma said.

Sloan leaned forward. "The night of the Pavlin & Co centennial party, I was surprised to see that the Electric Rose wasn't included in the exhibit."

"I know. You mentioned that the day we met at City Bakery."

"I've been making discreet inquiries about it ever since."

Gemma's eyes widened. "And?"

"Do you know that only one percent of all pink diamonds are larger than ten carats?"

Gemma did know this. Her mother had told her everything about the Electric Rose. She nodded impatiently. "Well? What did you find?"

Sloan shook her head. "Nothing. The trail is cold."

The assistant reappeared with a tall glass of iced tea and lemon. When she retreated, Gemma said, "How is that possible? It's one of the most famous stones in the entire world. I get it — brokers deal with discretion. But this seems extreme."

"Pieces do go underground. I've seen it happen many times. I have no doubt the Electric Rose will surface again but it could be decades."

Decades?

"Can you keep looking?" Gemma said, hearing the desperation in her voice.

Sloan stirred the tea with a long spoon.

"I can't keep putting time and resources into it. Especially if the auction isn't happening."

Well, that was direct.

"What are you suggesting?" Gemma asked.

"I'll keep working my contacts and searching for this diamond if you sign this contract."

Gemma looked at Sloan and knew she had nothing left to lose. Except one thing.

"I'll sign on two conditions: You add a stipulation that the Electric Rose will not be included in the auction. Not even if you find it and the new owner is willing to sell."

Sloan's pale eyes narrowed.

"And I want a cut of the proceeds." Gemma didn't know how much money an auction would make, but she was pretty sure even a fraction of the money would be enough to help her scale up her business.

"You drive a hard bargain."

"Is that a yes?"

"I need to work out the money part with legal. I think it can be arranged. But I need one more thing: photos of your mother wearing her famous jewels. For the catalogue and other auction promotion. Not photos from the ad campaigns of the 1990s, but candid, never-before-seen images. Do you have anything like that?"

Photos of her mother held a sacred space in Gemma's emotional life. Paulina had died before the world went social media crazy — before the iPhone had even been invented. Interestingly, and somewhat disturbingly, a few Paulina Pavlin fan accounts had popped up on Instagram where people curated the paparazzi and ad photos from the era just before Gemma was born. Paulina loved to be photographed, but once she became a mother, she lost interest in the spotlight. There were only a few truly candid images of her mother, and they were all held in her grandmother's photo albums boxed away in a storage space in New Jersey.

"I might," Gemma said slowly. "I'd have to look."

"Great! I'll loop in Elodie about the

photos and your cut of the proceeds."

On the surface, all of this made sense. There was something in it for both of them: The auction would boost Sloan Pierce's career. It would make Gemma some money. But as logical as it sounded, this wasn't the way she wanted to fund her business. In fact, it was the opposite. But all she could think about, the one thing she couldn't let go of, was the chance to see the Electric Rose again.

"I'm willing to give this a shot," Gemma said. "So . . . to be continued?"

Sloan uncorked the champagne, the cork flying off in the direction of the pool. She poured a glass and handed it to Gemma.

She sipped it uneasily. She felt like she was dancing with the devil. She wondered what her mother would want her to do. She suspected she would tell her to keep dancing.

48

Constance, 2004

Her husband had been right about one thing: All of Manhattan showed up to celebrate the tenth anniversary of the Electric Rose.

At one time, nights like this were the highlight of her year. But since her daughters had stopped speaking to one another, she couldn't enjoy any of it. A diamond might say love, but what did it say when a diamond divided the entire family?

All day long she'd gone through the motions, slipping into her Ralph Lauren gown, getting her hair done by Orlando Pita. Laura Mercier stopped by to do her makeup. Constance knew she'd never looked better. And she'd never felt worse.

Sitting in the back of the limo, one block away from the store, Alan reached for her hand. She snatched it away.

"What's with you tonight?" he said — as

if the problem were just that night. With their daughters locked in conflict, the family they'd built together falling apart, she felt their relationship withering.

"What do you think?"

Elodie bristled at even the mention of her sisters' names. Celeste had moved to some godforsaken beach town at the end of the earth. And Paulina traveled constantly with her husband and daughter, no doubt avoiding the tension in New York. Constance barely had any time with her only grandchild. It was a minor miracle that Alan had been able to wrangle them all together for the evening. She didn't know how he made it happen, because the topic of their daughters was now an emotional land mine in their marriage.

They hadn't been physically intimate in years. And no matter what any of the magazine articles said about aging and sexuality, she knew her body wasn't the problem. It was her mind, her unmitigated fury at Alan for putting the company first, for not listening to her when she said the competition for the Electric Rose was a bad idea. For his refusal to admit, even now, what a mistake it had been. Whenever she tried to mention it, he just pushed back.

"A mistake? You can't argue with results.

Sales have never been better. I just wish my father were here to see it."

His father? Elliot Pavlin had single-handedly changed the entire industry. All Alan had accomplished was a publicity stunt that destroyed the relationship between three sisters.

"You think your parents would be happy when our children no longer speak to each other? Pavlin & Co has always been a family business. What happens when the family falls apart?"

"Elodie is doing a fine job. The future of Pavlin & Co is secure. And the girls will grow out of all this silliness eventually. This will pass — you'll see."

She wasn't so sure — about any of it. And she felt very alone, even in that moment, surrounded by photographers and a flurry of invited guests as they made their way across the sales floor of Pavlin & Co toward the podium, where Celeste and Elodie were already waiting. The bright lights made her blink too fast, and she felt shaky standing by Alan's side in the center of the family. They were waiting for Paulina and Liam, who were late. She didn't mind the extra time to collect herself.

When she spotted Paulina making her way toward them, holding her daughter's little hand, she couldn't help but smile. They looked so beautiful in their matching butterfly dresses. Constance felt a surge of love for her youngest. And regret that she hadn't protected her more. Protected all three of her girls.

"Come along, everyone's waiting for you," Constance said, ushering them in place next to Elodie and Celeste. Then she walked back to stand on the other side of Alan. A photographer began clicking away, and a publicist asked for a pause so she could duck over and adjust the microphone.

She felt a tug on her dress and looked down to find Gemma beside her.

"What are you doing over here, sweetheart? You belong next to your mom."

"She told me to come over here," the girl said, her eyes filled with tears.

Oh, this was not good. She glanced over and sure enough, Paulina and Elodie seemed to be arguing. In front of everyone! As if they didn't have enough trouble with the tabloids. She wanted to run over and tell them to cut it out, but that would only attract more attention. Besides, the more important thing was to keep Gemma from getting upset. She'd failed to do the best thing for her own daughters, but she'd be damned if she didn't do things differently with her granddaughter.

"Oh, well, that's so nice of Mommy. She must know I need some extra-special company."

She gave a wink, and the little girl smiled. If only her older girls were so easily placated. She just hoped Alan was right: that the strife would pass.

She didn't want to think about what the future would look like if he was wrong.

49

Celeste practically floated her way over to Lidia's house. The diamond was gone! Sold.

The Pavlin curse was no more.

Fans whirred inside but seemed to do little more than move around hot air. Celeste wiped her brow with the back of her hand.

"Great party last night," Celeste said, accepting Lidia's hug.

"Should I turn on the air conditioner?"

"No, not on my account. I have to get back to the store."

Lidia poured two glasses of iced tea and they sat at the table.

She leaned closer to Celeste with a conspiratorial smile on her face.

"I'm glad you stopped by. Here's the burning question of the day: Do you think your sister and Tito are . . . involved?"

Celeste recalled the moment last night when Tito brought Elodie a drink — the way they looked at each other. She'd given her sister a teasing wink about it but had only been joking.

"Do *you*?"

Lidia shrugged. "I don't know. They do spend a lot of time together. Maybe I'm just being my usual hopeless romantic self."

Celeste suspected that was most likely the case. As far as she knew, her sister hadn't had a relationship in decades. Not that she was privy to any details about her personal life. Maybe Elodie had tons of love affairs. It was sad how little she knew of her only remaining sister.

But she wasn't there to talk about Elodie.

"Lidia, I need help planning the wedding. Jack is really eager to get things going."

"Thought you'd never ask! You could do it here on the water. Or, I was thinking the garden —"

The lights went off and the fans stopped whirring. Lidia walked to the foot of the hallway stairs.

"Manny?"

"Blackout," he responded from somewhere deep in the house.

"Can you get the generator on?" Lidia yelled back.

Celeste gulped her iced tea. She heard Manny thump down the stairs. He waved his phone at Lidia.

"I got a text from the power company. Apparently, the blackout is due to 'animal contact.' They're estimating about an hour or so."

"Well, Marco's oysters can't wait an hour, so you'd better get moving."

Celeste's heart beat faster. This was a sign. Even with the ring gone, there she was, in the middle of talking about the wedding, and the universe interrupted.

"I should get going," she said.

"Don't you want to finish —"

The conversation? No. She didn't.

Gemma dealt with the bad news about the diamond ring the way she dealt with most things: She got to work. Celeste had given her the go-ahead to sell her pieces in the store, and now she needed to create a display.

"Try using this for the chains," Jack said, setting up a Lucite "arm" he'd found in the back. "And then the charms can go on a tray in front."

"Yeah, that could work," Gemma said. She took a breath, telling herself to focus on the task in front of her. Still, her thoughts kept looping back to the Electric Rose. She didn't believe Elodie's explanation that the sale had been purely a business decision. It seemed like an act of spite — the same spite that made her aunt reject her. Maybe it even had something to do with why the family had cast her aside.

Suddenly, the lights went out. The fans stopped whirring. Jack's phone pinged with a text.

"The power's out," he said. "Animal contact."

"What does that mean?"

"Sometimes an osprey builds a nest near the power lines or something else and then we just have to wait for it to be fixed. It's pretty routine this time of year." He propped open the front doors and walked out back to get the generator going.

Gemma set her necklace chains on the arm, grouping them by metal: silver, gold-plated brass, and gold-plated silver. She put out two of each to leave room for the bracelets. Just a few minutes without the fans and already the shop was uncomfortably hot.

"Gemma. Hey."

She turned to find Sanjay.

"What are you doing here?" she said.

"I got to town two days ago."

She nodded, looking back at her necklaces. "Yes. I'm aware. I saw you at the parade.

Both of you." With her back to him, she put down the chain, took a breath, and said, "I don't get it. Is bringing her here some kind of payback?"

"What? No. I came to take more photographs. You mentioning me in the *Times* . . . I appreciate it. I really do. And I wanted to say hi to you before I leave tomorrow."

She turned around.

"Okay, well — hi. Is that it?"

"Gemma, don't be like that. We agreed to be friends, right?"

Friends. Right.

He walked closer, looking at the display. "You're selling your work here? That's a great idea."

"How long have you been with Monica?"

"Gemma —"

"I want to know. I want to know how long I've been needlessly blaming myself, feeling like an awful person, when you've already moved on."

She thought, fleetingly, of Connor. But that didn't count. She didn't have real feelings for him. She hadn't even slept with him.

Sanjay sighed. "It's pretty recent."

Two women walked in, both wearing patterned wrap dresses and strappy sandals, one blonde, one brunette, both with short haircuts and big sunglasses.

“We saw on Instagram that the GEMMA jewelry is being sold here,” the brunette said.

“Are you the designer?” the blonde said, pushing her sunglasses atop her head.

“I am,” she said. Then she turned to Sanjay. “Excuse me. I have work to do.”

50

Between the blackout and the heat, everyone had fled to the beach. With few customers, Celeste closed the store early and met Jack on the water.

The boat offered an escape. Out on the *Pacheco,* it was their own private P'town. Celeste leaned back on the bench seat and looked out at the horizon. The early evening light never lost its wow factor. Celeste had witnessed countless summer sunsets, and no two were ever the same. Once, she'd heard herself explaining this to a friend back in New York, and she realized she sounded just like her father talking about diamonds.

"Uh-oh. I know that look," Jack said affectionately from behind the wheel.

"What look?"

"That line between your brows. Never a good sign. Come take the wheel for a minute. I'm losing the wind."

She took his place behind the control

panel while he adjusted the sails. The truth was she felt more relaxed than she had in a long time.

"Elodie finally told me what happened to Paulina's ring," she said. "My parents sold it after she died."

Jack nodded thoughtfully. "You let all that go a long time ago. Now maybe your niece can, too."

Well, that's where he was wrong: She hadn't let it go. And now her sister and niece were stirring it all up again. She found herself thinking, again and again, of her last conversation with Paulina. It had been the morning after Gemma's eighth birthday party, her next visit after the stressful anniversary celebration for the Electric Rose.

The birthday party was yet another Pavlin extravaganza. Alan and Constance rented out the Plaza's Oak Room for an intimate family gathering of, oh, two hundred people. When Paulina invited her, she felt torn. She wanted to be there for her sister and niece but hated the thought of making small talk with strangers all night, explaining why she lived so far away, and why she wasn't married. Jack begged out of the spectacle, and she didn't blame him.

"Why don't you and Liam bring Gemma here for a visit instead?" Celeste had suggested with a trans-Atlantic call to Paulina a few weeks earlier. The three of them were still busy bouncing around Europe. Paulina and Liam's habits hadn't changed much in the years since becoming parents, and Paulina insisted she was going to settle in one place "soon." Constance was pushing them to plant themselves in the city so Gemma could have a proper education, but so far Paulina hadn't committed.

"Oh, please come to the party! I can't deal with Elodie's dirty looks without you as a buffer. You're honestly the only one I really want to see. And bring Heron — Gemma is begging us for a pet, so at least that might satisfy her for a weekend." At the time, Celeste and Jack had a rescue dog named after her favorite Cape Cod bird.

Celeste agreed to go for the weekend — without the dog. She was staying at her parents' on Park Avenue and Constance didn't like animals because they smelled.

She mollified herself during the long drive with the fact that at such a huge party, the tension between her sisters would be swallowed up by the crowd. Celeste should have known it wouldn't be that simple.

It wasn't enough for her parents to have a wedding-sized party for their eight-year-old granddaughter. They also hosted a dinner the night before, family only, at the apartment. When Celeste arrived, she found that Paulina and Liam were also staying there for the weekend. She'd had enough of the acrimony between her sisters during the last visit, but her adorable niece was some consolation; Gemma was a sweet, shy child who looked a lot like Paulina, with the same flaxen hair and bright blue-green eyes. But even at that age she was clearly her own little person. She talked about her love of animals and how she wanted to be a veterinarian or an artist when she grew up.

Gemma showed Elodie a drawing she'd made, and Elodie sneered that she'd better learn to color properly if she planned on becoming an artist.

"Ease up," Celeste had whispered, pulling her aside. "Whatever happened in the past isn't her fault. She never did anything to you."

"Her *existence* is doing something to me," Elodie said. "Something you'd understand if you ever took a second to consider my feelings."

It was hopeless. Years and years since the nuclear photos of Paulina, Liam, and Celeste on the beach, and Elodie was no closer to getting over it. She still hated Paulina, she resented the child, and she blamed

Celeste for not taking her "side." Celeste would have to just ride out the weekend, and the next time Paulina wanted to see her, it was going to have to be in Provincetown.

She had no idea that there wouldn't be a next time.

The table was set with crystal candlesticks and vases bursting with pink peonies. Paulina asked their mother if the birthday cake had pink icing, as she'd requested.

Constance turned to Gemma. "Your mother always insisted on pink frosting on her birthday cakes."

"It's the best!" Paulina said, giving Gemma a wink.

Her father praised Liam's latest boost to their marketing efforts. While Liam no longer worked for the ad agency, he never stopped sending ideas to Alan even as he and Paulina traveled the world. That night, he told Alan that the new popularity of "blogs" was something they should capitalize on. Specifically, he showed them that Paulina's blog got a tremendous amount of "traffic" and they should look at ways to monetize that.

"If she wears a piece in a photo on her blog, women will want to buy it. We need to figure out a way to integrate commerce so that her followers can buy with the click of a button."

"No one really buys jewelry online," Constance said. "Don't be ridiculous."

"I hate to say it, Constance, but they do," Liam said.

"Online shopping is the way of the future, Mom," said Paulina. Celeste agreed, but she kept her mouth shut. Getting involved in any conversation with the group was a lose-lose.

"The only future I want to discuss is when you're going to come home. Enough of this gallivanting around! My granddaughter needs a proper education. I've made some inquires and she can start at Spence in the fall." Constance turned to Liam. "And then you can come work for the company full-time. Save your ideas for the team in a conference room, not my dinner table."

"The *team* has it covered, thanks, Mom," Elodie said acidly.

After dinner, while her parents' kitchen staff set out the dessert, Alan asked Celeste to come along with him for his walk. He always took a walk between dinner and dessert no matter how hot or cold the weather. Even at a restaurant he would take a stroll around the block.

It wasn't unusual for him to tap one of

them to accompany him. When she was growing up, the walks had afforded her some of her best conversations with her father. After a good meal and a glass of wine — he never allowed himself more than one glass — he was at his most relaxed and amiable. But that night, she sensed an agenda.

Sure enough, as soon as they rounded the corner into Central Park, he said: "Celeste, no matter how far away you live, you're still the eldest sister. Everyone respects you. And I need your help."

Respect? Did he call cutting her off financially for moving away *respect*? Maybe it was a form of respect. Maybe it was a way of letting her make her own way in the world. She was happy to do so.

"Dad, whatever it is, I don't want to be involved."

"This isn't for me," he said. "This is for your sister."

"Paulina?"

"No. Elodie. I can't have Liam working at the company. It would drive her mad. And I need her focused. Elodie has become a vital part of our organization."

"So whatever you're about to ask me is for *you.* For the company."

"Your mother is determined to lure Paulina back here. I have a feeling this time

Paulina will say yes. And I can't have that."

"So tell all this to Mom."

"There's no reasoning with your mother. She wants her baby back in the fold. So I need *you* to convince Paulina to say no."

"How am I supposed to do that?"

"By example. You've decided that living at the farthest reaches of the earth is preferable to being part of our lives here. If it's best for you, isn't it best for Paulina?"

She told her father she'd think about it, even though she had no intention of getting involved.

The next morning, Paulina knocked on her bedroom door while she was packing up.

She carried a mug of coffee and was dressed in a T-shirt and faded red sweatpants with holes in them. With her long hair up in a ponytail, she looked like a teenager.

"I wish you could stay a few more days," she said, sitting on the bed and crossing her legs.

"Bring Gemma to P'town," Celeste said. "She'd love it."

Paulina nodded. "I will. But also I need to figure out everything else."

"What's everything else?"

"Well, Mom and Dad want us here full-time."

Celeste stopped folding her clothes. She'd already decided she wasn't going to do her father's bidding, but last night, seeing her little niece at the ostentatious party clearly planned more to impress her parents' friends than to please a child, Celeste started thinking that maybe it *was* best for Paulina and Liam to have their own family life away from the Pavlin & Co circus.

"Don't be pressured into moving back to the city just because Mom says so," Celeste said. "What do *you* want?"

Paulina sighed. There was a certain light missing from her eyes. It wasn't unhappiness. It was the absence of the complete carefree self-centeredness. It was motherhood.

"I almost feel ready to be here more of the time. But Liam wants to spend some time sailing. He's really into the idea of going back to the South of France. I just don't know how practical that trip would be with Gemma."

"You always take Gemma with you. Why would this be any different?"

Paulina shrugged. "I guess you're right," she said. Just like that: *I guess you're right.*

One month later, she and Liam were dead. A boating accident near an out-of-the-way village called Villesèquelande.

■ ■ ■ ■

Jack took his place back behind the steering column of the boat. When Celeste sat back down on the bench, her hands were shaking. Elodie had been right to be angry with her all these years, just not for the reasons she thought. Celeste hadn't done wrong by *her:* She'd done wrong by Paulina. She told Paulina to leave because that was her personal method of dealing with their parents. But maybe Paulina could have stayed in New York and found another solution. At least she'd still be alive today.

"Jack?" Suddenly she felt that if she kept this inside for one moment longer she would burst.

"Yes, my dear?" he said, smiling at her.

"Nothing," she said.

51

Elodie had long prided herself on her executive function. She not only had the ability to plan ahead, but to think two steps ahead of anyone else around her. Now, suddenly, she found herself two steps behind: The auction was not going as she had planned, and her room rental expired at the end of the week. She was surprised to find she didn't want to leave.

Partly because of work, but mostly — if not all — because of Tito.

She didn't want to admit this to anyone, not even to herself. Instead, she kept up the ruse that she wanted to open a Pavlin & Co summer outpost. Fortunately, the owner of the building was dragging her heels, so Elodie hadn't been forced to actually do anything yet.

Inside the Barros house the electricity was restored from yesterday's blackout; a fan whirred in the corner of the kitchen and the bright numbers on the stove clock blinked. But Lidia was nowhere to be found.

In the upstairs hallway, Tito stepped out from his bedroom with Pearl trotting behind him.

"She came running into my room," Tito said, smiling. "I think she was looking for you."

Elodie bent down and patted her stout little body and Pearl licked her hand.

"Shall we take them for a walk?" Elodie said.

He shook his head. "The mechanical sorter they use for the oysters is acting up, so I'm going to see what I can do. But how 'bout dinner tonight?"

Elodie looked up in surprise.

"Sure. That sounds lovely."

"I'm thinking we can go somewhere dog-friendly so we don't have to worry about a sitter," he said with a wink. "I'll pick you up at six."

"You're picking me up? We live in the same house."

"Well, that makes things easy now, don't it?"

Her heart beat fast watching him leave. And to think, just a month ago she thought that work would be the only thing getting her out of bed in the morning. Look at her now — excited as a high schooler invited to the prom. But her time at the house was coming to an end unless she hurried up and extended her room rental. She had to find Lidia.

She leashed up Pearl and walked her out to the dock. The heat had let up, beaten back by the wind blowing off the bay. Crowds of tourists were lined up for seal-watching tours and boat rentals. Lidia, wearing bright orange coveralls and water boots, helped Marco pull mesh bags full of oysters off a small boat and into waiting ice coolers. Her back was to Elodie but Marco noticed her and called out, "Hey there, Elodie."

Lidia turned around for a moment but went right back to feeding oysters into the ice bath. Elodie walked closer.

"Lidia, sorry to interrupt," she said, talking loudly over the rumble of a nearby boat motor. "I just wanted to say I'm going to take the room for the rest of the summer. I can give you the check whenever you want later but I just didn't want you to —"

Lidia looked stricken. "Oh, Elodie, I'm so sorry. I rented it out the day before the Fourth weekend, when you gave me notice you were leaving. I have new tenants moving in next week. But I think it's great that you're staying — just wonderful!"

Now what? She understood the town enough by now to know that finding another room would not be easy.

Tomorrow, she would have to go back and speak to that horrid little man at the real estate office. For now, she would stay focused on the positive.

She had a date tonight.

The restaurant Connor wanted to take her to, the Red Inn, was fully booked.

"I should have thought ahead," Connor said. "Of course, they don't take reservations. It's right on the water — totally historic. President Roosevelt and his wife stayed here when they came to lay the cornerstone of the Pilgrim Monument in 1907."

When Connor first arrived in town to start getting the gallery ready during the off-season, the locals had plenty of time and energy to share all sorts of Provincetown trivia. Now, with the summer in full swing, it was conceivable for someone to spot their spouse on the street and barely muster a wave hello.

"It's fine — honestly. Takeout is great."

Gemma wasn't in the mood for a crowded restaurant. After the unexpected visit from

Sanjay, she'd considered canceling her plans with Connor. But she couldn't give in to that impulse.

Connor's kitchen island was filled end to end with platters of chicken parmesan, pasta, and salads from Liz's Café on Bradford Street. They took their food to the front porch, drinking white wine out of clear plastic cups.

"This house is really spectacular," she said, trying to find something positive to say, to think — to feel. She couldn't let herself slide into a funk.

"It's pretty perfect," he said, leaning over to kiss her. "That's why I made an offer on it."

She looked at him in surprise. "It's for sale?"

"Isn't everything? For the right price, of course," he said with a wink.

He talked about the gallery and more Provincetown trivia. She liked looking at him while he spoke, the assurance of his gestures and the way he smiled as he told a story. Still, she felt her mind drifting.

"I'm sorry. What was that?"

"Everything okay?" he asked.

"Oh, everything's great," she said.

"Let me guess: You hate takeout."

"No," she said, forcing a smile. "I'm just

distracted. Family stuff."

It was partly true.

He made a "give it to me" gesture with his hands. "I know all about 'family stuff.' What's going on?"

She hesitated. But after the *New York Times* article, there was no use worrying about discretion.

"My aunt — not the one with the store, her sister — is auctioning off jewelry that's been in the family for generations. My mother died when I was young, and she left me her engagement ring. I was afraid it was going to be part of the auction, but it's worse than that: My grandparents sold it years ago."

"That's awful," he said, putting his plate down on the ground and reaching for her hand. "Have you talked to a lawyer?"

She shook her head. The thought never crossed her mind. Who could afford a lawyer? "I'm trying to track down the ring to start figuring out if I can ever get it back. Or even see it again. I know it's a long shot but I need to feel like I'm doing something about it."

"Well, you should go to the auction," he said.

"Why would I do that?"

"If there's something you like, bid on it.

That way you can at least have something from the collection."

Did he imagine she had that kind of money?

"I'll go with you," he said.

She laughed. "That's really sweet. But it's not for a while. And I'm not going."

He leaned forward and rubbed her knee. "Think about it. I'm more than happy to give you moral support. And I love a good auction. Maybe I'll bid on something. You'll have to tell me what's worth investing in."

Their eyes locked and she felt a powerful surge of desire. He leaned forward and kissed her so lightly it was like she imagined it. All at once she was tired of being cautious or protecting herself. She pulled back just enough to set her own plate on the ground, and then moved to his chair, onto his lap. They kissed again, more deeply, and her thoughts disappeared — she was all sensation.

"Do you want to go upstairs?" he said, his voice husky.

The question was like a record scratch. She felt the wall go up, her insides tightening like a fist. She took a deep breath, looking at Connor. He was definitely a man who was used to getting what he wanted. And by a third date, sex wasn't an unreasonable ask.

But she couldn't do it.

We agreed to be friends, right?

"Things are moving a little fast for me," she said.

He looked surprised — maybe even a little annoyed. But he quickly recovered. He reached for her hand.

"No problem. I can wait. You, Gemma Maybrook, are worth waiting for."

52

If Celeste and Jack had to name a favorite spot, the salt marshes at Herring Cove would be top of the list. Even at the peak of summer, they could usually find a moment of solitude amongst the great blue herons, osprey, and regal egrets. They dressed in waders and carried binoculars. Jack wore a whistle around his neck in case of coyotes.

Celeste pulled her straw hat lower over her face. The sun beat down as they walked the perimeter of a mud patch, bubbles popping up through small holes — a sure sign that quahogs were underfoot. She reached for Jack's hand.

"It never gets old," she said, flush with love for the staggering natural beauty of her adopted town. And for her partner.

Jack stopped walking, his dark eyes sharp and focused on her.

"It certainly doesn't," he said, pulling her close. She smelled the faint scent of the tobacco he was supposed to quit. That, and the briny musk of his sweat. "You're as beautiful as the summer we met. More beautiful. I love these." He traced her crow's feet with his finger.

"Oh, Jack," she said, kissing him. His hardscrabble New England exterior was no match for his romantic heart. A dragonfly landed on his shoulder, then alighted. "I love you."

"I know you do," he said. "Say, any thoughts yet about the wedding venue?"

"Well," she said, swallowing hard. "I started talking to Lidia about it but then the blackout happened and we got distracted." Okay, not exactly the truth. The blackout *did* happen right when they were set to talk, but she took it as a bad sign, and immediately called Maud for a reading.

Maud gave her unusual instructions.

"Go to the water tonight," she said. "Collect thirteen stones of similar shape and size. Keep them by your bedside overnight and bring them with you when you come for your reading."

Celeste did as she was told, carrying the bundle of stones to her lunchtime appointment. They sat across from each other at a small table and Maud marked each stone with a different symbol; one represented the sun, another the moon, another Mercury, and so on. Then she placed all the stones in a cloth, drawing it closed into a pouch. She then closed her eyes and asked Celeste to do the same.

"I want you to meditate on what concerns you, what questions you bring with you today," Maud said. After a few minutes, she told Celeste to keep her eyes closed, but that she was going to place her hand on the stones and she should retrieve three. "Now set them on the table."

The stones she picked were Venus, Mars, and the Universe.

Maud contemplated them, then looked Celeste in the eyes with her steady gaze. "Venus is connected to love and happiness. Mars suggests the need for courage and a potential battle ahead. The Universe suggests a reshuffling of your place in the grand scheme of things. So I would say that you're right to be on guard. Proceed with caution. Change is ahead."

"But what does that really *mean*? Should I go ahead with the wedding?"

Maud said she couldn't tell her what to do, she could only give her the information at her disposal. But the information wasn't enough; Celeste felt the universe was giving muddled signals just when she needed it to guide her the most.

"I was thinking we could have the wedding in the garden," Jack said.

"In our backyard?"

"No — not our garden: Suzanne's Garden."

Suzanne's Garden was a floral wonderland open to visitors for the past decade. It began as a private garden created by a longtime Provincetown resident named Suzanne, who hired a landscaper to plant a small orchard, and then a few years later began collaborating with a new next-door neighbor to create a joint flower garden. The pair even traveled to Monet's garden near Paris for inspiration. The result was both whimsical and thoughtful: pear trees, hazelnut bushes, roses, irises with shell pathways throughout, and a central wisteria arbor.

As she thought about it now, the arbor made it an obvious choice for a wedding, although Celeste had gone there to sit and read so many times and it had never crossed her mind. It was a perfect place for quiet contemplation, especially in the middle of the summer when so much of the town was overrun with visitors and every outdoor space seemed to be teeming with tourists. Most people didn't know about the garden, and even during the busiest theme week she could usually find an hour or two of solitude in the arbor.

Jack knew that she loved the place. It was a thoughtful idea.

"Um, sure," she said.

"We can go look at it tomorrow," he said, kissing her neck, then her collarbone, then gently tugged her down onto the muddy ground.

"Someone could walk by," she said, her body already responding to him.

"After all these years, you still pretend you're not every bit as adventurous as I am."

For the moment, her fears about the future were forgotten.

Race Point Beach was almost as crowded at eight at night as it was in the middle of the afternoon. Elodie and Tito had staked out their prime spot an hour earlier, setting down their folding beach chairs and the picnic basket they'd assembled together in Lidia's kitchen. Elodie, who had spent her life dining in the finest Manhattan restaurants — Daniel, Union Square Café, Danube, Le Bernadin — had perhaps never enjoyed a meal so much as the chicken salad sandwiches and potato chips she ate that evening.

The sky was already a kaleidoscope of

color: blues, purples, pinks, and oranges. It made her feel whimsical and girlish. It reminded her of the multi-flavored swirled sorbet her mother used to serve when she was a child.

Elodie swallowed hard. She looked into his deep dark eyes — so brown they were nearly black — and felt unmoored in a way that was unsettling and thrilling. A day ago, she would have told someone — if she had anyone to confide in — that her feelings for Tito reminded her of the way she'd felt about the one man she'd ever loved: giddy, unfocused, thrilled but also insecure. No one since Liam Maybrook had inspired such intensity. And yet, this was different. Being around Tito also made her feel enveloped in calm.

She didn't know what to do with these feelings. When she was younger, attraction led to sex and sex led to relationships and relationships were supposed to lead to marriage someday. But that hadn't worked out for her.

Besides, she wasn't sure how Tito felt. They were dog-walking buddies. Sure, a picnic dinner at Race Point at sunset had romantic overtones. Yes, he'd held her hand at the fireworks on the Fourth. But she still felt uncertain.

The sun inched lower on the horizon. People stood, phones held high, snapping photos. Elodie and Tito walked to the edge of the ocean. They stood, shoulders touching, watching the light change with every passing second. When the sun dipped out of view, everyone broke into applause.

"Penny for your thoughts," Tito said.

"Oh, even that would be overpriced, I'm afraid," she said.

"Are you worried about finding housing?"

She looked at him in surprise. Lidia must have mentioned her inquiry and the fact that she was losing her room at the house.

"No," she said quickly. "I'll find something."

"Now I'm kicking myself for renting out my house all summer," he said. "You could have stayed with me." Stay with him? *Definitely romantic.*

She smiled. "I would never impose. But thank you."

"It would be fun."

Fun? *Friendship.*

"I'm going to speak to the Realtor tomorrow," she said.

"Why don't you talk to your sister? She has space above the store. Unless there's someone else staying there aside from your niece."

"Oh — no. My sister and I don't have that kind of relationship. We're not like your family."

"Well, that's a darn shame," he said. "Maybe if you stayed there you could work on that."

"I'm doing just fine. There's nothing that needs working on," she said, a little defensive. He must have sensed her irritation, because he reached out for her hand. She went in to shake it — like a friend. *No hard feelings.* But then he held it — like *more* than a friend.

"Elodie," he said.

"Yes?"

"I only mention it because I want you to be happy. And part of that is selfish."

"Selfish? How so?"

"I figure the happier you are, the longer you'll stick around."

And then he leaned over and kissed her.

Romantically.

53

After weeks of distractions, Celeste finally got around to having Clifford Henry's antique walking stick restored.

She delivered it to his real estate office herself. The door heralded her arrival with a tinkle of the small bells attached to the interior knob. Clifford sat at his desk with a cup of coffee in one hand and an open laptop in front of him.

"Sorry to disturb," she said.

"Oh, not at all," he said, closing the laptop. "Just down the wormhole of the P'town Community Facebook page. Did you see the video of the seal getting eaten by a shark on Race Point Beach yesterday?"

"No. And I'm not sure I want to," she said with a laugh.

"Trust me, you don't. It's put me off my latte."

"Well, here's something that will hopefully cheer you up: your walking stick, your majesty."

"Oh, it's glorious! Just glorious. Looking at this, you have to wonder if we weren't born in the wrong century."

The bells on the door sounded again. She turned to see her sister walk in with Pearl on a leash trotting behind her.

"What are you doing here?" she said.

"What are *you* doing here?" Elodie crossed her arms.

"Ah, the lady returns," Clifford said.

"Yes, well, I lost the room I've been renting, so now I'm hoping you can find me someplace else." Elodie fanned herself with her hand, sat in the nearest chair, and pulled Pearl onto her lap. "It's exceedingly warm in here. Do you happen to have a water bowl for my dog?"

Clifford asked if she could work with a large mug and Elodie said that would be fine.

"How much longer are you planning to stay?" Celeste said.

Elodie hesitated for a beat. "The rest of the summer."

Clifford seemed even more surprised than she was.

"You want me to find you a place in *July* for the *rest of the summer.* Does it read 'Wizard of Oz' outside my door? Why do people expect me to work miracles?" Clifford said. Celeste glanced at Elodie and they shared a smile.

Celeste felt a rush of conflicting feelings: She was unnerved that Elodie planned to stay in Provincetown, but there was no denying the thaw between them these past few weeks. If Elodie was still blaming her for siding with Paulina all those years ago, she seemed to be letting that go, inch by inch. And now it was up to Celeste to forgive her for being pushy about the auction and lying about the ring. It was time to accept that they were all just doing the best that they could do. After all, Elodie was just as much a victim of their parents' manipulation as she was.

It was a relief on some deep, half-buried part of her psyche to be on better terms with her only remaining sister. Maybe Jack had been right all the years he'd been pushing her to have some relationship with her parents and, when it was too late for that, with Elodie. She could tell it was a relief for her sister to confess about selling the Electric Rose. There had been a tension on her face that Celeste recognized from when they were girls and she was caught in a lie. Elodie was fundamentally a decent person. No, it hadn't been fair of her to accuse

Celeste of being complicit in Paulina's relationship with Liam. In turn, Celeste went on the defensive, lumping Elodie in with their parents as someone she couldn't trust.

"I just need a room — not even a whole house," Elodie said. "I'll pay double the asking price."

Just a room. Celeste had a room down the hall from studio. What was the harm in handing out another olive branch?

"I have a room," Celeste said.

Elodie looked at her in surprise.

"See? What did I tell you?" Clifford said. "Come to Clifford Henry with an inquiry, and you walk out with a home."

Celeste and Elodie exchanged another hesitant smile and then burst out laughing.

The line for her jewelry stretched from outside Queen Anne's Revenge down the block.

Days after the *New York Times* article, Cardi B was photographed wearing a yellow gold Casterbridge "C" charm. Now Gemma was sold out of the letters. She had a few Rock Candy pieces left and a few recently made charms, including the cloisonné eggs. She had to find another estate sale as soon as possible.

"Celeste is looking pretty foolish about now for not selling jewelry sooner," Jack said from behind the counter.

Gemma, flush with the feeling of success, smiled at him. "Oh, you think just any jewelry would sell like this?"

When she'd gotten kicked out of her apartment building after graduation, she'd thought it would be months and months before she could sell in person again. Now there she was, up and running in July. She hoped if she could connect with one of Connor's money people, they would come by in person to see the action. Instagram numbers were one thing, but a line out the door on a flawless beach day was something else.

"You tell me," he said. "Is there some secret to your success?"

"My customers feel the pieces are made just for them. It's personal."

She handed one of the eggs to a customer about her age with a unibrow and blond undercut. The woman declared that her grandmother had one just like it. She also bought a gold-plated necklace chain.

"Are you the designer?" the woman said. Gemma nodded, and the woman asked for a selfie.

"Don't forget to tag me," she said, waving

over the next person in line. And then Elodie breezed in carrying a tape measure.

"Good heavens, are you giving these things away?" she said, peering at the display.

"I'm giving people what they want. When you do that, they sell themselves," Gemma said. Elodie checked the tag on a necklace chain.

"Your price point is very low."

"It's relative. For some people, it's a huge extravagance. But worth it to them."

She glanced at the charm tray, nearly empty. She'd hoped Celeste could take her antiquing tomorrow. Within the hour, she'd be cleaned out.

Elodie moved on, asking Jack to show her upstairs. Gemma found the request odd but didn't have time to wonder when her phone vibrated with a text from Sloan Pierce. *I hope you'll be in the city soon to fulfill your end of our bargain. I have some information I think you'll find very interesting.*

Gemma looked up at her next customer. "Excuse me for one second."

You located my diamond? she typed.

Not exactly. But I believe I know what happened to it. Need to discuss in person.

Her mind buzzed with logistics, like how soon she could go without leaving Jack and

Celeste shorthanded, and where she could stay in the city.

She was one step closer to the Electric Rose. One step closer to her past. Her birthright. Yes, jewelry was personal. And for her, it didn't get any more personal than her mother's engagement ring.

54

It took less than a day for Celeste to find her an estate sale in Truro. The sales manager granted Gemma and Celeste a preview before the general public.

The first floor had low ceilings and table after table filled with boxes of jewelry, figurines, and vintage shoes.

"I have another sale lined up for next week," Celeste said.

Gemma picked up a silver chain-link bracelet. "Actually, I need to go back to the city for a day or two next week. Can you and Jack manage in the shop without me? Maybe on Tuesday or Wednesday when things aren't peak?"

"Sure," Celeste said, glancing at her. "Is everything okay?"

"Fine," Gemma said quickly. "It's just jewelry stuff." Well, that much was true.

She examined a brooch shaped like a flower basket, wire inlaid with green and purple stones forming the petals.

"That's a hand-wired Sandor brooch," said a middle-aged woman with salt-and-pepper hair in a long braid watching from the corner. "From the 1950s."

"Beautiful," Celeste said, leaning over to examine it.

"Let me know if you have any questions," the attendant said. "Everything in that section is twenty dollars. We can also do bundles."

Gemma looked at a necklace of square-cut black glass. The segments were domed, with flat backs and set in black-painted metal. French jet. She'd take it if the price was right.

"So what's your process here?" Celeste said.

"I look for pieces that can be turned into charms or rings. Like this necklace: I can break it apart, add a brass or silver hook to each individual piece of glass, and they can hang from any of my necklace or bracelet chains."

"Such a fun idea. How long have you been doing this?"

Gemma smiled. "I mean, I've been making jewelry since I was a child. Even back when my mom and dad were around, I'd make necklaces for my Barbie dolls out of thread and tiny beads. I remember wanting to make her rings out of aluminum foil but the fingers on the doll weren't articulated and it was so frustrating."

"When did you start selling?" Celeste reached out and touched the subway token dangling from her necklace.

"Early in college. I spent every weekend scouring markets downtown or stoop sales in Brooklyn and Queens for knickknacks that could be turned into jewelry. I was always looking for pieces that could be personal to the wearer. Like this." She picked up a small gold vermeil owl with blue glass eyes. "I add a hook, and voilà — an owl charm. Maybe it's someone's favorite animal, a good-luck charm of sorts." She turned to the attendant. "How much are these?"

"Ten dollars each," the woman said. "I'll give you a ticket for all of your items when you're finished and you pay at the front door."

Even though Celeste insisted she was only there for Gemma and not to buy anything for the store ("Jack would have a fit!"), she drifted off to look at furniture.

The attendant beckoned Gemma over. "You might want to take a look at this piece — the best of the lot. You're lucky you're here early because it will get snatched up quickly." She held up a gorgeous purple necklace formed out of clusters of pear-shaped and octagonal stones, some translucent faceted crystal juxtaposed against deeper violet cabochon stones. But what really caught her eye was the clasp; bell-shaped and textured metal, it was a piece of art unto itself. It was the perfect punctuation to the beauty of the necklace.

"Schiaparelli?" Gemma said, naming one of the most famous jewelry designers of the last century. The woman nodded.

Gemma checked the price tag — way out of her budget.

"How's it going in here?" Celeste said, appearing in the doorway.

"I think I'm done."

"Perfect timing. I need help carrying something to the car."

"I thought you weren't going to buy anything?"

She shrugged. "It's a compulsion. What can I say?"

Gemma took her ticket from the attendant and followed Celeste into the hallway, where she pointed to a carved wooden chest with mother-of-pearl inlay.

"Ottoman Syria, 1800s," Celeste said. "I just had to buy it. Even though it doesn't go with anything in the house."

Gemma grabbed one end while Celeste lifted the other. Before they made it to the front door, two large men wearing name tags appeared and offered to move it for them.

Celeste showed them to her car while Gemma paid for her jewelry, already thinking of how to break up the black necklace into multiple charms to be fitted onto a chain. And that clasp from the Schiaparelli piece! It was a shame she couldn't afford it.

"Well, that was easy," Celeste said when the chest was taken care of.

"It's really pretty," Gemma said. "If you don't sell it you can always keep it."

"We don't have room for it. But I could give it to Maud. She owns a few places aside from the Victorian. There's a gorgeous house at the far West End of Commercial. You've probably noticed it. Shaped like an octagon?"

Gemma looked at her in surprise. "The guy I'm seeing . . . the one who came into the store. He's living at that house this summer. Such a small world. I noticed that the whole summer rental thing is interesting here — the way so many people in town rent their houses and then move somewhere else in town temporarily?"

Celeste nodded. "It's a big part of the economy here. But Maud's place is truly spectacular."

"I know. It's amazing. Connor made an offer on it."

Celeste looked at her funny. "That house isn't for sale."

"Are you sure?" Connor *had* said he made an offer — hadn't he?

Maybe she'd heard him wrong. She was probably confused.

Yes, she was definitely confused.

"Speaking of houses," Celeste said slowly. "I hope you're not too put out by this, but Elodie is moving into the room down the hall from you. Today."

Gemma blinked. "She's moving in?"

"Lidia rented out the room she's in and town is full, so . . ."

It was a little close for comfort, but there was one silver lining to Elodie staying in P'town a bit longer: She wouldn't be in New York when Gemma met with Sloan Pierce.

Tito carried Elodie's suitcase up the two flights to the top floor of Celeste's house. There was very little to actually move, and still he insisted on helping her. The past few days, they both found every excuse imaginable to spend time together, and yet their physical relationship hadn't gone any further than the kiss on the beach.

Last night at Lidia's, she lay awake in her bed, Pearl snoring by her side, fighting the urge to tiptoe down the stairs to visit Tito. She didn't know what was holding her back. Fear of rejection? Fear of being physical with someone after all these years?

"Watch that top step, it juts out a little," he said. She was a few paces behind him, coaxing Pearl to keep moving. Ultimately, she had to stop and scoop her up in her arms and carry her the rest of the way.

The small growl vibrating through her little body told Elodie that Pearl was displeased with the move. Frankly, Elodie wasn't too happy about it, either. As small as her room had been at Lidia's, it was downright palatial compared to the cramped closet of a space her sister had available for her. Yes, she was grateful for the place to stay. She should probably be grateful that Celeste had even thought to welcome her into her home. But on some level, way down with all her deep-rooted bitterness, she felt it was the least her sister could do after letting her down when she needed her all those years ago.

"I'm glad to see you and your sister patch-ing things up," Tito said.

"Yes," Elodie said. "Peace is certainly preferable to acrimony." She was thinking she should invite Celeste to dinner to thank her for her hospitality. It was the gracious thing to do.

"This is a cozy room," Tito said, lifting her suitcase onto the bed.

"I know beggars can't be choosers, but perhaps it's a bit too cozy," Elodie said. She sat down on the edge of the bed — a generous word for the narrow and wobbly piece of furniture. "I don't think I've ever slept on something this small."

Tito looked out the window at the view of the yard. When he turned around he said, "Well, if you have a hard time sleeping here, you can always stay with me."

She looked up at him in surprise. "Oh, I didn't mean —"

"I have to admit, on more than one restless night I thought about coming upstairs at Lidia's to pay you a visit."

Elodie smiled. "I had the same idea."

Tito sat next to her on the bed. "I like you, Elodie. I hope it's not too much to say this, but I've been hoping for someone like you for a long time."

The statement had the strange effect of making her delighted and uncomfortable at the same time. She wasn't used to such directness — not from a man.

"Is that why you never got married? You never found the right person?"

"When I was younger I was married to the sea. With my schedule, there was no time for a wife. It would have been selfish of me to even try. But things are different now — have been for a few years." He reached for her hand. "What I want to know is, how did a catch like you stay single?"

"My work took precedence, too," she said.

"That's it?" He seemed skeptical.

"Well, yes. There was one bad experience that perhaps made me gun-shy."

"What happened?"

"Oh, it's nothing. It was so many years ago I hardly remember." She wished that were true. Maybe, someday, it could be.

He leaned over and kissed her, and her heart beat so strongly she was sure he could feel it through his shirt.

"This bed might not be great to sleep in, but I think we could find some use for it," he said.

She stood and locked the door.

55

"Sorry I'm late!" Celeste said, running up Commercial and waving to Jack. He waited at the fence bordering Suzanne's Garden, their mutually agreed meeting time having passed about ten minutes ago. "I took Gemma to an estate sale."

"I thought we agreed we weren't buying any more for the season?"

"Gemma wanted to look for jewelry." She would break the news about the chest later. First things first. "But I did acquire one thing: another houseguest. Lidia rented out the room Elodie's staying in and she doesn't have anywhere else to go in town, so I offered her the second bedroom upstairs."

He smiled. "Celeste, I'm proud of you."

They walked past the gate into the garden. It was relatively empty considering how many people were in town. The flowers were a riot of color, peak bloom. Jack reached for her hand and they followed the white-shell path to the center of the gardens and ducked into the arbor. She sat on the stone bench while Jack stood in the center and looked around.

"This could really work, don't you think? Clifford could stand right here, and there's enough room for my best man and your matron of honor. We put some folding chairs right over there . . ."

It was a perfect spot. And he was her perfect man.

"So? What do you think?"

Celeste stood up and walked a few paces to stand next to him.

She looked down at the red bricks at her feet, the foundation of the pergola. And there, a stone inscribed with a French quote by Jean de la Fontaine: *Patience and time do more than strength or passion.*

She'd seen the words countless times before, and for the first time, she realized a word was missing: faith. That was all she could do — take a leap.

She reached for Jack's hand. "I think this is a perfect spot for our wedding. I love you."

He leaned forward and kissed her.

The cursed diamond had been sold. She and her sister were back on good terms. And Paulina's daughter was back in her life. She would ride the wave of positive momentum.

It was in the stars.

The more she thought about it, the more Connor's comment about buying Maud's house felt like a red flag. It bothered Gemma perhaps past the point of reason. Maybe it was a misunderstanding — a miscommunication. She wanted to clear it up by talking to Connor, but he was at the gallery and didn't like when she visited him there. Which, now that she thought about it, was another red flag: Weeks ago, when they first started to get to know each other, Connor asked Gemma — in the nicest way possible — not to visit him at work.

"You're just too distracting," he'd said, kissing her.

"Oh, come *on,*" she'd said, certain he was teasing her.

Today, she didn't care. She marched right in.

A pair of men wearing chunky glasses stood near the entrance, gazing up at a bright painting that took up most of one wall. The space was small — she could take it all in with one sweeping glance. She spotted Connor standing behind a small, modernist white desk near the back. He was talking on his cell phone but extricated himself from the call as soon as he noticed her.

He crossed the room with his long strides. "Hey, babe," he said, kissing her on the cheek. "Listen, now's not a great time . . ."

"I need to talk to you for a minute."

He seemed about to protest, took another look at her expression, and reconsidered.

"Sure. But I'm expecting an important client I have to deal with, so if she walks in . . . we'll pick up whatever this is tonight."

"You told me you made an offer on the house you're in, right?"

Connor nodded and crossed his arms. "Yep. That's right."

"Did the owner respond?"

"Why? Did you see another house you want to show me?" He grinned. "Because if you see something else you like, I could switch gears. As long as you promise to be spending a lot of time with me there." He looped his arm around her waist.

"No, Connor. I'm serious. I know that house isn't for sale."

"Oh?" He looked genuinely surprised.

"Yeah. My aunt's friend owns it. She said it's not for sale."

Connor's expression clouded. "Well, that pisses me off," he said. "My broker must be stringing me along. You know what? I bet he's keeping me on the line and is going to try to switch me over to another property. Thanks for letting me know." Connor kissed the top of her head and took her by the hand, leading her toward the front door.

"One more thing," she said. "I'm going to New York next week. So I guess I'll just touch base when I'm back in town."

Connor glanced between her and the front door, maybe checking for his client.

"Come over for dinner Friday night? I don't want to wait until you're back from New York to see you."

"Okay," she said, still feeling like something was off.

An older woman walked in, expensively dressed, extremely thin with silvery blond hair in a knot at the back of her neck. She looked to be in her sixties — it was hard to tell with wealthy women who did tons of skin maintenance. Sometimes they overdid it and actually looked older than their age. She also wore serious jewelry: a large pearl necklace, a gold coin pendant, and a ruby ring that had to be at least five carats.

This made her think, horribly, about who might be wearing the Electric Rose.

"My client," he said quietly. "Gotta go — but we're on for Friday night."

He didn't kiss her goodbye. He was essentially shoving her out the door, but she tried not to feel rebuffed. He'd explained the house issue. He'd invited her for dinner.

No need to look for trouble.

56

Napi's Restaurant was a Provincetown institution. It had a clubby, secret hideaway sort of feel nestled on Freeman Street. But with one quick turn off Commercial, you couldn't miss it, thanks to a sign strung with Christmas lights and featuring a giant red arrow pointing to the front door.

The dinner was Elodie's idea.

"I want to thank you for the accommodations," she'd said.

Celeste picked the restaurant. The dining room had a beamed wood ceiling, brick walls, and a long bar framed by panels of stained glass and decorated with more Christmas lights. The walls were filled with hundreds of paintings collected by the restaurant's owner, eighty-eight-year-old Napi Van Dereck.

"Interesting art," she said.

"All by locals."

That was the end of the conversation for

several awkward minutes until the menus arrived. Celeste knew it by heart but focused her eyes on it like she was reading a novel.

"What are you having?" Elodie said.

"The jerk chicken." It was her favorite thing on the menu, prepared with an apple-pear chutney and served with black beans, rice, and a crisp plantain fritter.

"Jerk chicken? Out of all these options?"

"There's nothing better. We've got a wonderful Jamaican population here, so the food is authentic."

"Well, I'm having the cod," Elodie said, closing the menu.

"That's good, too."

"I should hope so," Elodie said. "If you can't get decent seafood here, where can you?"

After their server took their order, Elodie sipped her Scotch. Suddenly, there was nothing to talk about.

"So what's going on with you and your Pavlin & Co popup?" Celeste said. With everything else that was happening, she'd almost forgotten about it. Probably because she'd tried to forget about it.

"It's on the back burner for the moment. Things certainly move slowly around here. Doesn't that ever bother you?"

"Why would that bother me?" Celeste said.

"It's just . . . why did you choose this place? Don't get me wrong — it's a charming town. A perfect getaway. But to never come back to Manhattan? I find it difficult to understand. And I know Mom and Dad always felt hurt by it."

"*They* were hurt? How do you think I felt — they never once came to visit me. They only wanted a relationship on their terms. They told us to do what they wanted, when they wanted, and how they wanted. All I did was choose to live my own life."

"They had strong opinions. But they earned it. Besides, they only wanted for us to be happy."

Where on earth had her sister gotten that idea? Celeste had certainly never seen any indication of that.

"Let me ask you something: Why did you give them a free pass when it came to Paulina and Liam, but you cut me out of your life?" Celeste said.

"Really? You want to get into all of that, now of all times? Because I'd rather not."

"You're here for the summer. We're under the same roof. It's the elephant in the room, and I'd like to address it." Celeste folded her arms.

"Perhaps this dinner was a bad idea," Elodie said with a sigh.

The silence returned. Across the restaurant, Celeste saw friends of hers seated at a table with their baby daughter in a high chair. They had struggled for a long time to become parents and it warmed her heart to see them happy. It made her think of her own life and her sister's.

"Did you ever want children?" Celeste said.

"Celeste, I'd like to enjoy my cocktail."

Celeste shrugged. "I figured since we haven't had a meal just the two of us in, oh, several decades, we might as well make the most of it."

"You don't have children, either."

"See? We have something in common."

Elodie seemed to consider this, fidgeting with her drink. "Yes, if it weren't for Gemma, the family line would be ending with us. How ironic: Paulina and Liam caused such a rift in our family, and now their heir will be the only one to continue it on." She looked up at Celeste. "Does she know that her father was my boyfriend first?"

Celeste's jaw dropped. "Oh, good heavens, Elodie. Come on."

"It's a legitimate question. What do you think?"

"I really don't know. I don't think so. Who would have told her? She was only eight when they died. Why even think of such a thing?"

"So now my relationship, the one that was stolen from me, is the dark secret? No wonder she's confused why I didn't welcome her with open arms. Well, she should know that I was robbed — by her *mother.*"

"Please, stop. This is ancient history. You're in a relationship now, right? Can't you just be happy with that?"

Elodie sipped her drink. A slow smile took over her face. She looked ten years younger.

"Tito and I are just friends," she said.

"Oh no, you don't. You're willing to talk about a guy who burned you a quarter of a century ago, but not about the guy you're involved with today?"

"Fine," Elodie said, reaching for the bread. "Go ahead. I give you one question, one get-out-of-jail-free question. And then I want to make small talk like regular civilized people."

But in that moment Celeste realized she actually didn't want to ask a question. What she really wanted, what she'd wanted for so many years, was to make a confession.

It was as if she'd been waiting to talk to her sister all this time.

"You know, it's my fault Paulina went on that trip. If she'd stayed in New York like Mom wanted, she'd still be alive today." She reached for her water glass, her hand shaking.

"What are you talking about?" Elodie said, covering her mouth full of bread.

"Paulina went to France because I encouraged her to. Mom was telling her to stay in the city, and she was genuinely considering it."

"Celeste, you can't possibly blame yourself. I never believed Paulina was going to settle down in one place. And Liam — that conniving opportunist — was more than happy to flit around the globe on her dime."

Celeste shook her head. "I'm telling you, there was a change in Paulina the last time I spoke to her. It was that weekend of Gemma's birthday party. I think if I'd encouraged her, she would have stayed in New York — at least for a while. She'd still be alive." Her voice cracked on the last part. She felt herself shaking.

"Paulina's death was an accident," Elodie said, leaning across the table and patting her arm. "She could have stayed in New York City and gotten hit by a bus, for heaven's sake. You have to let that go."

Celeste bowed her head, letting her sister's words wash over her. She waited to feel some sense of relief, but the guilt felt even more acute now that it was out there in the open. She appreciated Elodie's rush to absolve her, but she wasn't exactly objective.

"Did you mourn her at all? I mean, I know you were angry for all those years. But when she died . . ."

"I mourned the sister I loved when she betrayed me. I lost her when she took Liam away. I was stunned by her death — by both of their deaths. But I'd already mourned them. They were strangers by the end."

"I should have stayed in closer touch with Gemma. It was just so complicated with the Maybrooks . . ."

Elodie shrank back in her seat, shaking her head. "Celeste, you can't blame yourself. Honestly."

The server arrived with their food. The aroma of spices and butter distracted Celeste for a moment, but when she picked up her fork she found she'd lost her appetite. Elodie dipped into her cod and tasted it, declaring it delicious. It took her a few moments to realize Celeste wasn't eating. "You're not doing much to convince me the jerk chicken is the best thing on the menu," she said with a smile.

"I wish I could go back in time," Celeste said.

Elodie leaned forward and again reached for her hand. "Let's look ahead, okay? You know what: Let's go wedding dress shopping together. I'll call Vera Wang . . . we can spend a few days in the city."

Celeste shook her head. "Thanks for the offer but that's not really me."

"So what do you plan to do for a dress?"

"There's a vintage shop I like." She hesitated. "Do you . . . want to come with me?"

Elodie smiled. "Of course," she said. "What are sisters for?"

57

Elodie never understood the appeal of wearing vintage, which was really just a fancy word for old. Admittedly, she had no innate fashion sense. That's why she always relied on stylists at Bergdorf and Barneys and Saks to tell her what the must-haves were for each season. The result was that her wardrobe was impeccable, if not terribly adventurous.

And so the vintage shop in Chatham, with metal racks filled end to end with gowns from the 1960s and 1970s, left her cold. But this was what Celeste wanted. And for the first time in a long time, she cared about her sister's happiness.

"Can I ask you for a favor?" Celeste said, sifting through the gowns. She pulled out a satin shift and placed it back on the rack.

"Sure," Elodie said. "You're the bride-to-be."

"I'd like you to consider offering Gemma

a job at Pavlin & Co. Designing."

Elodie felt like she'd swallowed a mouthful of dust and coughed loudly before managing a brisk, "Are you serious?"

"Completely."

"What makes you think she's even interested?"

"Well, it's arguably the most prestigious design job in the industry. Who wouldn't want to be a part of it? And I have a feeling that this whole issue of the diamond ring isn't so much about the ring as it is about her own legitimacy as a Pavlin. There are other pieces of jewelry she could ask for, pieces Paulina wore. She's just fixated on that diamond because it represents so much."

"Well, I can't hire her just to appease her over a lost ring," Elodie said.

"She's talented, you know."

Even Elodie couldn't argue with that. There hadn't been a designer in the family since Isaac Pavlin, the founder, back in 1919. After his death, the company had always hired outside talent and prided itself on finding the Next Big Thing.

But what if the Next Big Thing happened to be part of the family?

Elodie thought about the mob scene outside of Queen Anne's Revenge the other day, tourists and locals alike lined up for Gemma's chunky necklace chains and one-of-a-kind charms. There certainly hadn't been organic, grassroots excitement like that for Pavlin & Co in a very long time.

"Her work appeals to the new generation," Celeste said. "Think about it — for me?"

With a start, Elodie realized she *had* thought about it. She'd thought about it deep down in places she wasn't brave enough to fully visit. She'd thought about it when she read the *New York Times* feature, and she thought about it when she saw the half-empty display at Celeste's store. She thought about it when she saw the necklace around Gemma's neck, and when she looked at the continuing decline in numbers on the weekly sales spreadsheets.

"Oh my goodness!" Celeste said. "A Bellville Sassoon!"

She pulled out an ivory-colored gown with long billowing sleeves and an overskirt. The neckline was quilted and the gathered bodice gave way to an ankle-length, waterfall skirt.

"That's . . . interesting."

Celeste, clearly reading her lack of enthusiasm, said, "Bellville Sassoon is a great British fashion house. It was founded in the 1950s by a woman named Belinda Bellville.

She became one of Princess Diana's earliest dress designers. They dressed absolutely everyone, from Jackie Kennedy to Madonna."

Maybe so. She still thought her sister would look best in a custom Vera Wang or Monique Lhuillier gown, but if she insisted on looking like a medieval flower-child bride, who was she to argue?

"Let me buy it for you. As an engagement gift," Elodie said.

"What? Oh, no. Thanks but that's completely unnecessary . . ."

"I want to! Please. It's the least I can do. I'm living at your house for free."

After Celeste tried on the dress and declared it perfect, Elodie took the gown and draped it over her arm. She headed down the stairs to pay, and it felt so good to be doing something for her sister after such a long time. It felt so good, in fact, Elodie had an idea for another gift — a wedding gift. It would be a fitting gesture to make peace with the past, and might assuage some of her own, more recent feelings of guilt. It would just require a quick trip back to New York.

The prospect should have excited her, but the thing was, she didn't want to leave town. Not even for a weekend. Not if it meant missing time with Tito. But she could invite him along. Yes, of course! She'd experienced his world, and now he could get a glimpse of hers.

Elodie felt Celeste's footsteps on the stairs behind her. She glanced back at her with a smile. Truly, she never imagined that someone else's engagement could be so much fun.

Tito took Elodie for a motorboat ride. He wanted to show her around the oyster farm, where the cages were set underwater.

The sun pummeled them. Elodie adjusted the wide-brimmed straw hat she'd bought at Mad As a Hatter for the beach. Then she rolled up the sleeves of her white linen shirt. Her golf shorts would stay dry and the borrowed boots offered enough protection for her to climb out of the boat and wade through a few feet of water to dry land.

Tito had just come from picking oysters on the flats and was dressed for action in rubber coveralls, boots, and a black baseball hat that read *Helltown.* One thing about Tito that was so different from other men she'd known was that he always seemed eager for activity. She couldn't imagine him paging through *The New York Times* or spending hours in a board meeting. Around him, she was forced to be a more energized, open version of herself.

For decades she had been most comfortable walking into the Pavlin & Co offices wearing a St. John suit and a string of twelve-millimeter pearls. But now she was wiping salt water off her face with the sleeve of her shirt. And she'd never been happier.

Still, it would be fun to show Tito around New York. She wanted to experience Central Park, the museums, even Café Carlyle with him. If she could don a pair of rubber boots for the afternoon, he could put on a tie for a few hours. Hopefully he'd enjoy the change as much as she enjoyed the things he was bringing out in her.

Tito used a contraption to pull up one of the "cages," a wire box filled with oysters. It was half covered in seaweed. The air smelled intensely briny and it was much cooler than it had felt in town. She could just make out the Pilgrim Monument in the far distance. An incredible feeling of calm washed over her. Sitting in the middle of the bay with the man she loved, she realized there was no other place in the world she'd rather be. And yes, she was starting to believe she was in love.

"This is also where Marco farms his seaweed," he said, pulling off a fistful of stringy, wet plant and handing it to her. She smiled at him like he'd given her a bouquet of roses.

"So you're going to be working with him more?" she said.

Tito nodded. "They're expanding and they need people they can count on year-round. It sounds like fun to work on an oyster farm, but then when their employees experience how labor-intensive it is . . . Well, they lose a lot of folks. My cousin tried to warn him it was a very difficult business, but he had his heart set on it."

"And his wife works with him?"

Tito nodded, sitting on the second crate next to her. "She was a city gal like you once upon a time." He leaned over and sprung open her cage.

"Speaking of the city: I have to go back soon to pick up a wedding gift for my sister. I was wondering if you might come with me."

He unzipped the knapsack and handed her a pair of thick work gloves.

"New York?" he said.

"Yes. You can see my apartment; we can have dinner at —"

"Thanks, but no thanks. I've never been to New York City and I don't intend to start now."

Had Elodie heard him right? "You've never been to Manhattan?"

"No. Why is that surprising? Before now you'd never been here."

"I know. But it's *Manhattan.*" A creeping dread made her heart start to beat faster. "It will be fun."

He started up the engine and they sped off toward Wellfleet, her heart pounding.

"So that's it?" she shouted over the hum of the motor. "You won't even consider coming with me?"

"Elodie, I care about you. But I'm not a city person. I don't want to go to New York with you because if this becomes a situation where you're in the city and I'm visiting you, it'll never work."

She couldn't believe what she was hearing.

"Are you seriously telling me that the only way we can spend time together is here in Provincetown? I mean, I'm sorry, Tito — that's incredibly narrow-minded."

He looked over at her. "We're old enough to know ourselves. And our limitations. I certainly know mine. I'm not saying it's right, but that's the way I feel. Me in New York — I'd be like one of the oysters in this cage."

Elodie felt her hands shaking. She couldn't

look at him. She felt like a fool.

How could she have let her guard down, opening herself up to this kind of hurt *again*? Now she couldn't wait to get back to the city, away from this mirage of happiness. Once she was back home, her relationship with Tito would be put back into perspective. It was a summer fling. That's all.

She looked around her. Solid land seemed very far away.

58

They ate takeout lobster rolls on Connor's front porch. By now, she felt bad about confronting him at the gallery. Her personal stress was making her cynical, and it wasn't fair to him. Afterward, they took a walk on the beach, holding hands, dipping their feet into the water.

When they returned to the house, she said, "Let's go upstairs."

The bedroom was warm and he opened a window and turned on the ceiling fan. She sat on the edge of the wrought-iron bed and patted the spot next to her. Connor moved to her side, tucking her hair out of the way so he could kiss her. She leaned into him. He smelled vaguely salty, the ocean air clinging to him. She tilted her face up to meet his lips.

The light in the room was fading with the sunset. All that was left was a golden cast on the white walls.

"You are truly beautiful," Connor said.

He pressed his body against hers, and she lay back. She felt shivers up and down her body when he moved his lips to her neck, his hands entwined in her hair. She knew that holding out on sex with him was getting absurd, and really, why not? It was time to let go of the hope that she and Sanjay would ever get back together. Sex with Connor would punctuate that. Maybe that wasn't the best reason to sleep with someone, but at least she and Connor were both getting what they wanted, if for different reasons.

Afterward, lying side by side and staring up at the whirling fan, he said, "Do you want company when you go to the city next week?"

She didn't. The trip would be emotional — good or bad, she didn't know. But she was certain she didn't want to bring Connor into it. Not yet.

"Thanks, but I have some family stuff I need to take care of."

"Oh, yeah?" he said, propping up on one elbow and looking at her expectantly.

"Yeah," she said. Then realizing she was being cryptic, added, "It seems a woman who's planning the auction might have a lead on my mother's engagement ring. Or she's going to tell me the trail is cold. And then I don't know what I'll do."

"What do you mean, you don't know what you'll do?"

She shrugged. "I mean, the ring is the only thing I have left."

He smiled and reached for her hand. "It's not all you have left. There's always the money."

The alarm bells returned, deep and loud. "What money?"

"Your family fortune. You're a Pavlin, Gemma. What are you worried about?"

She pulled her hand away. "I wasn't raised a Pavlin. I have nothing to do with that side of the family. Before this summer, I hadn't seen my aunts in over a decade."

Now Connor sat up. "You're telling me you're like . . . the poor relation?"

"That's one way of putting it."

He ran a hand through his hair. "Don't you think you might have mentioned this at some point?" His voice was low but clearly aggravated.

"It's not really any of your business," she said. "And besides, I've been telling you all summer I need an investor for my company. Why would I do that if I had my own money?"

"Everyone looks for outside money,"

Connor said. "I know I still am. And I was hoping you could help."

"Me? How?"

"I need an infusion of cash. I was hoping you'd be one of my investment partners."

Wait — she thought he could help her meet money people, and all this time he'd thought *she* was a money person?

"If you need money, then how did you make an offer on this house?" Oh, but he didn't. She hadn't been cynical earlier in the week — she'd been right. What else had he lied about? "Is that even your gallery?"

"It's my family's gallery, yes. But I want to go off on my own."

She stood up, pulling on her clothes as fast as she could manage.

"Don't contact me ever again, don't come by my aunt's store . . ."

She'd made a huge mistake. Again.

▪ ▪ ▪ ▪

PART THREE

▪ ▪ ▪ ▪

Love is simple. We make it hard with our trappings.

— IYANLA VANZANT

59

Constance, 2004

She hadn't left their bedroom since the funeral one week ago. It was hard for her to imagine ever stepping outside again. She didn't want to live in a world without Paulina.

Alan, dressed in a suit, walked into their bedroom, dark even in the middle of the afternoon. He pulled open the heavy custom brocade curtains and looked out at Park Avenue. She could imagine what he was watching: their doorman hailing someone a cab, parents holding the hands of small children, tourists carrying shopping bags. It was probably a beautiful mid-October day. The idea of enjoying a view, or a walk, or anything at all, was unthinkable to her.

"I thought you left for work," she said.

"No." Alan sat on the edge of the bed. "I didn't go to the office this morning."

"Where did you go, then?"

"I had a meeting with the Maybrooks and our respective attorneys."

Constance sat up, blinking against the intrusive light. "The Maybrooks? Why?"

"There are logistics to work out."

"Oh? What could possibly matter?" Constance sniffed and reached over to her bedside table for the Electric Rose. It caught the light streaming in from the windows and appeared to glow. But there was nothing beautiful about it any longer. There was now only an overwhelming sense of morbidity to the extraordinary stone; Paulina had been wearing it at the time of her death.

Fortunately, they'd managed to keep that detail out of the press; it wasn't exactly the association Alan wanted for Pavlin & Co's most famous diamond. When he'd shared his concern about public perception in the hours following news of Paulina's and Liam's deaths, Constance was appalled. How could he think of such a thing at a time like that? "It's my job, as head of the family, as head of a global business, to think of *precisely* such a thing," he'd said. "Public perception is fickle; once we lose control of it, it will be difficult — if not impossible — to regain control of the narrative."

"I knew you never should have given her this ring," she said now, looking up at him.

"What?"

"That stupid competition. The problems between her and Elodie. She was running away from it — from us — and it killed her." It was the one thing she'd been thinking over and over again, on a constant mental loop. She hadn't been able to articulate it to him until that moment. It felt good to say it aloud, even if Alan looked horrified.

He sighed and reached for her hand. "I know you want to make sense of this. I do, too. But the reality is, Paulina was driving the boat too fast. She had the motor on instead of using the sails and they were too close to the dock. The Maybrooks' lawyer made it clear that the toxicology reports don't work in our favor. The accident was just that — an accident. I know you're having a hard time making sense of it all, but it had nothing to do with the Electric Rose."

"Maybe those newspaper articles are right: There *is* a curse." She put the ring down.

"Oh, Constance. Don't start with that tabloid nonsense."

Constance pulled her hand away from him and jumped out of bed. "We have to protect Gemma from the press. She's our child now."

Alan held out his hand to her once again.

"Please. Sit down. We need to talk."

"We *are* talking."

"Liam's family is prepared to sue us for wrongful death. For millions. You're worried about the tabloids? Let me tell you, the Maybrooks are threatening to talk. Pavlin & Co, instead of being synonymous with glamour and romance, will become a symbol of wrongful death. And think of what this could do to Paulina's memory."

Sue them? How could those wretched people think of money? That wouldn't bring the kids back. And her husband seemed more concerned about the company than the fact that they'd lost their precious daughter.

"Paulina is gone. She was the face of the company. You can't sell your way around that."

Alan started to speak, then stopped. He looked at her with something that seemed like pity. "I hate to say it, but we've seen a sales spike since the accident. Paulina's become a tragic figure. But if she's seen as the cause of the accident, then she's the villain."

"What a horrible, horrible world we live in," Constance said, sinking back against the pillows. She put her forearm over her eyes, like she did when she had a migraine.

"So just pay off the Maybrooks. Whatever it takes. It's only money."

"They don't want money."

"What do they want?"

"Gemma."

Constance barked a bitter laugh, short and loud, a single syllable that sounded like a car horn. Alan furrowed his brow.

"I'm serious, Constance. They want to raise Gemma themselves, and they don't want us to have anything to do with her. No contact."

"That's not happening," she said.

"Yes," Alan said. "It is."

60

It felt strange to be back in New York. The minute Gemma walked into the Casterbridge, she regretted her decision to stay there. The art deco lobby, now renovated from the original Victorian, transported her back to the fall of her senior year, when she and Sanjay had been together. There he was, behind the front desk like no time had passed. But it had. And everything was different.

Still, when he noticed her walk in his dark eyes lit up.

"You made it," he said. "How was the trip?"

"Long," she said, smiling. "It's good to be here, though." The ferry had been crowded, and she spent most of the trip mentally kicking herself over her bad judgment with Connor. And as tough as that was to think about, it was still preferable to her anxiety over the meeting with Sloan

Pierce tomorrow.

She didn't know what to expect, what to hope for. What was the best-case scenario? That she'd located the ring, obviously. But where? If it had been sold, it was as good as gone. Even if it returned to the market, she couldn't afford to buy it back. Maybe it was on loan somewhere? She didn't know what she should be hoping for — what was realistic to hope for.

Sanjay slid her room card across the desk.

"Thanks for the help with the discount," she said.

"Anytime. So your meeting's tomorrow?"

"Yeah. But first I have to go back to my storage space. The auction person wants photos of my mom and in exchange she's going to tell me where I can find the ring."

"I'm off tomorrow if you need help."

She looked up in surprise. "That would be great. I'd love the company."

They looked at each other, eyes locking. Their connection was still there. It was nothing Connor Harrison or even Monica Del Mar could diminish. Or maybe Monica was out of the picture, too.

"How's Monica?" she said, aware of the couple standing behind her, waiting to check in.

"Great, great. She just got a job with Alice + Olivia." The way he smiled with pride made it clear they were still very much together.

"That's . . . great," Gemma said. "Well, I'll let you get back to work."

Elodie, never a fan of Manhattan in the peak of summer, found it even more oppressive after two months on the gentle shores of Provincetown. Fifth Avenue smelled like melting asphalt and the aromatic steam coming from the street food vendors turned her stomach. Her limbs felt languid and heavy, but she had to walk briskly to avoid getting jostled by the pedestrian traffic.

She threaded her way through a crush of tourists on the corner of Fifty-Third Street. The Pavlin & Co building was hidden behind scaffolding.

"Ms. Pavlin! Great to see you," said one of the security guards out front.

Elodie gave a queenly wave, then pushed through the revolving door into the frigid climate-controlled showroom. It was so cold compared to the blistering heat of outside that she wouldn't have been surprised to see frost on the glass display cases. Stores often set the thermostat low to compensate for all the body heat. But there were hardly any customers. Elodie remembered the days when there was a line down the block to get in, when people would press their faces up against the glass just to catch a glimpse of the famed Pavlin jewels or, if they were lucky, Constance Pavlin herself.

She headed to the elevator bank, texting her assistant that she was on the premises; they had a meeting set for noon so Elodie could confront the negative balance sheets in person. She was dreading it.

Elodie flashed her security credentials and electronic key card to an unfamiliar guard at the elevator banks.

The lower level was even more frigid than the sales floor. She stepped out of the elevator into the fluorescent lighting, the guard on her heels. She swiped her card to get past sliding bullet-resistant Plexiglas security barriers, remembering the days when her father would bring her down as a girl, a dozen keys jangling on a chain in his pocket.

Now, nothing but silence.

The Pavlin vault was similar to a bank's security box system, but the storage units were larger than the brick-sized cubbies in a financial institution. The jewelry was kept in numbered compartments, the contents all archived digitally. It would be easy to find what she was looking for.

The pink diamond eternity band, 6.5 carats, was the last remaining piece of the Electric Rose. It was the only thing she didn't sell after she had the large diamond cut into pieces. She kept the ring for herself, a token of the fact that the Electric Rose should have been hers all along. She wore it on special occasions, always on her right hand, lest it be mistaken for a wedding band. But now she would give it to Celeste as a wedding gift, to be worn as it was intended by design. There was no need for her sister to know the provenance of the stones.

The platinum band felt cool in her palm. She examined the ring, trying it on one last time. Even under the cold, artificial light the stones worked their magic, so radiant they seemed to glow. *Yes, this will do,* Elodie thought. *This will do just fine.*

She slipped the ring back inside the green velvet Pavlin & Co pouch, placed the pouch inside her Hermès clutch, and headed back upstairs for her meeting. Things had been running smoothly with her working remotely, but she couldn't sustain that forever.

I've never been to New York City and I don't intend to start now.

Tito's declaration was a deal-breaker. She couldn't spend the rest of her life in Provincetown when she had a Manhattan-based business to run. If she and Tito were both willing to travel, to bounce back and forth, their relationship could work. But if it was going to be a one-way situation? No.

So there she was, back in the store that meant everything to her. Back in her hometown.

The problem was, it didn't feel like home without Tito.

61

"I was half expecting all this stuff to be gone," Gemma said, surveying the piles of her boxes in the storage unit. It was oddly comforting to see it all again. Now, if she could just pull the metal door closed again and lock it up, she could merrily be on her way knowing that her things were safe. But she was there on a mission.

"Why would you think that?" Sanjay said.

She shrugged, putting her hands on her hips. "It just felt like I was leaving it behind in some way. Everything in my life feels so . . . scattered." She reached for a box but it was too high.

"Let me get that," Sanjay said. "This one?"

She pointed to a file box second to the top of a tall stack. She could just make out the words *Photos, Family,* and *Mom* scrawled in messy black Sharpie. Sanjay was tall enough to retrieve any of the boxes, and she realized with a pang that this was only because he had stacked them for her. He set the box on the ground at her feet, dusting off his hands.

"So, the woman at the auction house located your mom's ring?"

"I don't know if she found it yet, but she knows *something.* I'll find out in a few hours when I meet with her." Gemma looked around. "Ugh, of course I forgot scissors! How am I going to get all these —"

Sanjay reached into his messenger bag and produced two pairs of scissors and packing tape to reseal anything they opened. Gemma smiled at him gratefully.

She sliced through the top seam of one box, opening the cardboard flaps to find the photo albums. It was hard to imagine that people used to print out every photo and stick them in these heavy books. And her grandmother had left behind so many albums, it seemed like she must have spent half her time making them. But Gemma was thankful that she had; if all these photos had never been developed, or stuffed away in closets or old shoeboxes somewhere and lost, she'd really have nothing left. Still, she wondered what compelled her grandmother to send them all to her, when she'd heard nothing from the woman for years and years.

The leather-bound albums had thick white pages, double-sided with six photos to a side and protected under a clear sticky sheet. The spines were embossed with the dates, and she had all the albums memorized. Some of the pages had been turned so many times they'd separated from the binding. Her favorite year to look at was 1994, when her parents first got together, and at the turn of the millennium, when she was a little girl. The later albums, the ones just before her parents died, were too upsetting to look at.

Digging around in the box, she found the 1994 album and pulled it onto her lap. Her mother looked so cool, with her white-blond hair nearly down to her waist, dressed in flannel shirts tied around the waist of her sundresses. Even though it had been the grunge era, Paulina couldn't help but look glamorous.

Gemma's father, dark-haired and rarely smiling, looked like one of the Calvin Klein models from a Times Square billboard. He had the kind of handsomeness that called for black-and-white film. They were an "it" couple, the stuff of movies and perfume ads and novels. How could she not dream of a love like theirs? Her parents had been perfectly matched.

"May I see?" Sanjay asked.

She nodded, passing him the album while she reached for 1999 and opened to the first pages, images of herself as a shy, smiling tot always clutching her mother's hand. Page after page, photos of white-sand beaches and turquoise water, her parents tan and always touching. Her mother wore bikinis and sarongs, barefoot and bohemian except for the diamonds on her fingers and around her neck.

Sloan would want to see the 2004 album — photos from the night of the Electric Rose tenth anniversary. Her mother had worn a Chanel gown embroidered with butterflies, and Gemma wore a matching dress custom-designed by Karl Lagerfeld himself. She still remembered how it felt to step out of the car to the barrage of camera flashes, the sound of strangers calling her name to get her to look in their direction.

"Smile pretty," her mother said, squeezing her hand. The giant pink diamond on her mother's ring finger bit into her palm, reminding her of how it had felt to try it on earlier in the evening, how the weight of it had felt otherworldly and magical.

Gemma closed the album and tucked it

into her messenger bag.

"I want that ring back," she said.

"Gemma, it's gone. Sometimes you just gotta let go," he said.

She looked up, flush with irritation that he would suggest such a thing. But the look in his eyes told her he might not be talking only about the ring. She swallowed hard, meeting his gaze.

"I'm not ready to let go."

62

Sloan Pierce's office on the top floor of Whitmore's Auction House had expansive views of the East River. Gemma stared out the window while Sloan flipped through the photos.

"These are incredible," Sloan said from her desk.

"So tell me about the Electric Rose," Gemma said impatiently. The meeting was starting to feel like a ransom exchange, with Sloan demanding the photos immediately. She'd handed them over, and now she wanted her payback: news about where her mother's ring had ended up.

She moved from her spot at the windows to a seat in front of Sloan's desk. Sloan shuffled the photos absently, like a deck of cards, before placing them back inside the envelope. Then she looked up at Gemma, folding her hands in front of her on the desk.

"I mentioned before that I started searching for the diamond after your aunt's exhibit at Pavlin & Co. But every call I made, every email I sent, was a dead end. I figured the diamond had gone underground, as some pieces do."

"Yes, you told me," Gemma said impatiently.

"I almost gave up. But then a source came to me."

Gemma felt a chill run through her entire body. "Who?"

"A journalist. Regan O'Rourke. I believe you're familiar?"

Gemma nodded, her stomach tightening into a fist.

"Apparently, while Regan was doing background research for your interview, she came across a big jewelry collector — very well-known, but very private. Impeccable taste and reputation. And this collector told Regan that she had a pair of two-carat pink diamond studs that had been cut from the larger stone known as the Electric Rose."

"Impossible," Gemma said.

"The collector said she'd been told by a jewelry designer she'd commissioned to create custom pieces for her that the Electric Rose had been chopped up sometime around 2007 to make a few dozen pieces."

Gemma gripped the arms of her chair, her

mouth suddenly so dry it was difficult to speak.

"That can't be true."

Sloan looked at her with pitying eyes, her hand resting on the manila envelope.

"Maybe," she said, "you should speak to someone in your family."

Elodie drummed her fingers on her vintage brass and leather desk. Behind her, out the window, Fifth Avenue teemed with tourists braving the heat to shop. The day's *New York Times* style section was spread out in front of her. She hadn't thought about the press while she'd been away, but now that she was back in her seat of power — literally — the idea of the auction felt like fun, not just a necessity.

How had she spent so much time away from the office? It must have been a sort of temporary insanity. Sure, her subordinates had kept everything running smoothly. But even that delegation of work had maybe been a mistake. It was never smart to make oneself seem dispensable.

Now she was thankful Tito had been so obstinate about the trip. It made her decision very simple. She belonged in the city. She belonged behind that desk. Whatever had bloomed between the two of them, it was over. Now she just owed it to their friendship to tell him in person. She checked her watch; if she left the city in an hour, she could be back in Provincetown just as it was getting dark. She could collect her belongings, end things with Tito, and put her energy back where it belonged.

Her desk phone rang, a call from her assistant.

"Yes?" she said, the receiver cold against her cheek.

"A visitor, Ms. Pavlin. Your niece is here to see you."

Gemma. Since the day she was born, Elodie had never been able to see her as anything but the personification of Liam and Paulina's betrayal. But now, maybe because she herself had tasted happiness — however fleeting — or maybe because she saw that Gemma could be an asset to the company, that feeling had changed. And she found herself almost cheerful about seeing her.

"Show her up, please," Elodie said. Moments later, Gemma barreled in and slammed the door behind her.

"How could you?" she said.

"I beg your pardon?" Elodie said, confused.

"Really, I want to know how you sleep at

night." Gemma's cheeks were pink with emotion, her Pavlin blue-green eyes watery and red-rimmed.

"Gemma, come inside and sit down. I don't know what's got you so upset —"

"You stole my mother's ring from me and destroyed it! Chopping it up like scrap metal!"

Elodie stepped back, feeling behind herself for the desk to lean on. Her head buzzed with the competing frenzy of wondering how Gemma had found out the truth while trying to figure out how to calm her down.

"I can't have a conversation with you standing there shouting at me."

Gemma brushed past her into the next room, where she proceeded to pace in front of the settee with such vigor Elodie felt certain there would be a hole in the carpet.

"Why did you do it? Destroying something so beautiful . . ."

Elodie needed to sit. She moved to an armchair opposite the settee and wished Gemma would do the same. Instead, she insisted on standing, arms crossed, practically vibrating with fury.

"It was a business decision, Gemma. It wasn't personal."

"I'm sure it would have been personal to

my mother. Didn't you think about her at all?"

"The company was in a financial bind at the time. You don't remain a family-owned business for a hundred years without some sacrifices."

"Does Aunt Celeste know about this?"

"No," Elodie said sharply. "And I'd like to keep it that way."

She couldn't imagine a quicker way to fracture the reconnection with her sister than revealing her lie about the ring. It's not just that she'd made the unilateral decision to break up the gem in the first place, but she'd also explicitly lied about its fate to manipulate Celeste with the auction.

And really, she was trying to turn over a new leaf. The last remaining piece of the Electric Rose had been sitting in the vault, and she intended to put it to good use — a wedding gift, not a curse. Something both old and new.

"Celeste should know that you robbed my mother and me," Gemma said.

Elodie's shame gave way to a flood of anger — a tidal wave of anger. Decades' worth.

"Your *mother* was the one who was robbed? I don't think so," she said.

"What's that supposed to mean?"

Elodie knew she should stop, that she'd already said enough and this would only dig a deeper hole for herself. But she couldn't stop herself. For all these years she'd had to keep her feelings of loss and betrayal buried inside, in a little box in the corner of her mind, so that she could put on a happy face and deal with her family and build her career. But there was no reason to hold it all in any longer.

"Let me ask you something: Do you know how your parents met?"

"Of course. They met at a photo shoot. My father was the creative director and my mother was modeling for the company. It was love at first sight."

Indeed.

"Well, that's a nice little fairy tale. Sadly, it's not true. And I know it's not true because I unwittingly introduced them. They met at our parents' house when I brought my boyfriend to dinner. And that boyfriend was your father."

"What are you talking about?" Gemma said.

"Liam Maybrook was my boyfriend first. Your mother stole him from *me.*"

Gemma paled, then turned a flush so deep pink Elodie was alarmed for a second.

"You're delusional. That was just a silly

gossip item. You just want to justify destroying my mother's diamond. But you didn't just rob me. You robbed the whole world. And I know Aunt Celeste will agree."

That's exactly how Celeste would see it: Celeste, champion of forgotten treasures, ever mindful of preservation of all kinds. No, Celeste would not be happy about this news.

"Do you want to upset Celeste a week before her wedding? After how good she's been to you all summer? You'd be hurting her more than hurting me."

Gemma walked out.

63

She couldn't get away from Elodie fast enough.

Your mother *was the one who was robbed? I don't think so.*

Gemma rushed to Lexington and jumped on the subway to Park Slope. There weren't any seats and she grabbed on to a metal pole. It was forty-five minutes to Sanjay's — too much time to relive the childhood memory that was crashing in on her: She was at the Electric Rose party with her parents. Elodie said something to her, something like, "Did you know a thief can hide in plain sight?"

At the time, it had been confusing. Upsetting. She thought her aunt was maybe talking about the diamond ring, the fact that her mother got it. But no: She'd been talking about her father.

How was it possible that the most disturbing gossip item of all happened to be *true*?

And why did it hurt so badly? It didn't mean her parents loved each other any less. Really, it didn't mean anything at all. Except she realized now how much she had believed, her entire life, that her parents were perfect. They had a perfect love story, they were a perfect couple, and the life she was destined for should have been perfect. The boating accident was the single twist in the story — one so big, it was all she could handle.

By the time she reached Sanjay's brownstone, sweating from the walk and the heat, the impulsivity of the visit hit her. She stood at the base of the steps, looking up and mustering the energy to turn around and walk back to the Barclays Center for the train. And then the front door opened and his sister Daksha walked out lugging her cello case.

"Oh, hey. I was just . . . do you need help with that?"

Daksha shook her head no and proceeded down the steps. When she reached the street she set the instrument down and looked at Gemma.

"You're his ex, right?" she said.

Gemma nodded. "Yeah. Um, is he home? And is he . . . alone?"

"He's home," she said. "You should know,

you really broke his heart."

Great.

Gemma climbed the stairs and pressed the intercom buzzer.

"Sanjay, it's me. Gemma."

"Gemma?"

"I need to talk. Can I come in?" A beat passed, an excruciating twenty seconds or so during which she contemplated the six-block walk back to the train. But then the buzzer sounded.

She walked through the door leading into a vestibule, and Sanjay opened the interior door. He wore gray NYSD sweatpants and a black T-shirt. His hair was damp and curling slightly around his jaw. A lock of it fell into his face.

"Come in," he said, closing the door behind her. "Prishna's already asleep. She's got crazy hours, so we need to keep it down."

She followed him up the stairs to his bedroom. It was sparsely furnished, with a queen-sized bed, and a wooden desk and office chair from Housing Works they'd found together one weekend when they were a couple. Photography books were stacked in one corner, light boxes and cameras on a side table. It looked the same as the last time she'd been inside, seven months ago, except for a series of photographs from Provincetown propped up on his dresser.

"So, you really found a new muse in P'town," she said.

"I'm putting together a grant proposal. My parents keep harping on me that I need to work 'in the real world.' I think they were hoping that NYSD would help me get photography out of my system."

"What do they expect you to do instead?"

He shook his head. "Don't deflect, Gemma. You didn't come here to talk about my career. What's going on? The meeting with the auction woman didn't go well?" He pulled out the desk chair for her and then perched on the edge of his bed. She pressed her palm to her forehead, not knowing where to start.

"My mother's ring is gone. Destroyed. My aunt broke it up into pieces years ago and sold it off bit by bit."

Sanjay's eyes widened. "I'm sorry. I know how much that meant to you."

She looked up at him, feeling a sob deep in her chest but pushing it down.

"When I confronted her about it, she told me that she had a . . . thing with my father. Before my parents got together."

"A thing?"

"They were dating, and that's how my mother met him."

His brow furrowed. "Is that true?"

She pressed her fingers to her temples. "I don't know why she would make it up. To hurt me? That's just . . . it seems a bit much even for Elodie."

"How could it be a secret all this time?"

"It wasn't. That's the worst part. There were gossip items. But so many untrue things have been written about my mother and her sisters over the years, I just never took any of it seriously. And now it's like . . . the entire fairy-tale origin story of my parents is turned upside down. My mother, I mean, if she 'stole' her sister's boyfriend?" No wonder Gemma had been cast out; it was because of her mother's sin.

"She was just a person, Gem. These things happen," Sanjay said.

She looked up sharply. "These things *happen*? You can't forgive me for something far lesser that *I* did, but this? This is fine?"

"Let's not go there," he said. But something about the way his jaw shifted told her she'd struck a nerve.

"I'm totally lost." She felt her eyes tear up. "The past is a mess, and my future's a mess. The whole idea of competing with Pavlin & Co . . . it's a joke. I have no idea what to do. I can't beat them, and I can't join them."

"You're not lost. You're selling out online. You were just profiled in *The New York Times.*"

"I can't even afford to buy materials to fulfill the orders coming in. The publicity that seemed so great is actually hurting me because it came too early. I really don't know what I'm going to do now." Gemma felt tears in her eyes again and didn't bother fighting them off.

Sanjay walked over, bending down to hug her. She felt herself relax, as if she were unspooling in his arms. When he pulled away, it felt too soon. He rested back on his heels so they were eye level.

All this with her family, on top of losing him. She wiped her eyes with the back of her hand.

"My aunt Celeste believes there's a Pavlin curse — that we're doomed in love."

"Oh, come on. You don't believe that, do you? We make our own luck . . . out of our choices," he said pointedly.

"Well, clearly the women in my family make bad choices." She tried not to think of Connor. Or the way she kissed Noam at the party.

"I'm not going to argue with that." His

eyes locked onto hers and her chest constricted.

"I love you, Sanjay," she breathed.

He leaned forward so slowly it was like she was imagining it. And then his lips brushed against hers. She reached out to hold his face, feeling the hint of stubble along his jaw. She kissed him harder, and he reached up, winding his hand through her hair. She inched off the chair, sliding down so they were both on the floor, chest to chest, holding each other tight.

"I can't," he said pulling back.

"Why?" she said, catching her breath. She knew why: Monica.

For a moment, neither of them said anything,

"Gemma, if you don't know what to do next, go back to Provincetown. Keep working on your business. Live cheaply at your aunt's. Finish what you started."

She blinked, holding back the words: *That's what I was just trying to do.*

64

Elodie's driver deposited her back in Provincetown a few hours after sunset. She needed to tell Celeste the truth about the Electric Rose — and the argument with their niece — before Gemma got to her. But by the time she reached the house, Celeste and Jack were already asleep.

The small bedroom seemed even smaller with all her emotional baggage. Oh, that encounter with Gemma was regrettable. She'd completely gone off the rails. What had she been thinking to lash out like that? And lying about the ring — she should have just told them both the truth at the beginning. She was too focused on getting Celeste to sign the auction paperwork, not anticipating how the lie could come back and hurt her later.

Restless, she slipped down the back stairs and headed for Commercial. Even at this late hour couples and families with young children strolled up and down the street. A lone saxophone played somewhere nearby, and a drag queen stood in the entrance to one of the bars beckoning people to a late-night show. And then, a familiar face: Tito walked out of the piano bar Tin Pan Alley.

"You're back!" he said. "Why didn't you text me?"

"Oh, I really just got here," she said.

"I missed you," he said, reaching forward to hug her. She leaned into him without enthusiasm.

"Just not enough to come with me to New York," she said.

He stepped back, looking at her. "You can't teach an old dog new tricks, I'm afraid."

"A fitting metaphor since it was the dog walking that brought us together," she said. "I'm wondering if we shouldn't have left it at that."

"What do you mean?"

Looking at his earnest face and his warm dark eyes, she almost caved. But no: She'd been a fool for love once. That was enough.

"I think your refusal to come to New York was just an excuse to slow things down between us."

"What? No! In fact, while you've been away all I could think about was finding a way to spend more time together."

She shook her head. "I don't see how we can move forward, Tito."

"This is how: My rental the last week of August canceled, so I'll have my house back. And next summer, I'm not going to rent it out at all. I'm going to be working full-time with Marco on the oyster farm. He's expanding. It will replace my summer rental income perfectly. Anyway, the point is, in a few weeks we can live at my place."

"We?"

"Yes, Elodie. I want to know if you'll move in with me."

Elodie awoke tucked against Tito. He was still asleep, sunlight streaming through the bare window. The way the light fell across his face highlighted the white stubble on his jaw. She resisted the urge to reach out and touch it, not wanting to wake him.

She let herself luxuriate in that moment, to really take in the fact that after all these years, after having given up on love, she'd found it in the most unexpected place. In the most unexpected man. And yet, the issue of geography could not be ignored. There was no way she could move in with him. She had a home — in New York City. There could be compromises, there could be adjustments. But if he would never spend time there, it wouldn't work.

She voiced none of this last night. She'd just kissed him and said, "That's a lovely offer." He didn't press, and that was the end of it. Now, in the light of a new day, she'd have to deal with it. But first things first.

Elodie glanced at her nightstand, where she'd placed the gift box containing the pink diamond eternity band. She decided she'd give Celeste the gift first, then tell her that she'd lied to her about the fate of the Electric Rose. And confess that she'd told Gemma about her relationship with Liam.

Anticipating this talk made it impossible for her to lounge in bed. She dressed and crept out without waking Tito, walking to Celeste's.

She found her in the yard with a cup of coffee sitting at the picnic table.

"Oh, hi there. I didn't know you were back from the city," Celeste said brightly.

"You were asleep when I got to the house," Elodie said, sitting on the bench across from her. Celeste told her final preparations for the wedding were exhausting.

"I know Jack wants to get married on his birthday. But planning a wedding during our busiest month of the year probably wasn't the best idea."

Elodie cleared her throat. This was her opening. "Celeste, I want to give you your wedding present. I was thinking maybe you'd like to wear it on the big day. Something from the family."

"Aha," Celeste said. "Something old . . ."

"Exactly," Elodie said, her hand shaking slightly as she pulled the ring box out of her handbag. "I know you don't usually wear jewelry, but this is a piece of Pavlin history."

No, she hadn't intended on telling her sister the true origin of the diamonds. But now the secret was out.

"Elodie, this is thoughtful but really not necessary," Celeste said, holding the box in one hand.

"I had this made for myself. I thought I'd wear it on my own wedding day, but that day never came. I'm happy to pass it on to you."

"It seems like you could have a wedding in your future," Celeste said with a wink.

"Who knows. But if I do, it's because I came here to see you. And because you welcomed me into your home so I could stay here long enough to find out. So . . . thank you."

Celeste opened the box and gingerly removed the ring, placing it on the ring finger of her left hand.

"It's stunning, Elodie." She looked up. "It's so extravagant, though. I can't accept this."

"Please! I have enough jewelry for two lifetimes. I'd love to see you wear this on Thursday."

Elodie could tell that even though Celeste considered herself immune to the charms of precious gems, the stones dazzled her. She wished she could just leave it at that, but she forced herself to press on. "I do have one more thing to tell you," she said slowly. Celeste was busy holding up her hand and examining the ring at different angles. "I told you that I sold the Electric Rose years ago. But that's not the entire story."

That got her attention.

"But you did sell it, right?"

"Yes. Just . . . not all at once."

"What's that supposed to mean?"

"I had it broken up into pieces and made a collection out of the smaller stones."

Celeste's expression turned blank, then her eyes widened. She looked almost . . . afraid.

"Don't tell me . . ." she said, her voice low.

"Well, yes. That ring is the last piece I have of the original stone. And yes, I know you don't approve that I broke up the diamond. I admit, it wasn't the most ethical thing to do. It was one of a kind. But the company was in a real financial bind and —"

Celeste pulled the ring from her finger and dropped it like it was on fire.

"I should have known nothing ever changes with you people. It's always about money. Money, money, money! And don't you see the price we've paid for that?"

Elodie stared at her, stunned. What on earth was she talking about?

Celeste stood, her wedding magazine falling to the ground.

"Take that cursed ring and get out of my house."

65

It was late afternoon by the time the ferry docked at MacMillan Pier. Gemma sensed that Provincetown was more crowded than when she'd left. Even though Carnival, the annual theme week of costumes and parties, was still two weeks away, a few people were already showing off their creative interpretation of this year's theme, "Enchanted Forest."

The energy in town was so buoyant, she felt bad about returning with so much negativity. But Sanjay was right: The best thing she could do was return and get back to work. Work was always the answer. Still, she couldn't stand the thought of sleeping under the same roof as Elodie. And Elodie would surely be back this week for the wedding.

The front door to Maud and Alvie's house, like all front doors in Provincetown, was unlocked. If her request to stay for the night was an imposition, Maud didn't show it.

"Stay as long as you'd like," Maud had said the night before, jumping into Gemma's FaceTime chat with Alvie.

It wasn't just that she didn't want to see Elodie. She also wondered how she'd spend time with Celeste and avoid mentioning what happened during her trip. But Elodie was right: It would be selfish to dump her problems at Celeste's feet right before her wedding. The truth about the Electric Rose — and her questions about Elodie and her father — would have to wait.

"Welcome, welcome — I'm just on my way to the restaurant but make yourself at home," Maud said, emerging from the back of the house to greet her.

"Thanks so much," Gemma said. "Is Alvie here?"

"She's at the restaurant already. Then we're going to observe the blue moon later. You're welcome to meet us at the beach. A blue moon is very powerful — ripe for channeling our intuition."

Gemma's gratitude for a place to stay disappeared with a flash of irritation at her hostess. She'd been skeptical the day that Celeste brought her to get her cards read, but she'd let herself be seduced by the fantasy that some cosmic power could show her the way.

"By the way, your 'true love' prediction for this summer was way off," she said.

Maud smiled, glancing at her phone and then back at Gemma.

"In what way?"

"Well, for one thing, I was dating a guy here who turned out to be using me for my family money. And Sanjay, my photographer friend, the one who came with us to the Boatslip? He's the one I actually care about. But he's with someone else now. So, sorry to say but you were wrong."

Maud smiled, a twinkle in her eyes.

"The summer's not over yet."

Later that morning, the Barroses called a family meeting, summoning everyone to Manny and Lidia's. It wasn't unusual for them, but Celeste didn't have the energy today.

"You go and just fill me in," Celeste told Jack. She said she needed to keep the store open, but truly, she was just too upset over the conversation with her sister to deal with whatever the Barroses wanted to discuss.

She didn't know what upset her more: Elodie's lie about the diamond, or the fact that a piece of the cursed item remained in the family, like a floating cancer cell just waiting to metastasize.

Part of her confidence in moving ahead with the wedding planning was based on the ring being sold. If the cursed diamond was gone, it reasoned that the curse, too, was gone. Plus, the star alignment looked positive, and Maud's tarot reading didn't show any signs for alarm. But now, a major piece of her calculations had been false.

She stepped outside the store. A few customers milled around, but traffic had dwindled. It was too perfect a beach day for people to spend time indoors shopping.

I need a sign, she thought, looking up at the sky. *Is marriage the right next step?*

By the time Jack returned home, she had all but forgotten about the meeting.

"Hey," he said, walking in with those quick strides of his, eyes bright.

"So what was that all about?" she said.

"Here's the deal," Jack said, his face particularly animated. "Marco is expanding the business — the oyster farm. He's going to become a licensed reseller."

"What does that mean? Isn't that what he's doing now?"

"No. He's a wholesaler. He can't sell directly to restaurants. Now he could get a much higher price, and even sell direct to consumers at farmer's markets."

"Well, good for him." She didn't know why the family needed to call everyone over to announce that, but that was the Barros way.

"The thing is he can't just snap his fingers and become a licensed reseller. He's gotta get approved. They need a mechanically refrigerated vehicle, a walk-in refrigerator on-site, new sinks, stainless steel tables. Minimally, it's an eighty-thousand-dollar investment to convert the business."

"That's a lot."

"It is, but the increased sales volume and margins will let us earn that back within a year."

"You mean Marco and Olivia. *They* can earn it back in a year."

"He's offered us a chance to go in with him. Tito, too."

Celeste leaned forward, hands planted on the counter. He couldn't be serious.

"Why would we put money into Marco's oyster farm?"

"Well, it would become partly our oyster farm. And because this is a business that could be profitable enough in a few years to let us really plan our retirement."

Celeste couldn't believe what she was hearing.

"I have *zero* interest in investing in an oyster farm."

"Why not? My family has always earned a living off of the water, and Marco's done a great job taking it to the next level. It's incredibly generous of him to open it up to us."

"We have our own business to invest in," she said, sweeping open her arm.

"There's no way to grow this business — no amount of money will make it more scalable. We've only seen it shrink over the past few summers. We're getting older, Celeste. We need to think about security. Stability."

It was all too much. He wanted to get married, get involved in an oyster farm. It was clearly a midlife crisis.

Or maybe it was the curse.

"I'm not ready," she said to Jack.

"Well, now's the time. Marco says that —"

"I mean, I'm not ready to get married."

He froze. His face turned red — something she'd never seen before in his olive-toned complexion. It was alarming.

Without another word, he walked to the stairs.

She looked around the store, making certain there weren't any customers she hadn't noticed. Then she closed the front doors and put out her *Went to the Beach* sign. Heart pounding, she rushed up to their bedroom, where she found him piling clothes into his suitcase.

"Jack. What are you doing?"

"I'm going to Manny and Lidia's."

"What? Jack, no. Don't do that. We need to work this out."

"I don't see what there is to work out."

"I love you. And you love me, for one thing."

"Well, maybe that one thing isn't enough. Because you've been pushing back for years against the idea of marriage, and I always thought time would fix it. But now I know it won't."

"There's nothing to fix. We're happy together."

He looked at her sadly. "I'm not, Celeste. For me, something is missing. I want you to be my family. I want to make it official. I don't understand why you don't want that, too. But you don't. And I have to accept it."

"I'm sure we can find a way to work through this," she said slowly.

He stood still, looking at her. Their eyes met, and for a moment she thought she'd reached him, that he would let go of the idea their relationship had to be all or nothing. But then he walked out.

66

Gemma overlooked one small detail in her plan to avoid Elodie: All of her jewelry-making equipment was at Celeste's. By sunset, she couldn't ignore all the orders flooding her Instagram.

Queen Anne's Revenge was closed and she walked around back to use the private entrance. Before she reached the porch, she heard something that stopped her in her tracks: a woman crying. Gemma followed the sound to the yard, where she found Celeste at the picnic table, her head buried in the crook of her arm.

"Aunt Celeste! What's wrong?"

Celeste looked up, wiping her eyes and glancing around as if she'd been caught doing something illicit.

"When did you get back?" she said.

"A few hours ago," Gemma said, walking closer. "I'm staying at Maud's."

"Why would you — Oh. I understand. You

don't want to see Elodie."

Surprised, Gemma slid into the bench across from her. A stray shard of wood scratched her elbow.

"How did you know?"

"She's here, too. And she told me about the ring."

"She did?" Hadn't Elodie begged her not to tell Celeste? Hadn't she specifically guilted her — and rightly so — not to bring it up and spoil Celeste's happiness heading into her wedding?

"More than that," Celeste said. "She gave it to me. Or tried to."

Gemma leaned forward, avoiding the rough patch on the table. "Gave you . . . what, exactly?"

"The eternity band. Made from pieces of the Electric Rose."

What? "You're saying that Elodie still has one of the pieces made from the original diamond?"

"Yes. I'm sorry. I thought you knew. Anyway, I asked her to leave. She lied and manipulated us over that stupid auction! I believed her when she said she sold the diamond long ago. But it's not gone, so the curse is still here. And I can't get married. So Jack left."

Gemma sat up straight. "Aunt Celeste,

you don't really believe that, do you?"

"Of course I do. We've talked about this. As soon as my father launched that competition for the diamond, everything fell apart. And the one couple that didn't break up because of it *died.*"

Gemma's immediate thought was, *Yes, exactly:* It was the *competition* that hurt the family. Not the diamond itself. But it was clear her aunt was stuck in a kind of magical thinking, and there was nothing Gemma could say in that moment that would change her mind. If Celeste was so fearful of the curse that she was willing to break off her engagement, Gemma would need help.

She needed Maud.

Maud's restaurant, the Clamshell, was on the bay side of Commercial. Inside, the wraparound bar was hopping, with Steve Miller's "The Joker" playing on the sound system. Alvie stood sentry near the front door, holding a clipboard and checking off reservations. She was so busy she didn't notice Gemma walk in, and Gemma didn't bother her. She didn't need to: She spotted Maud behind the bar, shaking a metal cocktail mixer. The crowd in front of the bar was three deep, and Gemma had to bump her way through, getting spilled on in the process.

"Maud!" she called out over the music. "I need to talk to you."

Maud poured the cocktail into a martini glass. It was pale yellow and she garnished it with a maraschino cherry and a pink umbrella.

"I'm a little busy right now. We can talk back at the house. Wanna drink?"

"This can't wait," Gemma said.

Maud hesitated, but then blew a whistle that hung around her neck, summoning another bartender who appeared out of nowhere. She wore a referee shirt, cutoff jean shorts, and a backward Helltown baseball cap. Maud snapped her fingers at Gemma and pointed to the back of the room.

It took her a full minute to reach Maud at a pair of sliding glass doors leading to a deck. She followed Maud outside, past tables and busy servers carrying trays of burgers, crab cakes, and fries. Gemma's stomach rumbled; she hadn't eaten before getting on the ferry earlier. It seemed like an entirely different day.

"What's the emergency?" Maud said when they reached the end of the dock. A fat seagull perched on the railing and looked at them as if they were intruding.

"Celeste broke off her engagement."

Maud winced. "I'm sorry to hear that. I'm surprised."

Gemma crossed her arms. "Are you really? Surprised, I mean."

"Yes, of course. Why would you ask that?"

"Because she talks to you about everything — all that astrological stuff. Are you encouraging her to believe in this curse?"

"We've discussed it, but I've repeatedly told her not to put too much credence in it. I can only tell her what's in her chart or the cards."

Gemma reached out and touched her arm. "Maud, this is serious. Jack's a great guy. He loves her. They belong together, and now she's freaking out and messing it up. As her friend, you need to help her."

Maud nodded. "Of course I want to help her. I'm just not sure how. Do you know what happened?"

"Elodie told her our family's famous diamond — the one Celeste is convinced is cursed — was sold. But then we learned that it had been broken up into smaller stones instead, and one of those smaller diamond pieces is still in the family." The whole thing sounded insane when Gemma said it aloud.

"I see." Maud nodded as if it were completely reasonable — as if people walked in every day off the street talking about cursed diamonds. Maybe they did. "I have an idea," Maud said. "But we'll need your other aunt's help, too."

Gemma groaned. "Can't we do this without her? Elodie's . . . difficult."

Maud smiled at her with a gentle expression, as if she were a child. "There's no way around difficulty, Gemma. Only through."

She didn't need the cards to tell her that. The universe was giving her the message, loud and clear.

67

Tito was unusually quiet. Typically, they talked nonstop while the dogs frolicked on the beach at the municipal lot. Today, instead of sitting on one of the benches, they found two egg crates someone left in the sand and they used them as seats.

"Are you upset with me about something?" Elodie said.

"I'm not upset with *you,*" he said. "But your sister did break Jack's heart."

This was about Jack and Celeste?

"What do you mean?"

Tito looked over at her. "You don't know? Celeste canceled the wedding."

No, Elodie did *not* know.

"I'm sorry. I had no idea. To be honest, we had a bit of an argument yesterday morning and we haven't spoken since." A small crab scuttled out from the bottom of her crate.

"What's she mad at you for?"

"A business decision I made," Elodie said.

Tito shook his head. "I never understood that woman. They would've been hitched a long time ago if it were up to Jack. Celeste's a free spirit and that's fine. But in a relationship you gotta give a little."

She looked at him, incredulous. "In a relationship you have to *give a little*? Says the man who refuses to spend time with me in New York." Pearl, at the edge of the water, turned at the sound of her raised voice.

Tito looked surprised, then understanding dawned and he rubbed his brow.

"Okay, you got me there."

"Look," she said, her voice softening. "It was a lovely gesture for you to ask me to live with you. But I already have a home. If we're going to be together, I need you to be part of that life, too."

He looked out at the water. The egg crate underneath her suddenly felt very wobbly. She watched Pearl, trying to pretend she hadn't just given the man she loved an ultimatum. And really, who was she to push him to compromise when she hadn't been completely honest with him all summer? He didn't know that she was the one who lured Gemma to the Cape, or about any of the infighting in their family that might have given Celeste a damn good reason to be afraid of commitment. Tito believed she truly intended to open a Pavlin & Co outpost on Commercial Street!

"Well, Elodie," he said, turning back to her. "You drive a hard bargain. I'll think about it. But I warn you: You take this seafaring fella to the big city at your own risk."

Bart ambled over to them, impatient and needing attention. Tito waved a stick and tossed it, sending him dashing back toward the water.

If she was going to really go for it — change her life, figure out a way to work remotely, travel back and forth so she could have her relationship and her company — she had to know if it was for real. If he was going to stick around. One way to test that was to share the worst part of herself.

And so she told him. About her manipulations all summer. The lie about her intention to open a shop in town. About Liam. About Paulina. About the family infighting and decades of resentment. About how she took it all out on her niece, shutting her out and, maybe worst of all, tainting her memory of her father.

He listened calmly. Silently. When she was

done talking, he said simply, "You can fix this."

"I don't know," she said, shaking her head. But she knew she had to try. As long as she was fighting with her sister and her niece, the wounds of the past would never be healed. And they would all suffer because of it.

"Do you think terribly of me?" she said, feeling more vulnerable than she'd ever felt before. Sitting on that spit of sand, surrounded by water and with the taste of salt in her mouth and the wind in her face, it was as if her entire life had led to that moment.

"Of course not. How could I?" he said, his gaze soft. "I love you, Elodie."

Her heart swelled. He moved his egg crate closer to her, pulling her into his arms. She felt herself losing her balance, but he kept her steady.

"I love you, too," she said. And then, "Tito, if I do move in with you — or, at the very least, spend a lot more time out here — what would I do about my work?"

"Well," he said, seeming to ponder this. "A very clever businesswoman I happen to know said recently that this town needs a high-end jewelry shop . . ."

■ ■ ■ ■

Gemma wiped perspiration from her forehead, climbing the stairs to Lidia's front deck.

It felt like the entire town had descended on the marina. The line for boat rentals stretched almost to the street and there was a crowded queue of people waiting to board the seal tour boat. Behind the house, Manny and a few other men were repairing a pontoon. Carnival week was just around the corner and the streets and shops were already at maximum capacity.

If Gemma had her way, the argument with Elodie in Manhattan would be the last time they ever spoke. Just thinking about the self-righteous expression on her aunt's face when she spoke about her father still made her feel sick. But if she wanted to help Celeste, she had to put all of that aside.

She was so anxious about seeing Elodie, she wasn't prepared to run into Jack. He descended the stairs carrying a large cooler.

"Hi, Jack," she said, smiling awkwardly. Should she acknowledge what was going on, or just act normal, or what?

"Hey there, Gemma," he said with a faint smile. The usual twinkle in his eye was gone.

He looked tired, pale underneath his tan. She remembered his kindness to her the day she first arrived in town, so uncertain and unmoored.

"We're having a party here tomorrow night. I know Alvie's coming, so be sure to stop by."

With that, he continued on. She swallowed hard. Tomorrow was supposed to be their wedding day. She hoped there was some way to make sure it still was. She needed to see at least one Pavlin woman get her happy ending. She didn't believe in curses, but she did believe in love, even if she couldn't find it herself.

She knocked on the screen door before opening it. Lidia sat at the kitchen table, which was covered by long brown fronds of some sort. The room smelled dank and salty.

"Gemma, what a nice surprise. Come on in. Don't mind the smell — it's just fresh kelp."

Gemma had to resist the urge to cover her nose. She leaned against the counter.

"Is Elodie here?"

"She and Tito are out with the dogs. But they should be back anytime now. Have a seat."

"I saw Jack on my way in," she said.

Lidia frowned. "Yes. We have a full house

here. I'm usually happy to have the whole family under one roof, but not under these circumstances."

"I know. I'm trying to help Celeste see she's making a mistake. That's why I want to talk to Elodie. I need her help."

Elodie's pug, Pearl, ambled into the kitchen. Gemma tensed, knowing her owner wouldn't be far behind. It was hot in the kitchen, the window behind the sink open and a ceiling fan lazily stirring the soupy air. Pearl trotted over to a water bowl.

Elodie, dressed in madras plaid shorts and navy Tory Burch ballerina flats, walked in.

"Why don't you two go out on the porch and chat? I know you have a lot to discuss," Lidia said with a wink.

"Oh," Elodie said, caught off-guard. "Just a minute. I need to get something from upstairs."

68

Gemma watched a silver catamaran bobbing on the bay. Below Lidia's deck, seagulls battled over a discarded piece of bread. And on the chair next to her, Elodie rummaged through her handbag.

"It was inexcusable of me to talk about your father the way I did," she said. "Clearly, I haven't made my peace with the past, and it's impacted my judgment. And my treatment of you, I'm afraid."

Gemma looked at her. "I appreciate that, but I don't want to talk about it," she said. The more Elodie spoke of her father, the more three-dimensional their relationship seemed. It made the crack in her memory of her parents wider.

"I understand. But, as a token of my apology — and of good faith moving forward — I want to give you something. I tried to give this to Celeste but she didn't want it. And I realize now it rightfully belongs with you."

She passed her a pink diamond eternity band. The gems caught the sunlight and tossed it back to the sky. It was a perfect, pale rose hue, so sparkly it seemed lit from within. Her breath caught in her throat.

"It's the only thing I have left of the Electric Rose. I'm sorry I don't have your mother's complete stone. But I hope this is some small consolation."

Hands trembling, Gemma slipped it on her left ring finger. She was instantly transported to her childhood self, feeling her mother's one-of-a-kind diamond wobble on her small hand. Never wanting to take it off.

And she didn't want to take it off now. But she had to.

"I do want to talk to you about this ring. But not for me — for Celeste."

Elodie shook her head. "She doesn't want it. My sister, she's consumed with this idea of a curse and who knows what. I'd try to talk some sense into her but she's too angry with me. And now she's gone and done something stupid."

"Jack," Gemma said. Elodie nodded, and she could see Elodie was genuinely concerned. "I know. That's why I'm here. We're going to fix it."

"How?" Elodie looked skeptical.

Gemma slipped off the ring, holding it tight. She literally had, in the palm of her hand, the one thing she had wanted for so long — or, at least, the closest she would get to it. She had two choices: She could keep it, a piece of her past forever close to her. Or she could let it go for someone else's future.

It was low tide at Herring Cove. The beach was the most crowded it had been all summer even as it neared dinnertime, when the visitors usually thinned out except for the die-hards waiting for the sunset. Today, no one seemed in any hurry to leave. Dogs scampered into the waves, couples cuddled on blankets, beautiful young men drank up the last rays of sun to burnish their tans.

Celeste walked along the ocean edge, collecting beach stones, picking up all the green ones that were the least blemished and dropping them in a bucket. She tried to tell herself that no matter how sad she felt, how scared of what a future would look like without Jack, she could still enjoy Provincetown's unparalleled natural beauty. The sky was beginning to streak shades of peach, gold, and purple. How many times a season did she and Jack turn to each other and say, "That was the most beautiful sunset of all time," only to find themselves repeating the same words the next night. And the most magical thing was that no two sunsets ever looked the same. In a town filled with painters and writers and sculptors and photographers, nature was the most prolific and surprising artist of all.

Sunsets always brought her comfort. Growing up, spending summers out in the Hamptons, she'd shared countless memories of watching the light fade over the Atlantic Ocean with her parents and sisters. They sat out back on Adirondack chairs, her parents debating how best to tame the mosquitos while she and her sisters angled for a trip into town for ice cream. Celeste remembered the sting of her sunburns, the smell of the salt air, and a feeling of absolute security.

She hadn't cared when her father cut her off from the money. The thing she missed was the connective tissue between the five of them that had once felt as tight as a muscle. Every argument between herself and her sisters, every manipulation by her parents, every incident that made it clear that Pavlin the company was more important than Pavlin the family, set her further adrift until she had come to prefer the separation. And now, because of that, she was destined to be alone.

Celeste squinted into the near distance. Something about the sunlight bouncing off the ocean played tricks with her eyes. Or maybe it was the rush of nostalgia about the halcyon days of her youth. Either way, she thought she saw Elodie walking in her direction.

But then, it was Elodie, or a version of Elodie that she hadn't seen in thirty years. Elodie, her hair blowing in the breeze, barefoot. Elodie, noticing her, too, gingerly offered a wave. They hadn't spoken since their argument over the ring.

"I stopped by the store a few times today but I kept missing you," Elodie said.

A seagull circled them, pausing to peck at a cracked mussel shell still holding meat.

Celeste's impulse was to hold on to her anger about the Electric Rose. But she couldn't deny that she wanted — no, *needed* — to talk to her sister.

She felt tears welling in her eyes.

"Celeste. Are you okay?"

"No . . . I'm scared I'm losing Jack. I don't know what to do. And I can't talk to my best friend about it, because that's him. I can't talk to Lidia, either, because she's his family, so of course she has to take Jack's side."

Celeste put down her bucket and looked out at the sea, taking a deep breath. She needed to keep it together. Provincetown was a small place and news of a public breakdown would spread through town faster than you could say "community Facebook page."

"You can talk to me. I'm here. And Gemma, too."

Wait, had Elodie and Gemma patched things up? Had hell just frozen over?

She wiped her eyes with the edge of her caftan and looked at her sister in confusion.

"We've both realized that our shared affection for you overrides our differences," Elodie said.

"Well, that's a lovely thing to say." She looked at her, shielding her face from the sun as it sank lower, its splintering rays making it impossible to see even with her sunglasses.

"It's not just words, Celeste. Gemma and I are going to help you with this Jack situation."

Celeste didn't know whether to be moved by the naïve sentiment, or irritated that her sister and niece thought her issue could be solved so easily.

"And Maud, too," Elodie added.

Now, that got her attention.

"Okay," she said. "I'm listening."

"Tonight — the full moon — we all need to meet here at midnight."

Wait — what? Celeste had been fully expecting Elodie to jump into a plan full of logistics and strategy, her usual tactical approach to any problem. But her all-business sister was finally speaking her language.

The relief was so overwhelming, all she could do was throw her arms around her. Elodie, caught off-guard, tumbled back into the sand, pulling Celeste with her. After a stunned few seconds, they both broke out laughing. Celeste picked up her bucket, putting back the stones that had fallen aside.

"Wanna collect stones?" Celeste said. "I call the green ones."

69

Constance, 2015

Bucks County, Pennsylvania, was a two-hour drive from Manhattan. When her driver pulled up to the high school, Constance felt she might as well be in Kansas.

Her intention to go unnoticed — to blend in with the crowd — was undermined by her choice of attire. Constance was the only one wearing a Chanel suit. But what else would one wear to a graduation? As far as she was concerned, every important occasion called for Chanel.

Ten years earlier, at the lowest point in her life, she never would have imagined a time when she felt like celebrating again. But thanks to recent widowhood and modern technology, she'd found a way to be in her granddaughter's life. From afar.

Now, seated in the stifling, un-air-conditioned auditorium in the middle of Pennsylvania farm country, her stomach fluttered with anticipation at seeing Gemma in person for the first time in nearly a decade. All the images she'd seen on social media prepared her for the fact that Gemma could be Paulina's twin. Still, Constance was thankful to have her eyes — excessively emotional even for a graduation ceremony — hidden behind sunglasses. Her impeccably bleached blond hair, still the color of churned butter, was concealed by an expertly knotted Hermès scarf.

After a lifetime of having the best of everything, it went against her instinct to take a seat in one of the last rows of the auditorium. But she couldn't risk running into the Maybrooks. She didn't have the energy to battle them. Not while she was facing a far more daunting adversary: stage four cancer.

The terminal diagnosis forced some soul-searching. What was her final wish in life? It was both simple and yet impossible: to see her remaining daughters and granddaughter reunited. She had no idea how to make this happen, especially since she didn't want to use her illness to guilt them. Unlike her late husband, she didn't believe in emotional manipulation. Besides, she didn't want anything making its way into the press. Her image — glamour, beauty, power — was all that she had left. That, and control of Pavlin & Co.

The band began to play "Pomp and Circumstance," bringing tears to her eyes. Just about thirty years earlier, she'd watched Paulina march into a very different auditorium to this same song. Oh, how excited her daughter had been to finish school, so eager to get out into the real world, to live her life.

Her all-too-brief life.

The students filed in, dressed in dark blue gowns and matching caps with gold tassels. Constance had relegated herself to the back, but at least she'd gotten an aisle seat — the aisle the graduates used to make their entrance. Constance's heart began to beat fast; Gemma would be just inches away when she walked in. Would she see her in time?

She didn't have to worry: The hairs on her arms stood on end and she *felt* her granddaughter's presence seconds before she spotted the curtain of blond hair. As Gemma walked by, smiling and looking straight ahead, Constance reached out and touched the back of her robe, as softly as a butterfly landing.

No one noticed. But Constance knew she'd be reliving that moment until the day she died. And whatever time she had left between now and then, she'd find a way to use it to plant the seeds for her final wish to come true.

70

At midnight, the beach became a conversation between moon and tides, the stretch of sand untouched except for the sea birds and a stray coyote. Except for tonight, when the four women gathered at the water's edge.

Celeste couldn't remember the last time she'd been to Herring Cove at that hour. Maybe in the early days with Jack, when dinner turned into drinks which turned into a drunken stroll through town and ultimately to the beach. There had been a night or two when they'd made love in the sand. The thought of the way their bodies had responded to each other's back then — like magnets, like electrified cables — made her yearn for him now. The pain she'd been feeling for the past few days shot up again, just when she thought she couldn't feel any worse.

"The important thing is to stay in the moment," Maud said, as if reading her mind.

Maud, dressed in white jeans and a white T-shirt, was barefoot and gathered Celeste, Gemma, and Elodie into a tight circle. Celeste had dressed carefully for the occasion in one of her favorite pale blue tunics she'd found at a thrift shop years ago. It had lantern sleeves and went nearly to the ground, with slits on either side of her legs for easy movement. Elodie wore joggers and a gray cashmere wrap, while Gemma was dressed in denim shorts and a P'town hoodie. They stood as close to the ocean as possible before the tide licked their feet.

"Our intention tonight is to rid ourselves of negative energy and fear," Maud said. "The universe gives us signs — the stars can point us in the right direction. But the biggest factor in how our lives turn out is the choices we make. And the fact that the three of you are standing together here tonight is a powerful choice."

Celeste glanced at her sister and they shared a smile.

"I know that all three of you have the intention to be positive, to move forward in life. The challenge is that there are so few rites of passage for adult women," Maud said. "And it's a shame, because as we get older, we need to learn how to let go of the past in order to live fully in the present. So tonight, we form an Intention Circle." She told them to join hands.

"In order to dispel what has been holding us back, we each need to evoke the thing we want most to come *into* our lives. As we do that, we will pass this ring — a symbol of the past — to each speaker." She handed the diamond eternity band to Celeste. "Would you like to go first?"

"Yes," she said. She held the ring gingerly. Normally, she didn't feel the slightest bit self-conscious engaging in spiritual business. But she knew Gemma and Elodie were skeptics at best, making it all the more touching that they'd gone out of their way to help her in this way. "I want Jack to forgive me, and to trust me again. And to come back to me. I want to be able to get married tomorrow like we planned. But I don't know if it's too late."

It was one thing to ask the universe to vanquish bad energy. But human emotions were another thing; she knew Jack was deeply hurt. Because of *her* choices. Maud was right.

Jack wouldn't understand why she was afraid of getting married if she never really told him, and so he wouldn't understand how she let go of that fear. She'd just have to hope that somehow, talking to him tomorrow, he might not understand her but he'd at least believe her. If not, it wouldn't be because of the curse. She'd have only herself to blame.

Celeste passed the ring to Elodie, who hesitated a few seconds before taking it in her hand. She gazed at the ring, turning it between her thumb and forefinger in a way that caught the moonlight. When she spoke, it was so quietly that it was hard to hear over the rush of the waves.

"Our family fortune was built on the words 'A Diamond Says Love.' But it's obvious now how flawed that is. A diamond doesn't say love. Moments like this say love. Family says love. Forgiveness says love."

Celeste reached out to put her arm around her sister. And then Elodie passed the ring to her niece.

Gemma looked out at the sea. From her position in the Intention Circle, she had the best view of the water, liquid silver in the moonlight.

She held the remains of her mother's diamond in her palm, her fingers wrapped tightly around it. She had to resist the urge to slip it onto her finger one last time.

"Speak when you're ready," Maud nudged.

It was her turn to declare what she wanted to bring into her life. At the beginning of the summer, that would have been simple. She'd wanted to grow her company. She wanted her name to be synonymous with modern jewelry. She wanted the Pavlins to realize the mistake they'd made in casting her aside. And she wanted the Electric Rose, the symbol of all she'd lost — and been denied.

"I have . . . a lot I need to figure out," she said slowly.

"Gemma, may I?" Elodie piped up. "I'm sorry for turning you away from what's rightfully yours. I hope you'll forgive me. And you were right about what you said: The company has become stagnant. We need new energy. And I hope that energy will come from you."

"From me?"

"I want to offer you a design position with Pavlin & Co. It would be entry-level — you would be part of a team under our head designer. But there's room to grow. There's a future for you at Pavlin & Co if you'd like it."

Gemma, stunned, glanced at Celeste. *Where had this come from?* Celeste smiled.

"I don't get it," she said.

"I've seen you at work this summer. I've

seen how people respond to your designs. You'd be an asset to Pavlin & Co. It's as simple as that. I would offer this to you even if you were a stranger."

Here it was — a moment she had dreamed about as a teenager, only to realize it would never happen. But what if it could?

Gemma bit her lip. She knew, standing in the moonlight, flanked by her mother's sisters, that she didn't need to work at Pavlin & Co to make her life complete. She'd come to her aunts looking for a diamond, and instead found her family.

"Thank you, Aunt Elodie," she said. "I'll think about it. But first, can we agree on one thing? No auction. Tell Sloan Pierce it's off."

"Agreed," said Elodie.

"Are you two really negotiating right now?" said Maud. "Please, let's stay in the moment. Gemma, you need to focus on what you most want to bring into your life."

Looking at the silvery water, at the stillness punctuated only by the rolling tide, she missed Sanjay with a physical ache. What did she want most in the world? The answer was clear to her.

"I want Sanjay back." There it was. She couldn't deny it: She wanted the true love Maud had promised earlier in the summer.

"Good," said Maud. "Now we're ready to release the past. Gemma, since you're the last one holding the ring, I ask you to step into the water and toss it as far as you can manage. And in your mind, hold the thought that you are intentionally letting it go."

"Won't the tide just bring it back in?" Elodie said.

An amused smile played at Maud's lips. "We must trust the universe to accept what we're offering it," she said.

Gemma glanced at Celeste, who nodded at her. She walked a few feet into the water. It was cool and pebbly underfoot. She felt goose bumps rise on her arms and kept walking until she was up to her thighs, just before the water could reach her shorts. She felt herself squeezing the ring, as if afraid to lose it. Here it was, an object she'd wanted so badly for years. And she was about to toss it into the ocean.

Surrounded by black water and under the spotlight of an August full moon, all she could think about was her mother. The sea had taken her mother, and now the sea would take the remains of her ring.

Gemma pulled her arm back and then thrust it forward like she was pitching a ball, her fingers unfurling to release the ring into the pull of the outgoing tide. It was shocking to let it disappear, not even hearing it hit the water over the churning waves. She stood for a minute, as if expecting it to come back to her.

And then she realized she was happy to set it free.

71

She was the uninvited guest at the party that should have been her wedding.

Celeste had never felt so uncomfortable walking into the Barroses' house, not even on that summer day twenty-five years ago when Jack brought her — his "wash'ashore" girlfriend — to meet the family. They'd welcomed her with open arms. If Jack loved her, Lidia and Manny loved her. And Tito. And the kids, Marco and Jaci.

Today, all she got from Lidia was a tight smile.

Celeste set a few packages down on the kitchen table. Birthday gifts for Jack. She decided to leave them in the house; nothing more awkward than presenting birthday gifts while simultaneously begging for forgiveness. Jack wasn't big on extravagant presents. He usually asked her for something experiential, like, *Spend the day on the boat with me.* Or, this year's whopper, *Let's get married.*

"I know you're both hurting," Lidia said, standing against the sink while Celeste stood a few feet inside the doorway. "But I gotta say I'm Team Jack on this one."

Of course she was. That's why, first thing that morning, just six hours after leaving the beach, Celeste knocked on Elodie's bedroom door to fortify herself with one more conversation. Her sister, half asleep, patted the spot next to her on the bed and Celeste moved next to her. She felt like they were girls again.

"When I left for the city last week, Tito told me that he'd never visit Manhattan," Elodie said. "My first thought was, well, that's the end of that. And I think he knew it, and we both thought there's no way to compromise. But then, I was in Manhattan, and it didn't mean anything without him. And maybe, while I was gone, he realized the same thing because he asked me to move in with him. It was a gesture, something to show me he's all in. I don't know if we'll work or how, but it means a lot to me that he made the gesture. You need to show Jack."

"How?" she'd said. But of course her sister couldn't give her that answer. No one could.

Lidia busied herself slicing tomatoes on a cutting board.

Celeste sat in one of the chairs around the table. "Lidia, I would never ask you to be in the middle. That's why I haven't come over to talk to you before now. Before I wasn't ready to tell Jack that I was wrong. I'm really sorry, Lidia. I know deep down Jack is traditional, and that he tried to forget that to accommodate me. But I'm ready to be his wife now. If he'll accept me back."

Lidia put down the knife, her eyes softer now. "Celeste, I love you like the sister I never had. And I want nothing more than to see you and Jack together in the way that Manny and I are. But you can't get married to make someone else happy."

"I know. That's what I've struggled with. But truly, it's what I want, too. It just took me some time to get here."

"Well, then don't waste any more time yapping here with me. Jack's out back helping Manny set up the bar."

Celeste nodded, feeling buoyed by the conversation. One down, one to go. She stood to leave.

"Just one more thing," Lidia said. "I hope everything goes great. I hope we're all laughing about all this over drinks tonight. But just in case it doesn't . . . I think it's best if you leave. It's Jack's birthday and I don't want anything to spoil the day."

"Of course," Celeste said, swallowing hard.

Outside the house, neither Manny nor Jack noticed her approach. They weren't, as Lidia had suggested, attending to the bar. Instead, they were at the edge of the dock with Jack tying a rope on the back of a skiff.

Jack loved everything about the water, down to knowing the ins and outs of how the vehicles that transported him worked. It was just a testament to his love for her that he had spent most of the past two decades helping to build her dream of an antiques shop. Now he wanted to get back on the water. And if buying into Marco's oyster farm was the way to do it, didn't she owe him that same support?

She took a moment to gaze at him, the late summer, deep brown tan of his arms, the way his silver hair tufted around his ears because he'd been too busy to get a haircut. The gray T-shirt from Outermost Automotive stretched taut against his chest.

She didn't just love him, she was *in love* with him. The worst part of their whole predicament was that she'd led him to believe otherwise.

"Hey — sorry to interrupt," she called out, giving a nervous little wave.

Jack looked over, surprised. He seemed happy to see her for a second, but his expression became guarded. He said something to Manny, but the breeze and the squawk of a gull carried it away. She felt her heart race as he walked over to her.

When they were face-to-face, it took all of her will not to just throw herself into his arms.

"Happy birthday," she said.

"Thanks," he said stiffly.

"Jack, I love you. I'm sorry. I was letting fear hold me back, but I'm past it now. Please — I'm so sorry for hurting your feelings, for letting you doubt for a minute my commitment to you. Let's get married. I'm totally on board with the oyster farm. I want a life with you — that's all that matters. I want to be your wife."

Jack sighed. His expression changed from wariness to almost . . . pity.

"That all sounds great, Celeste. But how can I believe that when the time comes, you're not going to back out again? I can't set myself up to be let down."

She shook her head. "I won't let you down."

He seemed about to reach out to her, to

take her hand or touch her arm — something. She stepped forward. But then, he moved away. "I love you, too. And maybe you even believe what you're saying. But I'm sorry — I don't."

He turned and walked back toward Manny.

So that was it? No. She wouldn't accept it. He was being stubborn, as he was inclined to be. And she could be stubborn, too. But if they both gave in to their worst instincts at the same time, the relationship was finished. What could she do to get through to him?

Her sister's words from earlier that morning repeated in her head. It was as if an airplane flew a kite overhead with the words emblazoned on it: *It was a gesture, something to show me he's all in . . . You need to show Jack.*

Of course. It was so obvious!

She rushed back toward Commercial as partygoers began arriving in bunches. She didn't have time to say hi, so she kept her eyes ahead and moved quickly. But when she reached the alley she ran into Clifford and his husband, Santiago. There was no escaping a greeting from Clifford.

"Celeste!" he said, passing the large, extravagantly wrapped gift box he was holding to Santiago. "I'm so happy to see you here. Did you two patch things up?" His face was shiny from the heat, but he was dressed impeccably as always, in an eggshell-colored linen suit and lavender button-down with a matching pocket square.

"Um, no. We didn't patch things up," she said.

"Don't tell us you're leaving already," said Santiago.

"I'll be right back. I just forgot something."

And she had: her wedding dress.

72

The Barros boatyard was strung with twinkling lights and filled with dozens of friendly faces. Jack and Manny stood in front of one buffet table, drinking bottles of Red Stripe.

Gemma felt awkward, considering what was going on between Jack and Celeste. But he'd been so kind to her since day one. Of course she would celebrate his birthday.

"Happy birthday," Gemma said, giving him a hug.

They smiled at each other but fell into a silence that she was able to break only when she noticed Clifford Henry waving at her wildly, his arm linked with that of an attractive younger man. The younger man was talking to a familiar woman: She was in her sixties, extremely thin with silvery blond hair in a knot at the back of her neck. Gemma noticed she wore a yellow gold Pavlin tank watch.

"Clifford's calling me over," she said,

excusing herself.

The music changed, switching decades from Spice Girls to Phil Collins, "In the Air Tonight." She grabbed a glass of red sangria from the bar.

"Gemma," Clifford said. "This is my husband, Santiago."

Santiago smiled at her with beautiful big brown eyes that gave her a pang, reminding her of Sanjay.

Clifford leaned forward conspiratorially. "Such a shame about Celeste and Jack. But then, marriage isn't for everyone." He turned to the woman beside Santiago.

"And this lovely lady is Susan Harrison," Clifford said. "She rented out Maud's *jewel* of a house on the West End for the summer."

Gemma blinked, suddenly feeling overheated. Connor's place.

"Are you . . . related to Connor Harrison?" she said.

The woman gave a small laugh. "I'm his mother." She narrowed her eyes. "Have we met?"

Gemma realized why she recognized her. "I saw you once in his gallery."

"His gallery? You mean *my* gallery." She rolled her eyes and gave a wink to Clifford. "Though I'm done with that money pit.

Another failed venture courtesy of my son. Are you an artist?" Susan Harrison asked.

Gemma reached up and reflexively touched her charm necklace. She felt a hand on her arm and turned to find Elodie.

"Sorry to interrupt," Elodie said. "May I speak with you for a moment?" Elodie was dressed more casually than she'd ever seen her, in a khaki dress and wedges in red canvas that tied around her ankles. Her only jewelry was pearl earrings.

"What's up?" Gemma said, looking around. "Have you seen Celeste today? She was gone from the house when I woke up this morning and I haven't spoken to her."

"Well, you're not going to find her here, unfortunately. A little birdie told me her conversation with Jack didn't go very well."

Gemma closed her eyes. She felt awful for her aunt. She knew what it was like to make a mistake and not be forgiven. If she suffered this much after losing Sanjay after just a few months together, she couldn't imagine what it was like for Celeste after decades with Jack.

"I can't believe Jack won't forgive her."

Elodie crossed her arms. "Well, I suppose forgiveness is complicated. Can *you* forgive?"

Gemma sipped her drink. "I don't think

this is the time and place to get into all that, Elodie."

"I'm not asking for myself. I'm asking because I want you to really consider my offer to work at Pavlin & Co. I would hate to see you turn it down because of things that happened in the past. I know that your mother — and *my* mother, for that matter — wouldn't want that."

Gemma felt a lump in her throat. Of course she'd thought about the job offer. She'd thought about little else all day. And she believed Elodie was right: Her mother wouldn't want her to walk away from it just because it had taken this long for the Pavlins to welcome her back. But she also knew she couldn't accept *for* her mother. She'd spent too much time looking back.

"I'm not sure," she said. "I appreciate the offer. I really do. I just need some time."

Gemma smiled at her aunt. As she surveyed the crowd, she saw Maud and Alvie a few feet away, posing for a photographer.

And the photographer was Sanjay. Her first thought was, *This sangria is so strong I'm hallucinating.*

The music changed again, to the hypnotic slow burn of the song "Delilah" by Florence + The Machine. And then Sanjay looked up and their eyes locked. Gemma's chest constricted.

"Excuse me," she murmured, drifting away from Elodie. Each step felt like it was happening in slow motion, through water.

"Hey," she said. "What are you doing here?"

He started to say something about Maud but then looked past her. It took a second for her to realize everyone was gazing in the same direction, looking back toward the Barros house. She turned to see what everyone was staring at.

And saw Celeste walking into the party in her wedding gown.

73

Celeste knew it was a long shot.

The party turned quiet as she walked to Jack, not down an aisle, but across a paved lot, past the boat rental office, and toward the dock. Her pulse raced the entire way, and it took all of her will to put one foot in front of the other for the solitary, terrifying march toward a bewildered-looking Jack.

She glanced at the crowd, searching for Elodie. Her sister gave her a thumbs-up. Celeste knew that she, at least, would understand what she was doing. Trying to do.

Jack stood at the bar talking to Manny and Lidia.

Celeste caught the eye of Clifford Henry, and he began cutting through the crowd.

"Excuse me! Make way . . . wedding officiant coming through!"

People began murmuring. Elodie, realizing what was happening, made her way over to stand by her side. Manny, already next to Jack, gave Celeste a smile. The guests, confused and hushed in anticipation, gathered in a loose crowd before them. All she heard was the gentle lapping of the water and the old Bee Gees song "How Deep Is Your Love" playing on the sound system. A breeze stirred the lace of her dress.

"What are you doing?" Jack said, glancing around uncomfortably.

"I brought you something for your birthday," she said. "If you'll accept it."

She held out the two matching platinum bands Gemma made for them. He looked at the rings uncomprehendingly, then at Clifford. Then at her gown.

"Do you know what you're doing?" Jack said.

Celeste reached for his hand. "I do."

It all happened so fast. One minute, Elodie was feeling sad and uncomfortable around Jack. The next, he was her brother-in-law.

"Well, that was something," Tito said, handing her a flute of champagne. "Does this make us cousins-in-law?"

She laughed.

"I suppose." She reached down to pat Pearl. Overstimulated, she'd settled by Elodie's feet and wouldn't budge. Bart, in contrast, roamed around the party, visiting each cluster of guests like he was the host.

"I hope that doesn't mean we can't also be more," he said. "Have you given any more thought to moving in?"

Of course she had. But as tempting as it was to think of moving into Tito's house and living a romantic life by the sea, she couldn't. Pavlin & Co was a part of her. It was her legacy, one she'd set her claim on from the time she was a little girl. It was her first love, the one that had always been there — for better and for worse. She couldn't walk away.

"I have a life in New York," she said. "It doesn't have to be my whole life, but I can't just leave it behind. I can't live here full-time. As much as I want to be with you."

Tito reached for her hand.

"I was just thinking: If Celeste could change her mind about marriage after all these years, then the least I can do is visit the Big Apple."

Elodie set her glass down on the nearest table.

"Don't tease me."

"Is that a yes?" he said.

Elodie threw her arms around him. "You've got yourself a deal."

■ ■ ■ ■

The dock became a dance floor.

Tito was a nostalgic DJ: The music was 1970s heavy — Elton John, Tom Petty, Carly Simon. Celeste, the beaming bride, had kicked off her shoes while Jack twirled her around. Beside them, Tito and Elodie danced like they were the only two people in the universe.

Gemma watched from the sidelines as Sanjay moved around taking photos.

"Hey," Alvie said, beaming. She handed Gemma a glass of champagne. "A toast: to the summer of love."

Gemma held the glass by her side. "Alvie, what's Sanjay doing here?"

Alvie shrugged. "It's not my party. But I can say that a few days ago Maud became very interested in making sure we'd have some good photos from tonight. Unusually interested."

The sun was starting to set, a pinkish hue casting the boatyard in an almost surreal light. The bay was at high tide, the water lapping against the dock. Somewhere nearby, a cork popped.

The song "American Girl" poured out of the speakers, and Sanjay put his camera down long enough to take a break at the bar, downing a glass of water. She walked over, her heart beating fast.

"Hey," she said.

He poured a second glass of water and handed it to her.

"Hey. Sorry for just showing up like this. Maud reached out to me. She said they needed a photographer for a party tonight and for Carnival next week. She made me an offer I couldn't turn down."

The summer's not over yet.

Gemma bit her lip.

"Did . . . Monica come with you?"

His eyes met hers searchingly, and the surge of emotion she felt took her breath away.

"No. She didn't," he said, his voice low. He reached out and brushed a lock of hair from her face.

"Why not?" she said.

"Because I realized I had feelings for someone else. Feelings that made it unfair for me to be in a relationship with her."

Gemma swallowed hard. The sky was almost dark. A firefly glowed nearby, its tiny light like a winking star. She stepped closer to him.

"So . . . what now?" she said.

He kissed her, enveloping her in his arms.

The rest of the party — the rest of the world — receded. The music changed again, something slow and moody, a song she didn't recognize but knew would stay with her. In that moment, she felt — for the first time in a very long time — like the pieces of her life had come together. Like it was whole.

74

New York City, Three Years Later

The line of eager customers and press stretched an entire city block. The sun was just beginning to set on the late spring evening, and the barricades on East Fifty-Third Street had been in place since noon. Gemma stepped out of the Lincoln Town Car and was immediately met by a security guard in a dark suit and wearing an ear-piece. The entrance to Pavlin & Co was a yard away. With the swarm of photographers it seemed unreachable.

She pulled up the hem of her long white dress, keeping it from sweeping the ground. It was asymmetrical and wrapped over her left shoulder, with an embroidered butterfly above her heart. It had been designed by her intern, a current NYSD student. The dress was her award-winning final project.

"Gemma!" Elodie called, stepping out of her own car, followed by Tito. "What a spectacle," she said. She looked flustered, a sheen of perspiration on her forehead, her pale blue St. John shift dress rumpled from the short drive from Park Avenue. The sight of Tito in a suit put a smile on her face despite the frenzy around her; he hadn't even worn a suit at their beach wedding last summer.

"I'm honored you got so dressed up for the occasion," Gemma said to him.

"It's your big night," he said. "Both of yours."

Elodie gave her a wink. She was one of the few people who knew it was only the *second* biggest night Gemma was having that week.

Security hustled them to the front of the store, past the windows with the deep green awnings, under the limestone archway engraved with the family name.

Inside, the vast showroom had been arranged with seating for the press, where her NYSD friend Mae Yang, now an editor at *New York* magazine, sat in the front row. Gemma gave her a wave, thinking about the borrowed press credentials that set everything in motion.

Displays of jewelry open on tables flanked the speaker's podium. In a break from custom, they weren't encased in glass.

Gemma wanted people to be able to touch and feel and connect with the pieces — her first for Pavlin & Co as the lead designer.

The collection was called Gilded Butterfly, a celebration of precious metals and their versatility in conveying design. Every piece could be personalized, and some necklaces could be mixed and matched. The pieces ranged from affordable (a chunky sterling silver necklace chain) to extravagant (a twenty-four-karat gold cuff bracelet). Gemma's favorite pieces were the stacked rings, sleek and modern in brushed metals. Here, too, they had affordable single rings that could be collected over time for the dramatic look of half a dozen on a finger. On the higher end, customers could buy pave diamond versions with upcycled stones. The important thing was, there was something for everyone. A philosophy cemented by the company's first new tagline in seventy years: "Treat Yourself Like Gold."

Gemma's decision to work for Pavlin & Co had, ultimately, been a simple one. It was what she wanted. And then, one night over drinks with Elodie at the Carlyle, she learned she wasn't the only one who wanted it all along. "I finally realize why my mother made you one of the signatories on the private collection," Elodie said.

"So you couldn't sell?" Gemma said.

"No. She wanted you to be at Pavlin & Co. She knew it was your rightful place, even when I didn't want to see it."

Yes, GEMMA the brand had been her own. But Pavlin & Co was bigger than herself. And she knew she had the vision to bring it into the future and ensure that it was around for many generations to come.

The door opened again, revealing a frazzled-looking Celeste.

"Goodness. That was . . . challenging," she said, leaning against the closed door as if warding off a tornado. "Jack's looking for parking."

"Are we ready, Gemma?" asked security. She glanced over at Elodie and she gave a nod.

With that, the front doors were opened and the press flooded in like weary travelers discovering a roadside all-you-can-eat buffet. She knew Sanjay would have loved to be taking photos himself. But tonight, he wasn't a photographer. Tonight, he was her fiancé, and she needed him by her side.

He proposed just two nights earlier. She didn't see it coming. Sure, they'd been living together for the past year, and he photographed the new ad campaign for Pavlin & Co, and they were madly in love. But that evening, she was so stressed about the impending launch, she barely mustered the enthusiasm to go along with his idea to take a walk.

They strolled the East River promenade past Carl Schurz Park. It was one of those perfect spring evenings, with the tulip beds in bloom and the sunlight hitting the river in a way that made it look as dazzling as a Swiss lake. They were almost at Gracie Mansion when Sanjay got down on the ground. She thought at first that he'd dropped something, but then he looked up at her with those deep dark eyes that had become her home.

"Gemma," he said. At that point, the joggers, bikers, and parents pushing strollers realized what was happening and stopped to watch. Sanjay handed her a ring box. She opened it and gasped.

A pink diamond eternity band. *The* pink diamond eternity band.

"How is this possible? I tossed this into the ocean . . ."

Sanjay smiled. "Your aunt Celeste knew that the tide would bring it right back that night. Something about a full moon? She said she couldn't let you throw it away just to make her feel better."

"How long have you known she had it?"

Gemma said, barely able to process the fact that he'd proposed, never mind the reappearance of the ring she thought was gone forever.

"Only since I told her I wanted to ask you to marry me. She said she'd been saving it for that very moment."

When he slipped the ring on her finger, onlookers clapped and whistled. And when he said, "Will you marry me?" she barely managed to breathe out the word yes.

She was still on a high from it, reliving it over and over in her mind. But tonight was about work.

As the press filled in their cordoned-off seats, Gemma and her aunts discussed their positions on the podium. A familiar redhead pushed her way to the front of the crowd.

"I need a shot of the three of you," said Regan O'Rourke. Gemma obliged, acutely aware that she was standing in the spot where she'd first stood with her mother as a child, now wearing the engagement ring that was a piece of her mother's, flanked by Elodie and Celeste.

She smiled for Regan O'Rourke. And then it was time to address the room.

Elodie and Celeste moved to one side, leaving Gemma alone in the spotlight. She thought, briefly, of the night of her graduation, when she stood in front of the audience feeling so alone.

"Thank you, everyone, for being here tonight to celebrate. A special thank-you to my aunt Elodie Pavlin for carrying on the family legacy all these years and now inviting me to design in this new era of Pavlin & Co." She turned to look at her aunt standing beside her and saw the glimmer of tears in her bright eyes. Gemma swallowed hard and turned back to the crowd. "I dedicate this debut collection, Gilded Butterfly, to my mother, Paulina. She loved butterflies, and I embrace them as the perfect symbol of change . . . of metamorphosis. Pavlin & Co is now in its second century. The world is a different place, but jewelry remains a vital part of celebrating our milestones. My hope for the Gilded Butterfly collection is that a ring or necklace is the first piece of jewelry someone buys for themselves and never takes off. I hope people come back to Gilded Butterfly throughout their lives, for birthdays and graduations, for job successes, and yes, for engagements. My great-grandfather famously said that 'a diamond says love,' and I believe true love begins with ourselves. So, without further ado, I introduce you to Gilded Butterfly. Treat yourself like gold."

The room erupted in applause. Sanjay, seated in the front row, gave her a thumbs-up. She was instantly brought back to the moment at college graduation when she'd looked out at the audience and he'd given her the same gesture. But now, he wasn't the only one in the audience who cared about her.

She was surrounded by love.

ACKNOWLEDGMENTS

Thank you to my talented editor, Gabriella Mongelli, for pushing me through multiple drafts to the best possible version of this story. Gaby, thank you for your spot-on notes and patience. I love working with you! I'm grateful for the support of the entire Putnam team — my publisher, the brilliant Sally Kim; my publicist, Ashley Hewlett; Ellie Schaffer; Brennin Cummings; Nishtha Patel; Alexis Welby; Ashley McClay; the sales force; and the art department that created this dazzling cover. I know you were all responding to my emails while at home juggling children and pets and spouses, and I'm grateful.

My agent, Adam Chromy, read early drafts of this book and steered me away from a few cliffs. Thank you for being the one to always keep me on track and for believing I'll get there no matter how far off course I wander. I feel creatively safe knowing you are always there to catch my fall.

Every story begins with a spark, and for this book, that spark was the jewelry brand Lulu Frost, designed by Lisa Salzer. Lisa, your Plaza Collection reminded me that jewelry can tell some of our best stories. Thank you for the beauty you bring into the world. I also had great fun researching estate jewelry at Pippin Vintage in New York City and A. Brandt & Son on Main Line, Philadelphia.

But writing this book wasn't all glitter and gold: I'd always had this fantasy that somehow, if the world shut down and I had nothing to do but write, it would be easier to finish a novel. Well, be careful what you wish for. I started this novel in the summer of 2020, when the world had indeed shut down. I soon realized that it's the balance of life and writing that makes creativity possible. I never realized how much I fed off of the normal rhythm of my days until that rhythm was disrupted. I took for granted seeing my friends — especially my author friends — at dinners out and book events where we commiserated and shared notes and supported one another. I don't know what I would have done the past year and a half without my Thursday Zoom crew: Fiona Davis, Susie Orman Schnall, Lynda

Cohen Loigman, Amy Poeppel, Nicola Harrison, and Suzanne Leopold.

To my daughters, Georgia and Bronwen, you handled a time of change and loss with grace and fortitude. I love you and I'm proud of you.

A special thank-you to the booksellers and readers who have been with me on this journey. I appreciate each and every one of you.

Finally, thank you to my husband. In the very dark days of spring 2020, you brought me to live in a bright and hopeful place so that I could write this novel: Provincetown. You turned what could have been a disaster into something beautiful. You always do. And I love you for it.

ABOUT THE AUTHOR

Jamie Brenner is the author of six novels, including *Blush* and *The Forever Summer.* She grew up in suburban Philadelphia on a steady diet of Jackie Collins and Judith Krantz novels, and later moved to New York City to live like the heroines of her favorite books. Jamie now divides her time between Philadelphia and Provincetown.

The employees of Thorndike Press hope you have enjoyed this Large Print book. All our Thorndike, Wheeler, and Kennebec Large Print titles are designed for easy reading, and all our books are made to last. Other Thorndike Press Large Print books are available at your library, through selected bookstores, or directly from us.

For information about titles, please call:

(800) 223-1244

or visit our website at:

gale.com/thorndike

To share your comments, please write:

Publisher
Thorndike Press
10 Water St., Suite 310
Waterville, ME 04901